Praise

The Road to Frogmore touches on history with which most of us are unfamiliar—the history of transition. We are all exposed to stories of slavery, emancipation, civil rights, and so forth, but few of us know the story of transition between these. Transition is difficult for any society and Carolyn Schriber shares with us the intimate stories of the people involved in the transition from slavery to emancipation – the trials they suffer, the challenges they face, the difficulties that must be dealt with in relationships on all sides. The stories Schriber shares are emotional, sometimes humorous, and both familiar and unfamiliar. Schriber doesn't hesitate to get to the guts of the issues and reflect from all sides the genuine emotions involved

—Rev. Faith Nettleton-Scherer

A fascinating journey into a little known but emblematic chapter of the Civil War. *The Road to Frogmore* reveals how that epic struggle was not only to emancipate America's slaves but our very understanding of freedom and humanity. In vibrantly portraying the transformation from slavery to freedom, Carolyn Schriber astutely reveals how much we have still to learn from that struggle.

—Leila Levinson, author of *Gated Grief*

Learning about historical events through the eyes of the people that lived during those times is one of the most fascinating ways to approach history. *The Road to Frogmore*, a book of historical fiction, opened up lives and events from the Civil War era, of which I was totally unaware. Carolyn Schriber did a wonderful job of researching, along with using information from both diaries and letters to make discoveries regarding the women who made a huge impact on the lives and times of emancipated slaves.

—Joyce M. Gilmour, Editing TLC

In *The Road to Frogmore*, Carolyn Schriber is meticulous in her research of the events surrounding the mission of "Turning Slaves into Citizens". She uses imaginary journal excerpts written by Rina, a slave woman, as a way to bind the many stories gleaned from diaries and letters of volunteers that served. Carolyn's treatment of the Gullah language for the reader is brilliant.

—Elizabeth Egerton Wilder, author of *Granite Hearts*

If only history had been this spell-binding when I was in school! The title of Carolyn P. Schriber's recent release, *The Road to Frogmore: Turning Slaves into Citizens*, grabbed my attention immediately and never let go. The author has masterfully woven details from her exhaustive research into a book that reads like a well-plotted novel, yet all the characters are real people and all the events factual. I give the book five stars out of five and recommend it to history buffs as well as those like me who are looking for a good read with a bonus. I can see *The Road to Frogmore* used in high school or college history classes where it would spark many rich and lively discussions. It would also be an excellent book club pick for the same reason.

—Candace George Thompson, author of *Still Having Fun: A Portrait of a Military Marriage, 1941-2007*.

THE ROAD TO FROGMORE:

....

TURNING SLAVES INTO CITIZENS

Carolyn P. Schriber

Published by Katzenhaus Books
P. O. Box 1629
Cordova, TN 38088-1629

Cover Design by Cathy Helms

ISBN-10: 0982774524
ISBN-13: 978-0-9827745-2-6

Library of Congress Control Number: 2012948569
Katzenhaus Books Cordova, TN

Feb. 1866 – Laura m. Towne
Dick, Maria, Amoretta

Photo Credit: From the Penn School Collection. Permission granted by Penn Center, Inc., St. Helena Island, SC

"*The shepherd drives the wolf from the sheep for which the sheep thanks the shepherd as his liberator, while the wolf denounces him for the same act as the destroyer of liberty. Plainly, the sheep and wolf are not agreed upon a definition of liberty.*"

~ Abraham Lincoln

AUTHOR'S PREFACE

"Truth is so hard to tell, it sometimes needs fiction to make it plausible."

~Francis Bacon

This book is fiction, but its story is true, and its characters are real. How can that be? It is true because it is based on documented historical evidence. It is fiction because I have used my own imagination to fill in the blanks within the evidence. There is no shortage of sources material for the story of Laura M. Towne. For those who wish to explore the events of this story in more historical detail, I have included a short bibliography at the end of the book.

Laura, like most of her colleagues, kept a diary throughout the first years of her stay in South Carolina. All of her Gideonite colleagues were inveterate letter-writers, and much of their correspondence is still available. As a result, a researcher suffers from an over-abundance of material evidence. Almost every event during the Port Royal Experiment had multiple witnesses and participants. The problem, of course, is that when nine different people write their own descriptions of a particular event, they produce nine different truths—and all of them may be "true." Truth changes, depending upon who tells the story.

Diaries, too, can be untrustworthy. The diarist tells what she knows, but she may not be able to tell what she has chosen to forget or what she failed to see. In Laura's case, her diary entries often reveal a dark side to her character, and her fears come out to play in the dark. Her letters can seem cloyingly sweet and cheerful. She was very likely to write to her sisters to tell them she was bursting with good health, that she never felt better in her whole life. But a diary entry written the same night may indulge in descriptions of raging headaches, nausea, and muscle cramps that she feared were symptoms of terminal illness. Which one was the true Laura? That is the question her diary and letters fail to answer.

The Port Royal Experiment was marked by ongoing disagreements—religious differences, opposing political and economic theories, and widely varying reactions to the conditions under which they were all living. The result was, of course, a narrative of disagreement. In a novel, the reader wants to know how much is true, but there is a difference between truth and fact. Facts reveal details but can hide the truth behind a wall of distorted mirror images. Which image is true?

The writer of historical fiction must take the details and transform them into a story that makes sense. Sometimes that task demands a new search to ascertain the "truth" and sometimes it needs a healthy dose of imagination to make facts understandable. In *The Road to Frogmore,* all the characters are real, and I have changed no names to protect anyone from the consequences of his or her actions. Events are factual; dates are accurate; outcomes fully revealed. Is the story true? Perhaps. But it is also fiction because it reflects my own interpretations of how the characters felt and how they must have talked to one another.

I must add a word about Rina and the language she speaks. Rina herself is a real person. She served as Laura's laundress and housekeeper for a small salary. Her name appears throughout Laura's diary, increasingly so as Laura came to rely on her as a conduit into the slave community. She functions in the same way as a Greek chorus does—watching the action while remaining aloof from it and commenting on the behavior of those who don't fully understand the culture in which they are embedded.

Rina, like all of the slaves in the Low Country, spoke Gullah, a language in its own right, with its own rules of grammar, a distinct syntax, and a vocabulary that contained both English words and words from several African languages. It also used certain sounds that a speaker of a European language cannot pronounce. Linguists no longer see Gullah as patois, or a form of broken English. But for that reason, reproducing it for readers of English, while making it understandable, is a daunting task.

While I wrote, I kept by my side a Gullah dictionary and a wonderful translation of *De Gullah Nyew Testament* produced by the Penn Center's efforts to preserve the Gullah language. Yet the closer I came to being able to recreate the speech of a St. Helena slave, the more unintelligible it became for readers. With the help of my editor, Gabriella Deponte, we finally settled on a version of Gullah that preserves much of the authenticity of the original language while making it accessible to speakers of English.

We started by eliminating all apostrophes. An apostrophe suggests that there is a right way to pronounce a word, and that the speaker has failed to include all the correct syllables or sounds. It privileges the English form over the Gullah instead of recognizing that they are separate languages. An English speaker says "Tomorrow we are going to Beaufort."

A Gullah speaker says "Morrow we gwine fuh Bufor." Both are understandable. Apostrophes are unnecessary.

We included a few words that appear only in Gullah, such as *buckra*, which means a white man or white person. We also used the Gullah *fuh* in place of an English infinitive *to* and replaced all forms of *going to* with the Gullah *gwine*.

The verb *to be,* with all its forms *(am is, are was, were, have been, has been, had been)* appears in only two forms in Gullah (be or bin). A similar reduction occurs with pronouns, which for the most part are not inflected (no possessive or accusative forms). So a speaker of Gullah says, "He bring food fuh we" (not "for us").

Gullah speakers do not (perhaps cannot) pronounce a sound that would be an unaccented syllable at the beginning of an English word. This happens most often with words that begin with a vowel, such as accept, which becomes *cept* or exactly, which becomes *zakly*. The result is a speech pattern that always begins with an accented syllable and produces a strong rhythm similar to the poetic sounds of an English dactyl.

Finally, certain common English sounds are difficult for a speaker of Gullah. Our version changes all fricative *th* sounds to d (they becomes dey; other becomes udder). An aspirated th changes to a simple t (thing becomes ting; thumb becomes tum). Similarly, most v sounds change to a b (never becomes neber; very becomes bery). If you have trouble reading the Gullah portions of this book, try listening to how they sound out loud.

RINA ON "DE BIG SHOOT"
November 1861

Eberting change after de Big Shoot.

We knows dere be a war gwine on. Hard fuh miss dat, what wit de young buckra all gwine off, leavin dere driver an dere missus fuh run de plantation. We eben know summa our own folk what gone to war.

Ober on Lady Island, one uh de planter got a slave name Pa Polite. His son, name Prince, done tell he story. When de big war start, massa say, "You knows dis war be fuh free all you damned nigras. I gwine fight fuh muh own rights an de rights uh my State. You gwine wit me, or you gwine stay an take de fust chance fuh run away an git free soons I gone?"

Pa answer, "Massa, if I be free, I aint neber gwine fight fuh keep muh people fro bin free. But so longs I be your nigra, I be bound fuh do what you say." He say if Massa don trust Pa, Massa kin leave he, but ifn Pa always do he job good, den he want fuh go. "Sides," he say, "you aint neber gwine find sumbody who take as good care uh you as I duz."

So dey jumps on dey horses an gallops away. An we aint see dem since. Dey friend say dey be kilt in one uh de first battle uh de war. Dat be a good lesson fuh we, sho nuf! Black folk aint be gwine off fuh fight in a war. Life be hard nuf here at home wit Massa an his whip, witout udder buckra be shootin at de menfolk an killin dem dead.

When all de big boat start sailin roun Port Royal, Massa Pope, he say we gots nuttin fuh worry bout, cause de Yankee aint smart nuf fuh git hold uh Sout Carolina. But dere be mo an mo uh dem, an eberbody start worryin. When we hear de fust shot, de white folk all goes hustlin off fuh see what be gwine on.

De buckra goes off fuh a meetin at de white chuch, an de missus, dey goes off to de Chaplin House at Lands End. Fro de veranda dere, dey be watchin de battle. Dey could see Bay Point an Fort Walker, so dey be lookin when de flag come down an de Yankee flag go up.

Scairt? Dey jump in der buggy an head fuh home fuh do what dey an de buckra plan. Eberbody screamin an cryin an shoutin fuh help. We knows what fuh do. We skedaddle outta dere. De menfolk head fuh de wood, cause dey knows Massa want dem fuh drive de wagon an row de boat. Wimmun be tryin fuh stay outta de way uh de Massa.

Massa Pope, he want fuh take Zannah an Ol Bess an me wit dem, cause we be house slave, an he need sumbody fuh take care uh de clothe an de cookin an de chillun, but we aint gwine go. He keep runnin intuh de slave house lookin fuh we, but when he come in de front door, we jumps out de back door or de window.

Poor Ol Bess, she hab dis big ol sore on she leg dat not healin, so she caint run fast nuf. An she hab de baby Leah, what jis be larnin fuh walk. So she take Leah an go out in de cornfield an lay down between de row fuh hide. Poor baby hab a cough, so Bess keep her han ober she mout fuh keep she quiet. Near strangle dat poor chile.

De young missus catch Zannah in de kitchen tryin fuh hide sum food so de Massa not take it all. De young missus be cryin an say, "Oh, Zannah, de Yankee gwine kill you! Ifn you see a Yankee, it drive you crazy."

"Why, Missus, aint dey natural folk?"

"Oh, no, Zannah, they don look like we!"

So when soljers come, Zannah run to she man Marcus an say, "Oh, de soljers, dey come fuh kill we."

Marcus say, "Don be silly. Dey be jis mens." Zannah soon find out de soljers be such purty men, an so respectful.

Most uh we slaves, we jis listens to what de buckra says an den do nuttin, cause we gots bedder sense. Massa tell we fuh burn de cotton in de field when dey gone, but we say, "Why fuh we burn de cotton? Where we get money den fuh buy clothe an shoe an salt?"

Massa say ifn we don go wit he, de Yankees gwine kill we or send we to Cuba. We says, "Dat not true, cause we jis poor black folk who duz no harm an we only be guide by white folk."

So by de nex day, de buckra all gone. An we look round an say, "What now?"

Uncle Amos, Massa Pope driver, he call we all togedduh, an he say, "We be gwine keep doin zackly what we always duz. De Massa gwine come back, sho nuf, an ifn he don see work bin done, he gwine lick all uh we. Sides, we gotta chance fuh work de crops an git lots uh egg, an take what we needs fuh we."

So life go on, same as usual. Cept we hab mo time fuh visit wit udder black folk an hear what be gwine on udder places. We hear bout de mess sum black folk make in Bufor, when dey broke intuh house an stole de carpet an de curtain an de silverware. But dat dint happen here, less we was really needin sumptin.

We jis lives our lives an eats what we wants. An we be purty happy fuh a while, til food start runnin low. Den we worry, cause it be diffrunt. Nobody left who kin take care uh we.

Eberting change after de Big Shoot.

3

1
ABOLITIONIST DREAMS
March 1862

Laura Towne hesitated outside the family brownstone. She knew she was late for dinner, and she was in no hurry to encounter her sister's wrath. She debated for a few moments. Which was preferable—putting up with Lucretia's righteous indignation, or staying outside in the lowering fog and smoke-tinged air? Smoky fog almost won; then she shook her head and plodded up the stairs, resigned to her fate.

Just inside the front door, she carefully removed her heavy cape, shaking the water droplets back out onto the porch lest they spot Lucretia's polished floor. Resolutely, she pushed open the right-hand door into the dining room and stared down the four disapproving pairs of eyes that greeted her.

"You're rather late for dinner," Lucretia pointed out. "I left a plate for you there on the hob. It's probably spoiled by now, but there's no help for that if you insist on missing our scheduled assembly time."

"I'm truly sorry. I didn't expect to be so late."

"Well, where were you? Did one of those strange homeopathic courses you're taking run over its time?"

"No. Actually, I was at a meeting called by the Abolitionist Society. They were . . ."

"Bah!" William sneered at his sister. "Those idealistic young fops have no sense of time or place, do they? No wonder you're late, if you were out consorting with those types."

Laura took a deep breath and busied herself for a few moments retrieving her plate. The serving of stew had suffered from its time on the warming shelf—the gravy had begun to separate, the carrots looked dry and unappealing, and little puddles of grease were gathering around the edges. Laura gamely began to eat, stirring the contents on her plate into something that looked a bit more edible. Then, mopping up some of the grease with a small piece of bread, she focused on William, who was looking particularly self-satisfied.

"They are not idealist young fops, Will, which you would understand if you ever bothered to attend one of their meetings. Slavery is a real blight on our country, and the abolitionists seem to be the only ones willing to act on their beliefs in order to rid our nation of such injustice."

"What was today's meeting about, Laura?" asked Rosie, Laura's younger sister, trying to avert an argument between brother and sister.

"It was quite exciting, actually." Laura put down the crust of bread and pushed her plate aside in her enthusiasm. Lucretia frowned, but for once refrained from commenting about the waste of perfectly good food.

"The meeting was called by James Miller McKim. You remember him, Rosie. We met him at church not long ago. He called together all the leading ministers of Philadelphia, together with some prominent and wealthy businessmen, to discuss a new venture already underway in South Carolina."

"South Carolina?" Will interrupted again. "That hotbed of secession? What business is it of ours what is going on there?"

"Abolitionists have a role to play anywhere people are being enslaved, Will. Remember the stories in the newspaper last November about the great Union victory at Port Royal Sound? Where the Southern planters fled in panic at the first sight of the naval fleet sent against them?"

"Yes, I do. The South Carolina Expeditionary Force was a joint Army-Navy venture to establish a safe harbor from which to manage the blockade of the southern coast." Will loved to show off his superior masculine intellect to his sisters. "It was a tremendous logistical exercise. Lincoln simply instructed Secretary Chase to 'get it done.' So Chase put together an invasion involving 80 ships and 12,000 troops. No one thought the Confederate forces would give up that easily. We thought they had Port Royal Harbor well fortified. Instead, it turned out they had less than 200 men there and only a few operable guns, not one of which was able to swivel to attack a passing ship."

Laura saw a chance to enlist Will on her side and pounced on his story. "The white people fled, but they left their slaves behind—in effect, simply abandoned them to their fate. There are hundreds—no, thousands—of slaves on the coastal islands of South Carolina. They have no masters, no food, no clothing, no health care, no place to go, and no way to get there, even if they knew where to go. It's a disastrous situation."

"I'm sure it is. But what can be done about it?" Will shrugged, refusing to be caught up in the argument that easily.

But now sister Rosie stepped into the discussion. "Really? They didn't take their slaves with them? How heartless of them!"

Lucretia frowned at such silliness. "Heartless? The slave owners turned their slaves loose. Isn't that what you abolitionists want?"

"Yes, although some took their personal slaves," Laura explained, "and others dragooned a few of their men into driving the wagons and rowing the boats they were using to escape. But General Sherman reports that there are thousands of Negroes hiding in the interior of Hilton Head Island."

Will was back on the attack. "And the city of Beaufort, from all reports, has been overrun with blacks, rioting and breaking into the lovely mansions there to steal and ransack. The slave owners are gone, and the worst fears of what might happen if the slaves were freed seem to be coming true. There's simply no one to control them."

"Well, are they actually free?" asked Rosie.

"Nobody seems to be quite sure," Will replied. "There's been no official declaration from the government that they have been freed, and I don't expect one. But there's a difference between official policy and events of the moment. The image that keeps coming to my mind—degrading as it may sound—is that of a herd of cattle suddenly finding an open gate and starting a stampede. They're out of their pen and behaving as if they were free, but they are still domestic beasts that have to be rounded up. And who's going to corral them?"

"Well, Salmon P. Chase has already taken some first steps." Laura was in a lecture mode of her own now, eager to spread the exciting news she had heard at her meeting.

"He's Lincoln's new secretary of the treasury, you know. He has hired a cotton specialist named Lieutenant Colonel William H. Reynolds. He's a member of the First Rhode Island Artillery and came highly recommended by Governor Sprague of Rhode Island. He is said to have extensive experience in the cotton trade, and he is honest, highly principled, and fervently religious."

"And what is this wonderful man supposed to do once he gets to South Carolina?"

"According to the report we heard today, his first—perhaps his only—consideration is to get the cotton crop in as quickly as possible, before winter rain or rebel firebrands render it useless. General Sherman has already made some initial efforts to recruit the former slaves on each plantation to pick the cotton in exchange for a small salary. But Reynolds will have to organize them, set supervisors over them, make arrangements to gin the cotton, and ship it north. There's no time to waste."

"Sounds like more slavery to me," Will grumbled.

"No, Will, it's not."

"The Negroes are going back to picking cotton, aren't they?"

"Yes, for a little while. But Reynolds has a counterpart, someone to balance his efforts with compassionate care for the ex-slaves. Do you remember an article you read out loud to us last winter? I think it was in the *Atlantic Monthly*. A young soldier, Edward L. Pierce, was serving a three-month enlistment at Fort Monroe and thus had observed how General Butler handled the issue of contrabands. Pierce was duly impressed with the eagerness of the former slaves to learn to read and to serve their country. In his article he argued they were fully capable, as well as deserving, of American citizenship."

"Yes, I remember. It was quite an impassioned defense."

"Well, Secretary Chase apparently thought so, too. He contacted Pierce by mail, asking if he would be willing to postpone opening his planned law practice in Boston long enough to travel to South Carolina and assess the needs of the former slaves there. Pierce agreed to spend several more months in the service of his government before becoming a practicing attorney. He left New York in January and has been hard at work, traveling from plantation to plantation to learn about the former slaves and their current condition.

"Now he is back in Boston, with a preliminary report about the needs of the former slaves. He has the support of Reverend Jacob Manning, a minister at the Old South Church. Manning agreed to recruit missionaries and teachers to go back to South Carolina. He also promised to raise the money to support them, so that they would not be answerable to the federal government. Meanwhile, Reverend Mansfield French has been doing the same thing in New York City. They have established the Boston Educational Association for Freedmen and the New York National Freedmen's Relief Association."

Laura sat back to catch her breath. But Lucretia was still not convinced.

"Men just love to put together fancy-sounding titles for new organizations," she observed, "but what can they possibly be hoping to accomplish with these so-called 'relief associations'?"

"We can go there and put our theoretical discussions to a practical test." Laura had not meant to bring that up just yet, but her enthusiasm for what she had heard carried her ahead.

"Preposterous!" Lucretia snorted. "There's a war going on. It wouldn't be safe."

"One group has already gone," Laura countered.

"Really?" Rose and Sarah both leaned forward to question Laura in more detail.

"Elbows off the table, girls," Lucretia admonished.

"Oh, Lucretia, stop it. I'm the youngest person here, and I'm almost twenty-eight years old. If my manners don't suit you by now, it's probably too late to correct them." Sarah glared at the elder sister who seemed determined to rule the family as if they were all still children.

"Sarah." A single word from Laura was enough to squelch the budding argument. The younger women adored Laura for her gentleness and understanding. She alone of the five siblings still living at home had had the determination and ingenuity to venture out on her own, to make a life for herself that did not revolve around a family that had lost their mother during their childhood and their father almost ten years ago. Will sometimes resented her independence, but Rosie and Sarah looked to her for guidance in all matters.

"All right, Laura," Will said. "Tell us about this intrepid group of adventurers."

"Maybe not just now. I've already caused dinner to run late, and we'll need to be getting to the washing up." Laura began to gather the plates.

"No, I want to hear about it, too," Lucretia said. "We're this late—might as well sit here a bit longer. I'm not at all sure I like what I'm hearing, but I suspect we all need to know what's going on."

2
THE PHILADELPHIA CONNECTION
March 1862

L aura took a deep breath and plunged into her story. "A group of sixty-two missionaries and teachers from Boston and New York has just departed for South Carolina. The New York National Freedmen's Relief Association and the Boston Educational Association for Freedmen are working together to finance what they are calling 'The Port Royal Experiment'."

"New Yorkers and Bostonians working together? That's a wonder in itself," Will said with a grin, then shook his head and held up his hands to show that he hadn't meant to interrupt.

"Be that as it may, the two groups have a common purpose: to prove that they can take freed slaves and teach them to be independent and productive citizens of this great country."

"Of course that's what they think. Strong, capable men setting out to work wonders!"

"Please don't sneer at them, Will. And they're not all men. That was the idea at first, but Reverend French insisted on taking his wife along, and that opened the door for other women from New York City and Boston who also applied to go. Among them is a Miss Susan Walker, sent by Salmon P. Chase himself, who insisted that she go along to serve as his eyes and ears."

"I've heard of her," Lucretia said. "She's known as a staunch abolitionist, a fervent Boston Unitarian, and a philanthropist in her own right. She has traveled extensively in Europe and boasts about friendships with several senators, congressmen, and members of President Lincoln's cabinet."

Laura nodded. "From what I've heard, when she wants something she usually gets it, and she wanted to be a part of this Port Royal Experiment. She also persuaded Secretary Chase to send two of her friends, a Mrs. Johnson and her sister, Miss Mary Donaldson, along on the adventure."

"And who are the rest of these volunteers?"

"The twenty-five men from the Boston area are almost all Unitarians, I understand, most of them between the ages of twenty and twenty-five, and all well-educated in Boston's law, medical, or divinity schools. If they were not known abolitionists, they have been screened to make sure they have no sympathy for slavery. Edward Pierce handpicked them from over 150 applicants. The men from New York tend to be older, more experienced in the ways of the world, and more evangelical in their religious beliefs."

Lucretia snorted her disbelief. "Well, I wish them fair sailing, but I still don't see what was so important about that story that you would be almost forty-five minutes late for dinner, as well as being out in inclement weather after dark. You know better than to risk your health and your safety like that, Laura. Besides, what can we Philadelphians do about problems in South Carolina?"

"Quite a bit. Mr. McKim called this meeting specifically to organize a new group to be known as the Philadelphia Port Royal Relief Committee. We already have donations of over $5,000 to provide food and clothing for the ex-slaves. And plans are well underway to offer our services to give these long-suffering people some basic English instruction and to teach them the fundamentals of the Bible."

"We?" This time, Lucretia caught the telltale change of pronouns. "You mean you actually joined this committee?"

"I certainly did."

"What do you intend to be your role? You won't be taking time away from your medical studies to help raise funds, will you?"

"More than that, actually. I'll be going with the next group to set sail for South Carolina. I'm to be the committee's designated representative, traveling with the supplies we are sending."

"What?"

"No!"

"I won't hear of it!"

"You can't leave us!"

For the next few minutes, sheer emotion overran any attempts at rational conversation. Lucretia stomped off to the kitchen, expressing her disapproval by banging the pots and pans in a furious display of temper. The younger sisters dissolved into tears, clutching at Laura and begging her to reconsider. And Will set his jaw, folded his arms across his chest, leaned back in his chair at the head of the table, and looked daggers at all these foolish women.

* * *

Eventually, an uneasy silence settled over the small family. Evenings followed such a routine in this household that, even when they were fighting, the siblings automatically took their accustomed places around the fireplace in the sitting room. Lucretia opened her Bible and began to read silently. Will filled his after-dinner pipe and lit it with a splinter of wood from the fire before settling into the armchair that had belonged to his father. The younger sisters turned to their knitting and mending, while Laura stood at the window, staring off into the darkness.

At last, she spoke, facing her family and looking at each of them in turn. "I'm truly sorry to have upset you. You know that I love you all and that I would not intentionally hurt any one of you. But you should also understand that I am answering a higher calling. I must have a purpose in life, and right now something is telling me that I need to go to South Carolina."

"Seems to me your medical studies already have given you a purpose in life. You're too old to get married and have a family of your own, but caring for the sick seemed to be a good enough response to your inevitable spinsterhood."

"This has nothing to do with whether I ever marry, Lucretia!"

"Well, you won't." Lucretia seemed determined to focus on this particular failing. "No man would have you. You're arrogant, opinionated, and your feet are too big!"

"So's my nose. Don't forget that, sister dear. You've pointed it out often enough."

"Would you just stop bickering, both of you? You're spoiling a perfectly good pipeful of tobacco. Can't a man find a bit of peace in his own home?"

"Not until we settle this. Laura, I'm the oldest member of this family, and I forbid you to go. That's the end of it."

"You have no right to forbid me, Lucretia. I'm nearly thirty-six years old, and I will do as I feel I must. Why can't you understand?"

Lucretia recognized the stubborn set to Laura's shoulders and decided to try a different tack. "Somebody else can take this fool's journey and supervise the delivery of used clothes. That's a mindless task. You'll be wasting your talents by taking on that responsibility. I thought you returned from Rhode Island to work in a military hospital of some kind. You and your real medical skills can be of even more use to people who need you here in Philadelphia."

"I know you mean well, Lucretia, but I haven't been able to find such a position. And more training is not the answer. I already know all I need to know to take care of people. I'll never officially be a doctor or work in a military facility, because I'm only a woman. But I can combine my medical knowledge and the wealth of homeopathic remedies I've learned from Dr. Hering to reach out right now to people in need. The ex-slaves, I'm told, are almost completely lacking in medical care. My position as official representative of the Relief Committee is only a formality to authorize payment of my passage. Once in South Carolina, you may be sure I will put my medical knowledge to good use. Those people need me, and I must go."

3

IN SEARCH OF
A SEAL OF APPROVAL

March 1862

During the next few days, Laura had to restate her reasons for joining the Port Royal Experiment several times. Not surprisingly, her friends and associates were no more sympathetic to her decision than her family had been. So long as the war did not directly impact their lives, most people tended to think of it as someone else's responsibility. Few shared Laura's passion for abolition, and almost no one believed a single woman should go traipsing off on her own to get involved with slaves.

The people of Philadelphia supported the Union cause. Soldiers' Aide Societies were springing up in church congregations, while other women's groups took up sewing and bandage rolling for the troops. A massive new military hospital was under construction near the Chestnut Hill railroad station in northeast Philadelphia. Politicians and high-ranking Union officers passed through the city on their way to and from Washington, D.C. Local newspapers reported troop movements and described battles in gruesome detail. But for most ordinary residents of the city, the war was an event taking place many miles away and thus removed from their day-to-day concerns.

Laura had met Dr. Constantine Hering, the man who introduced her to the principles of homeopathic medicine, while she was a student at the Women's Medical College of Philadelphia. Although the college was beginning to award the degree of Doctor of Medicine to women, many of the enrolled students were taking only selected courses rather than seeking a professional degree. Society still frowned on the idea of women doctors in general, and even hospitals newly overrun by wounded soldiers would not allow a woman to treat male patients. Laura's course of study was motivated by a sincere desire to care for others, but she had little patience with classroom lectures that substituted for patient contact. She wanted clinical experience, and homeopathic medicine offered more opportunities for hands-on care. Laura knew that Dr. Hering considered her his brightest student, and, if she were going to give up her studies, she owed it to him to explain her decision.

Dr. Hering greeted her with a smile. "Ah, Miss Towne. What brings you to my office so early this morning? Shouldn't you be about your studies? Have you had any luck in finding a hospital position? Not feeling poorly, I hope?"

Laura wasn't sure which question to answer, so she plunged into her announcement. "I'm leaving the college, sir. I'm off to South Carolina to work with the newly freed slaves there."

"What?" Dr. Hering looked puzzled. "There's a war going on there, isn't there?"

"Yes, and there's also a desperate need for people with medical training."

"But not for women, surely?"

"Why not women?"

"It's dangerous, it's . . ."

"Please, Dr. Hering. You've supported my medical training for years. I thought you'd be pleased that I've found somewhere to put it into practice."

"Yes, I've encouraged your studies, but not so you could go off to some rebel-infested swamp and treat savages."

"Savages? I thought you were an abolitionist. Or did I misinterpret?" Laura was growing angry at the direction the conversation was taking.

"I am an abolitionist, in theory, certainly. But that doesn't mean I'm willing to send a young woman off alone to . . . to . . ."

"I won't be alone, sir. I'm joining a group of missionaries and teachers who have been sent by our own government to bring aid and comfort to thousands of Negroes abandoned on the islands along the coast of South Carolina. They need someone with medical training, and I can supply it."

"But you don't have your degree yet."

"I never expected to become an MD. You've always known that."

"But you could be. I have no doubt about your abilities. You could take your degree and become a real doctor, not an amateur practitioner."

"I thought part of the reason you introduced me to homeopathic medicine was so that I could bring practical care to people who were suffering. You yourself often treat patients outside the regular channels of medicine. Why is what I'm doing any different?"

"It's different because I have training and experience behind me, and a coterie of like-minded doctors and apothecaries to support me. Where do you think you'll get your homeopathic remedies down there? You don't know enough to concoct them on your own, certainly."

"Well, I . . ."

"You have no idea!"

"I haven't worked out all the details yet, but I plan to take a supply of medicines with me. There may be homeopathic doctors in nearby cities. There's a large military complex at Hilton Head, with a hospital and trained medical personnel. I'm not going to be dropping off the face of the earth."

"As far as you know." Dr. Hering walked from his desk to open the door. His eyes were sad, but his face was set in grim lines. "Goodbye, Miss Towne. I wish you Godspeed. I'm afraid you'll need it."

* * *

Laura found herself standing in the hallway, hands shaking and eyes brimming with tears. Why did no one seem to understand? Upset but still determined on her new venture, she decided to stop at the office of James McKim to find out about the travel arrangements she needed to make.

An officious clerk glared at her the moment she walked in the door. "Help you?" he asked.

"Ah, yes, I'm Miss Laura Towne, the Philadelphia Port Royal Relief Committee representative to the Port Royal Experiment."

"What?"

"I'm here to talk to Mr. McKim about my travel arrangements."

"Huh? This is a business office, lady."

"And I'm here on official business," she said. She handed the surly clerk a calling card. "Please take this in to Mr. McKim and tell him I'm waiting in the outer office."

In a few minutes, the dapper little gentleman himself emerged to greet her. "Miss Towne. Sorry to keep you waiting, but I was not expecting you."

"I know. I apologize. It was rude of me to barge in like this, but I am concerned about my voyage to South Carolina. I've heard nothing about arrangements, and, since all my acquaintances are trying to persuade me not to go, I felt in need of some positive reinforcement."

"Oh, dear, I hope you're not about to change your mind. We really need you down there to oversee the distribution of used clothing."

"No, my mind is made up. Although I hope you'll be able to use me as something a bit more inspiring than a rag lady."

"Such as?"

"You do understand that I am a medical student, don't you? I thought that was part of the reason you chose me."

"The Freedmen's Society is in the business of providing aid to the slaves in the form of food and clothing. We're paying your salary and providing your passage to South Carolina to handle that for us. If you want to practice medicine once you get there, you'll have to take that up with Mr. Pierce. Maybe he'll need you; maybe he won't."

Nobody's making this easy, Laura thought to herself. "Fine. When do I depart?"

"That's out of my hands. You should receive two letters—one from Mr. Pierce, confirming your appointment and their willingness to have you, and one from the New York Customs House, informing you of your departure date and the name of the ship on which you will travel. Then you'll have to report to the tax collector for the Port of New York. He will administer the wartime Oath of Allegiance and issue your passport. You need to be ready to go whenever the letters arrive. Now, if you'll excuse me . . .

* * *

Once again finding herself on the other side of a closed door, Laura considered her next move. Needing someone who would lend a sympathetic ear, she decided to leave a calling card with a dear friend from her boarding school days. Sarah Clarke was always ready to share a confidence or a word of encouragement. This time, Laura's visit was welcomed, as Sarah herself answered the door.

"Laura! How delightful to see you. I was just wondering what to do with myself for the rest of the morning when I saw you out here coming up the steps. I hope you can stay."

"If you're sure you're not busy. I only intended to leave a card with a suggestion that we meet soon for tea and conversation."

"Better yet—stay for lunch. Come in. I'll tell Cook."

Laura settled herself with relief on a small settee. The previous two interviews had left her standing, and her feet were beginning to protest. Sarah came bustling back and perched next to Laura, clasping her hand. "Are you all right? You look a bit—I don't know—sad, frazzled, tired?"

"Confused, I think. You were at the Abolitionist Society the other day when I agreed to represent the Philadelphia Port Royal Relief Committee, weren't you?"

"Yes, and I've been excited for you ever since! What an adventure for you!"

"What a hassle for me, you mean."

"Why? Has something gone amiss?"

"Only that everyone is angry with me—my family for going off without them, Dr. Hering for giving up my studies, and Mr. McKim for pestering him about my duties. I'm beginning to think it was a mistake to volunteer."

"Oh, Laura, it's the chance of a lifetime. What I wouldn't give to be going with you!"

"Humph. You're the only one who sees it that way. I was disappointed about the reactions of Dr. Hering and Mr. McKim, but my family's disapproval weighs on my conscience. What if I leave and something terrible happens to them?"

"What if you're here and something terrible happens? Either way, you're not responsible for what happens to anyone but yourself."

"But I owe them so much. You know that after Mother died we children were pretty much left to raise ourselves. We've formed a tight bond over the years, and I've always believed that I received more than I gave back. They've supported me in whatever I wanted to do, so now, when they are objecting to my departure, I feel a tremendous amount of guilt."

"That's understandable, but you don't owe them your life. What does Ellen say?"

Laura grimaced. "Ellen. That's part of the problem, of course. You were at the meeting. You know that she agreed to go with me as soon as her teaching job is finished. I haven't told my family that. They don't like my relationship with Ellen—never have—and I'm afraid they'll think I have chosen her over them."

"Haven't you?" Sarah smiled at her gently.

"Maybe so. I know I wouldn't go to South Carolina without her, although I'm willing to leave my family behind. See, that's another reason I'm feeling so guilty."

"Laura, I've watched you and Ellen together. If ever two people were soul mates, it's the two of you. I would be jealous of your friendship if it weren't so apparent that the two of you share an unbreakable bond. You mirror each other's posture. You finish each other's sentences. You belong together, and if you can find a way to live together permanently, I'm happy for you. The fact that you'll also be doing work fit for angels just makes the arrangement that much better. You'll treat the sick, she'll teach, and the world will be a better place. Your family will just have to accept that. So, Godspeed, my friend. Now, let's have lunch and talk girl talk."

4
SETTLING DIFFERENCES
March 1862

A clatter followed by a crash sent Lucretia Towne, with apron askew and flour in her hair, dashing up the back stairs to find out what had happened. She found her sister Laura sitting on a trunk at the foot of the attic stairs, looking disheveled and ruefully rubbing her knee.

"What in heaven's name are you up to now, Laura?"

Laura laughed despite herself. "I was trying to be useful without disturbing anyone. I guess I failed, didn't I? I'm sorry if I frightened you."

"What's in the trunk?"

"I've just finished cleaning out my room. I decided to store the things I'm not taking with me in the attic, so my room will be empty if you should want to use it for something else. But the trunk was heavier than I expected. I thought I could drag it up the stairs, but I couldn't budge it. So I came down to the bottom and tried pushing it up the steps ahead of me. That almost worked, but I couldn't figure out how to hold it in place and climb the stairs myself at the same time. I must have let go for a second, and it came barreling down on top of me. I've been sitting here trying to come up with a new idea."

"Here, let me help you. It's obviously a job for two. I'll go above and pull while you push from down here."

Together they managed to bounce the trunk from step to step until it rested safely on the attic floor, but both were panting from the effort. They sat side by side on the trunk to catch their breath. Lucretia made a small clearing noise in the back of her throat—one Laura recognized as an expression of disapproval. She peeked at her out of the corner of her eye to determine how angry her older sister might be. The frown on Lucretia's face was not reassuring.

"Thanks for your help, Lucy," she said, hoping to stave off the inevitable.

"Humph! The trunk is safely up here, but I don't understand what's going on. You've cleaned out your room? Why? I'm all in favor of neatness, but not to this extent. You make it sound as if you are not planning to come back. And what am I supposed to do with an extra empty room?"

"I don't know when I'll be back. I could be gone for a very long time," Laura said.

"Stuff and nonsense! How long does it take to sail from here to South Carolina? Three days? Four? And then how long will it take you to distribute the food and clothing supplies you are delivering? I understand that you're responsible for their safe arrival, but surely you'll be back within the month. And if you think I'm then going to help you drag this infernal trunk back downstairs, you . . ."

"Dear Lucretia, please try to understand. Mine is not a task that can be handled quickly. Yes, my ostensible job at the moment is to deliver the goods the Committee has collected. But that title simply justifies them paying my passage on the transport. Once I'm there, I have much bigger plans."

"Seems to me you always have 'big' plans. You just conveniently forget to tell anyone about them."

"Please don't be angry. I only have a few more days here at home, and I don't want to spend them fighting with you. Come, let's go down to the kitchen and put the kettle on for a cup of tea. I'll try to explain exactly what we have planned."

* * *

Laura settled herself at the kitchen table, but Lucretia refused to sit down. She returned to the sideboard, where she had been in the midst of kneading a loaf of bread. The vigorous punches and slaps she delivered to that lump of helpless dough made Laura cringe. She fully understood that they were also meant to express her sister's displeasure.

"Lucy, I know you understand the abolitionist position as well as I do. I've sat beside you in church as we listened to Reverend Furness preach about the evils of slavery, and I've seen you nod your head in complete agreement with what he says. Our country is fighting this terrible war to rid ourselves of an evil practice. But there's much more to the problem than simply putting down the Southern rebellion and telling the slaves that they are free."

"Of course I understand that, and I understand that our government will be faced with great difficulties in assimilating the slaves into normal society once the war is over. But that's going to take government policies and government action. You're just one woman—more intelligent than the average woman, I grant you—but still just one small woman against a very large problem. I fail to see why the solution has suddenly become your responsibility, when you have responsibilities right here at home."

"At Port Royal, the problems can't wait until the war is over."

"Why not? Surely the war can't go on for much longer."

"I'm afraid that's where you are wrong, sister. The Army has stopped signing soldiers up for a three-month enlistment. Now they sign on for three years, and even that may not be long enough, according to some of the speakers we have heard recently."

Lucretia whirled around and glared at her. "Well, if that is true, just how much do you expect to accomplish with a war raging all around you—if you even manage to survive?"

"Port Royal is perfectly safe, my dear. The Confederate forces abandoned it, and some twelve thousand of our boys are now stationed on the islands to protect the area. I'll probably be safer there than on the streets of Philadelphia. You keep telling me how dangerous our own streets are at night."

"So it's safe. And the Army is in control. And the slave owners are gone. What, exactly, do you think you are going to do, beyond the obvious, benevolent gesture of passing out some used clothing?"

"I'm hoping to set up a permanent resource center, where ex-slaves can come for all sorts of assistance. We'll provide food and clothing, of course, but I can also offer medical treatment. We'll have a lawyer or two to help them handle their legal affairs. There are already cotton agents in place to help with the selling of crops, and Ellen will start a school to teach both the children and their parents." Laura's excitement was so great when she talked about this idea that she could not help but smile in anticipation.

Lucretia simply stared at her for a moment. Then she spoke slowly, emphasizing each word. "Are you telling me . . . that you're taking . . . that young girl . . . with you?"

"Ellen Murray? Of course."

Lucretia turned away. She picked up the bread dough she had been working and slammed it into a pan. "Raise!" she ordered, and Laura could have sworn she saw the dough gather itself up to make a greater effort.

Silence dominated the kitchen for a few minutes that seemed like hours. Then Laura ventured a bit of explanation. "Actually, Ellen's not going with me right away. She's a teacher, you know, and she has to work at her current school until the end of the term. But then she'll be coming down to join me. She believes in our cause as fervently as I do."

"Nonsense! She's still a child, with a silly schoolgirl crush on you. You should be ashamed to take advantage of her."

"She's not a child, she's a grown woman. And she doesn't have a crush on me. We just happen to be very close friends who share a common goal. And I'm not taking advantage of her. She wants to come, and her mother approves."

"You haven't even known the Murrays that long, have you?"

"Just since I went to Rhode Island for that course in homeopathy, but Ellen and I spent long evenings together in her mother's boarding house last winter, and we found we had all sorts of things in common. It doesn't take long to know when you have found a real soul mate."

"Soul mate, indeed. Don't you realize how it may look to others? The two of you running off to South Carolina together? Abandoning your own families to . . . to . . ."

By now, Laura was angry, too. "What are you insinuating? That there's something wrong with our friendship?"

"Only if that friendship becomes a substitute for whatever else is missing in your life."

"Ellen is not a substitute for anything or anyone! We suit each other. We are very different, but each of us balances the other's weaknesses. I tend to take the quickest and most practical route to my goal, even if it sometimes means riding roughshod over those in my way. Ellen is more sympathetic and compassionate, so she balances my abruptness. She can, however, let her emotions get in the way of doing what needs to be done. That's where I can balance her by providing a bit of logic. Apart, each one of us can be weak. Together, we are strong. And we're going to need all our strength in the coming days, Lucretia. Please try to understand that."

Suddenly, Lucretia plopped herself into a chair across the table and buried her face in her hands. "I love you, Laura. For all your faults, you're still my baby sister, and I feel responsible for you. I know—that's absurd. But I do." Her shoulders shook, and she refused to lift her head.

Laura reached out and patted her hand. "I know you want only the best for me, Lucretia. But in this instance you are going to have to trust my judgment. I'll be as careful as I know how to be."

"That's not a whole lot of comfort, you know!" Lucretia almost smiled through her tears.

"I know, but you really have taught me well. When things get too tough, I'll just bake a loaf of bread and take my frustrations out on it."

5
VOYAGE SOUTH
April 1862

I nevitable paperwork complicated Laura's departure. New York customs officials finally sent her formal permission to sail with the *Oriental* on April 8th, provided she take the usual Oath of Allegiance and bring her paperwork to show that Mr. Pierce was expecting her in Port Royal. She set out from Philadelphia in high spirits, buoyed by the good wishes of her friend Sarah Clarke. Laura's enthusiasm even carried her through a potentially troublesome encounter at a hotel in New York, where the clerk tried to deny her a room because she was a woman traveling alone.

Laura Towne joined a group of twenty-three passengers as she boarded the *Oriental* for the voyage to South Carolina. Most of their small band came from Boston; Laura was the only representative from Philadelphia. She had initial doubts about the qualifications of some of the men, whom she found disagreeable, but, remembering her own experiences, she withheld all but private judgments.

Two other women made up their numbers. Helen Philbrick was traveling to join her husband, Edward S. Philbrick. Accompanying her was her dear friend Harriet Ware. Mr. Philbrick had specifically requested that his wife not make the trip until she could have Harriet with her, a precaution she privately thought rather silly. Nevertheless, she was happy for Harriet's cheerful companionship, and the two women quickly added Laura to their intrepid little group.

"You must be quite proud of your husband, Mrs. Philbrick," Laura commented. "I understand that he has been instrumental in managing the efforts of—what are they calling themselves now? Oh, yes, Gideon's Band."

"Leave it to Edward to manage any effort he joins," Mrs. Philbrick said. "I love him dearly, but his Harvard education has turned him into a real stickler for detail. I suspect, however, that the most important thing he has done has been turning the phrase 'Gideon's Band' into a badge of honor."

"That was his idea? I didn't know."

"The story he told me was this: when the original Freedmen's Relief groups from Boston and New York boarded the *Atlantic* to sail to South Carolina last month, they looked a bit scruffy and strange. One of the other passengers, a Mr. Forbes, made a disparaging comment about them being just another band of religious fanatics. He didn't mean the label 'Gideonite' as a compliment. Edward, however, turned it into one, telling the gentleman that he was proud to be carrying 'a pitcher of light and a trumpet' into the slave-owning South. He then began using the phrase with the rest of the group, and they soon adopted it with pride. By the time the ship reached South Carolina, Edward had managed to impress the skeptical Mr. Forbes, and Forbes volunteered to help the efforts of Gideon's Band. That's just the sort of thing Edward does."

"That's a wonderful story, Helen, but Miss Towne should also know about his other contributions," Harriet Ware said.

"Edward has left a blossoming career as an engineer and an architect in order to go on this mission. He's not only paying his own way but he has also contributed over $1,000 to the Boston Educational Commission to get its work started. His reputation was largely responsible for convincing other businessmen to join the effort."

Helen looked slightly embarrassed and proud at the same time. "Be that as it may, his benefactions don't change the fact that he can be something of a lovable old fuddy-duddy."

"Helen! You make him sound ancient, and I know he's not yet turned thirty-five."

"A young fuddy-duddy, then. But you should have seen all the instructions he sent me about making this trip. I received a complete packing list. Here—I have it in my hand satchel because I didn't want to forget anything. He's sure to check. Listen to this: 'Not over five dollars in silver money. Bed sacks and pillow. Three umbrellas with light covers, flypaper, tin cups, bowls and teapot, a set of wooden boxes for rice, sugar, and other stores. A spring-balance that will weigh about twenty pounds. A knife, spoon, and fork (plated, not silver). A thermometer and three pounds of tea'."

Laura could not help but grin. "It sounds to me like a shopping list of things he forgot and wished he had."

"Oh, I'm sure of it! There isn't anything very womanly there, you'll notice. I added a mirror, some soothing lotions and soaps, and some small pillows, but he won't appreciate those."

"He's a man, after all," Harriet said. "My brother Charles is much the same, as you'll all discover when he joins us in a few weeks."

"He has definitely decided to come, then? How wonderful!" Now it was Helen's turn to explain that gentleman's qualifications. "Harriet and Charles are the grandchildren of Henry Ware, the Harvard professor and pillar of the Unitarian clergy. They both inherited the family's dedication to the abolitionist cause. Charles is also an astute businessman, and Edward has been hoping that he would agree to come out and take over as superintendent of one of the most important plantations. He will be a valuable addition to Gideon's Band."

Laura was beginning to feel a little intimidated. "You are both so well-connected, and such an integral part of the Port Royal Experiment. I'm afraid I don't have much to recommend me, other than a sincere desire to help."

"On the contrary. I've been told something about your extensive educational background—in medicine, wasn't it?"

"It's true that if I were a man, I would be a doctor by now. I have taken all the training required, but I have not had the practical experience. Women doctors, as I'm sure you know, are not exactly well-accepted yet."

"Yet? You expect them to be?" Harriet asked.

"Yes, of course, particularly now, with a war going on and a critical shortage of military doctors. The change will come—perhaps too late for me, but not for others. Meanwhile, I've also been trained in homeopathic remedies, and I'm hoping I can put some of that experience to work among the freed slaves. I understand many of them suffer from poor health."

"They do. Your medical training is all you need to recommend you."

"That, and the complete trust of the Philadelphia Port Royal Relief Committee!" Helen exclaimed. "They've entrusted you with overseeing all their contributions. I assure you that neither Harriet nor I would be given such a prestigious position in the Boston Commission. You must be very well-qualified, indeed."

"Just another stickler for detail, I'm afraid, but I'm proud to be one of the carriers of Gideon's trumpet."

* * *

The *Oriental* arrived at Hilton Head on Monday, April 14th, and the new recruits traveled up the river to Beaufort the next day. Harriet Ware stared out at the scenery and was entranced. In her first letter home, she wrote: "The sail up was very beautiful, the green beyond description brilliant, and now and then the deeper shade of palmetto or live-oak. Some of the plantations were very picturesque. Roses and azaleas were plainly visible . . . the scent of flowers filling the air, everything like a June day after a shower."

Edward Pierce and his assistant, Edward W. Hooper, were waiting for them at the dock. Unfortunately, he had to tell the new arrivals that their lodgings were not ready for them. Without going into the details, he simply explained that there had been a mix-up with the cotton agents and the houses would not be ready until Saturday. In the interval, they would have to remain in Beaufort.

Pierce turned to Hooper and said, "Let's take the ladies over to the Forbes's place. I'm sure Mrs. Forbes can make room for them. Then the gentlemen can go out to the Fripp House with the others who are still working here in town. That should hold everyone satisfactorily until we can make better arrangements.

Helen Philbrick was the first to speak up. "Forbes? Is that the same Mr. Forbes who traveled with you on the *Atlantic?*"

"It is, indeed. John Murray Forbes has become our chief supporter here in Beaufort." He turned to the assembled missionaries to explain. "Mr. Forbes is a prominent Boston businessman with a shrewd ability to assess a man's character. Some of you may know him or his sons. He has been involved in the cotton trade for a number of years, and he agreed to come down here on his own to see to it that our government was treated fairly in the handling of the cotton crop. He and his wife have taken a house here until the next crop is safely harvested."

"But why should he care about us? Is he also an abolitionist?"

"Interestingly enough, he is not. Or at least he wasn't. I get the impression that he has been deeply troubled about the morality of the slave trade for many years. But he is also a businessman, and he recognized—as some of us have been very slow to understand—that the abolition of slavery would spell the immediate end of the cotton industry and cause a major economic crisis in this country. He considered abolitionists to be dewy-eyed dreamers with no understanding of the way the world functioned. He had also learned to fear the threat of a slave insurrection. As a result, he dismissed abolitionists as the lunatic fringe.

"Then he met us, and discovered that we, as a group, are well-educated, well-connected, and thoroughly reasonable. He even recognized several of the younger men in our group as Harvard classmates of his own sons. By the end of our voyage, he had given us a grudging vote of acceptance. When we arrived in Beaufort, he met Colonel Reynolds and his band of cotton agents. They are a thoroughly nasty bunch, by the way. They have no interest in anything except making money, and they are willing to adopt the worst practices of the slave drivers to get work out of the local black population. A few doses of their company, and Mr. Forbes was ready to become a Gideonite. He has been unfailingly helpful."

Laura was not particularly happy about the delay in reaching her assigned plantation. She was even more concerned that Mr. Pierce was imposing three guests on Mrs. Forbes without her consent. She knew better, of course, than to challenge her new superior before they had even been properly introduced. But her impetuous spirit took over. "Mr. Pierce? Excuse me. I'm Laura Towne, from the Philadelphia Committee. I don't like being a bother to strangers. Is there nowhere else we could go for a few days? I'm sure we could cope for ourselves."

Pierce stared at her for a long moment—long enough to let her know she had overstepped her bounds. "We are in a unique position here. We are strangers in a strange land, if you will. We all make sacrifices for the common good, without question or objection. Right now, you need to be in a safe place, where I don't have to be worrying about you. So you will come with me to the Forbes house. Someday I will ask the same sort of sacrifice from you, and I will expect you to accept it with the same smile you'll see on Mrs. Forbes's face when we arrive on her doorstep."

RINA ON "DE OAKS"
April 1862

It pinch muh heart how bad dis place look now. De Oaks usta be a purty place, but it jis stroyd now. An aint nobody fuh blame, cept eberbody. We jis lettin it fall part.

Dis be de onliest home I'se ever knowed. I growed up here, in de slave village an de fields an woods round here. I caint magine livin nowheres else. But it sho aint what it once be.

Massa Pope, he start stroying fore he run off. He say he dint want a damn Yankee drinkin he likker or eatin he food, so he go to de stohouse an he chop de necks right off de bottles uh likker an let it run out on de floor. Den he take a big ol knife an he punch holes in de bags uh sugah an salt an meal, an he stir dem all togedduh wit he boots.

Den he go to de cottonhouse, an he take a hammuh to de wheels what make de cotton gin turn. He knock off de teed what grab de cottonseed. An den he take de axe an chop up de frame, so de cotton gin aint neber gwine work agin.

Massa an Missus, dey try fuh loads up de good stuff in sacks an trunks, but dey jis leave what dey caint carry. So we be gedduh up de tings dey leave behind. We be usin oyster shells fuh spoons all our lives. Now we gots we sum real spoons. Dat not be stealin, cause Massa gone, an it look like he neber gwine come back. We jis usin he tings fuh de puposes Gawd meant fuh dem. Ifn dey come back, we

41

gwine gib back what we bin usin. Til den, we be keepin de good tings outta de hands uh de white folk what come truh here.

Like I says, most uh de Yankee soljers we seen here be nice an polite to we. But dey comes lookin fuh food, cause dey hungerd, too. Some uh dem breaks intuh de locked smokehouse an takes de sassiges an hams what be hangin dere. We aint gone dere, cause we aint gots de keys. But de soljers, dey jis busts de door down. Dey takes most uh de anmals, too. Dey takes de strong-lookin mules an de cows fuh roast.

But when dey try fuh take de chikkuns, den dey gots trubble. Aint nobody gwine take muh chikkuns. Dem hens, dey scrawny an tough. But eberday, dey be layin dem eggs an gibbin we food. Onliest soljer eber try carryin off a chikkun fro muh house, I tooks a broom to he head an runs he right off!

But de wurs fuh stroyin de plantation houses be de cotton agents. Dey don care bout nuttin cept bein comfy an gettin money. When dey comes here, dey jis moves intuh de big house like it blong to dem. Dat Massa Whitin what live here now, he move all de furniture round fuh set heself up in a couple uh rooms. Den he start cartin de res uh de beds an tables back to Bufor. Dey say he be sellin eberting he git he hands on.

An he gots a nasty temper, too. He be orderin we roun jis like he be de one what own we. An when he don git what he want, he scream an yell an pull out he whip or he pistol. Mebbe he be de Yankee de young missus be warnin Zannah bout.

I be very sad when I looks roun. I don know what we gwine do. Cept mebbe starve, less we gits sum help fro somewheres.

6
FIRST SIGNS OF TROUBLE
April 1862

For the next several days, Laura had time to explore the city of Beaufort, trying to imagine what it must have looked like before the invasion. She admired the huge oak trees that filled each yard, some of them so massive and gnarled that they seemed a part of the land rather than something planted upon it. She admired the flowers, many of them now growing wild beyond their original gardens. She breathed deeply of the soft air, enjoying the tang of salt and pluff mud at low tide. But she also lamented the destruction and desolation of empty houses, the sight of idle soldiers roaming the alleyways looking for trouble, and the prevalence of dirty and half-naked Negro children wandering aimlessly about the streets.

Mrs. Forbes, who had turned out to be a lovely and gracious hostess, took her around to visit some of the schools the Gideonites had already started for those who had been house slaves in the town. Laura was surprised at first to see as many women as children in the makeshift classrooms, many of them with babes in arms or toddlers clinging to their skirts. "It has been against the law in South Carolina to teach a slave to read," Mrs. Forbes explained, "so the adults are as hungry for lessons as the children. The mothers come during the workweek and their husbands show up on Sunday, when they have their day off."

"But how on earth do the teachers decide what to teach? Some of the children are much too young to learn even their ABCs."

"Then they learn about how to learn," Ms. Forbes replied. "Over at Miss White's school, she has a gymnastics class for the little ones who want nothing more than to tumble on the floor. We do what we can. After all, anything is better than the nothing they had before."

In the evenings, Laura talked to Mr. Pierce and Reverend French, asking questions about the soldiers and cotton agents, who seemed equally hostile to the Gideonites. "Don't they understand that you are all trying to do what is best for the Negroes?"

"What's best for the Negro is not their concern, Miss Towne," French replied. "The soldiers are bored most of the time, but occasionally rebels challenge them by trying to sneak back on to the islands, and then their only concern is defending the military boundaries. The darkies just get in the way. As for the cotton agents, their sole concern is securing the cotton crop, so they resent any attempt to distract the slaves from their work in the fields. We are all working at odds with one another, I'm afraid."

"What kind of school system are you setting up here?" Laura asked Mr. Pierce on another occasion. "Do the women who have already gone out to the plantations teach the same kinds of lessons as those offered here in town?"

"Oh, there is no system here, Miss Towne. We're all floundering through uncharted territory, just doing what we can."

"I understand, and I certainly don't want to be a cause of further bother to you. I am anxious, however, to go out to my assigned plantation. May I ask what is causing the delay?"

"Ah, there has been a bit of trouble out at Coffin Point. That's Mr. Philbrick's assignment, and he wants to be sure things have settled down before he takes Mrs. Philbrick and Miss Ware out there."

"Trouble?"

"A little rebellion, you might call it, among some of the ex-slaves who don't want to work the cotton fields. One apparently drew a knife, although he backed off when Mr. Philbrick met his challenge. A couple of soldiers have gone out to present a show of force, and the slaves are settling down nicely. They have been so beaten down by their conditions of servitude that they fear any white man who speaks forcefully to them."

Laura realized that his explanation was meant to reassure her, but, instead, it left her vaguely apprehensive. Until this moment she had not considered the possibility that the Negroes might resent the whites who had come to help them.

* * *

The journey to St. Helena Island took two full days. It involved a great deal of loading baggage onto carts for treks across land, followed by unloading and stowing the supplies on flat-bottomed scows to cross the ever-present slivers of water.

"Why hasn't anyone built bridges?" Laura asked.

"Watch the tide come in and out, and you'll understand," Mr. Philbrick said. "The water is seldom in the same place for more than a couple of hours. It's easier to wait for high tides and then row across."

Mr. Eustis, of the Eustis Plantation, welcomed the newcomers to his house for the first night. He was a Boston-bred Yankee who had inherited this piece of land from his stepmother, making him both a member of the Gideonites and a member of the slave-owning class. The combination was confusing enough to keep his slaves in perpetual submission. He had a large unused building on his property that the Gideonite women had turned into a storefront for the distribution of clothing and food supplies. The shipment Laura was escorting was unloaded here on Ladies Island, although she was to live on St. Helena Island.

"Don't worry," Eustis assured her. "There will always be a black man to row you across when you need to travel from house to store."

On the second afternoon, the small party of newcomers finally arrived at The Oaks, a large plantation that had been owned by Dr. Daniel Pope. This was Laura's final destination. The Philbricks came along, planning to spend the night there, since the journey across St. Helena Island to Coffin Point would take most of a day. Laura's first impression of the house was one of total chaos. Some rooms were closed off because a cotton agent was still in residence. Furniture was scarce, and crates served in place of chairs. Dark faces seemed to be everywhere, peering through windows and doorways, and then ducking out of sight. One parlor had been turned into a makeshift office for Edward Pierce, who used the house as his headquarters, and for Mr. Hooper, who acted as local superintendent. Miss Susan Walker was supposed to be in charge of the household, but a much younger woman, Nelly Winsor, was the one scurrying around to make arrangements for company. Two elderly women, Mrs. Johnson and her sister Miss Donaldson, had gone upstairs to finish packing their things.

"Packing?" Laura asked. "Are they being reassigned because of my arrival?"

"No, they're going home. The work has been too much for them, and Miss Donaldson has been ill the whole time."

"Oh." Laura was disturbed to realize that some of the original group were already giving up. Her first impressions of the Port Royal Experiment sank even further. Gamely, she tried to smile as Miss Walker stormed into the parlor from a day spent sorting used clothing.

Edward Philbrick introduced Laura to Miss Walker. "This is Miss Laura Matilda Towne, sent to us from the Philadelphia Port Royal Relief Committee," he explained. "She has brought us a huge shipment of clothing and supplies contributed by the good people of her city. And she has been charged by them to oversee the proper distribution of their contributions. Mr. Pierce says she is to work from here, since you already have a storehouse set up."

"I see," Susan said. "You are certainly welcome, Miss Towne, but this is hardly the time for us to discuss the nature of your duties. First, we will have to make arrangements for all of you to bed down tonight."

"Mrs. Johnson will remain in her room with her sister," Nelly Winsor said. "I thought the rest could make do sleeping here in the parlor, since it will just be for one night. I've sent two of the girls to find blankets and sheeting. And everyone is going to need supper, too," she added.

"Then I had better go and see what is available in the pantry. Excuse me, Miss Towne. We shall have to have a long talk, but at the moment, it appears I have inherited the housekeeping chores around here from our departing colleague." She stormed from the parlor as only an irate Susan Walker could do.

* * *

The next day, Miss Walker turned her attention to Laura. They sat in the parlor. Laura Towne's demeanor could strike a new acquaintance as intimidating or reassuring, depending on that acquaintance's own character. Miss Walker, however, had no intention of being intimidated. Both women sat with backs ramrod straight, hands primly folded in laps. Laura's gaze was forthright, and her full attention focused on Susan. "I have much to learn from you, Miss Walker. I hope you will be patient with me."

"Patient? I can't promise that. I am not naturally a patient person, and matters are always pressing here. I will need you to pitch in and do whatever needs to be done without asking too many questions."

"I will certainly try. Do I have quarters here?" Inwardly, Laura winced, realizing that she had just asked a question.

"You'll be sharing a room upstairs with Nelly Winsor. She makes a fine companion—neat, quiet, and helpful. She and I have been sharing a room ever since we arrived here because Mrs. Reynolds was the eldest of our group and deserved her privacy. Now I seem to have been elevated to the position of eldest, so I will have Nelly move into Mrs. Reynolds's old room with you. I hope that will be satisfactory."

"Of course. Whatever you say." Laura was trying very hard to assure this irritable lady that she was not going to be a problem.

"Fine. Then let me tell you about our duty roster. There will be only the three of us to handle the chores, since Mr. Hooper oversees the farming and Mr. Pierce is only here periodically as he tries to supervise all the plantations on the islands. We three are in charge of all the housekeeping here in the main house, the teaching and preaching in the slave quarters, and the distribution of food and clothing to all the former slaves on this side of the island. We alternate our positions every two weeks, so you will have to learn to perform all those tasks."

"That doesn't seem very efficient to me," Laura commented. "Wouldn't it be better for each of us to learn to do one job well?"

"No, that would be unfair. I thoroughly enjoy my work with the stores, but I hate housekeeping. Mrs. Johnson and Nelly both preferred to be in the classroom. So by switching positions, no one has to do the hated housekeeping chores all the time."

"Well, as Mr. Philbrick told you, my specific assignment is to oversee the distribution of goods sent from Philadelphia. However, if you already have the stores arranged to your liking, I will be happy to turn that task over to you while I assume the housekeeping."

"You don't mind doing the chores?" Susan cocked an eyebrow at her, looking skeptical.

"Actually, I hate housekeeping as much as anyone, but when my mother died in childbirth, the rest of us children had to learn how to care for ourselves. I'm used to cooking and cleaning. Besides, I don't think I'd be very good at teaching and preaching. My training has been in medicine, and I've been hoping that I would be able to use my medical experience among the slaves. Working here at the house will make me available if anyone is injured or ill."

Susan was tempted to argue further. She didn't really like this woman coming in and disrupting the way things were being done. But the promise of not having any more cooking and scrubbing duties was too tempting. "Fair enough," she answered. "We'll try it that way and see how it works out. Now, there are some other tough lessons you need to learn quickly about how things are done around here.

"It hasn't taken us long to discover that women are more warmly welcomed in the slave quarters than are our male counterparts, primarily because we are taking the place of the plantation mistress. The blacks find white women stabilizing and reassuring, a source of medical care, and conveyers of the education that is the key to their freedom. Therefore, they trust us. And they will particularly trust you because of what they will call your medical 'larnin.'

"The white men, on the other hand, are seen as the labor bosses. Because we newcomers know little or nothing about raising cotton, our men have to rely on the former slaves, first to teach them what needs to be done, and then to do it. However, that puts the blacks into their old roles as workers and automatically casts the whites as the masters."

"That concept makes me uncomfortable," Laura interrupted. "I thought we were here to free the slaves, not to take over as their masters."

"The blacks' reluctance to work in the cotton fields makes the problems worse. They labor readily enough when they are planting food crops, because they understand that they are thereby feeding themselves. But few appreciate the value of cotton because they have never shared in the rewards of the crop. So when the plantation manager has to order them into the cotton fields, the expected response is still, 'Yes, Massa,' and the work is just as backbreaking as it has always been. Yet everyone tells us that keeping the cotton crops growing is vital to the interests of our government. The need for cotton is what leads Congress and Mr. Lincoln's cabinet into supporting us in the kind of work we consider more important."

"Do the former slaves understand that at all?"

"I'm afraid not. Despite our best efforts, we are failing to communicate our basic message that whites and blacks are equal. Mr. Philbrick and the others remain convinced that the blacks can be trained for full citizenship, but they did not count on having to overcome the deference that the blacks express toward whites simply because we are white."

"Why is that? It seems a clear message to me."

"I think it's because we can't really understand the slave culture under which the blacks have lived for so long. As slaves, they lived in a strict hierarchy in which the ideal white man not only profited from the labor of his slave but also accorded him a kindly protection. If a slave had such a master, he learned to rely upon him. If the master was cruel, the ingratiating dependence of 'Sambo' was a superb defense for the helpless slave. We have had to learn that this dependence and deference is one of conscious playacting.

"With a few exceptions, the laborers have gone about their work as in the master's time. All understand the planting better than we can teach them, but they need encouragement. They have not yet become self-reliant. Many are well-disposed and work willingly when made to understand that the corn they plant is to furnish them food, but the cotton must also be planted for the government. For this planting wages will be paid them, and with their wages they must buy clothes, sweeting and tobacco, or have none. That's the first lesson we have to teach them. The meaning of freedom has to wait."

7
LAURA ADAPTS
May 1862

Laura Towne found the Sea Island climate more comfortable than she had expected. In Philadelphia, she had suffered every winter from the dryness of the air. Flaky skin, nosebleeds, and a dry hacking cough had been her chronic condition. Here, the moist sea air was both invigorating and soothing. She breathed it in huge gulps, tasting the salt of the sea and rejoicing in the softness of the air.

The scenery, too, she found beautiful. Oh, she admitted that the wild flowers of the island were a bit scrawny, but she had never seen such roses, camellias, and azaleas. "The island looks as if some imaginative painter has just spilled his entire palette of pinks, reds, and oranges across the landscape," she remarked. She even liked the soft silver sheen of the live-oak bark and the curly clusters of moss that hung from every branch.

Sometimes, her fingers itched to work in the yard, replanting some of the flowering bushes so that they would soften the bare wooden structure of their house. "Why in the world are all the roses out by the barn, where you can't even smell them over the peculiar tang of the stables?" she asked.

"I don know, missus," answered Joe, one of their house slaves. "Sumbody want dem dere, I spose. Slaves don ask tings like dat. We jis duz what we tole."

"Never mind. I'm sure I'll come to enjoy having a flowery barn." That was a typical Laura reaction, and the attitude served her well in this new environment. While many of Gideon's ladies complained bitterly about everything that was "not like it was back home," Laura thought the differences were invigorating.

She was finding the Negroes fascinating. At every opportunity she moved among them, her quick eye catching details of their lives that others did not notice. One day, shortly after her arrival, a house servant named Caroline invited Laura and Nelly Winsor to visit her mother's cabin because the older woman wanted to meet "dat missus wit all de larnin."

On the way, Laura observed for herself the natural deference that Caroline displayed. The black woman had dressed up for the occasion, holding a lace handkerchief at her waist and displaying a silver thimble on a string around her neck. She carried herself with obvious self-confidence, but she stayed two steps behind the white women, calling out directions when needed, but refusing to take the lead. At the door of the freshly whitewashed cabin, she reached around them to knock, but let them precede her into the main room.

Laura looked around with curiosity. The floor glistened with bright new boards, not yet nailed down but arranged carefully, side by side, over the original dirt floor. There were several rickety chairs surrounding a huge mahogany bureau. A crystal glass held a bunch of scraggly wild flowers. These recent additions, obviously borrowed from the main house, were such a focus of pride that Laura could not bring herself to ask about their origins. She simply appreciated the effort that had gone into making this tiny cabin seem more elegant than it could ever hope to be.

The clothing the slaves wore to church provided other examples of their need to show their individuality. One fellow always sported a jacket of many colors; its origin as an oriental rug was clear. It had to be scratchy and heavy and horrendously hot in the early summer months, but no manner of discomfort could persuade the old gentleman to remove his coat. Laura noticed another example of what it meant to these people to have new clothes: several came to church barefoot, carrying their brightly polished shoes in their hands.

"Why don't they put their shoes on?" she asked Miss Winsor the first time she noticed the phenomenon. "Don't they fit?"

"They probably don't know or care about fit. They don't want to get them dusty or dirty."

"Then why bother bringing them?"

"So that others will know that they have them. These people have enormous pride, and for those who have had nothing for most of their lives, a simple possession is a mark of real status," Miss Winsor explained. "Just wait until you work in the clothing store. You will be surprised, I think, to see what a highly developed sense of style the women have. They pick over our offerings endlessly, looking for just the right shirt for a husband or the most stylish dress for themselves."

"And then, I suppose, they don't wear those, either?"

"Sometimes not. They'll come to work wearing the dirtiest rags you can ever imagine, but it's almost impossible to sell them a good serviceable work dress. We have whole bundles of coarsely-woven shirts and drab dresses that no one wants."

Laura smiled. "Actually, I think I can understand that. I'm not thrilled about getting work clothes myself. For newly freed slaves, clothes meant to be worn in the fields or the wash-house must seem almost insulting. They become reminders of the past rather than promises of a brighter future."

The schoolroom offered more lessons about the slaves. The first time Laura visited Nelly Winsor's class, she was pleasantly surprised to hear how much the former slaves had learned in a brief period of time. They recited their ABCs with ease and grinned from ear to ear when they were asked to read aloud from a simple primer. They scribbled their numbers on pieces of slate and matched the numbers to their own fingers, beaming with pride all the time. These were signs of how much the slaves valued an education. After all the years when it had been against the law of the state to teach a slave to read and write, children and adults alike responded hungrily to their lessons.

Laura noticed again how many adults shared the classroom with the children. Mothers with babies at the breast and toddlers hanging from their skirts sat on the low benches and followed the teacher's every word. Sometimes a crying baby or a demanding toddler forced young mothers to get up and go outside, but as soon as the immediate problem was solved, they returned to their seats and continued their recitations as if they had never been gone.

When the missionaries had started a Sunday school, they quickly learned that "school" meant only one thing to a slave. "We don study dat!" was the belligerent response of one young man to a Bible story. "Dis be a school what happen on Sunday. We study de ABCs. Sunday be de onliest day we gots fuh do dat."

Laura left the classroom shaking her head in amazement at Miss Winsor's kindly instruction. She could not imagine the patience it took to teach such simple basics to all ages without being either condescending to the adults or too complicated for the children. It's a good thing no one expects me to teach, she told herself. I'd be crying along with the babies before the first hour was up.

* * *

Over a late and makeshift dinner one evening, Laura had a chance to talk to Edward Pierce and Mr. Hooper privately.

"How are you settling in, Miss Towne?" Mr. Pierce inquired.

"Quite well, thank you. Everyone has been so kind and welcoming. And I've never felt better or more energetic than I have for the last few weeks."

"No climate problems, then? The heat doesn't bother you?"

"Not at all. Before I came, I worried that the summer months would be intolerable, but I find that I quite like tropical weather. I seem to have found my geographic home."

"Well, it will get hotter than it is now. But you are right. The rumors about how unhealthy this area is are largely exaggerations. As long as you are close enough to the water to catch a sea breeze, it can be quite delightful. The slaves tell us that they stay here with no problem all summer long, but that their white masters found it necessary to leave. Personally,

I suspect that the plantation owners were just bored and looking for an excuse to get away for a while."

"I wouldn't be surprised at that," Laura agreed. "I do rather worry about my stay here, however."

"Why is that?"

"I came here hoping to make a real difference in the lives of the slaves. Oh, I believe in the cause of abolition, but I've never been one to make political arguments. I just care about reaching out and helping individuals. And I'm not experiencing as much contact with the people as I expected to."

"I've seen you out and about, visiting the clothing store and the school."

"Yes, but that's been just my way of learning about my surroundings. Standing at the back of a classroom or the church and watching how ex-slaves behave is not what I mean by contact. I want to feel useful, and, so far, the only use Miss Walker has made of me is as a housekeeper. I can do that. It's not the first time I've had to run a household. But it's not why I came here."

"Would you prefer to be a teacher?"

"No. Heavens, no! I'm a doctor, Mr. Pierce, or as close to being a doctor as a woman is likely to get. I should be out caring for patients, but we don't really have many who need doctoring here at The Oaks. I'm grateful for that, of course. I wouldn't wish anyone to become ill just to give me something to do. But my particular talents seem to be useless here. And if I'm not needed, perhaps I should be going elsewhere."

"Ah, but we do need you here." Mr. Hooper stepped into the conversation. "This is not for general knowledge yet, but we don't expect Miss Walker to stay much longer. She's been expressing her discontent for some time now, and, like those plantation owners who used the weather as an excuse for a vacation, I think she'll be packed up and gone before the next heat wave hits."

"Of course, I won't say anything to her, although I can't say I find it surprising. Miss Walker seems to be one of those people who simply can't be satisfied." Laura paused and cringed at the thought. "I apologize for that remark. It was unkind of me."

"Unkind? Perhaps, but also very true. Miss Walker has assumed the role of supervisor here, and she has done some good as an organizer of the various plantations under our control," Mr. Pierce said. "I can't take that job away from her, but we need more than she is willing—or able—to give."

"Edward's right," Mr. Hooper said. "We desperately need women here, but they need to be women who can command the ongoing respect of the slaves. Miss Walker tends to find fault rather than offer help."

"We all learned very early that the slaves recognize only one hierarchical structure," Mr. Pierce said. "Black folk do the physical labor, and they don't really object to that role. White men are expected to manage the plantation itself—purchasing seed, planning the year's work, laying out the fields, arranging the sales of the crops. And white women are seen as caretakers. They visit the slaves, provide them with their basic food and clothing needs, and treat their illnesses. The 'missus' must know every child's name and every family relationship."

"So there is a need for my medical skills?"

"Of course there is. Right now, Miss Walker rides out with us several times a week. She visits the slave quarters and fusses at them for not being cleaner. But she doesn't like touching the slaves. You can almost see her recoil when a black child runs toward her with outstretched arms. And not many are happy to see her coming."

"How sad."

"I look forward to taking you around to the slave quarters. In fact, I think we should start those visits immediately. Miss Walker will continue to go with us as long as she is here, but I'll tell her that we need her to concentrate on inventorying the plantation holdings while you talk to the slaves."

"Will she accept that, do you think?"

"Of course she will. She's a mathematician. Offer her a chance to work with numbers, and we might even see her smile."

* * *

Laura found her new duties frustrating at first. The former slaves did not yet trust her or expect her to behave differently than the white women who had come before her. Their reactions to her instructions stopped just short of insolence. If it happened to rain, Dagus failed to bring in the firewood. Robert, who made the butter, sometimes locked the dairy and went home, taking the key with him. Susannah had a habit of carrying off the leftovers from their meals, even when there would have been enough to feed the whole household for another day. Rina was never around when it was bed-making time, and the barn workers seemed to beat the mules harder whenever they thought Laura might see them.

Laura struggled to understand. One of John Fripp's slaves, a coachman who visited The Oaks regularly, justified their behavior this way: "Massas bin unfair to we. Dey takes all our labor fuh dere own use an gits rich on it, an den says we be lazy an caint take care uh ourselfs. Dat not be fair an dey not be fair to we, takin all our labor an gibbin we only two suits uh clothe a year fuh wages."

Laura agreed with the argument he was making. She had made her own effort to treat the former slaves as trusted servants rather than unpaid lackeys. She hired the slave woman called Rina as her personal washerwoman and chambermaid for fifty cents a week. Rina kept her house in the village as before and received the same food allowance that she had from the government. For Rina, her new pay was a welcome change because Susan Walker had always insisted that the free blacks be paid no extra wages.

The other slaves, too, indicated that they did not object to doing work; they just wanted to see some return. One woman was obviously grateful for the new state of affairs. "I be servant-born, ma'am," she said, "an now, cause de gubment be fightin fuh me, I gwine work fuh de gubment, dat I will, an welcome."

Her husband, however, was not so accommodating. "I craves work, ma'am, ifn I gets a lil pay, but ifn we don gets pay, we don care—don care fuh work." It was an honest statement, one Laura secretly applauded. If the cotton agents paid their field hands regularly, she was convinced that they would be more reliable than they were at the moment. There was little she could do to change the working conditions on the plantations, but at least she could make the household servants feel valued.

Laura was gratified to see that the servants repaid her own kindness with thoughtful gestures of their own devising. Susannah, the cook, brought food offerings to the house—frequently eggs, sometimes freshly caught fish or other food produced in the village gardens. She explained that she always did this for "ol Massa Pope," who in return would provide a bit of sweeting or other stuff from the main house. "It be a bit uh give an take, an de slaves be insulted ifn dere gifts not be accepted." Laura suspected the owners had taken more than they gave, and sometimes she felt as if the small bits she had to offer the servants were not a fair exchange, either. She tried to balance her own lack of resources with kindness and obvious gratitude.

Despite the atmosphere of suspicion and fear that hung over the plantations, Laura Towne was pleased with much of what she found happening at The Oaks. In one letter to her family, she wrote that she had never been so happy as she was at the moment. "We found the people here naked, and beginning to loathe their everlasting hominy—afraid and discontented about being made to work as slaves, and without assurance of freedom or pay, of clothes or food—and now they are jolly and happy and decently fed and dressed, and so full of affection and gratitude to the people who are relieving them that it is rather too flattering to be enjoyed." To Laura, it seemed that the slaves had already proved that they could and would work to support themselves, just as the abolitionists had long declared.

Laura was also finding personal satisfaction in being able to practice medicine among the slaves. She traveled happily out to the slave quarters on surrounding plantations to treat cases of measles and mumps, to dress a wound, heal a rash, or assist with a birth. She was even finding that she did not mind her housekeeping chores. She loved the challenge of setting a good table for the unexpected guests who frequently turned up at their door. She grumbled a bit about how far away the kitchen was, and how inexperienced the cooks were, but she labored willingly among them, showing none of Susan Walker's distaste for the slave quarters. If she had any complaints at all, they centered on her occasional teaching duties, which she found much harder than she had expected. Most important to her, she was constantly busy, and the feeling that many people needed her was satisfying.

RINA ON "DE
MEANING OF FREEDOM"
Late April 1862

I don unnerstan. What de white folk mean bout we be free? I tought I knowed de meanin uh de word, but I knows I don feel free. Nuttin bout dis way we be livin say free. De whole res uh de worl seem change, but we still be workin an doin what de Massa say.

When de white folk what belong to we go way, we dint know what we sposed fuh do. We jis kep livin we lives, cause here be where we always bin livin. Den de soljer men comes by, an dey say, "What you be doin here? You be free. Go on an leave. You don need fuh work here no mo."

But we say, "Where we sposed fuh go? Dis be we home."

Soljer say, "No, dis be de boss man home. You be free fuh go any-wheres. Dat be why we comes here—fuh set you free." Dey laughs at we, like we be stupid. An dey goes away, shakin der heads.

Nex come de cotton men, an dey says we not be free. Dey says, "De ol massa be gone, but we be de new massas, an we needs you fuh git out in de cotton fields an git de ol crop outta de groun an de new crop in."

Well, we don know what fuh do. Dese new cotton agents, dey don know nuttin bout growin cotton. Dey tellin we fuh do silly stuff.

De says we jis should pack de picked cotton in de sacks so dey kin ship it off.

We says, "Nossir, dis cotton, it need ginnin."

Dey says, "Sumbody mess up de gins, so we jis gwine send it nort fuh git it ginned up dere."

We says, "Nossir, dat aint right. Ifn you duz dat, dere aint gwine be no seed fuh plantin de nex crop."

Dey says, "We kin order mo seed."

We says, "Nossir, dat be special seed dat only grow here. You caint buys it elsewheres."

Dey says, "You shut up an do what you be tole."

Dey don know bout swamp muck what need fuh be raked up in de maash an spread on de dirt, neider. When de men heads off to de maash, de cotton men tink dey be runnin way, an dey says, "You gots fuh stay here. You aint free, no matter what de soljer say. Only de gubment kin says who be free, an dey aint done dat."

Den come dese teacher-folk, an dey be a fludduh-fedduh bunch. Dey be runnin round gibbin order an tellin we what fuh do, cause we be free. Der dat word agin, an it aint got no mo meanin den de las time we heard it. Trubble wit de white folk be dat dey don know nuttin bout Sout Carolina. Dey fro up nort, where folk do tings diffrunt.

Massa Pierce come here, an he say, "We be gwine gib you clothe an food an school." But de missus what come wit him, dey says diffrunt. Missus Johnson, she say she be startin school, but de chillun caint come less dey be clean an wearin dey bes clothe. She be sendin dem back to dey cabins, like dere be a basin fuh wash dey faces dere. An de chillun, dey don know what fuh do. Missus Nellie, she seem nice nuf, but she don say much atall. She jis wait in de room she call she school.

Den dere dat Missus Susan. Oh, she a piece uh work. She be full uh gibbin order, but she aint gwine do nuttin sheself. She say she come fuh see ifn we needs doctorin. I says, "Ol Bess do. She gots dat big ol sore on she leg what not be healin nohow." An I takes she to de cabin where Bess live. Missus Susan, she stop in de doorway an wrinkle up she nose. She say, "It smell bad in dere. I aint gwine in dere less Bess clean she cabin." But course, Bess ain't gwine clean she cabin cause she caint walk.

Missus Susan say she be gwine take ober de kitchen duties, but she don set foot in de cookhouse, neider. She say she kin eat de food, but she don want fuh see how dirty de cookhouse be inside. She keep tellin we fuh sweep de floor uh our cabins. But de floor be sand. She don know we caint sweep sand clean.

She don like we one bit bedder dan de cotton agents duz. She talk lots bout freedom, an how we gots fuh be eddicated fore we kin be free. But she make ugly face when she talk bout we. She say we stupid an dirty an smell bad, an we gots fuh start livin bedder fore she kin help we be free. She happy, I tink, when she go off by sheself to de place where dey hab all de clothe dey brung fuh we. She busy shakin dem out an makin piles, but she don want fuh gib any uh dem clothe to we. She say we needs fuh buy our clothe wit our own pennies, but where we get enny pennies? De ol massas, dey gib we our clothe twice a year. We neber needs money fuh buy dem. De cotton agents, dey says dey gwine pay we sumtime, but not less de crop git pick.

Dere be one mo group uh de new white folk. Dey says dey be preachers, come fuh teach we bout de chuch. We says we gots our own chuch, but dey says dat aint de right way. One uh dem, Missus Austa, she come here one aternoon in her buggy. She say we not lowed fuh go to our Praise House enny mo. An we aint lowed fuh do de Shout, neider. She say we comes to de brick chuch eber Sunday fuh lissen to she husband do de preachin, so we kin larn fuh worship de right way. She say now dat we be free, we aint free fuh do our own chuchin.

I means what I says when I says ebertin change after de Big Shoot—eben de meaning uh de words change. I know what free mean, when it mean dat a slave run away fro he owner an try fuh git to Canada. But now free jis seem fuh mean we not free fuh do ennyting cept what de white folk say. An what dey means by free keep changin, too.

8
COTTON AGENT WOES
May 1862

B y late spring, the rivalry between missionaries and
cotton agents was escalating. From the very beginning, Edward Pierce had realized that he and Colonel
Reynolds had very different goals. Pierce wanted whatever
was best for the Negro; Reynolds cared only for what was
best for the cotton crop. At first, the two men had watched
each other carefully while managing to avoid most arguments
about what they believed. By spring, however, Pierce had
found it impossible to control his anger. And the cause of his
concern was much the same as Rina's.

"Colonel Reynolds. Is it true that you are arranging to
ship all the cotton north to be ginned there?" he asked.

"I'm not sure why that should matter to you, but, yes,
that's exactly what I'm going to do."

"But the slaves could easily do that work, and they need
the income."

"They can't gin cotton if they've destroyed the cotton
gins," Reynolds said.

"The slaves say the plantation owners were the ones who
jammed the gins, and they are willing to help do the repairs

and get the machinery back in working order. There's no need to ship the cotton off."

"It will save us money and time. Both are important."

"But the welfare of the slaves is important, too. They can learn to take care of themselves, but they need employment. You're taking away the only jobs they know how to do."

"Then let them learn to work at something else. Isn't that what your fancy-pants teachers are supposed to teach them?"

"That will take more time than repairing the gins." Edward was dimly aware that this was becoming a childish argument, but he was helpless to control his indignation. "Besides," he said, "there's a more important consideration. If the cotton gets ginned in the North, you'll lose all the seed from this year's crop."

"So what? We can always order more seed for next year."

"Not this long-staple seed, you can't. Nobody sells it."

"Nonsense."

"It's not nonsense. The value of Low Country cotton depends on its quality. And that quality has long been determined by the careful cultivation of the seed crop from year to year, using only the local seed from the finest products. Nowhere else do you find cotton with such naturally long fibers."

"What's so special about that?"

"It produces a stronger thread and a smoother fabric. And it grows well only in fields like these, with long hot days and cool nights, and the unique fertilizer that comes from the muck the slaves dig up from the marshes."

"Well, well, well! Who turned you into an cotton expert?"

"The same people whose livelihoods you are threatening—the slaves who work this land. If you send the unginned cotton north, the seeds will be lost. They won't grow well anywhere but here, and the seeds you buy from a catalog will not produce the same quality of cotton that buyers are used to."

"Then that's the way it will have to be. I'm not concerned with keeping these ex-slaves growing cotton for the rest of their lives, and neither should you be. I've been sent to get this crop to market as quickly as possible, and that's what I intend to do. You have no orders to overrule me, so why don't you run along and worry about teaching the darkies their ABCs."

* * *

The rest of the Gideonites did not take long to realize that the cotton agents were at the root of many of their troubles, too. At The Oaks, Reynolds had installed a Mr. Whiting to oversee the cotton operations on the 500-acre plantation. When Pierce chose to establish his headquarters there, he and Whiting split the house between them. The Oaks, built in the late 1850s, featured a four-over-four floor plan, with the back rooms extending further to the sides, thus forming wings on a T-shaped house. A central hall with a staircase on either side made it possible for two households to share the building. And since the cookhouse and other outbuildings were separate from the main structure, each household could function independently with its own set of house servants.

But there the illusion of equality ended. Whiting had arrived first, and he plundered the house of its best furniture and conveniences to make a comfortable residence for himself and his wife, leaving only the bare necessities for the

Gideonites. At intervals, he also commandeered the front portico as a company store, at which the slaves working his cotton fields could exchange the scrip with which he paid them for items of food and clothing. The Gideonites could only watch in frustration as they saw the field hands being charged exorbitant prices for items the missionaries could have furnished more cheaply.

The agents were also causing great hardship among the slaves themselves by stealing their livestock. A woman who was carefully raising a pig in hopes of a litter of piglets found it missing. It appeared on an agent's dinner table the next evening. An old black man who made a living by moving goods with his horse and wagon was detained on the road by a cotton agent's employee; the white man simply unharnessed the horse and led it off. Chickens, lambs, baby calves—nothing was safe. As a result, the slaves, too, hated the agents, although they trusted the missionaries. The superintendents on the plantations tried to intervene to keep the agents away from the slaves, but that simply put up another barrier that irritated William Reynolds. He had no hope of achieving his own goal of a profitable cotton crop without the cooperation and labor of the slaves.

The same scenario played itself out on other plantations as well. The first time Susan Walker visited the Chaplin plantation, she recorded her impressions in her journal: "I fear the cotton agent, Salisbury, stationed here is not a good man. The Negroes complain of him, and they all look so neglected it is quite evident he has done no good upon the plantation. He drives the finest horses I have seen in Port Royal or St. Helena; gives good dinners; entertains largely; has appropriated all the furniture and nearly all the teams about the place and refuses to give anything to the superintendents placed there by Mr. Pierce."

Pierce blamed Colonel William Nobles, Reynolds's assistant, for much of the massive corruption that accompanied the cotton-dealing policies. His evidence came from an informant, James Adrian Suydam, who ran one of the company stores. Pierce confronted him one day, hoping to find an acceptable explanation for the activities that had aroused his suspicions. Suydam proved anxious to talk, but his revelations were even more disturbing than Pierce had suspected.

"The cotton agents are all going back on their promises to pay the field hands," he admitted. "There's such a push to get that old cotton out and the fields replanted that drivers have been promising the ex-slaves almost anything to get them to work. They're told that once the work is done, they'll be paid a real salary, based on how many acres they've worked or how many hours they've put in. But when it comes time for payday, they don't get more than a quarter of that amount in real coins. The rest is scrip."

"And where does this scrip come from?"

"Colonel Nobles issues it himself. He prints it on an old hand press he has, and it's worth less than the paper he uses."

"They can use it to purchase supplies, though, I understand."

"Yeah, but only in Nobles's own company stores. You don't accept it, do you?"

"Well, no, but . . ."

"Of course you wouldn't. Like I said, it's worthless. The slaves can exchange it for a few bits of food or clothing that Nobles has on offer, but the prices they are charged are much higher than retail values back up North."

"He's just lining his own pockets, then?"

"There's no doubt that he's getting rich on the backs of the slaves, but I think the reasons go even deeper. Nobles doesn't want to see the slaves freed, and he certainly doesn't want you people educating them. He's perfectly happy with using slave labor. I think he actually likes the whole idea of being a Southern plantation owner."

"If you feel that way, why do you work for him?" Pierce asked.

"Huh. I'm just another one of his slaves, albeit a white one. I've been promised a salary, too, but it will only be paid when I can make the company store turn a large profit. And to do that, I have to charge the slaves an exorbitant amount for items, so as to strip them not only of their scrip but also of the few actual coins they get. I'd like to go back North, but I don't have money for my passage. So I have to keep working. The other cotton agents and I are just carrying out orders."

"I can't understand the man's greed," Pierce said. "He's using everyone around him to serve his own interests."

"Yes. He strips the slaves of any money they think they are earning and deprives them of the ability to take their money and buy what they need at much lower cost from you missionaries. That keeps them under his tight control and out of your hands. He wants you and your band of teachers to fail and go home. You're interfering with his plans."

"I'm grateful for your honesty, Mr. Suydam, but why have you told me this?"

"I want to see someone get him fired. And I'm hoping that if his activities come to the attention of the military authorities, the Army will remove him and help me get back home. I just can't do much on my own. If he knew I'd been talking to anybody, he'd just see to it that I suffered an unfortunate but fatal accident."

"You really believe that?"

"Yes, sir, I do."

Edward Pierce was now determined to take action; he wrote a scathingly accusatory letter to General David Hunter, commander of the newly formed Department of the South. On May 7th, Pierce traveled down to Hilton Head to complain in person to the military officials, since the government failed to act on the matter. As he stepped onto the dock at Hilton Head, Nobles came rushing at him and began to punch him. Pierce fell to the ground under the onslaught, as Nobles shouted that Pierce was trying to run him out of the country like a dog. Soldiers managed to break up the fight, but not before Pierce had received a severe beating. The military police hustled Nobles onto the first ship headed north with orders from the commanding officer on Hilton Head that he not be allowed to return to the islands. That one firing, however, did not solve the conflict of interest.

Pierce recovered from his injuries under the skillful hands of Laura Towne, who managed to treat his wounds and listen to his frustrations at the same time. She worried about the scars the beating would leave. Not the physical scars—those would heal with time. Laura was more concerned with the mental ones. She could sense that much of Pierce's drive and enthusiasm had been dampened by the realization that others were actively opposing the goals he had set for his teachers and managers.

"Surely, now that Colonel Nobles is gone for good, conditions will improve. I have to believe that, since I just got here. I don't want my efforts thwarted before I even begin," Laura said.

"I wish that were so, but I'm afraid there will always be another like him," Pierce answered. "We work very hard, but we cannot hope to succeed in our goals without the basic necessities of life."

"I think we're all willing to do much for ourselves. We've planted gardens, taught the slaves how to manage the business of the plantation, and paid them a decent wage for working for us. We're making progress."

"But we arrived with little except our own few personal possessions. We need furniture in our houses, livestock on our plantations, and farming equipment of all kinds. And these are the very items that the cotton agents, directed by Colonel Reynolds, have carried off for their own use. No, I see very little hope for our endeavors."

9
GENERAL HUNTER'S GRAND EXPERIMENT
May 1862

While the members of Gideon's Band struggled with the moral implications of their relationship with the abandoned slaves of the Sea Islands and wondered if they were really doing any good for the slaves, Army officers were rapidly losing patience with the whole situation. Army personnel with too little to do and former slaves with no masters to control their behavior for the first time in their lives seemed bound to clash. Soldiers, many of whom were barely literate themselves, resented the fact that the government had sent teachers to educate the former slaves.

"If Ol' Abe spent more time thinking about us facing the Rebels down here and less time worrying about the dumb niggers," one soldier was heard to complain, "we'd of seen some fighting by now."

"You got that right. They don't know no more than a dumb brute," another agreed. "Why do they deserve more attention than we do?"

Such sentiments spreading through the Army camps led to the same sorts of comments being made directly to Negroes on the streets. Those who had been slaves had long before learned to close their ears to disparaging comments. They didn't dare talk back to their masters when they were in bondage; they didn't risk responding to soldiers who were carrying weapons. But such encounters poisoned the atmosphere of the town and only increased hard feelings on both sides.

The slaves' complaints about the soldiers were more than justified. The slaves had been accustomed to storing their food supplies for the winter and preserving the best of their seed corn for the following year. Soldiers, on the other hand, had been trained to live off the land, taking what they might need in the way of food wherever they happened to find it. The slaves witnessed the destruction in helpless dismay, as soldiers dug up their sweet potato fields, carted off their cabbages, and ground their seed corn to make johnnycakes.

Eventually, of course, such disagreements broke out into actual fights, particularly when a white soldier insulted a black woman, or worse, subjected her to indecent sexual advances. One night shortly after the Gideonites arrived, a group of soldiers decided to hold a party on the remote Gabriel Capers plantation on Ladies Island, where they thought their officers could not discover what they were up to. It turned into an outrageous drunken brawl, and the slaves who were still living on the plantation complained to the superintendent, Mr. Eustis. They accused the soldiers of beating up five black men, killing a cow, and trying to rape the black women.

There were often hard feelings between the soldiers and the missionaries as well. The typical soldier regarded the missionaries as shirkers. Many of the men among the Gideonites were recent college graduates, and most were in their twenties. Why weren't they in the Army, fighting to defeat the slave-owning South, the soldiers wanted to know? As for the missionaries, they suspected that the poor treatment the blacks received from the military was turning them against all whites. Both the soldiers and the missionaries were supposed to be against slavery, but the soldiers seemed to be against the slaves themselves, and that made the slaves distrust all white people, including those who were most anxious to help them.

When Edward Pierce tried to discuss the problems with General Isaac I. Stevens, commander of the Second Brigade, South Carolina Expeditionary Force, he discovered that in the literal military mind, freedom meant being totally free. The soldiers had driven the plantation owners away; therefore, the slaves were now free. The soldiers wanted them to be free enough to go away. Dealing with hordes of people who seemed incapable of taking care of themselves was not part of the Army's purpose or charge. The abolitionists blamed the military for not understanding what would be required to help the slaves make the transition to full citizenship. They had hoped to have military support for their efforts. All General Stevens could offer was a vague promise that, in time, things would get better.

General Hunter's solution was quicker, more expedient, and far less attuned to the anti-abolitionist sentiments still prevalent in much of the Union. He simply emancipated the former slaves. In an order issued from Hilton Head on 9 May 1862, he wrote:

The three States of Georgia, Florida, and South Carolina, comprising the Military Department of the South, having deliberately declared themselves no longer under the protection of the United States of America, and having taken up arms against said United States, it became a military necessity to declare martial law. This was accordingly done the 25th day of April, 1862. Slavery and martial law in a free country are altogether incompatible; the persons in these three States, Georgia, Florida, and South Carolina, heretofore held as slaves, are therefore declared forever free.

Both the North and the South regarded the proclamation with disapproval. *The New York Times* dismissed it as absurd: "His declaring freedom to all the slaves in three States, when he has no power to free a single one outside of his camp, is regarded in Washington as an act of stultification highly discreditable to anyone holding the rank of General, supposed to have ordinary intelligence."

* * *

On St. Helena Island, the missionaries were as surprised as anyone else to learn of the emancipation, and their reaction reflected their own ambivalence toward the former slaves' preparation for independence. Philbrick did not think that the emancipation decree was a very good idea, and he believed Hunter would lose his job over it. As for the blacks, he called the effect of the proclamation inconsiderable. "They don't hear of it, to begin with, and if they did, they wouldn't care for it," he wrote.

On the day the emancipation was announced, however, Harriet Ware overheard one of the house servants tell someone, "Don call me 'Joe'; muh name be Mr. Jenkins." It was a lovely expression of what freedom might mean to former slaves, but the reality was something quite different.

General Hunter immediately followed up his proclamation with an intensified drive to recruit soldiers from the newly emancipated slaves. On Sunday, May 11th, Susan Walker recorded what happened next: "Capt. Hazard Stevens, General Stevens's son, arrived at Pope's plantation on St. Helena Island bearing an order from General Hunter notifying the plantation that on Monday morning 'all colored men between eighteen and forty-five capable of bearing arms shall be taken to Hilton Head'—no explanation."

Susan was particularly horrified to discover that her duties as plantation manager required her to provide a list of all those who qualified: "I write the names almost as signing their death warrants. The saddest duty I ever performed." The next day she described the scene as Stevens came back for the men, lining them up at gunpoint: "The men were called from the field and thus hurried off without time for coat or shoes or a goodbye to their families . . . Women wept and children screamed as men were torn from their embrace. This is a sad day throughout these islands . . . Mr. Pierce has gone to Hilton Head to see General Hunter about it.

The same order to call up able-bodied Negroes came to Coffin Point on May 12th , and Harriet Ware described the pain it caused her: "You never saw a more wretched set of people than sat down to our breakfast table. I could not eat, for about the first time in my life." Here, however, the blacks were treated more gently, with the soldiers encouraging the men by telling them of the money they were going to make and the fine uniforms they would receive. They also allowed some house servants and drivers to remain for the "good of the plantation."

Edward Philbrick joined Mr. Pierce on his trip to Hilton Head to confront General Hunter about this latest move.

They received a plausible explanation of what was going on. Hunter had not gotten the black volunteers he sought, they were told, and so these were temporary measures, designed to give the men a taste of military life and drill, in hopes that more of them would be willing to volunteer. The Gideonites had no ready answer for that, but they did not believe the black men being marched off would ever be willing to volunteer.

Harriet Ware was one of the doubters: "If we can have blacks to garrison the forts and save our soldiers through the hot weather, everyone will be thankful. But I don't believe you could make soldiers of these men at all. They are afraid, and they know it."

William C. Gannett, superintendent at Coffin Point, echoed her sentiments: "Negroes—plantation Negroes, at least—will never make soldiers in one generation. Five white men could put a regiment to flight; but they may be very useful in preventing sickness and death among our troops by relieving them of part of their work, and they may acquire a certain self-respect and independence which more than anything else they need to feel, if they are soon to stand by their own strength."

General Hunter's effort to form a regiment of black soldiers immediately encountered almost insurmountable problems. Neither the military hierarchy nor the civilian missionaries had a full understanding of what the "land" meant to those who worked it. Northerners harbored an assumption that newly freed slaves would eagerly leave the plantations where they had worked against their will. The Gideonites were there to offer training for such freedom, and

General Hunter and his staff offered immediate employment in the Union Army.

None of them seemed to understand that, while the slaves might have resented their inferior status, they regarded their little cabins and the plots of land they worked as home—the only home most of them had ever known. Being free did not mean a chance to flee; it meant a chance to manage the land as they saw fit. They had refused to leave the Sea Islands in November, when their masters had fled before the arrival of the Expeditionary Forces. They refused to leave in May when General Hunter tried to lure them into military service.

RINA ON "DE FUST SLAVE DRAFT"
May 1862

Yestiddy be a scairt day. Soljer keep walkin past de house an standin in de yard. We hear dat dey be comin fuh take all de mens away. An we dint know what fuh do. Las night, after supper, I asks Missus Laura what she gwine do bout dem soljer ifn dey comes tomorra. She say she be gwine spend de day in de clothe house, cause she not scairt uh dem. I tought dat be a good ting, but de udders not so sho.

Las night, Zannah's husband warn de crowd at de Praise House. He say dey mus be jis like de birds when a gunner be bout, specting a crack eber minute —dat dey neber know what befall dem, an po black folk kin only wait an hab faith; dey caint do ennyting fuh demselfs. While he be gwine on, de soljer come, but den dey march on witout trubblin de meetin.

When he be finish talkin, me an Zannah go down by de creek fuh keep watch. Ol Bess tell me she shake all night wit fear: "Oh, I hab such a night, so fraid. Dey all runs an I aint gots a foot fuh stan on. Dey gwine leave me. What po Bess do when dey all take to de woods an I caint go—mus stay here fuh be kilt. Dey kill me sho or shoot me or lick me to death."

Today, de soljer come back an call de black mens togedduh. Capn Hazard Stevens say dey not gwine be soljer aginst der will an dat dey be lowed fuh return ifn dey wish, but fuh now, dey mus go. Missus Laura gib each man sum coins, an Missus Susan Walker gib dem each sum tobacco fore dey left. Sum uh de men escape, but all de wimmun an chillun be cryin.

De onliest black man I knows what be happy fuh go soljerin be Archibelle, Zannah's oldest boy. He be trouble fro de time he be a youngun. He work as Massa Pope peculiar boy, which mean he do whatever Massa Pope tell him fuh do. He eben cut he toenails fuh he. An we all knows he jis do it fuh de extras he git outta it.

After de Big Shoot, Massa Pope, he kep sneakin back to de Oaks fuh git mo stuff, like clothe an food, an he be lookin fuh carry off a few mo slaves. I knows he want me fuh do he laundry, an I hide eber time he come. But he also want Bella fuh take care uh his chillun, an dat Archie, he hep catch she. Archie find out where Bella be hidin, an when Massa Pope knock on de door uh de cabin, she run out de back an straight intuh de arms uh Archie, who be waitin fuh she.

Den he lef wit Massa Pope, cause he know he not be welcome here no mo. But den Massa Pope punish he fuh sumptin, an he escape. He gots heself lost in de maash, an done gone boggin fuh days wit nuttin fuh eat afore he get back here. Zannah take he in, cause dat what we duz wit fambly, but nobody like he much. So when Capn Hazard say he be takin soljers, Archie up an volunteer fuh go. I be tinkin he jis want sum free meal. He not gwine like takin order an marchin round like dey do.

Titus come back to de Oaks tonight. Missus Laura tink he be capture. But he say, "No, ma'am, not me, ma'am. Me at Jenkins, ma'am. If dey come dere an axed fuh me, dey'd had me, But I not here." Summa de udder mens, dey comes back, too. Marcus say he be willin fuh go back an serve at de fort. "I duz not wish fuh fight," he say, "but only fuh larn fuh fight."

I sho don know why mens always like fuh fight. Seems to me life be hard nuf witout makin it wurs by shootin at each udder. I heard Missus Laura talkin bout dis stuff, too. She an de young suptendents fro de udder plantation, dey say dis be de wurst day uh der life. Dey be worrit dat we not gwine trust no white folk fro here on.

Missus Laura, she be hopin dat Genral Hunter gwine get sumptin good outta all dis. I jis hope she be right.

10
REORGANIZATION
May 1862

Perhaps the most surprising development in May was the government's decision to reorganize the administration of the Port Royal Experiment. In one of those acts with unexpected consequences, Edward Pierce and Susan Walker had joined forces to convince Secretary Chase that he should remove Reynolds and all the cotton agents, putting Edward Pierce and his superintendents in total charge of the plantations of the Sea Islands. They argued that the cotton agents were still corrupt and could not command the loyalty or efforts of the slaves. They also cited their own successes, maintaining that if no one interfered with their efforts at training and education, the plantations could once again become profitable enterprises. Unfortunately for their case, however, they claimed that they got along well with the Army. Pierce confidently expected to be appointed as the new manager of the Port Royal effort.

Instead, Salmon P. Chase leaped at their acceptance of the military and appointed Brigadier General Rufus Saxton "to take possession of all the plantations heretofore occupied by rebels, and take charge of the inhabitants remaining thereon within the department" and to make "such rules and regulations for the cultivation of the land, and for the protection, employment, and government of the inhabitants as circumstances seem to require."

By June, the fate of the Port Royal Experiment seemed to hang in a precarious balance. Edward Pierce assembled his staff and several of the other superintendents at The Oaks. "I wanted to be the first to inform you that I am returning to my law practice in Boston," he announced.

A collective gasp went up. "Oh, no," Nelly Winsor said. "You can't! How on earth will we manage without you? You've been a part of this mission from the very beginning."

Mr. Hooper was a bit more practical. "Yes, Edward, that will be a problem. Who will take over the leadership from you?"

"Are they going to promote one of us?" Edward Philbrick asked, shaking off his wife's restraining hand on his arm. "If so, I'll want to apply for the position."

"Mr. Philbrick, this is hardly the moment for a 'the King is dead, long live the King' speech." Susan Walker frowned in ill-concealed disgust at his presumption. "You know as well as any of us that all such appointments come from Washington. And I assure you that I will be making my own recommendations to Salmon Chase."

"The man hasn't even left yet," Nelly observed. "Doesn't anyone else care that we are losing the one person who brought us all here?"

Laura Towne spoke up to redirect the discussion. "There are practical matters to be dealt with, too. We've lost several members of our household here at The Oaks already. Surely we will need to start moving personnel around now. Mr. Pierce, you are probably the only one here who understands the needs of each of the St. Helena plantations. Is there some way we could rearrange things so that your duties would be easier to handle? Would that persuade you to stay?"

"No. I'm happy with what we have accomplished, and my report to Secretary Chase will be a favorable one. But it is time for me to go home. I accepted this assignment with no expectation of spending more than a few weeks here. I did not make a lifetime commitment."

"None of us made a lifetime commitment, Mr. Pierce," Susan said, "and in many ways I share your desire to go home. But, while I have little more to offer this effort, there is much left for you to do."

"I can't afford to stay any longer," he said. "I am a poor man and need money above all things. This work did not pay and never could pay. I must return to Boston and rescue my law practice, which has suffered from my absence."

Susan may not have believed, or even understood, his plea of financial need, for money had never been her problem. She thought she understood his discouragement, however. "I know the newspapers back home are poking fun at us because we are trying to manage cotton plantations without having ever seen a cotton plant. They call us naive, condescending, and ridiculous visionaries, and that's unfair."

It was a sore subject among the missionaries, and their discussion veered off onto that new target. "I've seen those comments, too," Richard Soule, the superintendent at Frogmore, said. "Our political enemies accuse us of abusing the Negroes we are professing to help and of lining our own pockets by selling donated goods to the Negroes. Maybe we are wasting our efforts."

Edward Philbrick agreed. "Even the abolitionists criticize our efforts. I've heard it said that by providing for the former slaves' needs, we are reprising the role of slave owners and keeping the Negroes from advancing to full and independent citizenship. I mean no offense to you, Mr. Pierce, but perhaps we are in need of serious reorganization."

"In some ways, the criticisms are justified," Susan said. "We fall into the habit of referring to those who work for us as 'our people' and we let them refer to us as 'Massa' and 'Missus.' We make it easier for them to beg for help than to work on meeting their own needs. Those who call our movement a failure may well be right, but it's not Mr. Pierce's fault."

"I didn't say it was his fault."

"You implied it."

"Enough discussion." Edward Pierce held up his hands to stop the flow of conversation. "I depart at the end of the month. My resignation is already in the hands of Secretary Chase. He has appointed General Saxton to direct your efforts. In fact, the whole enterprise here will be reorganized, just as Mr. Philbrick suggested."

"Who is General Saxton?" Laura asked.

"General Rufus Saxton is familiar with the area from serving as Chief Quartermaster for the South Carolina Expeditionary Force responsible for the victory at Port Royal. He has enough standing with the Army to ensure its complete cooperation with your efforts. He is honest, reasonable, straightforward, and a thoroughgoing abolitionist. You could not ask for a better manager."

Charles P. Ware was not so sure. "He may have a certain authority, but I'm afraid a military man will accomplish little in proportion to our hopes and our needs. We need a civilian who is a first-rate businessman—a man of force, of forethought, of devoted interest in this undertaking."

"Perhaps so, but the appointment has already been made. The new organizational structure has much to recommend it. As I understand it, the plantations will be reorganized into neighboring groups, each with its own superintendent who will report directly to General Saxton. There will be no more need for independent cotton agents. The superintendents will direct the labor on the plantations and be paid from the proceeds of cotton sales. That, in turn, allows more government funds to be diverted to teacher salaries. The donations of the various supporting societies will be paid back, and more of the needs of the Negroes will come from the Department of the Treasury. It neatly removes the claws of the cotton agents who have been causing so much trouble."

"We'll see," Mr. Ware said.

"You should also know," Pierce continued, "that General Saxton offered me a position on his staff, but I will not reconsider."

"I fully understand," Susan Walker said. "I, too, feel a great need to go home. One person can do only so much, and you have given your share."

Some of the original band were determined to remain through the summer, but Susan Walker had lost her enthusiasm. Later that evening, she wrote in her journal: "I am not prepared to accept this as my life work—[I] doubt my vocation for it and do not feel a drawing toward it unless I can have such position and power as will justify my undertaking something beyond present duties. I do not wish to take the responsibility of the Clothing Department. I do not feel that I should satisfactorily fill the post of teacher, which I hold to be of first importance. There are duties I will not mention that I consider important and which, in all candor, I might undertake under different circumstances. Do not think I shall, but, *nous verrons*. I would not stand in the way of usefulness perhaps far greater than I can render, and so I will withdraw from certain conditions I am not willing to accept. I was unwise in accepting any responsibility in coming here, and I will not continue to act against my better judgment."

For his part, Edward Philbrick returned to Coffin Point with many misgivings. From the start of the Port Royal Experiment, he had realized that most of his colleagues were totally unsuited for the work they were undertaking. Some were simply young and inexperienced, some arrived already jaded by previous failures, and some were so wrapped up in their religious fervor that they failed to understand the nature of the work required of them. The missionaries, he had been known to complain, got up late in the morning, took their time with their ablutions, read their Bibles, said their prayers, dawdled over breakfast, and then discovered that their workers had been waiting for instructions all morning.

"Now they are complaining that the people back home do not understand what we are doing," he said to his wife. "It's a good thing they don't, if you ask me. If the government saw the meager results we're getting, they'd withdraw their support in a flash. But don't misunderstand, my dear. I am pleased with much of what we have accomplished here in a short period of time. We have 2,500 children in school for the first time, and a great many adults who are learning at least the rudiments of reading and writing. The blacks have demonstrated that they can support themselves, if at a fairly basic level. My concern is that those in power will fail to notice how much good we have done, and that they will concentrate too much emphasis on our meager material results."

"Will the departure of Mr. Pierce and the arrival of General Saxton make a difference, do you think?"

"I can only hope so. Edward Pierce is a fine Christian man, but he is altogether too idealistic to take the steps necessary to turn our efforts around. General Saxton? Only time will tell. I would have preferred to have a businessman in the position rather than a military man, but perhaps he will be more willing to give orders and see to it that they are carried out."

11
CRISIS AFTER CRISIS
May/June 1862

The Oaks plantation was a convenient stopping-off point for travelers between Beaufort and the far reaches of St. Helena Island. The islands of the Low Country were not all that large, but moving from one to another often meant hours spent hunting for someone to row a boat across or waiting for the tide to come in so that a boat could pass over the pluff mud without getting bogged. The Oaks offered two other attractions. Its larders were usually well stocked with provisions, so hungry travelers enjoyed stopping there for dinner. And because Edward Pierce used the house as his headquarters, news seemed to arrive there first. Laura Towne sometimes felt as if she were running a hotel, as missionaries, government officials, and military men came knocking at the door at all hours, looking for some gossip, a bed, or dinner.

Frederick Eustis, a Boston abolitionist and a graduate of Harvard Divinity School, was a frequent visitor. He had inherited the Eustis Plantation on Ladies Island from his stepmother, Patience Wise Izard Eustis, in 1860. He was in the unique position of being both a Gideonite and a Southern planter. He had spent much of his youth on the plantation, so slaves and South Carolina natives alike regarded him as one of their own. His house, which was actually just a tiny three-room affair, stood on the main road between Beaufort and St. Helena. It was, however, too small to allow him to bring his wife, Mary Channing Eustis, to live with him, and much too small to lodge more than one or two overnight visitors. As a result, Eustis provided the equivalent of a water taxi service across the creek to The Oaks. As often as possible, he accompanied the travelers, hungry for a good meal and the latest news.

Laura and the other permanent residents of The Oaks welcomed Eustis. His visits brought reports from Hilton Head, as well as insights into life in the Low Country. He was in constant contact with the officials in Beaufort. He could identify unfamiliar plants and wildlife, and recommend the best fishing spots. Because his slaves trusted him, he also was the first to hear of attacks against the blacks or brewing trouble over labor and wages. So it was natural that even Susan Walker turned to him for advice.

One evening in late May, Eustis brought the news of more imminent departures. "Have you heard," he asked, "that several regiments stationed in and around Beaufort have been ordered back to Hilton Head in preparation for an attempted assault on the city of Charleston?"

"Oh, no," Susan said. "I've always felt safe here knowing that we had 12,000 soldiers standing between us and any Southerners who might try to come sneaking back onto these islands. How many of them are leaving?"

"Six regiments that I know of—the Eighth Michigan, the Seventh Connecticut, the Twenty-eighth Massachusetts, the Twenty-sixth and Seventy-ninth New York, along with the Pennsylvania Roundheads. That's almost six thousand men." He ticked them off on his fingers.

"Not Colonel Leasure's Roundheads!" Now even Mr. Hooper was upset. "They have added a touch of civility to our surroundings. Who will be left to set an example to the other soldiers once they are gone?"

"We've all criticized the soldiers from time to time for their idleness and rough manners. But watching them pack up and march onto their transports will be a frightening sight," Mr. Pierce agreed.

"And who will defend us from all those rebels just waiting to return?" Miss Winsor wondered. The fear that the plantation owners would one day return had kept the Gideonites on edge from the time they arrived. Rumors of spies circulated almost every day, and imaginations conjured up the worst barbarities. "We've all heard that story about the discovery of drinking cups carved out of human skulls and labeled 'Yankee.' That happened just across the Coosaw River from this island."

"Well, almost 6,000 troops will still be stationed in the area," Eustis said, "but it does appear that most of them will be at Hilton Head. Beaufort and our plantations are likely to be on the outskirts of the area they can protect."

Ever practical, Laura Towne tried to steer the conversation away from panic and toward a solution. "What can we do to make ourselves safer?" She turned to Mr. Pierce. "Has there been any thought of providing arms to each plantation? I'm sure we could find several strong black men who would be more than happy to stand guard if they were furnished with weapons."

Several of the dinner guests stared at her in alarm. "Arm the Negroes? Wouldn't they be more dangerous than the rebels?" Mr. Hooper asked.

Laura was surprised. "Dangerous? I've never been afraid of our Negroes. I've found them to be embarrassingly grateful for all we do and almost childlike in their devotion to those of us who are helping them."

"Ah, childlike, yes, but you don't put guns into the hands of ignorant children—or the hands of women, for that matter," Mr. Hooper said. "No, if we have to arm the plantations, any guns would have to remain in the hands of white men, and I think we have quite enough to do without working all day and then standing guard all night."

"I would wager that I'm a better shot than you," Laura muttered under her breath.

Before more fuel could be added to that particular argument, Frederick Eustis stepped in. "No, weapons are not the answer. I do think, however, that we all need to be prepared to evacuate the islands quickly if it becomes necessary."

"Where would we go?" Mr. Pierce asked. "We are responsible for thousands of slaves. Where could we take them, and how could we move that many people?"

"The slaves would have to be left behind, of course," Mr. Eustis said. "I have over 150 on my small piece of property, and there's no way I could find other housing for them. But they wouldn't be any worse off than they were before we got here."

"But we came here to improve their conditions," Laura argued. "How could we abandon everything we've said we believe in?"

"Oh, you'll do it if it means saving your own life, believe me," Susan Walker said.

"Maybe you would. But don't presume to know what I would do."

"Ladies! Please!"

"The whole question is pointless," Mr. Eustis said. "Summer is nearly here, and you're at least going to have to move back to Beaufort. Everyone knows white people can't survive summer weather on these islands."

"That's not so. If black people don't die from summer heat, neither will whites," Laura commented.

"But the blacks are used to it, and they've already probably survived the kinds of diseases that breed in these swamps during the summer. I know my stepmother would not let us even visit our plantation during the summer months. We had to stay in Beaufort, where the houses are on higher ground and the sea breezes cleanse the air."

"I've heard about the malarial fevers around here," Susan said. "That's part of what is persuading me to go home."

"I didn't realize you were considering that, Miss Walker. I can't say as how I'd blame you, of course. Even Reverend Peck and his daughter are leaving next month, I hear."

"Are they? What's going to happen to their school?"

"I understand he's leaving it in the hands of the black teachers he's trained," Mr. Eustis said.

"How can he do that?" Laura was becoming more and more upset. "Maybe this so-called 'Port Royal Experiment' was just that—an experiment. Maybe none of you intended to do any more than make a gesture toward actually helping the freed slaves. But I made a commitment, and so did my friend Ellen Murray, who is just now on her way here. I don't want to leave."

"You will when it gets hot enough."

"But we have sea breezes here, too."

"Miss Towne, please try to understand. I'm not your enemy. I'm trying to save your life. Look around you. These

houses are not even built for summer living. This house—
and mine—and most of the others we have moved into have
southern exposures. Only the backs face the open water. That
helps keep them warm in winter, but it turns them into bake
ovens in summer heat."

"Then Ellen and I shall have to live in the back."

"Who is this Ellen person you keep talking about?"
Mr. Hooper asked. "Ever since you arrived you've been telling us about your little friend who will be joining you. But
you've been here for a couple of months now, and we still
haven't seen her."

"Ellen Murray is an accomplished and devoted teacher.
She did not come with me in April because she wanted to finish out the school year with her pupils back home. Now she
has all her paperwork, and she tells me that she will be sailing
just as soon as a ship heads this way."

"Well, that may be some time in coming," Mr. Eustis
said. "I don't like to be the bearer of ill tidings, Miss
Towne, but the spring has not been kind to ships sailing
along the Atlantic coast. A lone woman trying to gain
passage from New York to South Carolina has little hope
of succeeding."

"She won't be traveling alone. She is going to be accompanied by Mr. James McKim, who organized the Philadelphia
Relief Committee and has helped finance this venture."

"Be that as it may, the *Oriental* was wrecked, and the
Atlantic is in dry dock for repairs. There is high demand for
ships to transport troops. The whole focus of the war is moving away from this front toward Virginia. Transport cannot
be spared for the whim of a young woman who wants only
what she herself wants."

"No one has told me that," Laura said. Then, unable to contain herself any longer, she stood up from the table. "Please excuse me." Trying to keep her sagging shoulders steady, she headed to her room, where she could express her anger and grief in private.

Later that night, Nelly Winsor came down the stairs with a candle and stepped out onto the veranda. Black clouds sailed past and sometimes obscured the moon, and the wind whipped the trees. Lightning flashed in the distance. "Miss Towne? What are you doing out here in the dark? I almost mistook you for a rebel."

"I'm fine, Miss Winsor. I didn't mean to alarm you."

"You're not fine. If you were, you'd be safely asleep in your bed. You're worried about your friend, aren't you?"

"It's so stormy tonight. And I'm afraid Ellen is out in it somewhere."

"I'm sure she's safe, but it's really lovely of you to be so worried about her. You must care deeply for her."

Laura found it easier to talk in the dark. "Thank you for your concern. Ellen and I have a special bond. Neither of us is interested in marriage and children. We simply want to spend our lives together, doing something that will make the world a better place. We thought this would be it. We could come here, start over, away from the criticisms of our families, and create our own version of a family. We envisioned a small house, where she could teach little black children and I could treat their ills. It all sounded so simple when we talked about it back in Philadelphia."

"And now it doesn't?"

"No, it doesn't. Perhaps Miss Walker and Mr. Pierce are correct. This whole experiment could be doomed to failure.

Maybe we all ought to pack up and go home before it's too late."

"I don't believe for a minute that you really think that."

"Everything seems hopeless at the moment. I'm here running what might as well be a hotel. Ellen is God knows where, maybe halfway along but unable to find her way here. I face the real possibility of being evacuated and sent home because of disease or rebel invasion. And what if I've been wrong all along?"

"Wrong about what?"

"About the possibility of turning ex-slaves into prosperous citizens. About my own ability to play doctor in a strange and hostile environment. About the possibility that Ellen and I can create a life together. What if my errors of judgment have brought Ellen to harm? How will I manage to live without her if I've caused her death?"

"I think you are overwrought by the evening's discussion, Miss Towne. Your fears and doubts will surely lessen with the coming of a new day. Please come upstairs now, and try to sleep."

12
GOINGS AND COMINGS
June 1862

Although she had taken some comfort from Nelly Winsor's gentle words and support, Laura's relief did not last long. On Saturday, June 7th , Mr. Eustis came galloping to The Oaks on a borrowed horse to bring terrifying news. "Where is Pierce?" he shouted as he dismounted. "We must act at once!"

Laura and Mr. Hooper converged on the yard from opposite directions in response to the commotion. "Hold on there, Frederick. What's all the fuss about?" Mr. Hooper asked.

"There's been a rebel attack! We have to leave! I have to tell Pierce!"

"No." Laura was resolute. "Mr. Pierce is not here, and we're not going anywhere without his order."

"Where is he?"

"He left early this morning to escort Miss Walker to Beaufort. She's on her way to Hilton Head to catch a steamer headed for home."

"Well, when will he be back?"

"I don't know. But I'm fairly sure that if there is real danger, he will get the news and come back to tell us his wishes."

"You can't wait."

"Yes, we can, and we will."

"We can make some preparations, Miss Towne, just in case." Mr. Hooper stepped in, hoping to avoid further argument. "Please see to it that you and the other women pack your trunks, so that you can be ready to move quickly if we have to leave. I'll tell the hands to have the horses and the boats ready. Now, Frederick, please come in and try to calm down. I want to hear exactly what has happened."

Gradually the story came out. With the departure of the Union troops, no one had been guarding the outskirts of Beaufort for the past couple of weeks. A small band of rebels, said to have numbered about fifty, had made an attempt to cross onto Port Royal Island at the ferry. They had sent a few slaves ahead of them to flush out whoever was on guard. When the pickets challenged the approach, the Confederate troops rose up on their flatboat and fired. Several pickets died; the others fled to the relative safety of Beaufort. The panic spread rapidly. Army authorities ordered civilians, cotton agents, and women onto a steamer headed to Hilton Head. Rumors flourished.

"They're hiding in the woods right now, just waiting for nightfall so that they can creep up on us and kill us all in our beds," Mr. Eustis said.

"How do you know that?" Laura asked.

"Everybody says so. Officials at the Arsenal have announced that they are opening their doors this afternoon, so that anyone who wants to can come in and get a gun. We're all going to have to defend ourselves."

"That proves nothing," Laura said.

"Stop it, both of you. You've had this argument before. Miss Towne, please go ahead with your packing. And

Frederick, I suggest you head home to defend your own plantation. We'll handle things from this end until Mr. Pierce gets back."

"If he gets back, you mean. Somebody could have captured him."

"Highly unlikely, but we'll keep an eye out. You've done your duty, Frederick. Now, go home."

Laura went first to the slave cabin where Miss Winsor was holding a class. "Dismiss the children for the day, Miss Winsor. You are needed urgently at the house."

With her usual calm, Nelly finished her lesson and sent the children off with a smile and a pat for each of them. Then she hurried to catch up with Laura. "What has happened?" she asked.

"There has been another scare in Beaufort about rebel troops. I think it's an exaggeration, and it surely is not going to involve us out here on St. Helena. But Mr. Hooper has ordered us to each pack a trunk, so that we can be ready if someone gives the order to evacuate."

"But we can't just . . ."

"Shhhh. I know. I don't want to alarm the servants, but it's best, I think, to do as Mr. Hooper asks. There will be a worse problem if we're heard fighting among ourselves. Once everyone calms down, we can always unpack again."

Laura's advice was well meant but too late. Before she had even pulled out her trunk, Rina and Susannah were in the doorway of her room.

"Where you be gwine?"

"Is de bad mens comin back?"

"You aint gwine leave we behind, is you?"

"Is dere gwine be mo big shoot?"

"No. No. Don't worry." Laura sat down abruptly on the bed. What silly advice that was, she realized. But how could she explain?

"Missus Laura, you neber lie to we. What be happenin?"

"There has been a rumor of enemies in the woods, but . . ."

"Oh, Lawdy! We gwine die!" Susannah cried.

"No, you're not going to die, and I'm not going anywhere."

"You be packin dat dere trunk, aint you?" Rina stomped her foot as if Laura ought to have been ashamed of herself. "Why you be doin dat ifn you aint gwine ennywheres?"

"I'm packing because Mr. Hooper ordered me to do it, and I always try to do what I'm told. But I'm not planning to leave. It's just a precaution."

"What dat mean—pre-caw-shun?"

"It means 'just in case.' It's like . . . like . . . like that bucket of water Susannah keeps in the kitchen in case something catches fire. If she needs it, it's there, but she doesn't intend to start a fire. If I need the trunk, it'll be packed, but I don't intend to use it."

"Dat still don make good sense," Rina said. "You tinks de bad soljers be comin back, don you?"

"I really don't think they will. There's no reason for them to come here."

"Ifn dey's bad mens, dey don need no reason. Dey be comin fuh steal our food an take our anmals an lick we an . . ." Susannah was wringing her hands in the folds of her apron. "Oh, Lawdy! What be gwine happen to we?"

"Listen to me, both of you. I don't want you scaring everyone on the plantation. I really don't think anything bad is going to happen, and I am not going to leave unless the gentlemen force me to go. Furthermore, even if we have to leave, we'll come right back as soon as the danger passes, I promise."

"We kin hide ourselfs in de woods, ifn need be. But what bout poor ol Bess wit she gimpy leg? An de wimmun wit chillun? What be gwine happen to dem whiles you be gone?"

"All right. I promise! I won't leave. If trouble comes, I'll help you hide in the woods." The image was so unlikely that Laura grinned in spite of herself, and her humor broke the atmosphere of fear. Even Susannah chuckled.

"You aint be saying dat less you tinks you aint gwine nowheres."

"Right! So go along with you, now. Let me finish this, just to keep Mr. Hooper happy. Then we can talk more about how you can get prepared, too."

"As one uh dem pre-caw-shun?"

"Exactly."

The situation defused itself when Mr. Pierce returned around one o'clock. He confirmed the reports of plans to evacuate Beaufort if necessary, but was certain that the plantations were in no danger. "There's no reason we cannot stay here," he said. "I'm going to make one more trip into Beaufort, and I intend to bring back a few guns from the Arsenal. We might as well take advantage of that offer. I'm asking the plantation superintendents to set up patrols for a few nights, but there's not going to be trouble. This will blow over. Just you watch."

* * *

By Sunday morning, when the Gideonites gathered for worship at the Brick Church, most of them were able to laugh at their own foolishness. They lingered under the shade of the live-oak trees, gently teasing each other about their overreactions. The bands of marauding thugs had diminished to a couple of stray Confederate soldiers foraging for blackberries in the woods. The threat of imminent destruction of all they had built for themselves seemed more and more unlikely. And, once again, the long hot summer days stretched out in front of them.

"The most we have to fear," Mr. Philbrick observed, "is that black cloud moving this way. I'm afraid it is about to grace us with an unnecessary baptism if we don't move on from the church grounds."

"Why don't we adjourn to the Episcopal Church?" Mr. Soule suggested. "So far as I know, there's nothing going on there this afternoon. Miss Winsor could play their organ for us, and we could have a small musicale to celebrate our narrow escape from danger."

The idea met with enthusiastic agreement from all but Laura Towne. She had been awake most of the night, not sure whether she was listening for men creeping through the underbrush or simply imagining Ellen out on the ocean somewhere. "You young folks go along and enjoy yourselves. This middle-aged spinster is going back to The Oaks for a much deserved afternoon nap."

Her driver, Hastings, helped her into a small buggy, and they set off for home, arriving just ahead of the downpour that Mr. Philbrick had predicted. Laura went immediately to bed, fully admitting to herself for the first time that she felt dreadful. Her head ached, there was tightness in her chest, and her arms and legs felt too heavy to move. Despite the cool breezes that accompanied the rain, she was alternately sweating and shivering.

I probably have caught one of the swamp fevers, she self-diagnosed. It would serve me properly to die here after being so stubborn about leaving. I should have listened to Susan Walker and headed home with her. But then I'd be both sick and seasick.

She stirred uncomfortably on her lumpy mattress. Why did I ever think this was a good idea? I'll not stay a moment longer than necessary. It's not worth it. My family is unhappy. Ellen is probably never going to be able to join me. And the slaves we are trying to help only see us as other white owners who owe them protection in exchange for their services.

She drifted off, only to be awakened by Rina, who pushed the door open so violently that it crashed against the wall. "She here! Missus Murray! De one you bin waitin fuh. De mens jis be bringin she trunk fro de ferry. She be here enny minute. Oh, Missus Laura! Git up!"

Laura jumped up and then swayed as the room spun around her. She fell back against the pillow and squeezed her eyes shut against a beam of sunlight that penetrated the storm clouds.

"You be swoonin?" Rina hovered over her. "Or be you sick?"

"I'll be all right, Rina. Give me some room and some air. I just sat up too fast. You startled me with your dramatic entrance. Now tell me again. Is Miss Murray actually here?"

"I aint seed her. But de mens, dey says she gots off de boat an be on she way in a wagon."

"Where's Miss Towne?" another voice bellowed. Mr. Pierce poked his head into the doorway and then backed out hurriedly. "Excuse me, Miss Towne, but your little friend is on her way. I wanted to be the one to let you know, but I see one of your busybody servants has beaten me to it. Their traveling party took shelter at the Episcopal Church when it started to rain, but it's clearing now, and they will be on their way."

Laura hastily straightened her dress and hair. The excitement coursing through her had wiped away most of her symptoms. She made her way downstairs and was waiting decorously in the doorway when the wagon pulled up. Mr. Pierce was watching her every mood with a wicked grin on his face. He wants to see us together, she realized. Well, I refuse to give him a show.

As Hastings helped Ellen from the wagon, the two women looked intently at one another, but, as usual, Ellen read Laura's mood precisely. She walked slowly up the stairs, extending her hand for a warm but formal handshake. "Miss Towne," she said, bowing her head slightly over their clasped hands. "How lovely to see you again."

"And you, Miss Murray. Welcome to The Oaks. Won't you come in?"

The next few moments were filled with the usual formalities and introductions. Mr. McKim of the Philadelphia Commission and his daughter Lucy were also in the traveling party. The servants bustled in and out, jostling each other in their attempts to look busy while trying to get a good look at the newcomers. Finally Laura stepped in. "Miss Murray, I'm sure you would like to refresh yourself after your hard journey. Let me show you to our room." Still moving decorously, the two women ascended the rear staircase. Then safely inside the room, away from the watching eyes, they fell into each other's arms. For a few moments it was enough for both of them to stand locked in an embrace. Laura stepped back, clasping Ellen's hands in her own. "You're here. You're really here!"

"I'm here!" Ellen echoed. Then they were laughing, jumping up and down with glee, shaking their heads at the wonder of being together once again.

"I'm so sorry you've had such a miserable time arranging your trip," Laura said. "If I had known how hard it was going to be, I would never . . ."

"Don't you dare say it! It's been worth every minute of trouble."

"But we're not going to stay. I can't put you through all this. We'll go home and find somewhere safer to live and work."

"No! I won't hear of that! I'm here to stay!"

"I'm afraid for you, Ellen. There are dangers here—all kinds of dangers. There are rebel attacks. Strange diseases. Horrible bugs. Now that I see you, I know I can't risk your life here."

"And I know what you taught me a long time ago: 'Alone we are weak. Together we are strong.' We're going to have a wonderful life together. You may have gotten me into this experiment, but now I'm here. It's too late to change your mind."

13
LOW COUNTRY RELIGION
June 1862

Laura and Ellen had little time to relish their reunion while Mr. McKim and his daughter Lucy were visiting. The house was so crowded that, on the first night, Lucy McKim and Nelly Winsor shared the only bed, while Laura and Ellen slept on the floor of their room. The crowding situation eased the next day, when Mr. Whiting, the cotton agent, finally moved out of The Oaks. Mr. Pierce had ordered him to leave behind all the furniture he had appropriated, so the Gideonites now had twice the number of rooms, upstairs and down, and furniture for all their rooms. Within days, Laura wrote to her sisters that their accommodations were now comfortable and even elegant. Still, there was much to be done if Laura and Ellen were to make St. Helena Island their permanent home.

First, Mr. McKim needed to be persuaded that they were indeed safe here, a fact he seemed to doubt. As head of the Philadelphia Commission, he had the power and the right to cut off further funds and send the women home if he became concerned about their situation. Since Ellen seemed determined to make a go of it, Laura swallowed her own fears and discontents, plunging into a campaign to convince the McKims that their work was not only safe but necessary.

On the first night, she led the visitors out to Rina's cabin in the slave village to witness a "shout." Mr. McKim looked about him with a mixture of curiosity and dismay. "How many people live out here in these shacks?" he asked.

"We have about 150 blacks working on the plantation fields and others working as servants in the house, the stables, and the yard. With their families, that makes . . . oh, I don't know . . . maybe 300 or so."

"In these tiny houses?"

"They're not so small, really," Laura assured him. "Larger families have more room, and the people live so communally that they shift around as necessary. Their food comes out of the cookhouse, and most everyone is out and about their chores during the day. These are just overblown bedrooms."

"You referred to this area as the 'slave village.' I thought you were here to train the people how not to be slaves."

"It's been called the 'slave village' for as long as any of them can remember," she said. "That's one of the things we've had to get used to as well. We can tell them over and over that they are no longer slaves, but they're not ready to understand the difference. They still live in the same houses and do the same work. They still have white people telling them what to do. Yes, we now pay them, but I suspect they see those few coins as just something else that 'Massa' provides, along with food and clothing."

"That concept bothers me," Mr. McKim said.

"I understand. But that's why it's going to be necessary for us to stay here for a very long time. We can't just waltz in and create change. We have to move slowly and do a lot of educating along the way. Once you're here for a few days, you'll see how it all works out."

"So what's this 'shout' that we're going to see?"

"Ah! It's an amazing demonstration of slave culture. It's part religion and part pure exuberance—both chant and dance—music with a pounding beat—spontaneous but always in the same pattern. Sometimes it's joyful and other times mournful. You just have to see it to appreciate it."

As they approached, a crowd around Rina's cabin parted to let them enter. Mr. McKim looked around at the dark room illuminated only by the fireplace. Furniture—what there was of it—had been pushed to the walls to leave the middle of the room empty. Several black men stood among the pieces of furniture, looking somber.

"Now what?"

"Shhh."

The quiet deepened. Then came a single tapping of a hand against a tabletop. One by one, the other men joined in, clapping or pounding their knees, and the rhythm became progressively more complicated. Then five black women slipped through the doorway to form a circle in the middle of the room. They were barefoot, with their skirts hitched to make their steps more visible. Round the circle they moved, hardly lifting their feet but jerking their entire bodies in time to the beat. Other voices now joined, chanting the chorus of a spiritual.

"Are they singing?" Mr. McKim whispered. "It's quite musical, but like no music I've ever heard."

"Slave songs are like that," Laura whispered back.

Now the tempo was picking up. Faster and faster the women moved, perspiration flowing freely from their faces.

From outside came other voices joining in the chorus, and the drumming seemed to make the very walls shake. The women began to move more freely, some swooping to the ground, some dancing out sideways, and some whirling in place. Even the white people in the audience were breathing harder as they absorbed the sound. Just when it seemed that everyone must perish from exhaustion, a single crash brought everything to a halt. The dancers fell to the ground, and their accompanying chorus bent forward, heads bowed.

"I'm exhausted, and I haven't moved a muscle," Mr. McKim said.

"I know, but it's time for us to leave." Laura led the way out of the cabin and across the yard toward the house. "Sometimes they can go on that way half the night," she told the visitors. "When they get wound up, you can feel the vibrations all the way up here."

"It's their form of religion, then," Mr. McKim said. "It appears to be a remnant of African worship."

"Perhaps. Certainly there are native African elements in it. But I wouldn't call it their religion—at least, not their only religion. It's more like a creative outlet for impulses that the people keep in check all day long. It's an avenue of escape. Once you can understand the words of the chants, you'll pick up longings to go far away, to escape the present life, even if it means death. You'll also hear hostilities and fears that they can't express in other situations. It's the other side of the normally submissive slave. For serious religious ceremonies, the people go to the Praise House," Laura went on. "Just as Rina's cabin is the customary place to hold a shout, the Praise House is always the home of the oldest woman in the community."

"Sounds matriarchal."

"Oh, their social structure is certainly matriarchal. That's because mothers usually raise the children, while fathers go off to work at distant jobs or get sold to other plantations. You learn to obey whoever raises you. But at the Praise House, it's the men who speak as the spirit moves them. The Praise House is for discussing serious problems and asking for spiritual help and guidance. A whole lot of sharing goes on there—and a lot of praying."

"It still doesn't sound much like Christianity. Aren't the Gideonites supposed to be missionaries?"

"Attending Christian church services is the third element in the slaves' religious practice," Laura said. "But you have enough to absorb for now. Tomorrow we'll take the buggy out, and I'll show you our church."

The next morning, Laura repeated her suggestion about driving out to see the church. "Oh, we've already been there," Lucy McKim said. "That White Church is a lovely building with all those glistening walls. And the organ! I never expected to hear such music in a wilderness such as this."

"The White Church? Oh, you mean the Episcopal Church? I had forgotten that you were forced to take shelter there for a while on your way here. That's not the church I was referring to. Actually, the Episcopal Church is not used for worship at all any more. That's part of the explanation you need to hear."

"It's not used? Why? It appears perfectly serviceable."

"Serviceable, perhaps, but not a place of welcome for former slaves. Come along, I'll explain as we drive."

Laura called to Hastings to bring around the largest carriage, so that she could take Ellen and the McKims together. They went first to the Episcopal Church. Sitting in the shade of the overhanging oak trees, she pointed out the features of the grounds. "Out there among the trees on your right you'll see a Greek-looking structure. That's the Fripp mausoleum. It was built for Edgar Fripp and his family. It contains several graves, I believe. Just in front of it and slightly to our left, you'll see two other clusters of gravestones—all for Fripps."

"And who were the Fripps?"

"The most notorious slave owners on this island," Laura said. "Edgar owned most of the land around here, but once you start naming plantations here on St. Helena, you run into Edgar, Lawrence, Oliver, John, Isaac, Tom—there's just no end to the Fripp family. More significant, they were cruel. At Frogmore, Thomas Fripp had a whipping post erected in his dining room so that he could eat dinner while watching his slave driver punish the slaves for minor infractions."

"How do you know that?"

"The post is still there. Richard Soule, who is our superintendent there now, refuses to take his meals in the dining room because of it. Says the blood stains and gashes in the wood from the whip are enough to turn his stomach."

"Truly horrible! But what has it to do with the use of the White Church?"

"Must you insist on using that name?" Laura grimaced in distaste.

"Well, it is white, after all," said Lucy.

"Yes, but the color of its walls did not give it the label. It's known as the White Church because the Fripps would not let a Negro enter it. They didn't want it sullied. That's why we don't use it for religious services. We refer to it as the Episcopal Church, but the Negroes won't go there—ever. The Gideonites use it as a gathering place once in a while because they enjoy playing the organ, but it's no longer a house of worship." Laura urged the horses into a trot down the road. "Our church is down the road a bit."

At the top of a small rise—nearly the high point of the island—she drew to a stop in front of a two-story square building. "Welcome to the Brick Church," she said.

"It's rather boring," said Lucy. "I still prefer all that shiny white material the other one is made of."

"That's just beach sand and oyster shells stirred into the concrete," Laura said. "It is sturdy, and shiny, too, but not particularly valuable."

"If the white one was the Episcopal Church, what denomination is this one?" Mr. McKim asked.

"It started out as the Baptist Church back in 1855, when the Popes and several other families put their slaves to work building the structure you see here. When it was finished, the plantation owners brought their slaves to church with them."

"Good for them!"

"They were, perhaps, not quite so forward-thinking as you might suppose," Laura said. "They made the slaves sit upstairs in the balcony, where the owners couldn't see them. Still, the slaves felt ownership of this church, and they've been coming here ever since. When the whites evacuated this island, the slaves did their own preaching. Now we all share the building—Gideonites and freedmen alike. We have some very interesting worship services—sometimes Baptist, sometimes Methodist, sometimes Unitarian, and sometimes pure Gullah. One never knows whether we'll be led by a black preacher or a white one. What I can tell you, though, is that the worship that takes place here is sincere and heartfelt. It's one of the things I'm proudest of on this island."

"Well, I'm happy that the ex-slaves are learning about Christianity," Mr. McKim. "But is that enough to justify your staying here?"

"If that were all we were doing, perhaps not. But we have all sorts of projects underway. The men are learning about work done for wages. That's a big step, by the way. Until we came, they never realized that there was a connection between their work and their own comfort level. They thought they were supposed to do the least amount of work possible to avoid a licking, and they believed that the owners would give them the same amount of food, clothing, and shelter, no matter what they did. Now they are beginning to understand that the harder they work, the more money they earn and the more goods they can buy for themselves and their families."

Laura realized she was delivering a lecture, but she couldn't stop herself. "The women are learning about the connections between cleanliness and good health, about how to take better care of their children. And the children? They are learning the kinds of discipline and self-control that classrooms teach. All of them—young and old alike—are learning to read and write. Slowly, they are adopting some of our cultural values. We have weddings and baptisms nearly every Sunday at the church. Families are learning to live like families. We're accomplishing miracles here, Mr. McKim, even if most of them are too small for you to notice."

"I'm beginning to appreciate that," he agreed.

"Perhaps tomorrow we can drive out to Frogmore. Despite Mr. Soule's reluctance to use the dining room, I find it has one of the most beautiful views on the whole island. You ought to see some of the variety of plantations we're running, as well as some of the problems that are unique to each location."

"Oh, Lawdy, Missus Towne," Hastings spoke up. "Don you be takin dese folk out dat road fuh Frogmore. It be hanted. I aint gwine drive, dat fuh sho."

"Hastings!" Laura didn't know quite how to handle this situation. It was entirely out of character for Hastings to have anything at all to say to a white person. "I can find someone else to drive, but you are being ridiculous. I've been out there several times. I love that house, and it's certainly not haunted."

"It not be de house what be hanted, Missus. It be de road. Ifn you goes in daylight, you don see dem, but de hants an hags be dere, jis de same. After dark, dey comes out an runs up an down dat road under de hangin tree."

Laura shook her head in exasperation and turned away. "As I have been saying, we still have a lot of work to do."

14
LOW COUNTRY FEARS
June 1862

If Laura hoped the idea of a haunted road to Frogmore would pass unnoticed, she was to be disappointed. Lucy McKim excused herself to visit the slave quarters that afternoon. "I'd love a chance to meet the children," she explained. Mr. McKim used the same time to go to Beaufort for an interview with Reverend French. By the time they returned for dinner, both were agitated and apprehensive.

"I still don't think it's a good idea for you ladies to stay here any longer," Mr. McKim announced. "Mansfield French is a knowledgeable man, and he tells me that you will be facing grave dangers in the months to come."

"I think you're right, Father," Lucy said. "I've been talking to the slaves, and they tell me terrible tales of what goes on here."

Even Mr. Hooper was taken aback. "What dangers?" he asked. "We've never been in danger here."

"I'm more concerned with what the slaves told my daughter," McKim said. "Lucy, please go on. What have you learned?"

"Well, I started by asking what Hastings was referring to about Frogmore and a hanging tree."

"Oh, Miss McKim! That was just Hastings's way of getting out of work tomorrow. Slaves make up wild stories all the time." Laura shook her head.

"No, Miss Towne. With all due respect, I think you're wrong. I learned that there is an old oak tree with a strong branch that hangs over the road on the way to Frogmore. Before the war, the slave owners used it as a hanging tree to kill any slave who tried to escape. Then they would leave the corpse dangling there over the road as a warning to others. A slave woman named Judith told me that the spirits of the lynched slaves still live on that road. At night they come out looking like balls of fire, and they roll up and down the road, hoping to catch one of the slave owners."

"Surely you must realize how impossible that is."

"No, ma'am. She's seen them herself. She said the tree limb still shows the rope burns, where the bark is all stripped away. She says none of the slaves will walk past that tree. That's why Frogmore's slaves never come to church. They're more afraid of the haunts than they are of God."

"We'll just have to be sure that we don't go at night," Mr. Hooper said. "I wouldn't do that anyway. The road is in terrible shape, and I'd be afraid of the horse stumbling over roots and holes in the road. But balls of fire? I don't think so."

"Laugh, if you will, but she also told me about Graybeards and Night Hags."

"What in the world are you talking about?"

"All that stuff hanging from the trees. You told us that it was called Spanish moss and that it's some sort of miraculous plant that lives on air. I didn't ever believe that!"

"It's true!"

"Susannah says it's spirits that live in the trees. They're slave owners and other cruel people who have been punished by being trapped in a tree. They've been there so long that their beards have grown long and gray and straggly. When you see a tree with lots of graybeards, you're supposed to be warned to behave yourself. You can tell that this place is full of evildoers. Good people shouldn't be living here."

"I can see someone needs to have a long talk with our house servants. They must not be spreading such tales to our guests," Mr. Pierce said. "Miss Towne, will you see to that, please?"

"Of course. But, with all due respect to you, Miss McKim, I don't think our guests should be listening to the idle gossip of slaves and taking their word over ours."

Lucy was too wound up in her own story to notice that she had been rebuked. "There are Night Hags around here, too."

"Night Hags. And they are . . .?"

"They're demons who show up in the middle of the night. They look like ugly old women, and they sit on your chest and suck the air out of you, until you can't breathe. When you wake up gasping, they disappear into thin air." Lucy's eyes were wide with terror. "If one sits on you, you're likely to get sick, too. They spread diseases like swamp fever."

"That's enough, Lucy." By now even Mr. McKim was losing patience with his daughter. "These are just slave superstitions, I'm afraid. Good Christian people don't believe in haunts and hags. Although, the disease part . . ."

Laura pushed her chair back and stood. "Diseases are not caused by demonic old women sitting on your chest in the middle of the night! Why don't we move to the parlor and talk of something else?"

* * *

"Now, then," Mr. McKim began as soon as they were settled. "Let's talk about some more serious matters. Mr. French tells me that white people simply cannot exist on these islands during the summer months. He says the temperatures will be unbearably hot, maybe even dangerously so, and that the area will swarm with insects. He has frightening tales of people who have sickened and died from the malarial fevers that spread through the swamps."

"The slaves say only black people can live here in the summer, Father." Lucy still wanted to be heard, but her father ignored her.

"We've been told the same thing, but I don't believe it," said Mr. Pierce. "That's just a scare tactic the Army officials are using to try to run us out."

"Excuse me. Correct me if I'm wrong, but aren't you yourself scheduled to go home by the end of the month?"

"Yes, I am, but not because of the weather. I have a legal practice in Boston that will not wait any longer for my return. I am not a rich man, and I, like several other Gideonites, came here without the help of your commissions. The small salary I draw from the government may be enough to keep me alive, but it cannot also support a family and a house in Boston, or keep a business afloat. I must go home if I am to survive financially. I assure you that I'm not running away from the summer heat or some phantom disease."

"I jotted down other names here. Mrs. Johnson and her sister Miss Donaldson have already gone home because of illness. Miss Susan Walker departed less than a week ago. The Reverend Solomon Peck and his daughter Lizzie are scheduled to leave on the next steamer. All were concerned for their health when they resigned."

"People get sick. That doesn't mean the weather caused it."

"But the worst is still to come, so I understand. Reverend French tells me he is sending his own wife home in the next few weeks. And Mr. Eustis, who knows this area better than anyone . . ."

" . . . says that white people have always left the island to go to higher ground during the summer months." Laura shook her head in exasperation. "We know. We've heard it before. I fail to understand why Mr. Eustis tells us to leave here and go to Beaufort, while the Beaufort residents say they have to go to their summer homes here on our island. Mosquito netting and sea breezes go a long way toward making any location more bearable in the summer."

"But medical people say that . . ."

"I am a doctor, Mr. McKim. I didn't think I would have to remind you of that."

"Fine. But even if you manage to stay healthy, there is the threat of enemy attacks. Army officials seem to think the woods around here are full of rebel soldiers just waiting for the opportunity to attack. Why, Mr. French was telling me that just yesterday, several men were shot on Hutchinson's Island and others were taken prisoner. How can a bunch of women and a single man on each plantation defend themselves from military attacks?"

"We have guns and a great many defenders, both strong black men and other white men on neighboring plantations, should we need them, which I don't believe for a moment will happen."

"But just over on Hutchinson's I . . ."

"Do you know where Hutchinson's Island is, Mr. McKim?" Mr. Hooper had now lost his patience as well.

"Ah, nearby, I believe."

"No, it's not. It's separated from us by St. Helena Sound, and if you tried to reach it by land, you would be forced to travel for hours to get there. And when you did, you'd find that it is barely inhabited. It's not an established settlement such as this, and there are no defenses in place. It's an entirely different situation."

"Hooper's right," Mr. Pierce agreed. "We just weathered one such alarmist warning, which turned out to be entirely false. Perhaps no one told you about that because they are now all embarrassed. The Army and the cotton agents are falling all over themselves trying to prove that they were not the ones who were frightened. And whatever the threat was, it shall not happen again, for we now have gunboats stationed on all sides of the island. The ladies are probably safer here than they were at home, Mr. McKim."

"Still, I wouldn't be hearing all these warnings if there were not some element of truth behind them."

"Oh, there is an element of something, but it isn't truth." Laura fought to keep control of her temper. "The Army wants us gone so that they don't have to be responsible for us. And the cotton agents want us gone because we are keeping them from exploiting the labor of the former slaves. Our goals do not jibe with theirs. That doesn't mean we're in danger. It just means we're an inconvenience to them. But if we weren't here, hundreds of slaves would suffer. What we're doing here is good and moral and necessary. You must not send us home."

15
A TEACHING CHALLENGE
June 1862

While the McKims were taking tours of the rest of the Low Country, Laura turned her attention to Ellen. "Before you can start to work with our people, I need to be sure you are prepared for what you may encounter. You did have a smallpox vaccination before you came down, didn't you?"

"Uh, no, I didn't." Ellen looked sheepish as Laura whirled and glared at her. "You know how I react to the sight of blood, Laura. I'm deathly afraid of doctors, and when they pull out their instruments, I panic. That's one of the reasons I was so happy you were going into homeopathic medicine."

"Well, I have news for you. Homeopathy is largely responsible for the success of vaccinations. They use the same principle of treating a disease with a minute amount of the substance that causes it."

"But it involves scratching the skin and making it bleed."

"You have to do this, Ellen. Smallpox is endemic in the slave communities. I could take you through our own slave village here at The Oaks and point out a case or two. The slaves have been exposed so often that they have rather mild cases. But you! You could die, and I won't be responsible for that."

"You can't do it here, and I won't go home." Ellen was almost defiant.

"I can and I will. Let me get my bag, and we'll go out under the trees, where you can have lots of fresh air. I promise you it will only sting for a minute."

Laura arranged her instruments on a cloth-covered table in the yard and placed a pitcher of water and a glass nearby. "Now then. Just pull up your sleeve and then look off into the trees. Relax, Ellen."

"I'll try, but . . ."

Quickly, Laura scratched the skin and soaked a piece of cotton lint with the contents of a small vial. Swabbing the wound gently, she murmured, "There, that wasn't so bad, was it?"

But as she turned to find a sticking plaster in her bag, Ellen crumpled to the ground, catching the tablecloth as she fell and overturning the water pitcher, which poured its contents over her thin lawn blouse.

Laura knelt beside her to check her pulse as Rina came dashing over. "Be she dead?" she asked.

"Of course not."

"But she so white, an she not movin. Lawd uh mercy, Missus, you done kilt she!"

"She only fainted, Rina."

"Den wake she up."

"She'll wake in a minute. Step back so she can get some air." Laura waved her hands impatiently at the other slaves who were beginning to gather to witness the spectacle of a wet white woman, unconscious on the ground.

Laura could not take her eyes from Ellen's face as the younger woman began to stir. Gently she pushed a tendril of hair from her forehead. "Hush, my dearest. You are fine. I just wasn't prepared to have you swoon at my feet."

A faint smile curved the pale lips. "I warned you I might faint. Really, I tried not to. I tensed every muscle to remain upright, and then . . ."

"And by tensing your muscles you slowed your blood flow. The same thing happens to soldiers when they stand at attention. We see it all the time here in this southern heat. You don't need to apologize."

Ellen struggled to rise, but Laura restrained her. "Just relax a bit longer."

"But I'm all wet. Did you pour water on me?"

"No, you did that to yourself when you fell. But I must admit, you look very fetching in that wet blouse."

"Oh, pooh! I'm feeling positively bedraggled."

"And you look beautiful. I'm so fortunate to have you here with me. I'm sorry I caused you to faint, but I need to protect you from harm, my love."

* * *

Ellen Murray was eager to begin her teaching duties. For the first few days, she accompanied Nelly Winsor to her classes at the Eustis plantation, where Nelly was attempting to manage a mixed group of children and their mothers. The classroom was an empty slave cabin, with no seating except some boards supported by crates. The smaller children played happily on the dirt floors, and classroom activities frequently spilled over to the outside in good weather.

"How does she do it?" Ellen asked Laura after her first day. "I never saw such chaos. Some of the children do their sums and practice their letters on small pieces of slate, while others use a stick to write in the dust. The women and older girls have babies tied to their chests or toddlers clinging to their skirts. Someone is always crying or escaping through the open door. Mothers have to leave to take care of a hungry or injured child and then return, expecting school to have waited for them. Most of the time, I couldn't tell what was going on. Yet Nelly seems perfectly calm and organized."

"I understand how you felt," Laura answered. "I served as a substitute for Nelly one day when she was ill. There was one horrible incident when I heard a swishing noise outside and went to see what was going on. An older child with a willow switch was beating the legs of two smaller children. I demanded she stop, telling her that we had come to stop the beating of slaves, not to encourage it. Then Aleck, one of the older boys, stood up and lectured me, saying that sometimes little ones needed switching and the girl, Betty, had Nelly's permission to lick them. I was dumbfounded. It was the hardest day I have spent here so far."

Ellen sighed. "I knew teaching here would be difficult. I just didn't realize how different it would be. What worries me most, I think, is that I'm not sure the children are learning anything, and I'm almost positive the women are not. They're just mouthing back what the teacher says, with no sign that they understand a word. When I listen to them, they seem to be speaking an entirely different language."

"In many ways, it is a different language, Ellen. You're hearing a combination of English and some half-forgotten

African dialect, all blurred together with a laziness of pronunciation that gives it a droning rhythm."

"But how do you communicate with them if they don't speak English?"

"Oh, make no mistake. They understand English quite well. They have been hearing their masters speak it for generations. And most of them are quite capable of speaking English, too, if they make the effort."

"So why don't they do that in school?"

"Because they don't have to. It's a form of defiance, if you will, or a defensive reaction. If the teacher can't understand a child's answer, she can't say whether the child is right or wrong."

"Of course. I should have realized. I've had enough experience with mumbling like that in New England classrooms. Here, the sounds make it even more confusing. I still have my doubts, however, about whether or not they are actually learning anything. It's rather like teaching a parrot to recite his ABCs. He can do it, if he's clever, but you don't believe for a moment that he knows what a B is."

"What you're seeing, I think, is another part of the slave mentality that we are all just beginning to understand."

"They are not congenitally stupid, Laura. I refuse to believe that."

"No, and that is not what I meant. Not understanding is a survival skill. Imagine for a moment that you are a slave. Your master tells you to muck out the entire stable, but it is nearly dark and turning cold. If you refuse to do it, you'll be beaten, perhaps severely. So you go out and sweep up the area just on either side of the door. Then, when the master berates you for not completing the job, you can say, 'Sorry, massa.

I dint unnerstan.' You're still in trouble, but you're probably not going to be beaten and sold for disobedience."

"How do we overcome that attitude?"

"I'm not sure, Ellen. Perhaps when these people fully realize that they are free, they will feel more of the need for education. Right now, they're still very confused about their status, as well they should be. They know their masters could still come back to claim them. And if the owners return, they are not going to be happy to find educated slaves. The slaves know that, so they have little reason to make progress beyond the simplest things we ask."

"Then why do we . . .?"

"Because we can't do anything else. Someone has to try to get through to them. We can't predict their futures, but we can try to make them better."

* * *

Ellen puzzled over the problem for several days before she broached the discussion again. "I have an idea. Would there be any objection to my starting a class just for adults here at the house? We could use that back corner room, where the cotton agent stored his supplies."

"I don't see a problem with that, so long as it doesn't make you sneeze. The room is still full of cotton fluff. But how will it be any different from what the other schools are doing?"

"For starters, there would be no children tagging along. I don't want the women distracted. Then I'm going to ask them to write first and learn to read later."

"I can't imagine what you mean. Sounds impossible."

"Not really. It's an attempt to overcome that obstacle we discussed the other day—the lack of a reason to learn."

"I still don't follow."

"Let me give you an example. Call Rina in here, would you?"

When Rina arrived, looking puzzled, Ellen invited her to sit down. The former slave still looked the part, head bowed so as not to make eye contact, hands hidden by her apron, one foot twisted around the other ankle.

"Relax, Rina. You're on a break from your chores. Have a seat."

"Duz you mean me? I aint sposed fuh sit in de house."

"I'm giving you permission, Rina," Laura said from the corner, where she had settled herself to observe.

"No, tankee, Ma'am. I be gwine stan."

Ellen took out a small pad of paper. "Can you read and write, Rina?" she asked.

"No'm. I aint neber larned dat."

"Well, if you could write something—a sign, maybe—what would you like it to say?"

Rina shook her head. "I don unnerstan what you be wantin me fuh do."

"A sign, Rina. I'm going to make you a sign. A sign you can put anywhere to tell other people what to do. What do you want it to say?"

"Aint neber hab no sign," Rina protested.

"Now you're going to have one. It will be Rina's sign. What should it say?"

"I kin puts it ennywheres?"

"Yes."

"Den, maybe it be sayin sumptin bout muh chikkuns?"

"If that's what you want, yes."

"Den make it say, 'Dese be Rina's chikkuns. Leave dem be.'"

Ellen tried very hard not to laugh as she wrote down Rina's words: THESE BE RINA'S CHICKENS. LEAVE THEM BE.

"Dat what dose marks mean? Dat be writin?"

"Yes. That's what we mean by writing."

"An I kin takes dat sign an puts it on muh chikkun coop?"

"That's the idea."

"An dose lil marks gwine protect muh chikkuns?"

"I can't promise you that a dog won't get your chickens, since dogs can't read. But soldiers surely can read. If soldiers have been stealing your chickens, then this sign should keep them away."

"It kinda like magic, den?" Rina's eyes were wide with excitement.

"It is a kind of magic. It makes you very powerful." Ellen nodded toward Laura. "The ability to read and write is what gives women like Miss Laura her power to run this plantation."

"Kin ennybody do dat?"

"Anybody can learn how to write, yes."

"Den I wants fuh larn it. An kin we larn how fuh write udder tings, too?"

"Of course. Do you want another sign?"

"I wuz tinkin dat ol Bess mebbe like a sign fuh she taters."

"I can do that." Ellen took out another piece of paper and wrote: THESE BE BESS'S POTATOES. LEAVE THEM BE.

"What dat sign say?"

"It says, 'These be Bess's potatoes. Leave them be'."

"Jis like what muh sign say. Kin I sees dose?" Rina put the two sheets of paper on the table next to one another, and her eyes flashed back and forth between them. Ellen and Laura were both holding their breath.

Finally, Rina spoke. "Dese be Rina's chikkuns. Dese be Bess's taters. Dat word dere. Dat be muh name? An dat one be Bess's name?"

"You're reading them, Rina!" Laura said, her eyes stinging from the effort to hold back her tears.

"Yes'm. Make me annudduh sign."

This time, Ellen did not ask. She simply wrote out two more sentences: THESE BE JOE'S SHOES. LEAVE THEM BE.

"What dat word?"

"Joe."

"An what dat word?"

"Shoes."

"Dat sign, it say, 'Dese be Joe's shoes. Leave dem be'."

"That's right."

"Lawd uh mercy! I kin read?"

"Yes, you can read a little bit. And you can learn to read much more than just these signs."

"Kin I larn fuh make dem marks?"

"Certainly. That's called learning your ABCs. Some of the women have been already studying those. Would you like to have your own class?"

"Missus Laura? She be teasin me?" She looked at Laura for permission to believe the impossible.

"No, Rina. She's not teasing. If you and Susannah and the others would like to go to school, you can have some time off every afternoon to meet here with Miss Ellen. She will be your teacher. And I promise you, she's a good one." Laura smiled at Ellen, her heart nearly overflowing with love and admiration for the younger woman.

16
CLASH OVER COMMUNION
June 1862

It was a lovely summer morning, and Laura and Ellen were on their way to church. Laura drove the buggy herself, so that the two of them could have a bit of private time.

"I'm so proud of your new class, Ellen. The women seem to be absolutely lapping up their lessons."

"They are doing quite well, although it remains to be seen if their enthusiasm will last. They've only had a few days of instruction so far."

"But interest is growing. You'll have to move into the parlor soon, just to have room for all the mothers who want to be able to read and write better than their children."

"Wouldn't it be better to have a real school?"

"Of course it would, but there aren't many vacant buildings around here, you'll notice. We'd have to build a school from scratch, and who would do the labor? We've always had trouble keeping enough men out of the hands of the Army and the cotton agents to do the small handyman jobs around the plantation."

"Well, there's the Brick Church just ahead. What is it used for during the week?"

Laura pulled the buggy to a stop beneath a spreading oak tree. "This is your first day at our Brick Church, Ellen, and you haven't met the assigned preacher, Mr. Horton. I'm afraid he and I don't get along particularly well."

"Whyever not? Everyone is always charmed by you."

"Not when I clash with them at first meeting, I'm afraid. Mr. Horton may be a Baptist minister by occupation, but he is distinctly uncharitable. He's one reason I was glad that the McKims decided to visit Reverend French's church this morning in Beaufort. I didn't want Mr. McKim to learn how bad our relationship is."

"But the other day, you made it sound so idyllic. I don't mean to be critical, my dear, but is it honest to hide the problems from Mr. McKim? After all, that's why he is here."

"Yes, to find a reason to send us all home."

"But if there's trouble . . ."

"I'll handle it," Laura snapped. Then she winced at the tone of her own voice and reached out a conciliatory hand to Ellen. "Let me explain my dislike of Mr. Horton, and then you can judge for yourself whether I'm right or wrong. I came down to South Carolina with him on the *Oriental*, and at first I thought him to be a nice man. His preaching aboard ship was encouraging and comforting. But once he got here and took over the Brick Church . . . On my first visit to the Brick Church, Mr. Horton welcomed me to the service but made it clear that he knew I was not a Baptist and didn't really belong there. I told him that I had enjoyed his sermon, except for a couple of points."

"Not terribly diplomatic, my dear."

"No, but he had upset me. He kept telling the blacks in the congregation that they were not really free because the government of the United States had not recognized their freedom. He stressed their obligation to keep working in their old cotton fields because the Army needed the cotton. Then he tried to modify that by telling them what wonderful people the white missionaries are—that we had come down to do them good, that we had left our homes and comfort for their sakes, and that they should be grateful and obedient.

"I told him that I thought he was qualifying their freedom too much—that I much preferred the military message that tells them they are completely free and that they never again can be claimed as property by any master. His answer was that the slaves need to show us respect, and I responded that his method was not the way to earn their respect."

"He doesn't sound like much of an abolitionist."

"He's not an abolitionist at all. In fact, I would venture to say he is pro-slavery. And that worries me because almost all the Negroes are Baptists, since it was the only church open to them. He's their pastor, and as such has entirely too much influence over their opinions. To have him telling them to be grateful and respectful to all white people works against our efforts to give them confidence in themselves."

"I understand that. It doesn't sound to me as if he's much of a Baptist, either. I'm not hearing a great deal of Christian love coming from your description."

"You'll see for yourself," Laura said, as she jerked the reins to get the old horse moving again.

* * *

At first, Ellen thoroughly enjoyed the church service. She whispered to Laura that the women's Sunday turbans made them look like a flock of brightly colored tropical birds. She grinned when the people shouted out their agreement with something they heard from the Gospel. "Amen" had never sounded so sincere, she realized. She also delighted in listening to the spontaneous hymns that the Negro men started whenever they were so moved. Always, their feet and hands moved to accompany their own singing, adding an emotional rhythm that set the whole congregation asway.

She was still smiling when Mr. Horton mounted the pulpit and announced that he would be offering communion to all the baptized members of the church. "Those of you who have had a proper baptism by being completely submerged in the water are invited to stay. The rest of you must now depart until next Sunday's service."

"What!" Ellen exclaimed, causing several people to look her way. "What did he just say?"

Laura took a deep breath before answering. She was desperately fighting to maintain her composure. "You and Mr. Holt over there are the only Baptists among the Gideonite band, I believe. Therefore, you may stay and take communion with the baptized black members of this church. The rest of us will wait outside."

"I'll do no such thing! That's preposterous! He's advocating a closed communion table in a church that serves a mixed congregation? He can't do that."

"He just did. You may stay for communion, Ellen. You are entitled to do so. If you prefer not to stay, then come outside. It will do no one good to make a huge fuss at this moment."

"But why?" Ellen hissed as soon as they had left the building. "What is he trying to accomplish?"

"Actually, he thinks he will accomplish much," said Mr. Holt, as he approached the women.

"You didn't stay, either? Laura told me you are a Baptist, too." Ellen said.

"I am. I'm a lifelong Baptist, but I don't believe in using my religion as a weapon against others. I'm afraid Mr. Horton does."

"Why is he doing this?"

"First of all, it's a way to convince the unconverted blacks to accept baptism. Look around you. The Negroes out here with us are mostly young men and women, and, as you can see, they don't like being dismissed, either. But they are not seeing it as an insult; they see their dismissal as confirmation of their second-class status. They're ashamed, and Mr. Horton will soon tell them that they need to be dunked in order to be worthy to stay in the church."

"He doesn't try to teach them and encourage their belief?"

"This is much quicker." Mr. Holt sighed. "He hasn't done much to encourage me to remain in the church, either. He would like to see all us whites move down to the Episcopal Church and form our own closed communion, while the blacks have theirs here. Separate churches mean separate races, and that's just how Mr. Horton wants it. He says that's how the plantation owners kept the slaves under control, and he wants us to do the same."

"Let's just go home, Ellen," Laura urged.

"No. I'm going to stay here and tell him what I think."

"We've already tried to suggest that the Negroes don't understand why we leave. They think we just don't want to share communion with them, and of course that undermines our relationship with them. But Mr. Horton doesn't seem to care."

"Perhaps he will listen to another Baptist," Ellen insisted. "Here he comes now."

"Miss Murray, I'm so glad you are still here. I was very sorry to see you leave early. I wanted to welcome you to my church and tell you how happy I am to have you as a congregant."

"Your invitation to the communion table made it improper for me to stay," Ellen answered.

"You must have misunderstood me. All Baptists are welcome."

"I stand with my fellow Christians. I cannot countenance the kind of bigotry that shuts out so many church members from the Lord's Table."

"My dear Miss Murray. Your friends out here are Unitarians and the unconverted. They are not church members."

"They are better Christians than you will ever be. You just made a Unitarian out of me! I'm ashamed to be called a Baptist."

Ellen was still shaking with rage as she and Laura started for home. "What can be done about that man? He cannot be allowed to stay here."

"I agree with you, my dear, but your scolding will have little effect on a man with so hard a shell. He will have to be fired, and for that we need someone with authority."

"Mr. Pierce could . . ."

"Mr. Pierce will do nothing. One of the reasons he is leaving is that he has no real power. Even among the Gideonites, he cannot dismiss someone without the approval of their sponsoring commission. No, we shall have to look higher in the command."

* * *

Still, Laura sought out Edward Pierce at her first opportunity to ask his advice. "We must find a way to get rid of Mr. Horton," she said. "Whom should I talk to? How do I go about it?"

Pierce thought for a moment. "You know I can do nothing in that regard, but I can put in a good word for you. You need to go through General Saxton, but he will then have to consult General Hunter. So I would recommend that you get to know Hunter now. Then, when you talk to Saxton and he goes to Hunter, your name will be familiar."

"And just how do I go about getting an interview with the commander at Hilton Head? I can't just walk up to the gates and ask for him, can I?"

"No, but there is a way. The McKims are sailing on Monday from Hilton Head. You can accompany them to Beaufort and go along on the steamer to Hilton Head with them and Mr. French. I will tell Reverend French that I want General Hunter to meet you. He will take it from there."

The scheme worked, much to Laura's surprise and discomfort. Although General Hunter was pleasant and welcoming, she felt a bit of an interloper. General Hunter took the whole party on a tour of the camp of his new black regiment. Then they returned to his house, where Mrs. Hunter provided dinner. Laura was planning to return that same day to Beaufort, but the McKim's steamer was late in departing, and Mrs. Hunter insisted that she spend the night.

It was a sociable evening, and Laura began to relax. They sat late on the piazza, talking about the affairs of the Department, and then retired, only to be serenaded by a chorus of men from the camp. At breakfast, they shared a laugh about the serenade, and Laura found herself talking quite openly to the general about the problems the Gideonites were facing on St. Helena Island.

"I really liked him," Laura told Ellen the next day. "He is a generous man. Kind to a fault to his soldiers, and to my surprise, quite antislavery."

To Mr. Pierce, she added, "I now feel fairly confident of General Hunter's support. If you could arrange a meeting with General Saxton, I'm ready to broach the topic of Mr. Horton."

This time, Ellen accompanied Laura to speak with General Saxton. Her identification as a Baptist and the heat in her denunciation of Horton went far to convince Saxton of the depth of the problem. Within days, Horton had volunteered to depart.

"I don't know what happened during Horton's meeting with the generals," Laura told the household at dinner one evening, "and I really don't want to know. I'm just relieved that the problem has been solved."

RINA ON "DE CONFUSIN WHITE FOLK"
June 1862

I be feelin all mix up bout dese white folk what come here fuh hep we, or so dey says. Dat ol Missus Susan, she be a nasty one, an I be glad fuh see she leave. But Missus Nelly, she aint no problem. She quiet an grateful when we duz sum work fuh she.

Missus Laura, too. She be as good to me as ennyone eber be. She pay me sumptin fuh muh work, an she nice an patient, too. I be watchin her fro de time she come, an I neber see she git mad at we slaves. Oh, she scold Erric when he don haul in de wood fuh de fire, but he deserve it. An I hear she yell at Joe when she ketch him beatin on an ol horse. But I figgers she be jis defendin dat horse, not pickin on Joe fuh no reason. She good to me, an I feels comforble round she.

I likes Missus Ellen, too. I be glad she come, cause Missus Laura feel so much bedder when she be here. Dem two, dey like muh chik-kuns. Dey jis fludda round each udder, an squawk when one git lost or don come home on time. Dey's fambly, I tink, eben ifn dey not be related.

Dat Missus Ellen, she gots lots uh larnin. She be teachin me fuh read, an I aint neber tawt I could make sense uh dem lil marks. But she good!

Some uh our people still gots trubble. Zannah, she be worrit bout she son Archie. He done run off fro de army, jis like I tawt he

149

might, an he keep comin back here to he mama. Mr. Pierce, he say he not gwine turn he in fuh a deserter, cause de army aint bin paid. But now, Archie, he got heself a band uh udder young mens who be at loose ens, an dey be killin cows on de plantations at night, an den sellin de meat to de soljers.

Dat dangerous nuf, but now de army mens, dey gots wind uh who be killin dose cows, an dey after Archie. Dey says dat soljers be de onliest ones lowed fuh kill cows. An since Archie done run away fro de army, he aint no soljer an caint kill no mo cows. Dat don make no sense to me. De soljers still be eatin de cows. What diffrunce it make who kilt um? Even Mr. Hooper, now, he say he gwine arrest Archie an turn he in.

Now, what mixin me up be dis. Dere be diffrunt rules fuh diffrunt folk, an de same ting can git you praise by one white man an punish by nudder. Preacher Horton, he keep on tellin we how we still gots fuh work fuh de white man. De wimmunfolk, dey be tellin we dat we be free an should only work fuh pay. We don know who fuh trust.

What be eben wurs, sum uh de white folk, dey say one ting an do anudder ting. We all goes to chuch togedduh, an we acts like we all blong in de same place. But den de preacher man, he say we gots fuh go to de munion table. Dat when we sposed fuh go to de front uh de chuch an drink sumptin sour fro dat big ol cup. An we gets a lil chunk uh dried bread, aint hardly big nuf fuh feed a bird. I sho don unnerstan what dat all bout. Not much uh a table, you ax me.

But dat when all de white folk gits up an goes out in de grave-yard. What dey do dat fuh? I members when Massa Pope an he fambly be here. Dey all goes to dat table togedduh wit we, an we all drink outta de same cup.

I be sulted when eben Missus Laura an Missus Ellen be leavin de chuch. Duz de Yankees tink dey be too good fuh drink outta de same cup wit we? Or aint dey eben Christians? Massa Horton, he say dey aint good Christians cause dey aint bin baptize right. He say dey jis be sprinkled. I don know what dat mean, but it don sound nice.

Now, Massa Horton, he be gone all uh sudden like, an we aint got no preacher atall. Now de white mens, dey takes turn doin de preachin, an dey all says sumptin diffrunt.

I guess I jis be confuse. White folk says one ting, an I spec dey tinks dey beliefs what dey says. But den dey acts like dey don belief it atall. Mebbe dey don know what dey tinks.

17
EDUCATING GENERAL SAXTON
June 1862

"You liked the new general, didn't you?" Ellen commented as she and Laura left Saxton's Hilton Head office and headed home.

"I hope I didn't appear too accommodating. I did find him congenial, although I suspect we still have a lot of educating to do. He's obviously antislavery, but I'm not sure that he understands everything that entails."

"Is that why you invited him to dinner? So that you can give him a firsthand glimpse?"

"He needed a place to bring some of the Gideonites together, and The Oaks is always the favorite meeting place."

"Yes, but we can also let him know what plantation life is really like. Maybe you could talk Rina into being especially uncooperative and Susannah into burning dinner," Ellen suggested with a grin.

"Susannah will probably burn dinner without any suggestion from me. I'm going to have to do something about her horrendous cooking, but I hesitate to insult her. That might only make matters worse."

"Seriously, Laura, what do you think the general wants to talk about?"

"He's a new broom, and he will have lots of sweeping to do. Mr. Pierce is leaving a huge hole in our organization—assuming it has any organization! At the moment, nobody knows who is in charge of anything. I'm hoping Saxton will move some people around. For example, Mr. Hooper is now the only man at The Oaks, and he can't fully protect us while running around to all the other plantations, trying to fill Mr. Pierce's shoes. And I'm not sure I'm old enough and homely enough to be a satisfactory chaperone for two lovely young women such as you and Miss Winsor when we are there by ourselves."

"You're neither old nor homely to me, you know, but I agree that we could use a few more people on our staff."

* * *

As it turned out, Laura was exactly right about General Saxton's intentions. Two days later he arrived at The Oaks announcing that he had invited several of the other Gideonites to join them. "I've asked Mr. Ware, his sister Harriet, Mr. Eustis, Mr. Soule, and Mr. Fairfield to be here. I hope that's not a problem," he said.

Laura took a deep breath before she answered. "Of course not. We're used to having unexpected company at all hours. If you'll excuse me for a moment, I'll need to tell the cook how many to prepare for."

Ellen smiled one of her knowing little smiles.

She's thinking that five more dinner guests will be more than enough to throw Susannah into a fish-burning tizzy, Laura realized.

Once all the guests were seated at the table, they had a long wait for the soup to appear. After a few minutes of small talk, General Saxton looked expectantly at the door to the dining room, and sighed. "Shall I go ahead and get started, then?" he asked.

"That's probably a good idea," Laura said.

"Well, then. You all know that we are shorthanded at the moment and that some of our plantations are functioning better than others. I say that not because any of you are doing a bad job, but because too many of our superintendents have given up and gone home just when we needed them the most."

"I know I'm not very successful," Richard Soule said. "I thought I could be a farmer, but I know nothing about raising cotton, as I guess I have amply demonstrated."

"No one has criticized you, Richard," Mr. Eustis said. "Not even after you used the cotton seed for cattle feed."

"I'll never live that down, will I?"

The general was laughing with the rest of them. "You have enormous talents, Mr. Soule. Cotton growing just doesn't happen to be one of them. So let's start with your new assignment. I'd like you to move into Mr. Pierce's quarters here at The Oaks. You will take on the responsibility of managing the stores and Army rations for all the plantations on this side of the island. That will free Mr. Hooper from handling the logistics of running the plantations, and you will provide the ladies here with protection at the same time."

"And what will I be doing?" Mr. Hooper asked. "Am I being fired? You can't do that, you know, because I came here at my own expense."

"Indeed not, Mr. Hooper. You are perhaps the most valuable man on our staff. I am breveting you to the rank of captain on my staff."

"Wait. I'm not a military man, general."

"You are now, son. Your country is at war, and she needs you. I need you. As you probably realize, staunch abolitionists are in short supply in the Army. I need a man I can trust to see to it that the Negroes are protected and their interests served. There is no one on my staff who fits that description. General Hunter and I are alone in our sentiments. You, Captain Hooper, add a third member to our intrepid band. You will report directly to me, serving as my eyes and ears here on the island. Your rank will give you the authority you need to requisition supplies and discipline any wayward young soldier who interferes with your efforts or those of the superintendents and teachers."

"But I stay here? I don't have to move into an army camp?"

"No, you are needed here on the ground. You will simply turn over your other responsibilities to Mr. Soule here, to free yourself to assist me."

Mr. Soule was still looking dubious about the whole idea. "You want me to manage all these plantations, after I've made something of a hash of Frogmore?"

"Why not? Mr. Philbrick will be handling the upper portion of the island, and it's my understanding that you work well with him," Saxton said.

"That's true. We get along remarkably well for being relatives."

"Wait a minute." Laura was surprised. "You're really related to Edward Philbrick?"

"Helen Philbrick is my niece."

"But that will leave Frogmore—as well as the Jenkins and Chaplin plantations along the Seaside Road—without anyone living there," Mr. Hooper said. "Without any supervision the slaves won't work, and we'll lose all those acres of cotton."

"I've thought of that," Saxton assured him. "Charles and Harriet Ware are moving into Seaside Plantation, which will put them right next door to Frogmore. They plan to combine the two operations."

"We've heard terrible stories about Frogmore," Ellen said. "Are you sure you won't be afraid to go there, Harriet?"

"I'm not sure I know what you mean," Harriet said, looking alarmed. "What don't we know?"

"Well, Judith says that there are ghosts that . . ."

"Ellen, that's just Judith's nonsense." Laura glared at her, silently pleading that she drop the topic.

"But . . ."

"Miss Ware, I promise you there are no ghosts at Frogmore. And I should know. I've been living there for three months and pass along that road under the Hanging Tree nearly every day," Mr. Soule said.

"Hanging Tree? Ghosts? Did you know about all this, Charles?"

"They're just slave superstitions. I can't believe anyone would take them seriously."

"But many do," Ellen warned.

This time Laura aimed a sharp kick at Ellen's ankle. "If you'll excuse me, I'll just check on dinner."

Rina thwarted Laura's plan to escape when she came in bearing a soup tureen. Without stopping to think, Laura asked, "Where on earth did you find that tureen, Rina? I've never seen it before."

"Yes'm. You sho nuf aint. Hastins hab it hid down in he cabin an I sends he fuh fetch it back."

Laura took the ladle to serve her guests, only to make another unexpected discovery. "Rina, this soup is cold."

"Yes'm. It done bin hot once, til I sends Hastins down to de slave village. Now Zannah say she be cookin de res uh de dinner an caint reheat it. Y'all jis kin eat it cold."

Ellen tried so hard to muffle her giggles that she choked and required a bit of back-pounding from Laura. The rest of the guests helped themselves to small portions of soup. Even cold, the beginning of the meal was a welcome diversion from the impact of General Saxton's new assignments.

After gamely sampling a few spoonfuls of the unidentifiable broth, General Saxton resumed his explanation of the new assignments. "Mr. Fairfield will be responsible for the other plantations south of Seaside, at least for a while. We are expecting some new recruits by the end of the month, but until they arrive, Mr. Fairfield, you will have to be something of an agricultural circuit rider."

"You do realize, don't you, that I'm already handling the two Capers plantations and some of the Fripp lands as well? I'm grateful for your confidence in me, but I have no other assistance. Since the cotton agents and their wives left—and I'm not saying I was unhappy to see them go, especially that Mr. Salisbury—we haven't had a housekeeper or a teacher at any of those locations."

"And that's why Miss Winsor here will be taking over more of the teaching duties. In fact, I've been told she is so capable that she can actually handle the superintendent duties as well.

Nelly sat with mouth agape, looking at Laura with a desperate plea for intervention.

"Miss Winsor is already helping us with our teaching and running Mr. Eustis's school at the same time," Laura said.

"And doing a top-notch job of it, too. The Negroes on the Capers lands will benefit from her talents."

"But, sir, I don't think I can . . ."

"Of course you can. We all have to juggle a bit these days. If you take over the Capers plantations and combine their schools, I'm sure it will all work out. I'm not asking any more of you than I'm asking of Miss Towne, who travels all over the island to do her doctoring."

"But I'm a woman."

"I've noticed."

"Superintendents have always been men," Nelly protested, but she was blushing prettily.

"Only because we have more men than women. I'm a great believer in the talents of womenfolk. You'll do fine."

"An here come de croakers an de homny," Rina announced from the doorway.

The general turned in alarm. "Croakers? Frogs?"

Now even Laura was laughing a bit. "No, General. A croaker is a kind of freshwater fish. Hastings pulls them out of the creek nearly every day so that we have a steady supply for our dinners. They're quite mild and flavorful."

"You have your very own fisherman?"

"Well, he's supposed to be our man of all work, but he'd rather sit by the creek and fish than haul wood and muck out the stables, not that I blame him much. And since we need the food, I'm willing to overlook the fact that he's out enjoying himself."

"This is my first real taste of local cooking," the general said. "Can you tell me what all's in this side dish? It's very tasty, but I'm a bit mystified by the consistency."

"It's too thick. Susannah's overcooked it again," Ellen said.

"Ellen's probably right, but that's part of the beauty of grits. You can't really spoil them."

"Grits?"

"Grits are made from dried hominy, ground right outside the kitchen door, so they're always fresh. You boil them up slow and toss in little bits of whatever else happens to be lying around. Tonight, I think I detect a few slivers of salt pork, onions, peppers, tomatoes, and okra—a real feast because it's summertime. In the winter, they tend to have nothing but root vegetables in them, and maybe some shrimp or leftover fish."

"So you eat well."

"Relatively speaking. We've only had fresh meat once since I've been here, and, that time, I learned too late that it came from a lamb that our cotton agent's wife had stolen from a neighboring farm. And we rarely have bread, other than cornbread or rice waffles. Of course, we can get all the oysters we want, and shrimp and clams. Once in a while, somebody catches a turtle, too, which makes a tasty soup—when it's hot, that is."

The general nearly choked. "That was . . . turtle soup?"

"Yes, it was. Sorry. I should have told you. Never fear, however. We have some lovely melons and figs for dessert, all raised right here on the plantation."

"It's been a delightful and informative evening, Miss Towne. I hope we can do this often. Perhaps I can even do something to add a little variety to your diet. If you'll tell me what you can use from our Army stores, I'll have it delivered."

"That's quite generous of you, sir."

"Nonsense. It's my way of making sure you invite me back. In the meantime, I meant to mention something else. The Fourth of July is coming up in a few days. They're planning a huge formal ceremony at Hilton Head, but it seems to me that it would be a good idea to hold a celebration here on St. Helena as well. If we are training these former slaves to become fully functioning citizens, they need to start learning about our country's birth. Can you manage to set something up on such short notice?"

"Certainly. Our people love a party. And you'll join us, I hope?"

"May I come for breakfast?"

And so he did, bringing his staff with him. The women of The Oaks had been up since 4:00 A.M. making their preparations. Nelly had taken care of erecting a flagpole, so that the Stars and Stripes welcomed the guests. After breakfast, the whole party traveled to the Episcopal Church, where another flag waved proudly over the road. The Army men and the Gideonites first assembled inside, where Nelly played several patriotic songs on the organ. Then they moved to a platform built under the trees. They watched as two of the superintendents marched the people from their plantations toward the church. The Negroes waved palm branches and sang "Roll, Jordan, Roll" as they marched.

Nelly lined up her classes to sing a song, and one of the men preached a little sermon to the children. General Saxton spoke about his pride in seeing how far the people had come from their slave status, and Mr. Philbrick carried on for a while about the virtues of hard work, especially when it involved the raising of cotton. When the formalities ended, the blacks were treated to hardtack and herrings, accompanied by one of their favorite beverages, water flavored with ginger and molasses. The whites returned to The Oaks for a cold lunch.

The afternoon was spent in leisure. General Saxton and his staff went on to Beaufort. There was singing on the porch for a while, before the Gideonites dispersed for friendly visits with each other. Laura and Ellen retired to their room for some much-needed personal time.

"You decorated the parlors beautifully, Ellen."

"I thought they looked nice enough. After making such fun of the general at our last dinner, I wanted to do something to let both of you know that I really do welcome him here. I'm impressed by his attitude toward the people. He seems to enjoy them and their culture, just as you and I do."

"I only hope his attitude lasts, once he fully realizes some of the problems of the freedmen."

18
EDISTO REFUGEES
July 1862

L aura did not have to wait long to see how General
Saxton would handle a real slave crisis. Even as the
Gideonites and their military comrades were enjoying
a placid July 4th afternoon, trouble was erupting on Edisto
Island, just across St. Helena Sound.

Edisto Island had been a prime agricultural oasis in the
years before the war. The planters themselves were from some
of South Carolina's oldest and wealthiest families. Long-staple
cotton thrived there, as did most other agricultural produce.
The island's location helped it to catch every ocean breeze,
which drove the bugs away and cooled the residents. Herds of
cattle grazed on the long marsh grasses, while cadres of slaves
tended the acres under cultivation.

But all that changed in November 1861 with the Battle of
Port Royal. For all its beauty, Edisto was isolated and poorly
situated to defend itself. Beauregard, the Confederate general
in command at Charleston, moved quickly to cut his losses by
ordering the evacuation of all the islands that were vulnerable
to attack. Despite the richness of the land, Beauregard simply
did not have the troops to defend these hard-to-reach areas.

Colonel Drummond delivered the bad news to Edisto Island. He ordered the planters to pack up their families and slaves and retreat to the mainland. Before they left, they were told to set fire to all their crops, particularly the cotton, to keep such valuable commodities from falling into the hands of the enemy. A delegation of Confederate soldiers arrived to round up all the cattle and drive them to the mainland, where they would be slaughtered to feed the Southern army.

The orders were drastic, and disobedience was widespread. Slaves refused to go, and their owners were secretly relieved, since they would have had no way to support the hundreds of field hands some of them employed. Some planters refused to burn their crops, making elaborate plans to sneak back to the island to save their harvests. In the end, 2,000 head of cattle were evacuated, along with all but one of the white people on the island. Remaining behind were some 1,600 slaves, who were for most purposes immediately freed. Tom Black, the one white man who stayed, was harassed by the freed blacks, who threatened to lynch him as so many of their numbers had been lynched. Within a few weeks, the freedmen captured him and turned him over to the Yankees as a prisoner of war.

Edisto became a black island, where no white man dared to set foot for nearly three months. The blacks survived by moving into the abandoned homes of their former owners and appropriating the stores of foodstuffs they found in the cellars. They continued to work the crops and their own small gardens. They raised their pigs and chickens, and relied on the bounty of seafood at their doorsteps. However, they knew they needed help, so when Yankee soldiers finally showed up on the island in February, they welcomed them.

The Forty-seventh New York Regiment, supplemented by one company of the First Massachusetts cavalry, and the Fifty-fifth Pennsylvania Regiment found wide-open spaces in which to build their camps. The soldiers served as protection from the former owners who might have been thinking about returning. They were not as much help with the agricultural challenges the former slaves were facing. For that, Edward Pierce sent out four of his most capable Gideonites to act as superintendents on the plantations—Jules de la Croiz, J.W.R. Hill, C.E. Rich, and Francis E. Barnard. Under their direction, the plantations thrived.

Something of a military crisis erupted in June, when Union forces made their first foray against Charleston. For a short while, eight other regiments joined the troops on Edisto, and then they departed, taking all but the Fifty-fifth Pennsylvania with them. The crisis deepened when another division of the Union Army suffered severe losses in Virginia. General Hunter received orders to reinforce General McClellan by sending 10,000 men north. That deployment left Hilton Head Island practically defenseless, and Hunter recalled the Fifty-fifth Pennsylvania to beef up his main camp.

As a result, while Fourth of July celebrations continued, General Hunter sent his troops to offer evacuation to the 1,600 blacks now living on Edisto. He promised them his personal protection if they would consent to being relocated to other islands where defenses were already in place. This time, the blacks rushed to accept the offer. They were allowed to bring their families, their household possessions, their pigs, and their chickens. The superintendents helped to keep the evacuation orderly. One by one, the former slaves loaded their families and belongings onto flatboats, covered everyone with branches to protect them from any random rebel gunshots, and allowed themselves to be towed across St. Helena Sound and up the river to Beaufort. After a one-night stopover, during which it became apparent that Beaufort could not handle such a crowd, they boarded another steamer and arrived at St. Helena Island.

A seemingly perfect solution had offered itself. The village of St. Helenaville stood on a patch of high ground on the northeast side of the island. The plantation own-ers had their summer homes there, but the houses had been unoccupied in November when the Yankees captured Bay Point. The Gideonites who had come to take over the plantations had not yet found it necessary to seek higher ground. So it was that the 1,600 former residents of Edisto Island found themselves in possession of a town all their own.

* * *

Francis Barnard settled himself on the front porch of the general store that stood at the north end of Land's End Road. Inside, he knew, were stockpiles of supplies that would help his charges turn this abandoned village into a home. He watched with relief as the Edisto transplants claimed empty houses as their own. With almost no discussion, fam-ily groups took over the largest houses, while couples or indi-vidual slaves settled happily into smaller cabins.

"Massa Banard? You feelin bedder?" The speaker was an elderly slave woman. She leaned on a stick she had picked up along the road and stared at him closely. "I bin watchin you. You gots de swamp feber, aint you?"

"Oh, you don't need to worry about me, Tessie. I'm just a little tired from our trip, that's all."

"No, dat aint true. I sees you all shivery-like an den flush an febrish. You needs a doctor."

"I'll be fine as soon as I have a good night's sleep."

"An wheres you gwine do dat? You caint sleep on dat dere rockin chair."

Barnard forced himself to laugh. "Who's the master and who's the slave here?"

"I aint no slave no mo. You says so yoself. I jis be sayin I tinks you blongs in bed."

"And so I will be, Tessie, just as soon as all our people get settled. I have a few more empty houses on the list here to point out to our stragglers and late arrivals. I'll be staying here, in rooms above the store. The building will make a good headquarters for me and the other superintendents."

"Dat good, den. We preciates what you done fuh we. We don want nuttin happenin to you."

"Thank you, Tessie. Now you go and take care of yourself, hear?"

Barnard leaned back in his rickety rocker and closed his eyes for a moment. Tessie had been right. He felt deathly ill, but the responsibility for nearly 1,600 people so weighed upon him that he dared not give in to his own needs.

"Massa Banard? Jis one mo ting." Tessie was back again. "Is you gwine open dis sto in de mornin? Dere lots uh folk running outta supplies an needin clothe."

"Uh . . . no, not for a while. But there's a plantation back down the road we traveled. It's called The Oaks, and the man in charge of this entire island lives there. They have supplies that they dole out right on their porch. You and the others will be able to visit them with your pennies and buy whatever you need."

"Tankee, Massa."

Inwardly, Barnard cringed at what he had just done, hoping Mr. Soule and his fellow Gideonites were prepared for the onslaught he had turned loose.

* * *

Edward Philbrick was furious when he learned of the arrival of the Edisto refugees. "What are we supposed to do with 1,600 more mouths to feed?" he complained to Charles Ware. "Did the Army think of that before they dumped them here?"

"Probably not, Edward. But I think General Hunter means well. He was concerned that the latest troop movements were leaving Edisto with no means of protecting itself. He has saved countless lives by moving the people out."

"And what has he accomplished by abandoning some 700 acres of prime long-staple cotton and 900 acres of corn and potatoes? Does he not realize that the rebels will now come sneaking back onto the island to grab those crops?"

"Now I think you are exaggerating, Edward. Without their slaves, the rebels are not able to harvest the crops and put them to use. But you are right that the loss of food and cash crops will be a tremendous blow to the economy of this region."

"And what will Washington make of it when we have even greater losses?"

"Didn't Mr. Pierce send a completely favorable accounting to Secretary Chase before he left? Surely that will count to our credit."

"Yes, he did, but that report was so sugarcoated as to be unrecognizable. For example, he praised the slaves for raising 6,000 acres of corn and 1,500 acres of potatoes—and so they have, which is only just enough to keep the local Negro population from starvation. But the cotton yield? God in heaven! The plantations here on St. Helena only managed to plant some 3,000 acres of cotton, and the yield will be about 26 pounds of cotton fiber per acre. Before the war, the average yield on these plantations was about 137 pounds per acre. Nobody but a blithering idiot could call that success."

"Doesn't Secretary Chase understand the implications of that low yield?"

"Oh, he understands all right, but the true figures would have been an embarrassment. So instead of taking steps to put the work of these plantations on a more business-like footing—which, in my opinion, is what they need—Chase compounded the deception. When Congress asked him for an accounting of our profits and losses, he took the yield figures from the 1861 crop and added them to this year's figures, presenting the total as our year's income."

"But that's an open lie."

"Of course it is. Chase justified it by saying we had to reap that crop before we could plant this year's fields, so it counted in our production figures. Believe it or not, he managed to convince the House of Representatives that we have produced a half-million-dollars worth of cotton. The truth? We have already spent some $75,000 more than our crops will bring in."

Charles Ware walked to the windows to stare out over the marsh. "I had no idea the situation was that dire. Whatever are you going to do, Edward? You sound as if you are ready to give up on this enterprise."

"No, I won't quit, because I truly believe that, despite all our discouraging circumstances, we are doing important work here. It is wonderful to see what our people have done and how much improvement they have brought to the lives of the Negroes. Our freedmen have already demonstrated that they can support themselves on the land by their own labor and initiative. We now need more time to prove that the system of free labor can grow cotton more cheaply than slave labor ever could.

"About all I can do for the moment is continue to argue for the kinds of improvements we need—more diligent superintendents, a stable policy of government payments to our workers, a replenishment of our supply of seeds that produce long-staple cotton, and some guarantee that the Army will quit trying to steal away our best workers to turn them into cannon fodder. And in the long run, perhaps, these Edisto refugees will provide the extra labor boost we need to make our claims a reality."

"I know I can put many of them to work on my newly assigned plantations. My new lands lie so close to the scrutiny of the Army that my best workers have, as you say, been stolen off."

"And now see what you and your unbreakable good humor have done! You've managed to talk even me into seeing the latest disaster as opportunity. We'll work with what we have, Charles. We can do no less."

19
THE WEIGHT OF THE WORLD
July 1862

"Ellen, what are you doing out of bed? It's not even light out yet."

"Tell that to all the people who are milling around out there in our yard."

"What? Who's out there? Soldiers?" Laura was fully awake now, scrambling to find a wrap as she joined Ellen at the window.

"They're all Negroes, I think, but I don't recognize any of them."

"They must be Edisto refugees," Laura said. "But they are supposed to be in St. Helenaville. Perhaps they're lost."

Just then, Rina came bustling into the bedroom. "You missus bes be gittin yoselfs downstair," she said. "We gots ourselfs a problem."

"Rina! How many times do I have to tell you to knock?"

"Sorry, Missus, but dis be portant. An you be up ennyhow, aint you?"

"Yes, but . . . oh, never mind. Who are all those people out there? Do you know them?"

"I aint neber seen dem before. But dey says a Massa Banard send dem here fuh food an stuff."

"Oh, my word! We'll be right down, Rina. Go get Mr. Soule and Mr. Hooper. And don't let any of those people into the house."

"No, ma'am, I aint gwine do dat. Dey kin wait outside."

Ellen had been listening to their conversation with alarm. "What are we going to do, Laura?"

"I haven't the faintest idea. Obviously we can't feed them, but maybe we can hold them off for a while. I can't imagine that Francis Barnard really sent them here. He must have known we aren't prepared to deal with his refugees."

"Maybe they need clothes. We do have extra supplies of work clothes that our own people didn't want."

"Good idea. It's worth a try."

* * *

By the time the ladies were dressed, Mr. Hooper had managed to corral the crowd into a semblance of order. He stood on a chair to be seen. "We welcome you to St. Helena Island," he said. "But these are private plantations. Your basic needs will be taken care of back in St. Helenaville."

"But Massa Banard, he say we comes to de Oaks fuh hep." The crowd seemed to have elected a spokesperson: a tall young black man stepped forward to confront Mr. Hooper. "Aint dis de Oaks?"

"Yes, but . . ." "Den we be in de right place. Massa Banard, he say you gots clothe send down fro up Nort an dat we gwine find jobs here, too."

"I'm sorry, but we're just not ready for you. Where is Mr. Barnard? I think we need to talk to him."

The man shrugged. "Dun know, massa."

"He be sick," an old woman said as she hobbled out from the crowd. "I be Tessie. Massa Banard, he gots de swamp feber. He say he not sick, but he caint git heself outta bed fuh two day."

"Where is he?"

"At de village sto. He gots a room upstair."

"All right. We're going to help. Just give us a bit of time to get organized."

"Dat good, massa. We aint gwine nowheres."

* * *

"Rina! Susannah! Get us some breakfast. Quick. We'll think better once we've had something to eat," Laura said. As the serving women scurried off to the cookhouse, the others moved into the dining room, where Mr. Soule belatedly joined them.

"This is your problem, Richard. You agreed to be superintendent of the village. You're going to have to find a way to deal with these people," Mr. Hooper said.

"I . . . I . . . I don't know where to start," he confessed.

"Massa Eustis jis arrive," Rina announced from the doorway. "You wants him fuh come in dere?"

"Thank God! Yes, Rina, send him in."

"What's happening out there?" Eustis asked as he found a seat at the table. "You folks got yourselves a problem?"

"Yes, and you can help us solve it," Mr. Hooper said. "Can you go to Beaufort and send a message to General Saxton?"

"Certainly."

"Tell him we have 1,600 black refugees with no food and no clothing. He sent them here. He's going to have to help supply them. Immediately."

Laura stepped into the discussion. "If Mr. Barnard is ill, as that old lady said, I'd best go check on him. I'll take Hastings with me, and we'll ride over to the village this morning. In the meantime, Ellen has offered one solution. In Mr. Eustis's warehouse, there are boxes and boxes of work clothes that none of our people were willing to purchase. They all saw the dressier things we had and wanted to buy those. If you could send a couple of your men over here with those clothes, Mr. Eustis, we can offer them for sale and keep the people happy for a day or two while we hope for a shipment of food supplies."

"Did you say Mr. Barnard is ill?" Mr. Soule interrupted. "If so, perhaps I ought to go to the village with you to see what I can do."

"Good idea, Richard. You and the other superintendents will need to organize the people out there in the village. Find out how many of them are looking for work, and get recommendations from the supervisors who know them. You might make several lists—laundresses, cooks, stable hands, field hands, drivers, and so forth. Then we can check with the plantations to see how many they want to hire. But make it clear to all concerned that hiring will be done in the village, not in our front yard."

Mr. Hooper looked around the table, trying to organize the staff into some sort of order. "Here's what I need the rest of you to do. Miss Towne, as you suggested, you need to check on Mr. Barnard, and while you are in the village, look for others who may need medical care. If you can find a spare building—maybe even a room in the general store—you could establish one morning a week to hold a clinic there. We don't want the sick to be coming here for help."

"Yes, I think that will work well. I'll just add a village clinic to my regular circuit."

"Now, Miss Murray, can you handle the clothing distribution for us?"

"Certainly. I'll have Rina round up a couple of girls to help me. We'll use the front porch for sales, just as soon as Mr. Eustis's boxes start arriving."

"Next, Miss Winsor. You need to get some idea of how many children, and adults, too, are interested in starting school. I think we have some extra teachers arriving, perhaps as soon as next week. We'll try to use facilities in the village for their classes, too. But I need some idea of how many pupils there will be."

"I guess I can do something of a hand count," Nelly suggested. "Or ask all the mothers who want their children in school to line up and give me names."

"That should do it, I think. We're taking care of clothing, education, employment, and medical care. Now, if the Army will do its part in provisioning us, we can maybe get some rest around here tomorrow morning."

* * *

At dinnertime, the little group of Gideonites reassembled, all of them drooping from the intense summer heat and the frustrations of dealing with so many needy people. "I want to hear reports from each of you," Mr. Hooper began, "but first I think we need to eat. Will someone check with Susannah and see if she is preparing anything for supper?"

Ellen held out a hand to restrain Laura as she started to rise. "I'll go. You rest for a bit. You look tuckered out. I've been busy but not really out in the hot sun, as you have been."

Just then, a clatter of hooves announced some other arrivals. Mr. Eustis and General Saxton shouldered each other as they pushed into the dining room. Ellen turned and fixed them with a none-too-happy grimace. "Just in time for dinner, I see. Don't the two of you ever get tired of burned fish and cold soup?"

"Ellen!" Laura admonished her with a look, but the general was grinning, oblivious to the proffered insult.

"I've come to assure you of the Army's help in dealing with the Edisto refugees," he said. "And if you'll feed me one more time and furnish me with a bed for the night, I'll have sufficient supplies here by morning. Maybe even with a few special tidbits for your headquarters."

Laura was beaming at him, despite her exhaustion. "Thank you. I knew we could trust you to follow up on this problem."

"How did you find conditions in the village?" the general asked her, ignoring the others.

"Well, Mr. Barnard is indeed very ill. He has a malarial fever, which means he is not prostrate every day, but he is much too weak from the cycles of chills and fever to be able to accomplish much. Not that he has not moved mountains so far; just getting the people here and settled was a huge job. But now, the rest of us are going to have to step in for him. As for the general well-being of the other refugees, most are remarkably healthy. They've been well nourished, and they are now living in clean and comfortable surroundings. They should be fine."

"I suspect I have the best news of all," Mr. Soule announced. "I have a list of five cooks, all of whom are eager to come and work for us. I think we'll be able to give Susannah some time off while we try out their cooking to see which one we want to hire."

The others had similar reports. Mothers were ready to send their children to school, and some were clamoring to learn along with them. The work clothing had proved popular, and most everyone went home satisfied.

"A good day's work," Mr. Hooper concluded.

But once alone in their room, Laura's mood flagged, and Ellen watched her in alarm. "What is it, Laura? What is making you so unhappy?"

Laura slapped at her neck. "I'm tired of being drained. If it's not these infernal mosquitoes, it's a newly freed slave wanting me to do something for him. Or it's Mr. Hooper with his lists of chores for each of us, or Rina's laziness, or Susannah's terrible cooking, or a new patient with an incurable disease, or Bess's leg ulcers, or temperatures hot enough to boil our blood away. I'm tired, Ellen. Used up. And I'm never sure I can summon the energy to get through another day."

"It's not like you to be so despondent. Yet you were quite animated at dinner, talking to General Saxton. Are you and he . . .? Is there something . . .?"

"What? Oh, no! How could you think that? You know me better, Ellen."

"You do like him."

"Of course I do. He's a good man, and he's genuinely interested in helping our cause. I'm grateful to him. But even with his help, I keep wondering if we are just wasting our time here, if the problems are not too big and too deep for any of us to be able to bring about change."

"Maybe you're just exhausted from this influx of Edisto refugees. That's not something that will happen every day. Things are sure to get better."

"Are they? What makes you think there are not thousands of other slaves out there, all expecting us to rescue them and do for them what we are trying to do for the ones we already have?"

"If there are, we'll deal with them."

"Until we're all drained to mere husks."

"You used to tell me that God never gives us more than we can bear. Have you forgotten that?"

"Maybe I just don't believe it anymore."

"And I don't believe you when you say that. You're tired, and you think you have the weight of the world on your shoulders. You're not thinking clearly, or you'd see how many people you have around you to help with the burden. Look how smoothly everything went today, once we got ourselves organized. Food will arrive tomorrow, along with soldiers to help with the work. New teachers are coming to pick up the new students. It's not a load you have to carry by yourself. You need to trust the rest of us to do our part."

"You're right, I know. But this miserable country has a way of slapping me down every time I feel a bit hopeful. I can't bear the thought that you will suffer because of my decision to come here. Will you promise me, Ellen, that when you have had enough of South Carolina, you will tell me so? I would take you home to Philadelphia tomorrow if I thought you wanted to go."

"I have no home but the one I share with you, and no purpose other than our shared goals. We're going to be fine here, and we'll do something that the world will remember. I promise you that. So you can quit fussing."

"Thank you, my dear, but I intend to rage against mosquitoes as often as I like!"

20
LONG HOT SUMMER
July/September 1862

ollowing a pattern that Laura was coming to think of as "typical Low Country" behavior, nothing seemed destined to go as planned that summer. The plantations finally received their much-requested guns, only to find that the Army had also stationed gunboats in all the creeks, so that there was much less need for the plantations to arm themselves against the threat of invasion.

Comforted at first by the appearance of the Union gunboats, Laura invited the officers of the nearest one to dinner. Much to her alarm, the officers turned out to be rude and deliberately provocative. They spoke so approvingly of the Southern plantation owners and their treatment of the Negroes that Laura asked them to leave. Then she found good use for the new guns, arming herself and several of the Negro men against the possibility that the boat's crew might return to do them some mischief.

Laura continued to rage against the mosquitoes, not that it did any good. The women found that they could do almost nothing in comfort unless a storm drove the mosquitoes away. Once or twice, she and Ellen tried taking their candles and writing materials under the mosquito netting, only to set it afire when a bit of a breeze tossed the netting too close to a candle.

"Now look what we've done," Ellen sighed. "Our only defense against the wretched little things now has gaping holes in it."

At church, the troublesome issue of communion raised itself again. A newly introduced preacher, Mr. Phillips, arrived, only to cause more trouble. Within days, he had told his black parishioners that they should not be taking communion with Unitarians, who were not true Christians. The Negroes accepted whatever the preacher told them and refused to allow the Gideonites to attend their baptisms. Laura reported the problem to General Saxton once again, and Mr. Phillips was warned not to encourage the idea of a closed communion. Then she discovered that two of the superintendents were really behind the communion controversy, and that Mr. Breed and Dr. Wakefield were now enemies not only of the Unitarians among them but of General Saxton as well.

Controversies between the missionaries and the military multiplied. General Hunter, who had been so kind and courteous to Laura earlier in the summer, now saw the missionaries as antagonists. He was still trying to develop his plans for recruiting black regiments to supplement his own troops. But the men he recruited were usually the strongest and best-behaved men on a plantation. The result was a lack of labor in the fields, and many of the superintendents actively discouraged their former slaves from joining Hunter's army. Breed and Wakefield were more vocal, striding into Hunter's office to demand that he remove his soldiers from prime agricultural land.

General Saxton arrived at The Oaks to talk out his own frustrations. "I've just been called on the carpet to explain why my superintendents go right over my head to complain. General Hunter is now convinced that I'm not doing a good job overseeing you all."

"Oh, surely he knows better than that," Laura said. "The two of you have very similar views on abolition. He should see you as an ally—maybe his only ally in the military, if what I'm seeing lately is any guide."

"Yes, he spoke in the heat of the moment, I know, but he was threatening to call an evacuation of all these islands and send the Gideonites home. I thought you had better be aware that the behavior of some of the superintendents is putting you all in danger."

"There's not much we can do about Breed and Wakefield. They work under Mr. Philbrick on the other side of the island," Mr. Soule said in his usual mild manner. "I'm afraid they are just more interested in the money they can get for the cotton crop than they are in the welfare of their workers."

"I'll go to General Hunter myself if I have to," Laura said. "He can't make us leave here. This land has become our home, and its people, our families. We are doing so much good for them. It would be criminal to make us abandon the black population of the island. They're learning fast, but they couldn't survive without us."

Ellen smiled at Laura. "I thought you were fed up and ready to go home."

"Oh, I may have said that, but I didn't mean it. Most of the time I'm quite fond of these mosquito-infested swamps."

* * *

Toward the end of July, Edward Pierce dropped in for an unexpected visit. He arrived around midnight, frightening everyone in the house when he knocked at the door. But he was his old exuberant self, much happier than he had been before he resigned.

"What on earth are you doing here?" Laura exclaimed. "We thought you were busily practicing law in Boston."

"Our friend Salmon P. Chase had other plans. When I got to Washington, he was already laying out a couple of diplomatic trips he wanted me to take on his behalf. At least, this time, he's paying me well. I'm on my way to Jacksonville, but the ship arrived early and I thought I'd take advantage of the chance to visit with you."

"You're welcome, of course," Laura said, pulling the collar of her wrap a bit closer around her neck. "But would you mind terribly if we postponed our visit until breakfast?"

"Ah, I've gotten you out of bed, I see. Sorry. I always find traveling more enjoyable at night. I keep forgetting that other people sleep when it gets dark."

In the morning, Laura and the other missionaries clustered around the table, eager to hear reports from home. One question was foremost on all their minds. "We were promised some replacements. When are our new teachers arriving?"

"Not for a long while, I'm afraid. I'm finding travel easy enough, but the Relief Commissions seem to think it is too dangerous to send new people down here at present."

"Why? What are they afraid of? We haven't had any major battles nearby, and the rumors of rebel invasions usually turn out to be one or two rebel AWOLs looking for a handout."

"They're hearing the same old stories they've always heard—the climate is too unhealthy, the former slaves are dangerous and uncooperative, disease is spreading. And, I'm afraid, those of us who have returned home have not reassured them. No one ever comes right out and asks why we've come home. They just assume that it's because we couldn't stand it here any longer."

"You're there to tell them different."

"Yes, but what do they see? Dedicated fellows like Reverend Peck and staunch abolitionists like Austa French went south, stayed a few weeks, and came home. And, of course, there are those who are genuinely ill when they go home. I know the Phillips family is desperately afraid that their young Sam is dying of the malarial fever he contracted here. If he couldn't survive the conditions here, maybe nobody can."

"But . . ."

"Not everyone is as logical as you, Miss Towne. There's one lovely and talented young woman who wants more than anything to be here. Charlotte Forten is a mulatto from a prominent and historically free black family. She's very well connected, too—even has a personal friendship with the poet John Greenleaf Whittier. She made just one big mistake. She chose to have Reverend Peck represent her plea for passage before the Boston Relief Commission. They looked at him, remembering how eager he was to go to South Carolina and how thin and pale he was when he returned. And they said no to sending a young woman into whatever furnace so melted him down."

"So she's not coming at all?"

"I think she'll find a way. She's just as stubbornly determined as the members of the commission are. But it's going to take some time. The same is true of a Quaker gentleman named John Hunn. He has plans to bring a huge shipment of goods from Philadelphia and open a store here. He and his daughter have everything they need to depart, except for permission, and I don't foresee that coming anytime soon."

Later, in the privacy of their room, Ellen turned to Laura for reassurance. "In other words, there will be no relief. So what are we to do about the new scholars who are waiting for their own school?" She looked discouraged for the first time.

"We'll do what we always do—make do. Your adult class is going really well, I know, but you're about to overflow that back room. And the little cabin where Nelly teaches the younger children is filled to capacity, too. I had hoped that when we had more teachers we would be able to spread the scholars out among other locations. Instead, I think we'd better start looking for a building we could use as a regular schoolhouse."

"When we talked about this before, you said there was no building large enough."

"And, if I remember correctly, you suggested that perhaps we could use the Brick Church during the week." Laura had a look on her face that suggested she was considering an evil plot. "Maybe that's not such a bad idea after all."

"Would Mr. Phillips go along with it, do you think?"

"If it's put to him correctly, he might. Phillips knows that he has angered General Saxton, and it's to his benefit to make a conciliatory move. If we convince him that it would please the general if he offered the use of the church to us, he might just do it. He'll have to believe that it's his own idea, but he's easily manipulated."

"Oh, Laura, think what we could do with that building. It has its own outhouses and a well, even its own bell. And the meeting hall is so large that we could easily hold four different classes there. It's centrally located, convenient even for the Edisto people in St. Helenaville."

* * *

It was, indeed, the ideal solution, providing room for the classes they had and allowing for expansion in the future. It also meant that the living spaces at The Oaks could be put back to their original purposes instead of being strewn with benches and slates. Laura handled the negotiations and found Mr. Phillips to be even more agreeable than she had expected. "We can even give the school a name," she said. "Let's call it the Penn School, in honor of the spirit of cooperation in which the building has been given over to our use. This arrangement is exactly what one might expect from the natives of the City of Brotherly Love."

Had it been too easy? Probably. Still, Laura was caught off guard by the next developments. On September 28th, Laura and Ellen attended church services at the Brick Church and were pleased to hear Mr. Phillips issue a call to the communion table that included all who were in attendance. Laura glanced at Ellen's bowed head and downcast eyes, poking her gently. "We won another one," she whispered. Then came the following announcement: the service would also include baptisms and a wedding, both of which would be conducted before communion. Each of these rituals included the Baptist rites and the Negro customs of the parishioners. Baptisms alone took almost a half hour per person, as the candidate was questioned at length about his individual beliefs.

The congregation squirmed. Small children cried. Older children snickered. All over the room, individuals stood and made their way to the aisles to get to the outhouses, occasionally stepping on toes and eliciting an "ouch." Here and there a snore echoed. More and more people began to leave. The service lasted all day. Laura might have marveled at the pastor's ability to keep going for so long, but she was more moved to anger at what she saw as a ploy to test the Unitarians. Hobbling from the church on legs that had long grown cramped and stiff, she gave the pastor only a tight-lipped grimace in response to his ingenuous greeting.

One week later, Laura and Ellen arrived at the church to discover that Mr. Phillips was holding services out under the oak trees. It was a lovely fall morning, and, under normal circumstances, they might have enjoyed the departure from the usual. In this case, however, suspicions clouded their enthusiasm—suspicions that were confirmed when Mr. Phillips announced that he would be serving communion inside. "I'm sorry to report, however, that the church elders have requested that only Baptists be invited to participate."

Closed communion had won, after all. The black Baptist parishioners paraded dutifully after their appointed minister, leaving the missionaries standing in the yard. "So be it," Laura pronounced. "I am done fighting this battle."

21
NEW ARRIVALS
September/October 1862

Laura had hoped that the coming of fall would bring with it a time of settling in and an easing of the conflicts that had kept the Gideonites from uniting toward a single goal. At least, she thought, the mosquitoes would disappear and the dangers of swamp-bred disease would lessen. Instead, their little island continued to seethe with disturbances.

"We gots fuh be on guard aginst de bugs," Rina cautioned Laura. "Soon's it git cooler, dey starts lookin fuh a warmer place fuh settle, an dat likely be in de houses, not de yard."

"Do they ever go away?" Laura asked.

"No, ma'am, dey don, least til de frost come, an dat don happen sometime til after Christmas."

"Well, at least the fever months are over. The next few months will be healthier, surely."

"Um, um, don tink so. Some uh dem Edisto folk be here yestiddy, an dey says dat Massa Banard be sick agin. An de slaves ober on Cat Island, dey gots a whole run uh sickness. Don you be puttin your doctorin bag away, missus."

Laura soon confirmed Rina's report. Mr. Barnard's bout of malaria had returned in force, and he was prostrate with the recurring fevers and chills. By mid-October, he was dead. Captain Hooper also fell victim to malaria, and Saxton requested that Laura attend him. Soldiers reported epidemics of typhoid. Black children spread whooping cough, which did not completely debilitate them but caused so much racket in the classroom building that teachers were forced to shout over the hacking. And in the harbor at Hilton Head, several ships lay at anchor, under quarantine because of yellow fever aboard.

Nor did the threat of invasions fade away. It sometimes seemed to Laura that the Army was being stirred by some giant stick. Troops moved in and out of Hilton Head, and rumors that both General Hunter and General Saxton were going to be reassigned circulated. Captain Hooper, on those days when he felt well enough to work, worried that he might be left as the only antislavery officer on the island. Evacuation orders were issued and then countermanded. The cavalry troops from Hilton Head were already aboard their ships when they were ordered to disembark and return to patrol duties. And taking advantage of every internal disturbance at Hilton Head were bands of rebels, who made repeated attempts to land on Port Royal Island.

On St. Helena, the Gideonites had armed their most reliable Negroes and put them on picket duty at night to guard the plantations. On at least two occasions, rebels landed at Eddings Point and entered St. Helenaville before they were driven back by armed guards. But instead of cooperating with the Negroes who were performing heroic duties there, the soldiers assigned to the same areas harassed them and stole from them. Military officers made occasional forays to St. Helena to round up able-bodied blacks and recruit them for the new black regiments. On one occasion, twenty of the former slaves were dragged from their beds in the middle of the night and shipped off to Fort Pulaski to serve as laborers there.

"I feel quite helpless," Laura complained to Ellen. "I am run ragged by the demands of patients; the guests of our household have nearly depleted our food supplies, so that we have barely enough to stave off real hunger; and all we try to do seems to be at counterpurposes with those in charge of our well-being. I'm sick, tired, and cross."

Not even the news that President Lincoln promised emancipation by January 1, 1863, alleviated the stress of these months. It was, to be sure, a great victory for the cause of the abolitionists, but in the lives of those who were about to be emancipated, it made no difference at all. As Edward Philbrick pointed out, "The President's proclamation does not seem to have made a great deal of stir anywhere. Here the people don't take the slightest interest in it. They have been free already for nearly a year, as far as they can see, and have so little comprehension about the magnitude of our country and are so supremely selfish that you can't beat it into their heads that anyone else is to be provided for beyond St. Helena Island."

* * *

One evening in late October, Mr. Eustis arrived at The Oaks just at dinnertime. "I have some grand news, just in from Hilton Head," he said.

"And it just happened to be timed so that you could announce it over dinner, I presume." Laura grimaced at him. "Have you completely run out of food at your place?"

"No, but you have to admit that your new cook puts out a tempting spread."

"Nonsense. You showed up even when Susannah was burning everything she cooked."

"If it's a problem . . ."

"No, no, I'm cranky. I'd do almost anything to hear some good news for a change. Go in and sit down. We'll be serving in a few minutes."

Eustis waited until after the usual soup to make his report. "You are about to receive shiploads of help."

"Really? From whom?"

"The steamer *United States* sailed from New York on Friday, October 24th. Aboard is Mr. John Hunn, sent by the Port Royal Relief Committee, to take over your duties as storekeeper here. That will free you to tend to your doctoring on the island, Miss Towne."

"And Mr. Hunn is . . .?"

"A Quaker, with experience as a shopkeeper in Philadelphia. Accompanying him is his daughter Lizzie, who will assist her father, but who also wants to work directly with the slaves, if you can use her."

"That will certainly be a help. I wrote a letter to Mr. McKim some time ago, complaining about how short-handed we are. But during the summer, all the ships were tied up with troop movements, and civilians were not being granted passage."

"Apparently, that crisis is over. This steamer should be arriving within a day, and we have been notified that others will follow shortly."

"It will be wonderful to have someone here who actually understands how to run a store. I've been doing my best to keep track of what we are selling and what we need to have shipped in, but I know I've done a shoddy job of it. I'm grateful for the help."

"Ah, but that's not all. Accompanying the Hunns is a young woman named Miss Charlotte Forten."

"I've heard that name . . ."

"She's the free black woman that Mr. McKim has been trying to send us for some time. She's a trained teacher and is anxious to work in your school."

"A free black? Now I remember. Mr. McKim called her a mulatto and said that her family is historically free. I wonder how she will work out in this setting?"

"She won't be the only new teacher, either." In his hurry to spread the rest of his news, Mr. Eustis entirely missed the worried note in Laura's voice. "General Saxton says he has approved the arrivals of a steady stream of volunteers coming in the next month. You may have your hands full, Mr. Soule, making all the new assignments."

"A chore I relish, I assure you. We have more than enough plantations that still need staffing."

"General Saxton says to tell you that he wants the Hunns and Miss Forten assigned to open up Oaklands."

"Oaklands? There are a few slaves there, but the main house has not been lived in for months. I imagine it's quite empty of furniture and supplies by now. It's been easy pickings for slaves, soldiers, and cotton agents."

"Nevertheless, that's where General Saxton wants them. Mr. Hunn will take over the general store there at The Corner and use it as a central distribution point for our charitable donations. It's been empty since Mr. Barnard died, so it's a perfect opportunity for us to put it to better use. And, of course, that will allow Miss Forten to live within easy walking distance of the Penn School."

"Even if they have to eat and sleep on the floor," Ellen whispered to Laura, who responded with a small shrug.

* * *

The newcomers arrived Tuesday night, after a moderately uneventful voyage. Lizzie Hunn was still pale and thin from being seasick the entire trip, but Miss Forten was wide-eyed and smiling with excitement.

"I hope you've had a safe passage up from Hilton Head," Laura said.

"It has been beautiful. My first glimpse of the South Carolina shore was not too inspiring. Hilton Head seemed to be a dismal, tent-filled island, populated by soldiers and a motley collection of contrabands. But then we arrived in Beaufort, and I got a look at those wonderful houses with their verandas and the huge oaks and magnolias. They are quite breathtaking. There were a few rude soldiers trying to scare us with talk of rebel attacks and yellow fever, but they didn't succeed in frightening me."

"Ah, you'll hear a lot of that from the military. We're not popular with them, primarily because they have to protect us, and they don't fully understand the importance of our work here," Mr. Soule explained.

"I forgot all about them when I saw the sunset," Miss Forten went on. "What a magical end to our day it was. The clouds all turned to crimson and gold, reflected in the water, as our boatmen rowed us across the river. They serenaded us, too, and their music was so sweet and strange and solemn. I was quite moved."

"The men always sing as they row," Laura explained. "It keeps them in cadence, but it also gives them a chance to express some of their deeper longings. Once you can understand them, you'll hear a full explanation of their faith."

"Yes, I caught 'Roll, Jordan, Roll,' which seemed fitting for the end of our voyage, and then a long group of verses, with a refrain of 'No man can hinder me.' I fully felt their need for freedom in that piece."

Laura was grateful that the candlelight was dim enough to hide her blush. That was my first blunder, she thought. I just insinuated that a black woman could not understand the language of our freed slaves. How insensitive of me.

"You must be exhausted from your travels," Ellen commented. "Let me show you and Miss Hunn to your room, while Mr. Hooper gets Mr. Hunn settled. It's quite late for us here, I'm afraid, and you'll find that the household will be up and bustling by sunrise. We'll talk more tomorrow."

RINA ON "DAT MISSUS CHARLOTTE"

October 1862

I don know what fuh make uh las night's goins on. I sho don. De new folk arrives an one uh dem be a brown gal. I be spectin sumbody fuh send she fuh de cookhouse, but she jis set sheself down in de parlor like she blong dere. Dat aint right.

Missus Ellen come out fuh git sum water an I ax she who dat brown gal be. She say she not brown—she be a mulatto. Well, I knows what a mulatto be. Dat mean yo pappy or granpappy be a buckra, an yo mammy or granmammy be a black slave who aint gots no say bout who be crawlin intuh she bed. Dat may make she skin light, but she be a black woman all de same.

Des white folk, dey still don unnerstan bout de way tings work round here. Jis de udder day, we hab a commotion bout who be ridin to chuch. De white folk be gittin ready fuh go to chuch, an ol Aunt Phyllis say she be wishin she be strong nuf fuh walk all dat way. Dat Massa Hooper, who be workin fuh Genral Saxton now, he jump down fro de carriage an push she up intuh he seat. He say he kin walk or hang on behin de seat.

Harry stop de horses an say, "Massa, muh massa, don do dat." He tole Aunt Phyllis fuh git off. He not gwine drive no carriage fuh no black woman. But no matter how hard he beg Aunt Phyllis, she not be movin, an Massa Hooper, he not be gittin back in.

Harry be downright mortify when he drive on. Dat what de white folk don unnerstan. We be willin fuh work fuh dem, jis like we works fuh de ol massa, cause dey pays us, jis like de ol massa gib us our food an our clothe an our cabins. But we don work fuh each udder. We may not be equal wit de white folk, but we be equal wit each udder.

Now what gwine happen wit dis new Missus Charlotte? She be sleepin upstair, in de same room as de udder white wimmun, an Missus Ellen, she say she gwine be a teacher. Dis mornin I goes intuh de dinin room an dere she sit, big as ennyting, right at de table. An dey spectin me fuh wait on she, same as de white folk. Why she not stickin wit she own kind?

I dint want fuh bring her enny breakfas, but Missus Laura, she come stormin out to de cookhouse an say I bedder git movin, or else.

Aunt Becky don want fuh make up she room, neider. She say, "Why I hab fuh wait on dat brown gal? She not be bedder den me. She kin make up she own room."

An Aunt Phyllis, she say dat brown gal don blong here no ways.

Finely, Missus Laura, she git tired uh hearing we complain. She say dat Miss Forten be a missionary fro Philadelphia, jis like she be, an she hope we gwine show she de same spect. She say dat brown gal come here fuh hep we, an we best be treatin she nice.

Don know what dis ol world be comin to. Eberting change now, an I don know who be sposed fuh work fuh who. I know we be bedder off now. I wants de missionaries fuh stay, an I don want de ol owner fuh come back. We have mo fuh eat, an good clothe, an nobody be beatin we no mo. All dat be good. But I don unnerstan all de rules yet.

22
SOUL SEARCHINGS
October 1862

Ellen Murray waited until she and Laura were alone in the buggy, headed out to see patients at Frogmore and Seaside. The road was full of ruts and old tree roots, and the horse himself was listless and reluctant to pull. Usually, she and Laura took turns—one whipping the horse into motion while the other read aloud to pass the time. Today, however, Ellen pushed the book aside.

"What's eating at you, Laura? You've been an absolute grump for the past two days. Wouldn't it help to talk to me about it—whatever it is?"

"Sorry. I'm not angry with you. I'm frustrated by the reception we're all giving Miss Forten."

"I'm not sure I understand. You said yourself that you liked her very much, and she seems enchanted with South Carolina. Is there a problem I don't know about?"

"I do like her. She's absolutely charming. But I've been having constant battles with the servants, none of whom want anything to do with her. I was hoping they would be happy to have a Negro teacher—one of their own. I thought they'd be more comfortable with her than they are with us. I even hoped that if they saw us treating Miss Forten as one of us, they'd start to understand what we mean when we tell them they are free and under no obligation to anyone—that they would see that we look on everyone equally."

"Oh, I think they understand that. Charlotte mentioned the oarsmen singing 'No Man Can Hinder Me,' and I, too, have noticed that it has become their favorite song."

"That may be, but they don't understand equality when it comes to work. Rina as much as told me that she would work for white people, but she wasn't going to wait on a black woman, no matter how nice she happened to be."

"Yes, I've noticed that table service has been a little slow and spotty."

"Downright rude, if you tell the truth. Aunt Becky comes in with the serving dishes, but she just plops them on the table now instead of carrying them from person to person. I've been trying to pass the food quickly around the table, so as not to call attention to the fact that Aunt Becky won't wait on Miss Forten, but it's awkward at best."

"Don't you think their attitudes will improve as everyone gets to know each other? Perhaps it's just because she's a stranger."

"No. We've had lots of strangers to dinner, and the servants have never treated them like pariahs."

"Are you saying that our servants are prejudiced against their own race?"

"Perhaps."

"As a result of self-hatred, do you think? Have they become so inured by slavery that they think of themselves as lesser beings—as a result of that disgraceful governmental decision that said they were three-fifths of a human being?"

"Yes. That's part of it. They don't see themselves as having any self-worth, and we haven't done a very good job of changing that."

"It will come in time, I think. You're trying to overcome centuries of mistreatment in just a few months."

"Humph."

Laura grew quiet and withdrawn. Finally, Ellen could stand the silence no longer. "Here," she said. "Take the whip. If you're going to engage in browbeating, at least direct it toward this infernal beast who wants to nibble on every available weed."

"You know I don't approve of mistreating animals."

"Well, then, feel free to use the whip on yourself. You seem determined to take all the blame for the tension at The Oaks upon your own shoulders. Might as well take the punishment for it, too."

Laura glared at her and then lapsed into silence again until the Hanging Tree loomed up before them.

"I know there are no ghosts around here," Ellen commented, "but this section of the road to Frogmore always makes me uncomfortable. It's dark and so overgrown that it's hard to believe there can be anything pleasant at the end of the road."

"I think you've just described the state of my mind," Laura said. "Things are dark, and I'm all closed in, with little hope that I'm going to accomplish anything at the end of the road."

"Why so pessimistic? I think we are accomplishing miracles every day."

"Tiny ones, at best."

"Who would have thought that self-sufficient, fiercely independent Rina would be sitting in a schoolroom studying her ABCs? That's not a tiny change. It's huge."

"But I haven't changed. I'm afraid I'm going backward."

"You? Is that why you came here? Because you wanted to change something about yourself?"

"It should have been the reason I came, but it wasn't. I arrived all confident in my abolitionist theory. I believed the Negro was capable of great things—that all we had to do was put an end to slavery and then pave the way a bit so that all those former slaves could move into our society as successful and productive citizens. I was sure all men were equal. I just needed to prove it to the ignorant ones around me. Now I'm beginning to realize that I knew nothing, not even about myself."

"I don't understand. You haven't given up on abolition, surely."

"No, I still see it as an ideal. But the goal seems ever more distant. I didn't know how hard it would be. I thought that the slaves were just like me, except for the bonds of slavery that were holding them back."

"And you no longer believe that?"

"I think years of slavery have crushed their spirits in some way. They've adapted their own techniques to cope with abuse and oppression, and they've built up a society all their own. That society helped them to survive when owners were brutal. Their workaday world was on the outside. When they returned to their little slave villages, they entered a safer place, one whose rules protected them against the outside, but whose restrictions now do not allow them to mingle freely on the outside. Sometimes I think they don't even want to be free."

"I can see all that," Ellen agreed. "But I still don't understand why you are so down on yourself."

"Because trying to enter and understand their world has made me realize that I don't always practice my own preaching."

"For example?"

"My own reactions to Charlotte Forten. When I first heard that a mulatto teacher was coming to join us, I heard *mulatto*, not *teacher*. From the very beginning, I've been aware of her race, and that awareness makes me look at her—and treat her—differently. I've tried to be color-blind, but I just can't manage it."

"Laura, I haven't noticed a single thing that would suggest you are treating her differently because she is a Negro."

"But I know I think of her that way. And I'm ashamed of myself."

"You know, I wish I were perfect, too. But I'm not, and I accept that as the price I pay for being human. That may be the lesson you have still to learn. Give yourself—and her—some time. I'm betting that, someday, you'll realize that you've forgotten about her color."

Meanwhile, Charlotte Forten was facing her own struggles, for many of the same reasons. On her first visit to the school, she was deeply moved by how much the children had learned and how beautifully they sang. She wrote in her diary that night: "Dear children! Born in slavery, but free at last? May God preserve to you all the blessings of freedom, and may you be in every possible way fitted to enjoy them. My heart goes out to you. I shall be glad to do all that I can to help you." They were prayers of sincerity and goals of lofty dimensions—setting standards she would find difficult to maintain.

She had also enjoyed her first day of substituting for Laura, who had needed to travel to Beaufort. She found the children well behaved and eager to learn. She was sure she was going to like her fellow teachers. But during those first few days, reality had not yet had time to settle in. On Sunday, after services at the Brick Church, two weddings, and an organ concert at the Episcopal Church, she wrote: "It is all like a dream still, and will be for a long time, I suppose; a strange wild dream."

But after her first full day with her own class, Laura Towne found her slumped over a makeshift desk, head buried in her arms and shoulders shaking with sobs. "Miss Forten, whatever is the matter? Has someone harmed you?"

Charlotte lifted her head and gulped bravely. "No, I'm fine. Just a bit tired."

"That's not so, and you know it. What's wrong? I promise you, it will help to talk it out."

"The day was so awful," she wailed. "You must be aware of that, since we were all teaching—or trying to—in the same hall. I have that curious mix of young children and mere babies, and I have no idea of how to keep the babies amused while the older ones are trying to learn. They were squalling and tottering about, getting into everyone's way. I saw you glaring in my direction several times—and I deserved every glare for letting the children make such a racket. But I don't know what to do. I'm going to be a total failure at this!" Despite her struggles, the tears began again.

"I do understand, believe me. My first day was a disaster, too. You need time to get to know the children and to figure out what they need. When you get that far, you'll be able to provide them with activities to keep them busy. Nobody expected you to be perfectly in control today—and we would have probably hated you if you had been that organized."

Charlotte stared at her. "Sometimes I do think everyone here hates me," she confessed.

"Oh, my dear, I hope we haven't given you that impression."

"Not you. You've been nothing but kind, and Miss Ellen is delightful. But the servants want nothing to do with me, and when I walk out to their cabins, they turn their backs. The children look at me as if I have a huge wart on my nose. The adult students obviously prefer white teachers. They don't seem to believe that I can know anything because I'm not white. And I've heard what they call me—'dat brown gal'—as if I'm a race all to myself. I've never felt so isolated."

"Believe it or not, I've felt the same isolation here." When Miss Forten cocked a skeptical eyebrow at her, she tried to explain. "Look, I'm a middle-aged white lady with a bulbous nose and big feet, living in the midst of a world inhabited by two different cultures—one full of black people who know nothing but slavery, and the other full of frisky soldiers looking for a pretty young thing. Nobody likes me, either, because I don't fit anywhere."

"That's not so. You are the most indispensable person on the plantation, and the people are devoted to you."

"That may be partially true now, but it certainly wasn't when I came. So I do understand how isolated you must feel. You know, I think I like you even better, now that I see that you suffer the same doubts and fears as the rest of us do.

We must try to make you more comfortable. May I call you Charlotte?"

"Actually, my friends used to call me Lottie."

"Then Lottie it shall be. Now dry your eyes, and let's head back to The Oaks for supper. There are few troubles that are not eased by a good meal."

23
HUMAN WEAKNESSES
October 1862

General Saxton had been gone for most of the late summer months. He returned to South Carolina just before Charlotte arrived. The two had met on board the little steamer that carried them from Hilton Head to Beaufort. Within days, Saxton had invited himself to lunch at The Oaks and sat down to evaluate current conditions on the island with Laura and Mr. Soule.

"I'm anxious to learn how your newest teacher is working out," he said. "I encountered her when she arrived and found her to be quite intelligent and eager."

"She's adjusting, I think," Mr. Soule said. "Your request that she and the Hunns open up Oaklands plantation added some stress to their arrival, I'm afraid. The plantation house was almost completely stripped of furniture. The first time they went over to see it, they found only two bureaus, three small pine tables, and two chairs, one of which had a broken back."

"What happened to the rest of the furniture? From what I've seen, the other plantations are adequately furnished."

"Carried off and sold by cotton agents, I suspect, just as happened here in the months before you arrived. We've all had to struggle to piece together our own furnishings, some of which we have found in the slave quarters, and other pieces we've reclaimed when the cotton agents left."

"I've heard stories, of course, but I didn't realize the situation was that bleak."

"Believe me, it was," Laura said. "Lottie and Lizzie managed to piece together a floor covering out of some old plaid stuff they found in the attic. They've hung pictures and brought in flowers, trying to make it look a bit more home-like. They even convinced an old black man on a neighboring plantation to hammer together a bed frame for them so they didn't have to sleep directly on the floor. They still don't have mattresses, however, or a table to eat on. Lottie arrives at school some mornings looking tired, as if she hasn't slept all night."

"Do they have servant help?"

"Oh, yes, although the three they have are pretty inexperienced. Rose and Amoretta are teenagers who ought to be in school. They can do chores, such as sweeping and laundry, and even some simple cooking, but they are far from being able to run a household without supervision. And Cupid, their 'man of all work,' does little beyond carry wood and collect oysters. He's still in school, trying to master his writing skills so that he can clerk for them."

"Unfortunate. Maybe we can find her more comfortable lodgings as we move our own people around. She's too valuable an asset for us to risk losing her."

"I agree. I've watched her teach, and she has a deft hand with her students. She took it upon herself to write home asking for toys for the littlest ones, but in the meantime, she's fashioned rag dolls for them and simple games they can play in the dirt. The older children tested her at first, but they soon learned that she could be kind and strict at the same time. Now they hang on her every word."

"No problem with the fact that she's a Negress, then?"

Laura winced. "That was a major problem at first. Our people didn't want anything to do with her because they didn't understand how someone could look like them and behave like white people. Our own servants, even the best of them, were reluctant to work for her. That's part of the reason the Oaklands servants are so young. The older women refused to go there. But most everyone is used to having her here now. I don't expect it to be a problem in the future."

"Well, let's move on to some of the other arrangements. How are Charles Ware and his sister making out at Seaside?"

"Doing well, I think," Mr. Soule said. "Charles isn't much of a farmer, although when he first arrived he claimed to have agricultural experience. He's much more interested in music. He's making a collection of slave songs, which he hopes to publish someday. And that has made him popular with his workers. He encourages them to sing in the fields, so that he can listen and write down what he hears. The workers love being listened to, and their music makes their work go faster, too. It's an ideal working situation."

"Harriet Ware is a fine teacher, too," Laura added. "She helps out in our school and conducts her own classes at Seaside. In fact, she and Lottie get along quite well. We might consider moving Lottie out there to help with the children at Frogmore next door."

"That's a possibility," Saxton acknowledged. "It would also relieve your Miss Winsor of some of her responsibilities. And speaking of her—what's happening at the Capers plantations? Every time I mention them, there are knowing little looks being exchanged among the other superintendents. It's as if everyone's in on a secret that I know nothing about."

Laura and Richard Soule exchanged a brief glance, and Saxton pounced on them. "There! Just like that. What's going on?"

"Rumor has it that Nelly and Josiah Fairfield are . . . friendly."

"Friendly?"

"Well, maybe courting? Look, I really don't know anything, except from what I hear from our people, many of whom have relatives on the Eustis plantation. They say that the two are spending more time together than absolutely necessary. Here at home, Nelly never says a word about Mr. Fairfield. And when we are all together, as at church, the two of them stay on opposite sides of the room. I've never seen them talk to one another," Laura said.

"Which is, in itself, a bit unusual," Mr. Soule added. "We are all rather starved for more worldly conversation after spending days on the plantation, so all the Gideonites come together as often as possible to socialize. Everybody talks to everybody, usually all at once. Except for those two. And that makes their avoidance of one another all the more noticeable."

"If they are not getting along, it could interfere with the operation of the lands over which they have responsibility," the general said. "Perhaps I'd better have a talk with them."

"No, General, there's no problem with the running of the plantations or their schools, I assure you. It's just that these are two young people who need to work out the nature of their relationship. Best we leave them alone to get on with it."

"I hope you are right. No other problems, I assume?"

"Uh . . ."

"Uh oh. I recognize that look. Where are the problem areas, then?"

Laura drew one of her characteristic deep breaths. She was torn between her desire to speak no ill of her companions and her responsibility to let the general know if trouble was brewing. "T. Edwin Ruggles, who is reclaiming the Fuller lands just west of the village, is a superb farmer. That's what he claimed to be when he signed on, but some people, I understand, doubted his abilities because he had just graduated from law school. He has really made a noticeable improvement to the Fuller place. He's also acting as Mr. Philbrick's second-in-command. We have heard nothing but good things about him."

"But . . .?"

"His sister Amanda is not doing as well with her school. She wants to have a school there, and she complains loudly if any of their blacks try to attend our classes at Penn School. But the truth is that while she wants a school, she doesn't actually want to teach in it—or doesn't know how. Her children tell us that she only meets with them occasionally, and that when she does, she doesn't teach them anything. She just demands that they tell her what they already know. The poor little tykes come to classes with us so that they have something new to recite when she asks them."

"That's pathetic."

"I know. But she's not interested in our offers of help, either. She has gone so far as to accuse us of stealing her pupils.

I don't want to antagonize her, but neither do I want to see those children suffer because she can't or won't do her job."

"How can I help? Should we send Miss Forten over there?"

"No, Lottie deserves a more supportive environment. But if we have additional teachers coming this fall, you might consider sending a couple of them to organize a more consolidated school in that area."

"Isn't that close to the Thompsons' land?"

"Well . . . yes it is, but . . ."

"Oh, dear. More trouble there? The Thompsons hail from Philadelphia, don't they?"

"They do, and they came highly recommended by Mr. McKim, who described James Thompson as a zealous young newspaperman with strong antislavery principles. I wish that had been so."

"And it's not?"

"No, I'm afraid it isn't. At least, he may have had strong theoretical principles, but he seems to have changed his mind now that he has seen the reality that is the South."

"Meaning?"

"He didn't like the Negroes once he met them. They shock and revolt him. He visited here not long before Lottie and the Hunns arrived, to demand that he be allowed to take over the store there at The Corner and sell all the Philadelphia goods from there as well. From what I gathered, he thinks it is a waste of time, effort, and money to try to clothe our ex-slaves. He kept saying that if he could turn the store into a form of private speculation, he could make a tidy profit at it. He despairs of ever civilizing a man who has once been a slave. He even went so far as to say that all former slaves needed whipping to keep them in line. I was horrified and told him that, if that was the way he felt, he should go straight home. But, no, he sees South Carolina as a land of new opportunity for himself. He isn't about to leave."

"What about his sister? Does she feel the same way?"

"Matilda? I'm not sure there has ever been a thought in her pretty little head!"

"Miss Towne." Mr. Soule's voice carried a note of warning.

"I'm sorry. That was ungracious of me. But I meant it, too. Matilda is lovely, clearly the belle of St. Helena Island, and she plays up her good looks to the exclusion of anything else. She dotes on her older brother and is content to believe anything he says. I don't think she is vicious, as he is, but she'll never stand up to him. And the thought of actually working with the slaves has never crossed her mind."

"Hmmmm. Sounds like a woman I need to meet," the general said, giving his best imitation of a leer.

"You go and do that," Laura snapped. "You'll fall under her spell, just like every other man around here. Just don't ask her a question that takes more than a few words to answer."

"Perhaps I'd better find some place to stash the Thompsons, out of the range of your righteous wrath. He was a newspaperman, you say?"

"That's what I've heard."

"Maybe there is an opening for him in Beaufort that would take him out of immediate contact with the former slaves. Would that help?"

"Anything that gets James Thompson away from St. Helena Island will help."

"I'll see what I can do. As soon as our replacement teachers begin to arrive, we can make adjustments. And I thank you, Miss Towne, for your honesty."

24
HATCHING PLANS
November 1862

S everal days later, Saxton returned. "Problem solved!" he announced as he came in the door. "James Thompson has just been appointed lead reporter for Beaufort's little newspaper, *The Free South*. He'll have to write about the Negro problem, of course, but he won't get overly harsh words past his editor. Once he doesn't have to deal with driving former slaves back to the cotton fields, perhaps he won't see them in such a bad light. And even if his attitude doesn't change, he'll no longer be in a position to do actual harm. Whipping them with words won't bother former slaves."

"You're a miracle worker," Laura said.

"Not at all. Just putting people where they fit best, rather than trying to cram the square ones into round holes. Besides, every Army officer in Beaufort is now in my debt. They will have the privilege of watching the lovely Matilda as she walks around town."

"Men!"

"Yep. Might as well make their weaknesses work for us, don't you think?"

Laura couldn't help but smile at his guilelessness. "Any more word on the next shipload of teachers?"

"Not a lovely face among them, I hear."

"Stop. That joke's wearing thin. Do we know how many are coming?"

"My last communication with Mr. McKim said that he was sending several persons from Philadelphia, and that all of them had been training and reading up in preparation for what they will be doing here. He's been of much greater assistance after his June visit."

"I was afraid he was going to send us all home when he saw the conditions here. Luckily, he chose instead to focus on what he could do to help out."

"I understand from what he said that he and his daughter may be returning themselves after Christmas. In the meantime, I think we can look forward to some congenial additions to our numbers."

"We need them. Is it true that six or eight of the superintendents are headed home before Christmas?"

"Fraid so. Most of them are from the outer islands, or from Philbrick's side of St. Helena Island."

"Why are they all leaving?" Mr. Soule asked. "Have they given you any reason?"

"Most plead ill health. It's hard to argue with that. But I suspect some of them just don't like it here."

"You know, general, I don't think any of us realized what we were getting into. I'm sure I didn't. I wasn't expecting to be put in charge of acres and acres of cotton plants, when I had never even seen one. I guess I made that pretty obvious when I fed the cotton seed to the cows." Richard Soule looked embarrassed again as he remembered that day.

"Another problem was the age of our first recruits," Laura added. "Although I wasn't in the initial band, I understand

that almost all the Boston men were recent college graduates, unmarried, and under the age of twenty-five. They were
available, but they were completely green, and nobody told
them they were signing away the next several years of their
lives. They thought they'd come down here for a couple of
months, solve the problems, and then get back to their real
responsibility of building their own careers and families."

"Mr. McKim would agree with you. He tells me he's
sending older people now, ones that have free time and independent means of support."

"But he hasn't given you any names? The abolitionist
community in Philadelphia is not so large that I wouldn't
recognize the names if I heard them."

"Patience, Miss Towne. You'll meet them soon enough."

Laura thought that the general was looking particularly
sly and proud of himself, but she understood that there was
no use pushing him further. He was a man who loved his
secrets. Whoever the new arrivals turned out to be, they
were sure to be better than Mr. James Thompson and the
loathsome Matilda, she thought. And with that, she put her
curiosity out of her mind and returned to folding packets of
medicine for her patients.

* * *

The next week, General Saxton called for an all-day meeting with his superintendents on St. Helena Island. Nothing
had dimmed Saxton's antislavery convictions, but he was also
enough of a military man to recognize that compassion and
dedication were not necessarily the most important qualities
for his Gideonite staff to exercise. The ex-slaves reminded

him of new army recruits, set in their own ways, independent enough to chafe at any restrictions placed on their behavior and too inexperienced in the ways of the world to understand the necessity of orders being hurled at them. As for the superintendents and teachers he was trusting to bring order out of chaos, they suffered from a lack of clear understanding about what the government and the Army were trying to accomplish.

Not that they were entirely to blame in that regard. President Lincoln had made a hash out of his early policy toward emancipation. Offers of freedom, hedged in by forced labor and the threat of being carried off into the Army, left the ex-slaves confused about their positions. Superintendents who tried to establish rules of work and behavior found that there was no way to enforce those rules, unless it was by using the same methods the Southern slave owners had employed. Pupils who had to haul their younger brothers and sisters with them hindered the teachers who tried to bring order to their classrooms.

Saxton often found himself discouraged when he looked at the day-to-day problems that confronted them all, but he was also buoyed by examples of courage and dedication among the Gideonites. They had an impossible goal, he knew, but few of them were willing to acknowledge the possibility of failure. People like Laura Towne amazed him with their resilience.

For her part, Laura watched with admiration as Saxton struggled to balance his responsibilities on St. Helena with the military expectations of the staff at Hilton Head. She was well aware that he had little support there, except from General Hunter. Soldiers and officers alike tended to blame the slaves for the war itself. They reasoned that they had done their job by invading South Carolina, driving off the plantation owners, and freeing the slaves. Now they expected the slaves to go off in their newly found freedom and fend for themselves. Resentment blossomed when they discovered that they were expected to keep right on protecting those slaves and delivering free army rations to them, while the slaves did little or nothing to help themselves.

* * *

Saxton opened his meeting by calling attention to the date. "It was one year ago today that our South Carolina Expeditionary Force arrived at the mouth of Port Royal Sound. We faced two Confederate strongholds guarding the richest area of cotton and rice production in South Carolina. The aristocracy of the South and several of the fathers of secession lived here. It was an enormous gamble, but within two days we were in complete possession of the Low Country, and we had freed over 10,000 enchained black men. What an amazing victory it has proved to be!

"Four months later, some of you arrived as the forerunners of the Port Royal Experiment, that grand abolitionist effort to bring their highest aspirations to fulfillment. You came to prove that a black man, once freed from his chains, could become a full, productive, and loyal citizen of the United States. Your efforts are ongoing, but your accomplishments continue to mount. I'm here today to ask you what I can do to make those efforts even more successful." He stopped, full of pride in his own eloquence, and waited for the applause that did not come.

Instead, he faced a room fairly seething with resentments of its own. "You might try getting control of your own soldiers," Charles Ware said. "The pickets who are supposed to be guarding our coastline seem to spend most of their time stealing our chickens and tearing down our fences for firewood. When the slaves are constantly harassed by white soldiers, it makes it hard for us to command their loyalty and obedience."

"Exactly so!" Mr. Gannett said. "And while you're at it, you might stop Hilton Head from passing more foolish regulations controlling the behavior of the ex-slaves."

"I'm sorry. I'm not sure what you are referring to," Saxton interrupted.

"Well, for one example, Hilton Head just issued an order that no Negro is to be on the roads without an official pass from the superintendent of his plantation. And I'm supposed to enforce the rule. How silly is that? As if I had time to patrol our roads and check to make sure every one of my blacks carries a pass from me?" Charles Ware shook his head in disgust.

"Yes, and furthermore, you might spend more time seeing to it that we have enough rations to feed these people instead of interfering with our choice of a pastor for our church," Dr. Wakefield mumbled.

"No, what's most important is money." Mr. Philbrick spoke for the first time, and the others yielded the floor to him. "My biggest problem is paying my field hands. We've promised them that if they work the cotton fields and produce a good crop, the government will pay them a fair salary for their labor. That's the standard any potential citizen has a right to expect, and a former slave is no different. These men have been hoeing cotton in the hot sun all summer, and their families have helped with the picking and ginning. They were not paid for all their spring planting efforts until the crop was nearly grown in August, and they haven't been paid since. Last month, I finally paid their promised salaries out of my own pocket, in hopes of recouping my losses when the government money came through. But I haven't seen a sign of it. I can do as fine a job of running the plantation as any man here, and I've agreed that the resultant crop must go to the government. But I expect the government to keep its end of the bargain."

"I'll contact Secretary Chase immediately," Saxton replied, "but I can't make the money appear by magic."

"Well, maybe I can make that cotton disappear by magic. If I've paid for it, it's mine."

"I don't like threats, Mr. Philbrick."

"That's not a threat, General. It's a statement of fact. If the government will not do its part, we'll turn this into a private enterprise and cut you out entirely."

"Gentlemen, please." Laura Towne was the controlling voice of reason amid the growing hostilities. "We all know we face multiple problems, but we must not lose track of our primary purpose. We are here to bring protection, education, medical care, and compassion to people who need us. We need support from you, General Saxton, and reasonable assurance that you will do all you can to see to it we have the wherewithal to do our jobs. That's all we really ask, although I realize it's a big order."

"That's what I just said."

"Yes, I suppose it is, Mr. Philbrick, but I intended to balance it with another statement. I promise, and I hope my colleagues agree, that we will do our best to concentrate on our own responsibilities and not burden General Saxton with the blame for matters over which he has no control."

At the end of the meeting, General Saxton reached out his hand to detain Laura as the others filed out of the room. "Once again, I am in your debt. I understand the levels of frustration you all deal with, but it takes a woman's gentle voice to smooth them over. Perhaps I should hire you as my constant companion."

"Heaven forfend! I wouldn't face your responsibilities for any remuneration. I'll settle for handling my own little rebel raids, slave rebellions, and internecine bickering."

"Not exactly what I had in mind," Saxton said. "I was just hoping for a way to manage more time in your company. I'm headed to Fort Pulaski tomorrow to attend a ball celebrating the Battle of Port Royal. I would be happy to escort you there."

"And set the whole island aflame with gossip? I hardly think so!" Laura squinted at him, trying to decide if he was just teasing or being deliberately provocative.

"Perhaps it wasn't such a good idea—just a moment's whim," the general said, backing away.

"Well, if I was supposed to be flattered, I am, but . . ."

"Never fear. We'll have a dance yet." Saxton swept an elaborate bow in her direction and hastened off to his waiting horse, leaving Laura standing in bemusement at the door.

"Whatever was that all about?" Ellen asked as she approached the porch from the yard.

"I don't know."

25
FAMILY MATTERS
November 1862

Less than a week later, one part of the mystery unraveled. Laura was still puttering around her bedchamber one morning when Rina came dashing in. "Missus Laura, you bes be gittin yoself downstair. You gots company."

"Rina, how many times do I have to tell you . . .?"

"Fuh knock? I knows it, but dere aint no time fuh dat formal stuff."

"You mean we have company before breakfast? It better not be Mr. Eustis or General Saxton. We simply have to ask them not to pop in at such early hours."

"Aint nobody I knows. But I knows who dey says dey be, an you be wantin fuh see dem."

Shaking her head at Rina's characteristic panic at the first sign of change, Laura took her time straightening her dress and wrapping her hair into its usual bun. Then she descended the stairs, hesitated as she caught a glimpse of the foyer, and took the last few steps at a dead run. "Will! Rosie! When . . . how . . . what are you doing here?"

The next few minutes dissolved into such a flurry of squeals and hugs and tears that no one could have heard a question or an answer. Even Rina appeared a little teary-eyed as she watched the family reunion. Finally, Laura pushed away, her hands clasped in a gesture of prayer in front of her lips. "I cannot believe this! Rina, why didn't you say that my brother and my sister were here?"

"Cause I don know you eben hab a brudder or a sistah." Rina shrugged.

By now the other members of the household were coming downstairs, awakened by the commotion. As introductions were made all around, only Ellen hung back at the edge of the crowd. As soon as she saw an opening, she drew Laura to one side.

"I'm thrilled and excited for you, my dear. But . . . do they know I am here? I don't want to cause any . . ."

"Nonsense, Ellen. Of course they know. I don't hide my relationship with you from my family. They may not fully understand, but they do accept my choices. Now come and say hello, or they will think you are unhappy to see them."

A moment later another voice boomed from the doorway. "How do you like your new recruits, Miss Towne? Didn't I tell you you'd find them satisfactory?"

"Ah, good morning, General Saxton. I should have known you were behind this."

"I traveled with these folks from Hilton Head yesterday, but the tide turned and we were so late in reaching Beaufort that we spent the night on board. Then I had us rowed over first thing this morning to surprise you. Did it work?"

"What? The surprise? It certainly did. But you told me we were getting permanent replacements. I would never have guessed at a visit from my family."

"This isn't a visit, Laura." Will stepped to her side. "Rosie and I are both here to work for as long as you need us."

As Laura stared at him, the general broke in again. "What about my thanks? At least you could offer a starving man some breakfast!"

* * *

After a thrown-together meal, Saxton left feeling very proud of himself, and the family reunion moved to the front porch, where they could enjoy the still warm weather and talk in private.

"Now tell me everything," Laura demanded. "How did you manage this and how long can you stay?"

"We've been talking about the move ever since you left," Will admitted. "Nobody wanted you to come down here, but we were all a bit envious of your gumption. Rosie and I, in particular, found ourselves going to more and more abolitionist meetings, as if in that way we could be a part of your efforts. But in the long run, it became obvious that saying 'Yea, verily' to the lectures we were hearing was not enough. We could either be a part of your mission or not. We chose to sign up."

"But Lucretia must have been furious."

"Surprisingly, no, she wasn't," Rosie said. "She was supportive and agreeable. She even made sure we met all the right people and had all the proper paperwork."

"Why the difference, I wonder. She was so angry with me . . ."

"And angry with herself for wanting to hold onto all of us. For whatever the reason, Lucretia has loosened her grip on our little family. Maybe she has finally realized that we are all adults, capable of making our own decisions. At any rate, she has found a new outlet for her mothering instincts," Will said.

"Really? And that would be . . .?"

"John Henry's brood. Our nephew and nieces are growing up, and John Henry's wife is none too interested in them. Lucretia has taken over the search for a college for young Henry, and I swear she's already on the lookout for a beau for fourteen-year-old Helen. Little Alice is not getting the full Lucretia treatment yet, but she will as soon as she quits losing her baby teeth and becomes a teenager."

"John Henry and Maria ought to be grateful for her assistance," Laura said.

"Oh, they are. It's a happy relationship all the way round, and it has freed us to make something more of our lives. Even sister Sarah has started a new project. She's trying her hand at writing, and, who knows? Without Lucretia standing over her every moment, she may actually succeed."

"So you're really serious? You're planning to join our little Gideon's Band?"

"Yes, we are. I've spent the last few months in Boston and the surrounding area, getting acquainted with the needs of the cotton industry in New England. I can tell you all about your long-staple crop, and rate the worth of a bale of cotton by rubbing it through my fingers. In my correspondence with General Saxton, I've assured him that I am as prepared as possible to take over as a superintendent of a small plantation."

"I've been studying, too," Rosie said, "only I've been learning about how our local people work with new immigrants to help them adjust to a new culture and language. Mr. McKim put me in touch with the Sisters of Charity. They run a school for little Irish children, where they help them get rid of their Gaelic brogue and learn to speak standard English. Along the way, of course, they are also teaching reading and writing, and the children thrive in their lessons. I'm hoping that experience will help me teach some classes with your young speakers of Gullah."

"You have been sent from God, my dears. You are exactly the kinds of people we need here. And, oh! It will be so good to have you nearby. I wonder where General Saxton will place you?"

"He's already given us our assignment. Didn't he tell you? He said a place called Frogmore is your favorite plantation, so he thought we would enjoy it there, too."

"Perfect! It is one of my favorite places, and it desperately needs good people to whip it into shape. I won't tell you it will be easy, but it will reward your efforts, I'm sure."

"Can we see it? I'm dying of curiosity about what makes it so special." Rosie was fairly bouncing with enthusiasm. "I want to get to work."

"The general will want to take you out there and formally install you as the new overseers, but until he's ready, I'll be happy to show you around. The house has been empty for several weeks, but the slaves have been hard at work in the cotton fields. I go out at least once a week to treat their minor ailments. If I can round up Hastings, we can probably drive out there this afternoon so you can see it for yourselves."

* * *

As Hastings steered the large carriage off Seaside Road onto the long approach road to Frogmore, Laura instructed her siblings to draw deep breaths. "Can you smell it and taste it?" she asked. "There's something different about Frogmore air."

"Dat be de hants you be smellin," Hastings mumbled.

"What?"

"Hastings! Not another word. You're getting to be as bad as Judith."

"What did he say? What are hants?"

"You'll hear the stories soon enough, I suppose. The blacks here on the island are full of superstitions. They believe that all that gray moss you see hanging from the trees is a sign that ghosts live in the trees. The gray stuff is their beards because they've been trapped in the trees so long. They also think this road is haunted because there's a tree that used to be used for hanging runaway slaves. We just passed it a ways back."

"Well, there is something different about the air," Rosie said uncertainly.

"Yes, but it's not ghosts, I promise. The sunlight is very filtered because the trees here are so old. Frogmore plantation is located right on the water, so the onshore breezes carry the mist inland, where the light reflects off it, giving the whole woods this curious shimmery effect. It may have scared the pants off the slaves, but I love the otherworldly atmosphere. In another couple of minutes, we'll emerge from the trees and you'll see the house overlooking the sea. It's one of my favorite views."

"Is there a beach?"

"Yes, there is, and a lovely little cove where the water is clear and blue. I've always wanted to go for a swim there. Perhaps once you have moved in, I'll be able to manage that. There's the house now."

"It's . . . a bit small for a plantation house, isn't it?" Will was frowning.

"Not for its age. The Stapleton family built this house and its tabby barn around 1810. Just before the war, the whole plantation was part of a much larger complex that belonged to Thomas Coffin. He had an overseer living here, but it wasn't actually designed to house a family."

Hastings drew the horses to a halt so that the visitors could take a lingering look. "Inside, it's a pretty basic four-room floor plan—central hall, two parlors, a dining room, and a back room. Upstairs there are two small bedrooms crammed under the eaves, but the roof is designed to be raised, so that a second story can be added. I envision that upper front area as a sleeping porch that catches every sea breeze. It's wonderfully quiet here, except for the sounds of the waves and the sea birds."

"If you're so fond of it, why haven't you asked General Saxton to assign you here?" Will asked. "I got the distinct impression that you have him wrapped right around your little finger."

"Hardly! But I can't stay out here permanently—not just yet. Right now, I have responsibility for doctoring all the slaves on the island, so I have to be more centrally located. But someday . . ."

"You talk as if you were planning to stay here permanently," Rosie said.

"I would be content to do exactly that, Rosie, but we'll see what time brings. For now, Frogmore is just my occasional escape hatch. And if you two are living here, I'll have an additional excuse to visit more often."

Laura was about to say more, but the carriage came under attack by small black children, all reaching up to greet Missus. "Missus! Muh missus! You brings sweetin? You gwine stay?"

"It doesn't sound so quiet any more," Will observed, raising his voice to be heard over the chatter.

"That's enough, children. I'm not here to see you this afternoon. I'm just showing some visitors around. Back off now and go back to your chores. I'll visit with you next week."

As quickly as they came, the crowd of children disappeared. "Are they always that obedient?" Rosie asked.

"Not always, but they tend to be afraid of strangers. That's why it will be best if General Saxton is the one to bring you out here. We'll head home now, Hastings."

"Yes'm. Dat be good. We gits dere fore de hants gits us."

* * *

The travelers retired early, exhausted from their adventures, but Laura found that she was too excited—and worried—to sleep. As she had the night before Ellen arrived, she made her way to the veranda. Staring out over the marshlands illuminated only by the moon, she tried to sort out her feelings. One part of her was comforted by the presence of her family. Rosie's love encircled her, and Will's strong masculine confidence gave her a shoulder to lean upon. I didn't realize how much I missed them all, she thought to herself. I've enjoyed their letters, but having them here makes such a difference. There had been times she had felt very much alone; now she remembered the importance and the strength of their family bond. We'll do this together, she vowed.

Still, when she sank into one of the porch rockers and tried to relax, she found that every muscle was still tight. Something else was going on. What am I afraid of? she wondered. I'm as tense as if I had just seen one of Hastings's hants. She shook herself with impatience.

Then she recognized the fear. It was the same fear she had felt with Ellen's arrival. It's my own lack of confidence in my decision, she realized. It was bad enough when I thought I might have gotten myself into an untenable position here— that I might have thrown away a career and a settled life for an ephemeral goal, one I could never accomplish. I was more frightened when Ellen joined me because she trusted my decisions. I was then risking two lives instead of just my own. And now, I'm responsible for drawing two more of the people I love most into this mess. What if it's all a spectacular failure? What if the North loses the war? If the government just cuts off our support and leaves us stranded here? If the slaves turn against us? If we all come down with horrid tropical diseases that I am unable to treat? How can I face the possibility that I have led my family into untold dangers?

Laura had long insisted that she did not want the term "martyr" applied to her or what she was doing. But now, the possibility of martyrdom hovered before her in the shadowy darkness. She realized that all the bonds of love that now surrounded her had committed her to move forward. The unknown that lay ahead offered the possibility of failure and death. But there was no turning back without destroying the faith and trust of those who loved her.

26
ROMANCES BLOOM
November/December 1862

G ood weather had always bolstered Laura's spirits, and this November was no exception. The danger of hurricanes was past, as were the heat and humidity of summer. The sky remained a deep blue, sprinkled with little powder-puff clouds. The onshore breezes held no winter chill as yet, and the flowers that had been dormant or shriveled in August now burst into a final frenzy of blossom. Add to the weather the continuing arrivals of friends and family members and the excitement of the approaching holiday season, and even the gloomiest soul could find a reason to rejoice.

Laura was particularly encouraged when young Sam Phillips returned to St. Helena in November. She had watched him depart in midsummer, wracked by swamp fevers and near death. She had despaired over her own inability to treat his illness, and had worried that his abolitionist father might lose faith in the Port Royal Experiment when he learned what it had done to his only son. Now Sam was back, still looking a bit pale and much too slender, but apparently restored to health by his stay in the North. He stopped by The Oaks, bringing Laura a bunch of camellias along with greetings from his mother and her best friend, Sophia, Laura's eldest sister. He bubbled with enthusiasm as he described his return, and how the children he had been teaching came tumbling around him to welcome him home. "And it is home, Miss Laura," he said. "You must never doubt that. Home is where we are most needed. That's where we will always belong."

Lottie Forten had settled into her teaching routine with ease. Although, in private, she missed her friends and mourned the fact that letters from home did not arrive often enough, she was quickly falling in love with her students. She wrote of their small triumphs in the classroom and their beautiful voices. One friend, the poet John Greenleaf Whittier, responded by writing a special hymn just for the children. He sent it to Lottie, hoping her pupils could learn it in time to sing it at their Christmas celebration.

Lottie was also delighted to find that she was not the only free black in the area. Harriet Tubman, that little powerhouse who fought tirelessly to deliver her people out of the bonds of slavery, was working in Hilton Head. Laura also made sure that Lottie met Robert Smalls, the enterprising young slave who, back in May, had managed to steal a Confederate ship and sail it out of Charleston Harbor and into Yankee hands. Reverend French had taken Smalls to Washington and introduced him to Secretary Chase as evidence of what a black man could do for his country. As a result, General Hunter's plans to recruit colored regiments within the Union Army seemed at last to be coming to fruition. Lottie watched with delight as one of her dearest friends arrived to work with the new recruits. Dr. Seth Rogers was their regimental surgeon, under the command of Colonel Thomas Wentworth Higginson.

* * *

Back at The Oaks, more good news enlivened the season. Nelly Winsor finally announced to her friends that Josiah Fairfield had proposed.

"Proposed? As in . . . marriage?" Laura asked.

"Yes, Miss Towne, he has asked me to marry him."

"And you said . . .?"

"I haven't given him my answer yet. I didn't want to seem too eager. But I'm definitely inclined to say yes."

"Oh, that's wonderful, Nelly." Ellen was the first to give her a congratulatory hug. "When will the wedding be?"

"I don't know. I haven't thought that far. I'm still trying to get my head around the idea that someone wants to marry me."

"It was never a question of 'if'—just a matter of 'who' and 'when.' You'll be a lovely bride."

"Perhaps, but I'm more concerned over whether I can be a lovely wife."

"If you have any doubts, my dear . . ." Laura began to deliver a lecture and then stopped herself.

"No, say what you were going to say," Nellie urged her. "Do you think I shouldn't marry?"

"No, and I would have no right to do so. It must be your decision. I only hope you will take your time before you take that final step. Don't let any of us, Josiah included, talk you into something you are not sure of."

"I won't. There are too many other matters that need my attention right now. Nothing will happen before next summer, I suspect. But it does cast an interesting glow over the prospect of the coming holiday season." Nelly's eyes sparkled with impish glee at the thought.

Laura had been dreading the holidays because everyone would be so far away from home, but now, with Will and Rosie here, the prospect was more exciting. Realizing that many of the Gideonites would be expecting a Thanksgiving dinner at The Oaks, she tried to talk to Rina about a menu.

"I don know what you Yankees eats fuh Tankgibbin," Rina said. "Ol massa, he always want turkey, but dese birds we gots in de woods round here not be fit fuh good eatin. Dey all tough an stringy, an dey tastes like acorn, cause dat what dey eat."

"We're used to turkey, too, I'm afraid, but you don't make it sound too appetizing."

"We kin stuff um wit oysters an cornpone, but dat don hep much."

"Maybe some sausage to give them a better flavor?" Laura asked.

"Sound like a waste uh good sassige."

"How about some sweet potato pies?"

"Yes'm. We kin do dat."

"Fine. Let me think about the rest of the menu for a while. We need to find something for which our guests will be grateful."

Laura recounted the conversation at dinner one evening, hoping that someone would come up with a solution, but she was not expecting the one she received.

"I have your answer," Mr. Eustis said, "but you'll have to promise that you'll invite me."

"When are you ever not here?" Laura answered. "I'm hoping to have all our staff members, if I can come up with enough food."

"This will do it, I think. General Saxton has ordered that one head of cattle be slaughtered for each plantation, so that everyone, black and white alike, can have meat for Thanksgiving."

"Meat? Real beef? Heaven!"

* * *

Excitement increased daily. On the day before Thanksgiving, Lottie and Ellen went for a walk in the woods and gathered bright red leaves and clusters of berries to decorate the tables. On Thursday morning, everyone attended a service at the Brick Church, where General Saxton spoke to the young men, urging them to express their thanks for their freedom by enlisting in the new colored regiment. The services concluded with jubilant singing and a wedding, after which the blacks had the day off and the Gideonites gathered at The Oaks to enjoy their roast beef and to take stock of their many accomplishments.

At the end of the day, Lottie wrote: "This has been the happiest, most jubilant Thanksgiving day of my life. We hear of cold weather and heavy snowstorms up in the North land. But here, roses and oleanders are blooming in the open air. Figs and oranges are ripening, the sunlight is warm and bright, and over all shines gloriously the blessed light of Freedom—Freedom forevermore!"

The joy did not last. Two deaths on the same day, December 5th, temporarily muted the building excitement. One was a small black baby named Hercules, who succumbed to whooping cough and fever as the weather turned sharply colder. He was the grandchild of an old man who worked at Oaklands, and Lottie recorded the gloom that settled over the little slave village. After his burial, the slaves gathered outside the grandfather's cabin and sang something Lottie described as a kind of funeral chant. She was particularly concerned about the effect the chanting must have on the mother of another tiny baby suffering from the same illness. Pleading the cold, the village children avoided school for the next two days, although Lottie suspected they were still in mourning.

The other death affected the Gideonites more directly. Young Sam Phillips had taken suddenly ill after Thanksgiving. Dr. Wakefield came from Beaufort to treat him and diagnosed him with bilious colic. Laura suspected yellow fever, but Dr. Wakefield would not let her visit his patient. She could only wait helplessly as the young man suffered and died.

The teachers and superintendents gathered for a funeral service at the Episcopal Church, their numbers now reduced further by a second martyr. The black casket, wreathed with pine boughs and camellia blossoms, was placed temporarily in the Fripp Mausoleum on the church grounds. Slaves had stripped the tombs earlier, taking their revenge on one of the most hated of the slave owners. Now it stood empty, its gaping entrance a mockery of the fine carved lintel stone, and could be used as a temporary resting place for those whose bodies were to be shipped home.

The group of mourners retired to The Oaks, unwilling to head home to their isolated plantations so soon. Many of them were worried about the effect of Sam's death on his devoted parents, who had now lost their only son. Laura was fighting a mixture of grief and anger over what she considered an unnecessary death. Charles Ware, who had been particularly close to Sam, offered some comfort.

"Sam told me that he did not expect to live long," he said. "The doctors back home had given him a terrible prognosis, but he chose to return to South Carolina despite their warnings. He believed his parents understood his decision, even if it was hard for them. He loved this land, he loved his people, and he believed in the work we are doing. He didn't want to die, but if that was to be his fate, he wanted to die as he lived—serving those who needed him most. We honor him best by continuing his work, and he would not want any vestige of grief to mar the great celebration that awaits us on New Year's Day."

* * *

The Gideonites went to work preparing for a Christmas celebration, although it seemed almost unimportant in comparison to the coming proclamation of emancipation, the goal for which they had been laboring so long. There would be a church service, of course, and the women decorated the Brick Church with wreaths and garlands of greenery, American flags, and fringes of Spanish moss. Since the children were attending classes in the same hall, they watched the proceedings with growing excitement. Every afternoon, Lottie assembled her chorus and worked with them to memorize the hymn Whittier had written just for them. And in the evenings, the teachers were busy assembling small toys and packets of candy so that every child might receive a Christmas gift. Still, talk was not of Christmas but of New Year's Day.

There was to be an outdoor ceremony at Hilton Head, one to which the military, the civilians, and the former slaves were all invited. The speeches would be followed by a grand feed for soldiers and former slaves alike, while the military officers and the Gideonites would celebrate that evening with a formal banquet and a cotillion, after which the ladies of St. Helena Island would return home by way of a moonlight cruise.

It all sounded quite romantic, and General Saxton made sure that Laura understood that she would be his special guest. "We have ten oxen to roast, a new dining hall to christen, and an event to celebrate that outreaches anything our country has ever known. We owe it to ourselves to make this a special celebration."

"I'm sure it will be lovely," Laura said.

"Not just lovely, although with you and the other ladies there, it will certainly be that," Saxton replied. "But it is also a grand victory, one in which you—and I—have played a part. You will join me at the head table to symbolize our joint endeavors."

"I shall be honored."

"Besides, I promised you a day would come when we would have a dance." Saxton swept an enormous bow at Laura's feet and then gave her an outrageous wink as he left.

27
A NEW YEAR
January 1863

A *Proclamation: Whereas, on the twenty-second day of September, in the year of our Lord one thousand eight hundred and sixty-two, a proclamation was issued by the President of the United States, containing, among other things, the following, to wit:*

"That on the first day of January, in the year of our Lord one thousand eight hundred and sixty-three, all persons held as slaves within any State or designated part of a State, the people whereof shall then be in rebellion against the United States, shall be then, thenceforward, and forever free; and the Executive Government of the United States, including the military and naval authority thereof, will recognize and maintain the freedom of such persons, and will do no act or acts to repress such persons, or any of them, in any efforts they may make for their actual freedom."

Most people in the Low Country could recite the opening lines of the Emancipation Proclamation by heart, long before it went into effect. For the Army, it meant a rich new source of manpower. For the Gideonites, it was the culmination of all their years of campaigning for abolition. And for the former slaves, it was a guarantee that Uncle Sam himself had declared them forever free.

The provisions of the proclamation reassured the whites that the former slaves would abstain from violence except in self-defense. Even long-time abolitionists found that something of a relief. It urged the freedmen to work hard in exchange for reasonable wages. The field hands saw a guarantee that wages would be paid on time; the superintendents put their faith in the blacks' instruction to keep working at jobs where they were needed. Permission for former slaves to enter the armed services meant that the newly formed black regiments would have a steady supply of enlistees. Everyone was happy, with the possible exception of the die-hard former plantation owners, but, for everyone concerned, there was a need to hear the proclamation read out in official terms.

Flatboats had been making their way across the water to Port Royal and the new encampment of the First South Carolina Volunteers all night long. By sunup, whole families of Negroes, dressed in their most colorful outfits as they might have been for church, were taking up their positions around the open-air platform where the ceremony was to be held. General Saxton had predicted a crowd of 5,000 souls, and the early numbers suggested there might be even more. Colonel Higginson worried briefly whether the ten oxen turning on tree-trunk spits would provide enough meat for all.

Lottie Forten and the Hunns had set out very early to be sure they caught the steamer *Flora*. It was a beautiful morning for a river cruise, and the crowd on deck was already in a celebratory mood. A band played music all the way, while the former slaves clapped and sang along. After a stop at Beaufort to pick up more passengers, they sailed on to Port Royal. At the dock, Lottie was met by her dear friend Dr. Seth Rogers, who promptly whisked her away from the Hunns to take an impromptu tour of the camp.

"Isn't it wonderful, Lottie?" Dr. Rogers said. "Who would have believed a year ago that we could have a whole regiment of trained black soldiers fighting for the freedom of their brothers?"

"From what I've seen of them, they look quite impressive with their blue coats and scarlet pants. And the camp is surprisingly well-equipped."

"Well, we've had to make do a bit, but this is the site of a very old fort, as well as a former cotton plantation, so there were already fortifications and a few buildings in place. My hospital is a converted cotton gin, but it has room for a dozen or so beds. And Colonel Higginson has inherited a lovely old plantation house to use as his headquarters. I'd wager we are as well situated as any regiment in the South, and better than most. Ah, there he is now. Have you met Colonel Higginson, Lottie?"

"Of course. I mean, no," Lottie stammered in embarrassment. "I've heard him speak and been introduced on several occasions, but I'm sure he doesn't remember me."

"Sir, I have the pleasure of introducing Miss Charlotte Forten of Philadelphia."

"My pleasure, Miss Forten. I have heard much about you since your arrival in our overgrown paradise here. I hope you are enjoying the day?"

"Oh, yes, it's already been wonderful and it hasn't even started yet. I mean . . . I'm so pleased to meet you."

"Perhaps we can have time to talk about your work here after the ceremony. Will you stay? Right now I need to get these men organized and in place. You will excuse me?"

"Yes . . . I mean . . ." Lottie watched as Higginson made his way toward his troops.

"Oh, dear. Why can I never say something coherent when I meet a hero in person?"

"Better get used to it down here. We are surrounded by heroes. And we had better get you to your seat on the platform. You are one of the honored guests, you know."

"A place in the crowd would suit me better."

"No, indeed," Dr. Rogers said. "You are a shining example of what your people can accomplish, and the men will want to get a good look at you. Up you go. I'll meet you after the ceremony, and we can chat more over lunch."

The women from The Oaks were not so prompt and efficient. All of them had been invited to attend the ball General Saxton was giving, and there were ball gowns to be packed in a trunk for later. Laura was in a tizzy. "I just don't know," she fussed at Ellen. "I want to look presentable if I'm to sit at the general's table, but I don't want to be seen as trying to be something I'm not."

"You'll be fine, Laura. I declare, I've never seen you so fludduh-feddered, as Rina would say. Are you sure you don't have a secret crush on the good general?"

"No! How can you, of all people, think that? But see? That's exactly what I'm afraid of. I'd better put this silk dress back and find something less showy."

"That blue silk is gorgeous, and it sets off your eyes. You must wear it."

"But look at you—you're planning on wearing that modest dove-gray gown. Next to you, I'll look terribly bright and fussy."

"Ah, but you won't be 'next to me,' my dear. You'll be next to the general in his dress uniform. You mustn't look drab in comparison."

"Drab would suit me just fine. Then I could fade into the background."

"No. You must be lovely and a fitting companion for a general."

"I'm not his companion," Laura insisted, but she carefully smoothed away the wrinkles as she placed the blue gown into the trunk.

Such indecisions and delays meant that the women's carriage arrived at the dock just in time to see the *Flora* steaming away toward Beaufort. "Now I don't have to go at all." Laura breathed a sigh of relief.

"Oh, yes, you do. The men will just have to row us across."

"That will take too long."

"Perhaps so, and we may be late for the ceremony. But you are going to be there, and you're going to be the belle of the ball, Laura Towne."

The band of the Eighth Maine took their seats on the platform. Steamers sent upriver to pick up the white teachers and superintendents from Beaufort began arriving around ten o'clock, while other civilians and regular Army officers added their carriages and horses to the throng. The companies of Colonel Higginson's colored regiment marched out in some sort of order and took their positions, sitting or standing, around the base of the platform. The ceremony was scheduled to start at 11:30, and thanks to military discipline it did so, although newcomers were still arriving.

By the time Laura and her companions reached the camp, the opening speeches had ended. But they were in time to witness the most moving moment of the ceremony. Reverend Mansfield French had just presented Colonel Higginson with the new flag of his regiment. Higginson unfurled it and held it high for all to see. Then, from somewhere within the crowd, an elderly black man with a wavering and cracked voice began to sing, "My Country, 'Tis of Thee." One by one, the people around him joined in. Those on the platform, startled at first by this unscheduled moment, stood transfixed as the notes swelled and flowed around them.

Higginson wrote of the moment in his diary: "It seemed the choked voice of a race at last unloosed. Nothing could be more wonderfully unconscious; art could not have dreamed of a tribute to the day of jubilee that should be so affecting . . . Just think of it!—the first day they had ever had a country, the first flag they had ever seen which promised anything to their people."

When all the verses of the song had been sung, the program continued. Higginson handed his new flags off to two black members of the color guard, and with one or two more songs from the regiment, the crowd dispersed to their late, beef-laden luncheon. The people were unusually quiet and orderly, but everywhere one looked there were smiling faces and children with wonder in their eyes, as a multitude of former slaves now began to realize the real meaning of the word *Freedom.* Many of the attendees ate quickly and started their long journeys home, but for those honored guests who remained, there was a sumptuous sit-down midday meal followed by a dress parade and band concert. Lottie was delighted to visit Colonel Higginson's tent and to have some private conversation with him now that she felt less flustered.

Laura and her companions reboarded the steamer to go back to Beaufort. General Saxton was on horseback at the dock to wish them a pleasant sailing and a brief farewell until he should see them again at his reception that evening.

246

Spotting Laura, he rode close and pulled his horse into a rear and then a bow, although he came dangerously close to falling off. Laura smiled and relaxed a bit, deciding at last to enjoy his attentions without worrying about what people would think.

* * *

That evening, Laura looked resplendent in her blue silk gown as the general led her into dinner, seating her at his right hand. After dinner and some congenial discussion in the parlor, Laura and the general opened the dancing with a cotillion. Laura had not danced those elaborate figures for years, but she found that the steps came back to her. Flushed and smiling, she accepted the general's finishing bow and gratefully took his arm back to her seat.

"That was delightful. I enjoyed it immensely, but now you must pay attention to your other guests."

"I would rather spend the whole time with you."

"And have the entire island talking about us? I think not." She tapped him lightly on the arm with her fan, stopping for just a second to wonder where that flirtatious gesture came from. "Go on with you now. Nelly Winsor over there is perfectly safe, since she is firmly committed to her Mr. Fairfield. My Ellen would share a step with you. And there is always the beauteous Miss Thompson."

"Tilly? She can't hold a candle to you tonight, my dear."

"General . . ."

"All right. I will do as you say, but it would be more fun with you."

Laura turned to Mrs. Francis Gage and began a conversation about the efforts of the Sanitary Commission, while watching the goings-on from the corner of her eye. When the general and one of his captains pulled Nelly and Tilly into the center of the floor and began draping them in military scarves and swords, she swallowed a pang of jealousy and tried to look even more fascinated with the long story Mrs. Gage was telling her.

As the steamer delivered them to the dock below The Oaks, long after midnight, Laura was unusually quiet. Ellen watched her carefully but said nothing until they were in their room. "You had a good time tonight."

"Oh, I did. I had forgotten how much I loved dancing when I was a girl."

"And how much you enjoyed the company of an attractive man?"

"Ellen . . . I . . . I ignored you tonight, and I apologize. This should have been a night for us to rejoice in the achievement of a mutual goal. Instead, I let my head be swayed by the general's attention."

"And his intentions are . . ."

"I don't know!"

"What do you want them to be?"

"Again, I don't know. I'm flattered when he singles me out. He makes a charming companion. But I have no desire to go further than that. I can't even imagine being any closer to him than I am now. I'm not looking for a beau or a husband. I don't think I could ever bring myself to put his wishes above my own. I just . . . just . . ." She stumbled to a halt, unable to express herself more clearly.

"You enjoy feeling admired. And why not? There's nothing wrong with that. But don't lead him on, Laura, unless you are willing to make more of a commitment than you seem to be."

"There's little danger of that. I don't believe he's the marrying kind, any more than I am. He's married to his job. All his flirtations are just a nod to the joys of the season, I think. Now let's get some sleep before the sun comes up. The year ahead promises to keep us busy enough without worrying about a single romantic evening."

RINA ON "EMANCIPATION"
January 1863

Missus Laura done tole we dat we gots New Years off work ifn we wants fuh go fuh de Emancipation program. Not eberbody care bout dat. Zannah say she aint gwine nowheres, an ol Bess, she still caint walk good, but me an Hastins both wanna see dis ting fuh ourselfs. Sides, dey says dere gwine be meat an lasses water fuh eberbody. So we gits up as soon as de sky start fuh lighten, an wake de udders who gwine, an we all walks to de river. Hastings an de udder mens, dey rows we cross de river to Buford, an we waits at de dock.

Dere be a big crowd uh our people dere, all wantin fuh ride dat ferry fuh de fust time. When I sees de size uh dat boat, I aint so sho I wants fuh git on, but Hastins push me up de plank. He say jis don look at de water an don tink bout how deep it be. So, uh course, dat be jis what I does. But den de boat be movin, an it be too late fuh jump off.

Sumbody start singin "No Man Can Hinder Me," an we alls start singin long. We goes truh all kind uh verses—must uh bin de whole Bible dere—all bout dat Moses, an dat Jonah, an Noah, an all dem folk. Fore we knows it, we be comin to de dock at Port Royal.

Den we hasta walk some mo to de big army camp uh de new colored troop. Who'd a blieved dat dere could be a whole camp full uh colored soljers, all dressed up in uniforms an actin like white

251

folk? Hastins, he say he know where we be gwine cause he kin smell de beeves a cookin.

It were a sight fuh behold. All dem black people dere, all dressit up in dere Sunday best, an de black soljers in dey uniforms, an de white folk ridin in on dere horses an carriages. Dere be a band on de platform in front, makin hand-clappin music, an eberbody be in a good mood.

Course, de white officers, dey all hasta make speeches, mostly bout what a great day it be, an why we should all be happy an grateful. Hastins mumble dat he be grateful when he git sumptin fuh eat, but I tells him fuh hush. Den dey start wavin flags round, an dat ol man Zekial, from Mr. Eustis's place, he start singin "Muh Country 'Tis uh Dee." Eberting gots real quiet, an den folk start joinin in. Eben I starts singin, an Lawd know I caint sing much.

Bout den, dis all start makin sense fuh me. Dey sayin we be really free, an dat nobody caint hinder we no mo. I bin singin dose words long time, but I neber blieved dem fore. I looks round an sees people cryin fuh joy. Aint dat be sumptin!

Ater de ceremony, we alls goes ober to a grobe uh oak trees where dey hab tables settin. Some uh de white folk, dey's pourin out dat lasses water an slicin de beeves fuh we, stead uh we waitin on dem. Dat taste bedder den de food. Hastins be wantin fuh leave when we done eat, but I says I wants fuh walk round a lil mo. We hab de whole day off, don want fuh waste it. We may be free, but work be waitin fuh us tomorra.

All uh sudden, I pokes Hastins. Lookit ober dere, I says, pointin to sum uh de black soljers. Aint dat be ol Archibelle? Sho nuf, dere he be, all proud like in he blue coat an red pants.

Hastins wonder how he gots outta jail fuh killin dose cows, but I says dat jis like Archie. He know how fuh gits in on ennyting good.

So now I be ready fuh go home, cause I wants fuh tell Zannah dat I seen she boy. I tink she dint want fuh come today cause, as far as she knowed, he still be locked up. She gwine be happy fuh hear he be free, too.

28
LAND SALES
January 1863

The Emancipation Day celebrations continued all week. On Sunday, the Brick Church overflowed with guest speakers who had come to wish the freedmen well and offer them their advice. General Saxton was there, of course, along with a newcomer, General Truman Seymour, recently assigned to the Department of the South and commissioned by General Quincy Gilmore to assess the progress being made by the Port Royal Experiment. After the services, Laura invited all the guests to dinner and rode back to The Oaks with General Saxton, much to Ellen's amusement.

Conversation around the table started out congenially enough. The civilian guests had been delighted to hear the children sing at church, and Reverend French, feeling justifiably proud of the accomplishments of his fellow Gideonites, praised the work being done by the teachers. For the teachers and superintendents themselves, the major discussion was how word of the successes being realized there in the Sea Islands could make its way north to reassure their supporters.

Laura Towne, seated at one end of the table opposite Mr. Soule, the host, looked from Saxton on her right to Seymour on her left. "We are fortunate," she said, "to have the unwavering support of our military leaders. If it had not been for General Saxton and General Hunter, we might have had a much more difficult time. It's been quite hard to make our needs known when we are located so far from the centers of government."

"You must understand, my dear, that Mr. Lincoln has many other crises to deal with," General Seymour commented.

"And we are well aware of the recent challenges as a result of the Battle of the Peninsula," Mr. Soule added. "Still, our people have trouble understanding that they are free when they are not being paid for their labor."

"Military needs must take priority."

"Perhaps now that Lincoln has removed General McClellan from command, our armies will be more success-ful," Laura said, not meaning to set off an argument. Too late she realized that she might have done exactly that.

General Seymour pulled himself upright, almost quiver-ing with indignation. "And a rude job of it he did, too. A president needs at least to have a civil tongue."

Laura's eyes widened. "Rude? More like a determined commander, I would have thought."

Seymour postured himself into his best presidential imi-tation. *"My dear fellow, if you're not going to use your army, I'd like to borrow it for a while."* He glared around the table. "That's exactly what he said . . . to the finest general this Union Army has ever known . . . a true patriot . . . a man who has been desperately trying to find a way to hold the union together after this war has run its course."

And now it was General Saxton's turn to bristle. "You won't find much sympathy here for a general who is willing to preserve the institution of slavery in order to save that union."

"McClellan has not condoned slavery, and he is willing to make it forever illegal in any state that is not now tradition- ally based on that peculiar institution. But he is not will- ing to alienate the thousands of fine, upstanding gentlemen whose livelihoods rely on the labor of slaves."

"And how is that not condoning it?"

"He recognizes slavery as a necessary evil," Seymour said.

"There is no such thing. Evil is never a necessity. And those who employ evil means cannot be considered fine, upstanding gentlemen for doing so," Laura said.

"I spent a great deal of time in Charleston before the war, and I assure you that the slave owners I knew there were as decent a group of men as ever graced a dinner table."

"Or whipped a slave," Laura mumbled.

"It's a moot question, isn't it?" Saxton said. "The slaves have been freed by presidential decree, and no opinion, whether it be yours or General McClellan's, can change that now or in the future. Like water rushing over a waterfall, time moves on, and there is no way to stop it."

The dinner party broke up with everyone being civil, but Laura was left with a feeling of foreboding. The future did not look as rosy as it had on Emancipation Day.

* * *

Several days later, General Saxton arrived at The Oaks in mid-afternoon, hoping to catch Laura alone. They sat on the veranda, enjoying the cool air.

"I'm happy you came by, General Saxton. I've been hoping for a chance to apologize for introducing McClellan's name into the conversation the other day."

"No apology necessary, my dear, but I do wish you would learn to call me Rufus."

"Oh, I couldn't possibly do that. You are my superior, and I owe you my respect."

"I'm not your superior. In fact, I am your humble servant. And as your humble servant, I come bearing a small invitation."

"An invitation? I've been hoping the social scene is over for a while. It's past time for me to be back to work."

"But surely you need a day off once in a while. I was hoping you would accompany me on a tour of Admiral DuPont's warship, the *Wabash*. Miss Thompson has asked me to take her to see the ship, and I thought . . ."

"Miss Thompson! Matilda? Why in heaven's name is she interested in a ship all of a sudden?"

"Ah, she said she was just curious about it after hearing all the stories of the Battle of Port Royal, but she doesn't want to go see it as an unaccompanied lady. So she asked me to escort her."

"I'm sure she did—as if she didn't have a male member of her family to do that sort of thing!"

"Well, James is busy with his reporting duties for the paper, and she doesn't like to take him away from his important work."

"Of course not. While you, on the other hand, are only a general with all sorts of spare time on your hands." Laura shook her head in disgust. "You men really fall for a line like that, don't you?"

"I know how I've made it sound. And that's exactly why I'm inviting you to go along with us—so I don't look like I'm favoring her."

"You want me as a chaperone? I don't think so. I'll be busy that day."

"I haven't told you what day I'm talking about," the general pointed out impatiently.

"It doesn't matter. I'll be busy."

"Laura, please. You know I would rather spend time with you, and I was hoping, after our lovely dances on Emancipation Day, to increase our meetings. I'm very fond of you, you know."

"Please don't pursue this, General Saxton. You seem to be seeking a level of friendship with me that I am incapable of returning. I like you very much, sir, and I admire your principles. I enjoy our conversations. But we shall never be more to each other than we are right now."

Saxton looked startled. "I didn't mean to offend."

"And you didn't. But I know my own heart, and I know it is firmly committed to another. I don't want to hurt your feelings or lead you on. I would like us to remain on a business-like footing."

"Your wish is my command, fair lady."

Laura whirled on him in exasperation, and then laughed. "I'll take that as a bit of good-natured teasing."

"Among friends?"

"Among friends. Now, back to General Seymour and his obvious pro-slavery attitude. Whatever are we to do about him?"

"I don't think he is as bad as he came off sounding on Sunday. He and George McClellan are old friends, and no soldier enjoys seeing another put out to pasture, so to speak. At the moment, he resents Lincoln and supports McClellan in everything he has said. You simply walked into that tender topic at an inopportune moment."

"But isn't Seymour here to work with Colonel Higginson and the new colored regiment? How can he do that effectively if he doesn't accept emancipation? Is he going to treat the First South Carolina Volunteers as a band of slaves?"

"No, he's quite pleased with them, as a matter of fact. Fortunately for them—and for us—his pro-slavery sentiments apply only to the continued existence of the peculiar institution, not to individual slaves."

"How can he separate the two?"

"In his mind he can. And for that, we should be quietly grateful. I'm certainly not going to challenge him on his beliefs again, for fear of antagonizing him further. Besides, we are facing a much more difficult challenge."

"What's that?" Laura looked at him in alarm.

"I'd like to discuss it with all of you at dinner—if I am invited to stay, that is."

* * *

The announcement, when it came, caught the Gideonites off guard. At the end of dinner, Saxton commanded the attention of everyone at the table. "The tax commissioners have set February 11th as a day for land sales. All of St. Helena Island will be on offer."

"Except for our plantations, of course," Ellen said. There was more hope than conviction behind her words.

"I'm sorry, Miss Murray, but no. General Hunter and I have both been pushing Secretary Chase and the antislavery commissioners to add a provision to that effect, but so far, our protests have had no influence. Anyone who can come up with the cash will be able to buy a piece of this island, in any sized lot up to 320 acres."

"But what will happen to our efforts here?"

"It could well mean the end of the Port Royal Experiment, I'm afraid."

The assembled teachers and missionaries sat for a moment in stunned silence.

"They can't do that!"

"I'm afraid they can, Miss Murray. I'm not saying it will happen, but it would be wise for us to be prepared for that eventuality. Congress passed a law at the beginning of the war that gave the government permission to tax all the states, north and south, to support the war effort. Washington recognized that seceding states would ignore the levies, so the law provided a mechanism by which, once the Union Army took control of any rebellious area, the land could be confiscated for nonpayment of taxes and put to public auction to raise the local assessment."

"But what about all our people?"

"The law did not address that issue. In early 1861, no one had any idea that the slave owners would abandon their slaves or that so many Negroes would be living on the land when it was confiscated."

"But the tax commissioners have been in Beaufort since last fall, and they have all seemed like reasonable men who sympathized with our efforts."

"Yes, and we've been quietly hoping that their antislavery sentiments would protect us. But in the end, they are government employees charged with carrying out the letter of the law."

"But land speculators could come in here and . . ."

"It will all depend on who bids on the land. They could be good people with our best interests at heart, or they could be greedy land sharks just trying to make a quick profit when the war is over."

"There is one other possibility," Mr. Soule said. "I'm not sure I am at liberty to reveal this, but you should be aware of it. Mr. Philbrick has a plan to preempt the sale."

"Philbrick?" General Saxton asked. "He's your nephew, isn't he, or rather, he is married to your niece?"

"Yes, which is how I have come to know about the arrangements being made."

"I think you owe it to us to reveal what you know," Laura said. "This is too important an issue for us to keep secrets from one another."

"That's true, Miss Towne, but there's another consideration. This is no time for our little band to take different sides." Mr. Soule was still reluctant to break a confidence. "My niece told me of her husband's plans, but I have not talked to Philbrick about them myself. Perhaps I shouldn't have mentioned it at all."

"I am not optimistic about our chances of holding this island," General Saxton said, "but we must at least present a united front against anyone who would drive us out. Let me talk to Philbrick and learn what course he has in mind. Then perhaps we can work together to turn this happenstance into an opportunity for all of us."

* * *

Neither Ellen nor Laura could sleep that night. Into the small hours of the morning they worried about their future. The prospect of losing their schools just when they were beginning to show results was not something they were willing to face.

"And what about all the others who have made sacrifices to help us?" Laura fussed. "Will and Rosie are just settling into Frogmore. They've put up with so much hardship already—sickness, uncooperative slaves, the lack of furniture, difficulties in procuring rations from Hilton Head. If we now tell them they have to go home, they will surely regard this whole venture as a fool's errand."

"Your family loves you. They will understand that it is not your fault."

"Perhaps so, but they will still question my judgment in coming here in the first place. I would so like for them to stay long enough to learn to love these islands as I do."

"I understand how you feel, my dearest. So much good has taken place here already. And you are not alone in loving the area. Look at how many others have brought their mothers, their sisters, their fiancées here to establish permanent homes."

"Or very temporary homes, apparently!"

"It hasn't happened yet, Laura. And hand-wringing is not going to help. Perhaps we should be thinking more like Mr. Philbrick. Whatever his plan is, I give him credit for taking some sort of positive action."

"How do we take action against the U.S. government? It's hopeless."

"Things are never hopeless. Perhaps it is not my place to mention this, but don't you have a small trust fund?"

"Of course. Father left each of us enough to live on for our lifetimes. It was his way of avoiding the problems involved in trying to marry us off."

"So . . ."

"So? You mean, use it to participate in the sale?" Laura sat straight up in bed. "We could! We could bid for Frogmore and make it our very own." Then she hesitated, and her smile faded. "But would it be right? There's something of a moral issue here, isn't there? Seeking our personal desires and getting them simply because we can afford to pay for them? Wouldn't that be stealing the land from the Negroes who have worked it all these years? Don't they have more right to these lands than we do?"

"I'm not telling you that's what you should do. But it is one possibility. Perhaps there are others, too, if we just look for them."

29
CHALLENGING PHILBRICK
January 1863

eneral Saxton set out the following week to confront Edward Philbrick. The general's horse was frisky, happy to be out in the springlike breeze. Although the road was little more than a sandy path beaten through the fields, the first part of the trip across St. Helena Island was easy. I quite like this island in the winter, Saxton realized. It's quiet, the heat has not had a chance to build, and the bugs are gone. Or perhaps I just appreciate spending a January without ice and dirty slush. It's ironic that we should all be learning to appreciate our subtropical climate, just when the government threatens to drive us all out in the name of economy and protection from unseen dangers.

As he neared the spot where Mr. Hunn had established his Philadelphia store, a figure emerged from the heavy undergrowth that separated the road from the fields. Saxton pulled sharply on the reins to draw his horse to a skittish stop.

"Be you dat Genral Saxby I be hearin bout?" the man demanded without any preliminaries.

"Yes, I am. Uh, it's Saxton, actually. And you would be . . .?"

"I be Harry."

"I see. Well, Harry, is there something I can do for you?"

"Yessir. I need fuh talk wit you bout dese lan sales what be gwine happen."

"The land sales? You know about that?"

"Course I duz. I aint no dumb nigruh. I be a buyer."

Saxton stared at him for a moment and then dismounted. "It's time for a stretch. May as well take it here. Is there somewhere I could get my horse some water while we talk?"

"Yessir. Dere be a trough right ober dere, nex to de sto what blong to Massa Hunn. We kin squat a spell under dis tree whiles you waits fuh de horse fuh finish drinkin." To illustrate his point, he dropped easily to his haunches.

Not to be outdone, Saxton lowered himself carefully, smothering the groan that threatened to reveal how little he was used to sitting on the ground. "Now then, what's all this about? You are interested in purchasing some land, I take it. Tell me what it is you hope to buy."

"I be gwine buy me a reglar plantation ober on Ladies Island. I jis wants fuh be sho I knows how I sposed fuh do dat."

"Really? You have a place in mind?"

"Yessir. I be gwine buy me De Inlet."

"The Inlet? That's a 300-acre plantation."

"Yessir. Dat be what I be wantin."

"But . . . but . . ." Saxton floundered for a way to handle this situation. "Surely not, my good man. That's much too expensive an investment for a slave."

Harry glared at him. "I aint no slave. I be a free man, eber since Massa Pierce gots here an hire me fuh be he guide. Massa Pierce, he tell me I be as good as enny white man. I works fuh wages an I be savin muh money. I be a hard worker, an I neber spend none uh muh wages, neider. I jis be puttin all muh money in a jar fuh safe, an now I hab nuf fuh buy me de lan I wants." He finished his little speech with a defiant toss of his head.

"And exactly how much money have you saved?" Saxton asked.

"I hab zackly tirty-seben dollar an sixty-tree cent. I works hard fuh dat, true."

"I'm sure you did, Harry, but have you talked to anyone else about this purchase? How did you hear about the sale?"

"Massa Pierce, he tell me fuh talk to Massa Philbrick, but he aint be answerin muh question. Dat why I popped out at you de way I don. I hear Massa Philbrick tellin Missus Hayiat dat you be comin fuh visit dem purty soon, so I be watchin de road. I figures dat you be knowin much as ennybody roun here. But talkin fuh you be like talkin fuh Massa Philbrick. You be axin all kind uh question, but you aint be tellin me nuttin bout what I needs fuh know."

"I'm sorry, Harry. You are right. I do understand your concerns, and I wish I could be of more help. But the truth is, none of us knows what is going to happen with these land sales. That's why I'm heading out to Coffin Point to discuss it with Mr. Philbrick. I'll promise you this: as soon as we know exactly how the sale will be managed, I'll get word to you. But in the meantime, I think you ought to rethink your decision. I don't want to see you lose your money if it turns out that it's unwise to buy land right now."

"I be buyin me sum lan." Harry jumped up to emphasize his point. "It be jis a matter uh how I goes bout it. Don you goes tryin fuh change muh mind!"

"Harry, you don't know me, and you're right not to trust me. But you can trust the Gideonites who teach your children, can't you? Talk to someone like Miss Towne or Mr. Hooper before you decide."

"Neber mind." Harry stalked off and disappeared into the underbrush.

* * *

Much disturbed by the encounter, General Saxton remounted and urged his horse into a canter until they reached the overgrown road that led off through the woods to Coffin Point. Here they had to go slowly so that the horse could pick his way through the roots and brambles that clogged the road. The ancient oak trees blocked much of the sun, and their twisted branches loomed overhead, reminding the general of all the troubles that threatened this primitive island.

Saxton found Philbrick in what was, at one time, the dining room of this graceful and welcoming plantation house. The table now groaned under its weight of ledgers and stacks of papers. Small clumps of cotton decorated what had once been a service buffet. Chairs held piles of books. Edward himself sat hunched forward over a sheet of paper, carefully writing what appeared to be a letter. Saxton watched for a few moments, admiring the man's concentration and diligence. Then he cleared his throat gently, being careful not to startle Philbrick when his pen was touching the paper.

"What? Oh! General Saxton. I was not expecting anyone so early this morning."

"There was a lovely sunrise, and I enjoy an early gallop through the countryside. Opens the passages, you know."

"Well, do sit down. Oh. Here, let me move some of these things. And you'd best avoid that side of the room. Cotton lint gets everywhere when I'm trying to teach my superintendents how to tell when their crops have been properly ginned. Gracey! Bring some coffee for the gentleman, and make sure it's hot before you serve it this time." Philbrick bustled about, obviously a bit uncomfortable with his visitor.

Fully aware of his host's discomfort and more than a little puzzled by it, Saxton plunged directly into the question at hand. "Mr. Philbrick, I understand that you have been developing a strategy to deal with the upcoming land sales. I'd like to hear about it."

"Who told you that?"

"Does it make a difference? This is a matter that concerns everyone on this island, and I am responsible for the entire region. I need to be kept informed of any and all business matters. Since you did not see fit to come to me, I have come to you." Having thrown down that conversational gauntlet, Saxton stared fixedly at the younger man, waiting to see—and judge—his response.

Philbrick glanced at the papers on his makeshift desk and then studied a hangnail for a few seconds before appearing to make up his mind. He sat, leaned back in his chair, and steepled his fingers—a pose designed to appear professorial.

"I welcome the upcoming land sales, General. I believe it is a move that can help us prove the very concept I came here to demonstrate—"

"And that is?" the general interrupted.

"As a fervent abolitionist, I believe in the Negro's innate ability to take actions that are in his own best interests. I also believe that a system of paid labor produces better results than any system of slavery. From the beginning of my tenure here, I have had only one goal—to introduce these former slaves to the value of hard work and free enterprise. I want to see them fully employed in jobs they are well-suited to do, and I want to see them fairly compensated for their labor. I want them to learn how good it feels to be entirely self-sufficient—to be able to support their families through their own efforts without having to rely on handouts from anyone, no matter whether slave owner or government."

"You've been accepting government handouts here at Coffin Point from the first day of your arrival, have you not?"

"Yes, but only because our government has not made it possible to do otherwise. You should know that I came here at my own expense, and that I have already paid my workers once out of my own pocket. We have not yet established a system that will allow the Negro to take control of his own life; therefore, I have had to accept food doles and clothing handouts for them. But this is a system that will not—cannot—work in the long term."

"It's a noble goal, but far from realization, I'm afraid."

"It doesn't have to be. Put the land here into the hands of self-interested owners who will benefit from the hard labor of a well-paid workforce, and this land can blossom. Its people can blossom."

"So I will repeat my original question: What is this plan you have concocted?"

"I have been putting together a consortium of well-respected and honorable businessmen who are willing to make an investment in the future of South Carolina and its Negro population. With the help of John Murray Forbes, I now have fourteen such investors—abolitionists all, and all but one proper Bostonians. They have promised me the use of some $12,000 to buy up land on this side of St. Helena Island, where I know that there are healthful living conditions, rich soil, and an available work force.

"I intend to assume management of the plantations we buy with those funds, and I will entrust their day-to-day operations to superintendents I know and trust. I am personally guaranteeing that the plantations will make a profit. The workers will be paid regularly and well. The first profits beyond our labor expenses will go to repay the investments of the members of the consortium, including six percent interest on their funds. After that, I will take twenty-five percent of the net profit and reinvest the remainder. Once this terrible war is over, we will sell the plantations to those of our workers who wish to have their own lands.

"There is my so-called nefarious plan, General. All parties benefit. The cotton gets raised. The slaves become landowners. And, God willing, I will accomplish my purposes and be able, at last, to go home."

"I'm not convinced. Why not postpone the sales for a bit until we are sure that this is the course we want to follow?"

"I'm already sure of that, General. In fact, my experience tells me that we have already left the sale far too late. If it had taken place before the end of last year, Emancipation Day would have had an even deeper meaning. As it is, the plantations have been left in limbo. The current superintendents have had no authority or reason to stock their plantations with cattle or mules or fresh seed or new equipment. Fields have not been dressed. Our new purchasers are going to be facing a huge backlog of tasks at the same time as work in the fields must begin in order to assure a profitable crop."

"I would still prefer to see the land put directly into the hands of the Negro people who have poured their sweat and blood into it for the past two hundred years. It is by rights their land, and they have earned it just as truly as the American colonists did and as the settlers on our western frontiers are earning possession of their properties."

"There's a huge difference there, General. You are comparing ignorant slaves to people who founded this land out of their strong stores of knowledge and experience. The Negroes of South Carolina aren't ready yet. They are uneducated and barely Christianized. They can raise enough crops to feed themselves, but they can't handle the high-level negotiations needed to market a cotton crop. They don't have the capital to equip their lands with the tools necessary to produce and gin cotton. And they certainly do not have the sophistication to provide self-government."

"That's what the Gideonites are here for. You know that, Philbrick. You came as part of that band. But this plan you support will drive them away. If the lands are sold as the law is now written, our teachers and missionaries will lose their homes and their schools to land speculators who will have no reason to continue their work."

"First of all, the idea that land speculators are going to come swarming in here to buy up all the land is simply nonsense. I don't have to remind you that there's a war going on. Land speculators are not inclined to spend their funds on an unsafe investment. And until the war is over, we can't be sure that the old plantation owners will not return and claim their lands. Some of the people I have approached back in Boston have warned me about the real possibility that any sales will be nullified at the end of the war. Even if a few speculators do purchase the properties, there is little likelihood that they will actually come down here to work the fields. They'll be content to leave conditions as they are for the time being. Life as you know it will continue as usual."

"Perhaps so, but . . ."

Philbrick did not like being interrupted on his soapbox and held up a hand to silence Saxton. "Furthermore," he said, "the Gideonites are going to go home anyway, as are the soldiers and the cotton agents, and the freelance plantation managers who have come here ostensibly to help. None of them have an abiding interest in the Low Country or its people. They are here to make themselves feel useful, to do a good deed or two, or to feather their own nests. Not one of them has a permanent stake in seeing this land succeed. Only property ownership can provide that, and I don't see any of them lining up to put their own money into the effort needed."

Saxton shook his head in dismay. "I think you are being unfair to some very good people. I grant you that not all the Gideonites have done a good job here, but I believe their motives are pure."

"And I think you are confusing 'do-gooders' with those who do well. The Gideonites are the former, and I am an example of the latter. I am the only one of the plantation managers who made a profit in the past year. And that is precisely because I had my own money invested in it. Human motivation has always required a system of rewards, and the most effective reward is monetary. Landownership is the only solution to the problems that exist here in the islands, and I intend to see that we implement it as quickly as possible. I advise you not to try to stop me by preventing the land sales."

General Saxton left Coffin Point feeling dejected. He knew that much of what Philbrick had said was accurate, even though he did not like hearing it. The Port Royal Experiment had become a personal crusade for him, and his friendships with several of the Gideonites themselves caused him to worry about their futures. Slumped in the saddle, he allowed his horse to pick his way through the forest paths without guidance. When he reached the village, however, he suddenly kicked the horse into a gallop, hoping desperately not to be stopped again by Harry.

30
A PRAGMATIC WOMAN
January 1863

At The Oaks, everyone's nerves remained on edge throughout January. Even Laura and Ellen caught themselves snapping at one another. It's just the letdown after all the excitement of the holidays and emancipation, Laura told herself. That, and the winter doldrums, even if winter isn't so very nasty down here. We'll all feel better once spring arrives. But that excuse did not stop her from rounding on Ellen at the slightest provocation.

"We haven't seen much of General Saxton lately," Ellen remarked one evening at dinner.

"And good riddance!"

"I thought you and he were getting along famously. Didn't he invite you back to Hilton Head for some fancy occasion?"

"That 'fancy occasion' was nothing more than a tromp around the admiral's flagship and a pick-up lunch in the officer's mess. I didn't bother to go."

"Laura! You stood him up?"

"No, I simply told him I wasn't feeling well and wouldn't be able to attend."

"But . . ."

"But nothing. He had the lovely Miss Thompson to hang on his arm and bat her eyelashes at him. He didn't need me."

"You would sound almost jealous if I didn't know better," Ellen teased.

"Jealous? How dare you!"

"I was joking, Laura."

"I'm sorry, my dear, but I do get tired of people trying to make a couple out of us. If the truth be known, I think we'll hear about many more occasions when he and Miss Thompson get cozy together. Apparently, the man is indeed looking for a wife, and Matilda certainly is ready to sink her claws into any available man she can get her hands on. Mark my words. They'll be the talk of the island before long."

"I, for one, think that would be lovely," Charlotte Forten commented. "It's very lonely down here for all those men cooped up together with so few available women."

"Ah, Charlotte," Nelly said. "Is that why you've been getting so many letters from Hilton Head lately? Every time I have to sort the mail packet, I find an envelope addressed to you."

"They're just from Dr. Rogers. I told you we knew each other back in Philadelphia when I was his patient. He keeps in touch to make sure my health remains good."

"How unusually kind," Nelly said. "And then he tells you how lonely he is?"

"He's mentioned that it is a problem among his men, yes. There's nothing more to it than that." But Charlotte felt herself beginning to flush and gave silent thanks for her dark complexion.

* * *

General Saxton returned to The Oaks on February 1st, arriving just at suppertime, but he was so sunk into his own gloom that he did not even notice Ellen Murray's sharp little jibes about his meal mooching. The others at the table soon picked up on his mood as he shoved the hominy around on his plate. As usual, it was Laura who stepped in to break the uncomfortable silence.

"Come, General Saxton. Something is obviously wrong. Why don't you tell us what you learned from Mr. Philbrick when you visited him last week?"

"It's nothing but more bad news, I regret to say."

"He didn't tell you about his plan?"

"Oh, he told me. He told me in great detail and in emphatic terms. But it's a plan to benefit Mr. Philbrick, not a plan to save the Port Royal Experiment."

"But surely he understands—"

"The man understands money. Don't try to talk to him about anything else."

"I think you're being unfair to Edward," Mr. Soule said. "He has worked hard at Coffin Point to take care of the people on the plantation. He provides schools, just as we do here, and he has treated his workers more than fairly."

"So he told me. He believes in the abolitionist cause, and he is dead set on proving that a well-paid Negro can produce a profitable cotton crop. But his interest stops there. I didn't see any evidence that he is concerned about the Negroes themselves."

"Come, General. We still haven't heard his idea. What is he planning to do to preempt the land sale?" Laura was growing increasingly impatient.

"He's not trying to preempt the sale. He wants it to take place as quickly as possible. His only plan is to turn it to his own advantage."

"How?"

"He has backers. He described them as 'a consortium of well-respected and honorable businessmen'—Boston abolitionists who have given him access to some $12,000. With that money he is planning to buy up all the plantations on the far side of St. Helena and turn them into cotton-producing bonanzas. He'll be hiring away our best plantation superintendents to run his plantations for him, and luring the best Negro workers with the promise of high wages paid on time."

"I can't believe he plans to become a Southern planter!"

"Only until the end of the war, apparently. He's going to limit himself to taking a mere twenty-five percent of the profits, turning the rest into more land purchases. Then, when the war is over, he'll sell the land to whoever wants it and go back to Boston a wealthy man." Saxton was fairly snarling as he finished his description.

"You mean he's going to make the Negroes work the land for him, pocket the profits, and then force the workers to pay him again for the privilege of owning the land that should have rightfully been theirs from the beginning?"

"That's right. And he justifies it by saying the Negroes do not know enough to be ready for landownership. I didn't hear him explain why they'll be any more knowledgeable at the end of the war."

"Wait." Ellen stepped back into the discussion. "Didn't you say that he is planning to purchase the plantations on the far side of the island—those near where he lives now? Maybe he's counting on our schools to provide that training."

"You're always the optimist, Ellen dear." Laura smiled at her.

"I just can't believe that he has not taken our positions into account."

"He hasn't, Miss Murray. He doesn't care about your schools, any more than he cares about his workers' desire to own their own land. He has no plans for the rest of the island. The most he would say was that he thought the people who buy up the rest of the land will not bother to exploit it until after the war. That, of course, would mean that you could go right on with what you are doing until . . ."

"Until somebody throws us out." Laura pushed herself away from the table and strode to the window, staring out into the darkness. After a few moments, she returned to the table, leaning on her hands to glare at the assembled dinner guests. "We have to do something—anything—to stop this sale."

"There's nothing to be done, Miss Towne."

"Nonsense. Good people can always find a way to combat evil."

"That's a nice sentiment," Mr. Soule said, "but not very practical."

"On the contrary, sir. It is nothing if not practical. What Mr. Philbrick is planning is wrong. Therefore, we have a responsibility to prevent his actions. Who has the ultimate authority to stop the sale, General?"

Saxton shrugged and shook his head. "Congress, I suppose, but you can't get to them in time. The sale is just weeks away."

"But the sale will be taking place right here in Beaufort. Isn't General Hunter the one in command here?"

"I've already talked to Hunter, Miss Towne. You know he is on the side of the slaves and a supporter of your efforts, but he can't countermand a congressional decision."

"Yes, he can! Think back for a moment." Laura's face was suddenly animated as she worked through the idea that had just occurred to her. "When Hunter issued his emancipation decree back in May, didn't he also declare that all these islands now fall under martial law?"

"Yes, he did so, but you know how that decree ended up. The president stepped in and voided it."

"Not exactly. Hunter claimed that martial law in South Carolina was a military necessity. And then he claimed that slavery and martial law were incompatible. Lincoln said that Hunter had not been authorized to make proclamations about slavery and voided that part of the decree, but the president never questioned Hunter's right to exercise martial law here, and he never punished or censured Hunter for what he had done."

"You're talking technicalities."

"Yes, sir, I am. A technicality is exactly what we need. Someone needs to present General Hunter with a rational plan to stop the sale on grounds of military necessity."

"I fail to see—"

"General Saxton! Would you please quit telling me that this thing is impossible while I'm busy doing it?"

Saxton's face had such a startled expression that Ellen snorted into her cup of tea. Laura glared at her, and then the two shared a conspiratorial grin before Laura launched into her plan.

"I can think of at least three reasons why the sale of our lands will adversely affect Hunter's military mission. First, he has granted the plantations the right to arm our own guards against any incursions by rebel troops or returning planters. Every plantation guard means one less soldier who needs to be deployed to protect the borders of his military district. If this land passes into the hands of absentee owners, there will be no one here to stop such an invasion."

"That's a good point," Mr. Hooper agreed. "I've heard the general speak about the good job the Negro guards have been doing. He was delighted not long ago when they caught those Rebs trying to sneak into the village."

Laura nodded in his direction but held up her hand to prevent further discussion. "Second, the encampment at Hilton Head has, from the very beginning, relied on local produce to help feed the troops and provide timber and building materials for the camp. If this half of the island falls back into rebel hands, that supply line will be cut. Even if Mr. Philbrick manages to keep his plantations in production, it sounds to me as if he plans to concentrate on his cotton crop, not corn or vegetables, not poultry and cattle, and certainly not timber. Our continued existence here can be accurately described as a military necessity on those grounds."

By now, Saxon was paying close attention. "Go on," he urged.

"The third military necessity is manpower for his new First South Carolina Volunteers. Hunter has been trying to build that regiment ever since he arrived. He needs strong black men who are willing to accept military regulations in exchange for the promise of a regular source of income. But you know how hard it has been to convince our Negroes to join the Army. Military life is totally foreign to their nature. Even when they do join, desertion is an ongoing problem among young men who go off without warning to visit their families. How much greater will the problem be if Philbrick is offering those same men a steady wage and the promise of land to buy at the end of the war?"

"No arguments on the grounds of moral responsibility?"

"No, not this time. General Hunter understands the moral grounds for our opinion, but he also knows that he is almost alone in his sympathy for the freed slaves. He needs an unemotional argument, and that's what you can offer him— three reasons why the land sales will threaten the stability of the Army's hold on the Sea Islands."

"You never cease to amaze, Miss Towne. Who would have thought that such a gentle little lady could be so hard-headed?"

"I'm not hard-headed, general. But I am a pragmatist. I believe in doing what has to be done. Will you take my case to Hunter, or do I need to do it myself?"

"I'll talk to him first thing in the morning. And thank you. I find the way your mind works to be perfectly frightening, but I'm glad it works on the side of the angels."

31
A PARADE OF VISITORS
January 1863

The women of The Oaks had settled themselves for a light lunch, enjoying the novelty of being together without any guests or the conversation-dominating presence of their male colleagues. Laura looked from her beloved Ellen to Lottie Forten and Nelly Winsor, smiling privately at the camaraderie that had developed among these four very different women. "What a nice change," she remarked. "I scarcely know how to eat in companionable peace and quiet."

"I agree," Ellen said, "but I'm really surprised that we have not heard from General Saxton about his meeting with General Hunter."

"We don't know that the meeting has even taken place," Laura responded. "I trust him to gauge the right moment to present his arguments. I know the matter seems pressing to us, but the sale is not scheduled for almost a month from now. We can bide our time."

"Perhaps so," Lottie said, "but I'm not sure my people can. There's a great deal of unrest out in the slave village. I'm hearing the same question over and over—'What be gwine happen fuh we?' The sooner we can answer that, the better."

"I understand that, but I'm not going to push the general into precipitous action and risk jeopardizing our case."

"Scuse me, missus, but dere be a gemmen out here. He be axin fuh Massa Soule. What does I tells he?"

"Who is it, Rina?"

"Dat buckra dat be livin in de house at Coffin Point."

"Mr. Philbrick?" The women exchanged startled glances before Laura pulled herself into her best stiff-spined posture. "Bring him in here, Rina, and set an extra plate. We can be gracious for the sake of finding out what's on his mind."

"Maybe he won't want to talk to us," Nelly said.

"He's a well-bred Bostonian. He'll be polite."

Laura stood and moved to the doorway. "Mr. Philbrick. How nice to see you. Won't you join us for our midday repast? We've just been remarking how strange it feels not to have any gentlemen at our table."

"I thank you kindly, but I'm really looking for those missing gentlemen. Will they be back soon?"

"I'm afraid they are occupied for most of the day. Mr. Soule has gone to the village with some supplies. Mr. Hooper is working in Hilton Head this week, and Mr. Fairfield, of course, is teaching his classes over on Ladies Island. Perhaps we can be of assistance, or at least pass on a message?"

"Actually, I'm here with a petition. I'm hoping to get every one of our band of Gideonites to sign a request that the land sales be carried out without delay for the good of the citizens of St. Helena Island."

Laura took a deep breath to give herself time to formulate an answer. "I doubt very much that you will get any such signatures on this side of the island. Our staff is much opposed to the coming land sales."

"And I don't understand why that is!"

"Such sales threaten our mission here, Mr. Philbrick. If our plantations are sold to land speculators, our schools will close and our Negroes will either be driven out of their homes or reduced once more to the evils of slave labor. We'll be forced to abandon the very people we have come here to help. I refuse to countenance that."

"You're exaggerating the dangers, I believe. Land speculators are not going to move in while there's a war going on."

"Then why hold the sale? What's your rush?"

"Look, Miss Towne. The government has badly mismanaged this entire region. They have a war to run, I understand, but they have neither the financial resources nor the needed expertise to train these ex-slaves for productive citizenship. We need to get the land into private hands so that it can be made profitable again."

"Then why not make it possible for the people who have actually raised the cotton here for generations to purchase the land?"

"Because they're not ready."

"Nonsense!" Lottie glared at him.

"You're still struggling to teach them the alphabet and to count to ten."

"They're making tremendous progress."

"But not enough to take over complex matters of marketing their crops. No, my dears, you don't understand what all is involved in agricultural productivity."

"Please don't be condescending, Mr. Philbrick. We're quite aware of the problems. That's why we don't want to see the land sold until our people are ready to claim their rightful inheritance."

"Inheritance? What an unusual term."

"They do have an inheritance here. They have poured their labor and sweat—and yes, even their blood—into this land for generations. It's rightfully theirs, and I refuse to let anyone take it away from them."

"With all due respect, ma'am, you don't have a voice in this matter. You are only a woman. I will be asking that the sales go on as soon as possible. Even February 11th is too late if we want new owners to have time to equip their plantations properly before the start of the growing season. I will be asking for—and I expect to get—the signatures of every white male on this island. You ladies will just have to tend to your knitting and trust me and my colleagues to manage the affairs of the plantations."

"Mr. Philbrick." Laura's voice was cold but steady. "You came here as a missionary to take on a humanitarian task—to help the abandoned slaves, not to become a cotton entrepreneur and line your own pockets."

"I'm not interested in 'my own pockets.' I simply want to prove what I have always believed—that with proper management, the Negro can be taught to farm this land successfully. I am still a supporter of that humanitarian cause you speak of. I simply see a different path to its accomplishment."

"I do not believe that any man can serve two masters. You must either be interested in making a profit—and using the slaves to do that to your own advantage—or you must care more about the long-term welfare of the people involved than about your personal balance sheet. I wouldn't trust myself to do what you are suggesting, and I doubt you are a better man . . . uh . . . a better person than I am."

"And you are an irritating and opinionated woman! I came here to discuss this matter with rational gentlemen. I'll excuse myself until such time as I can do that."

The encounter left the women feeling unsettled and concerned about the strength of Mr. Philbrick's plan. Even Laura was more worried, now that she realized how deeply involved he was. As she later explained to Ellen, "I thought he was purely interested in the money. That made him easy to attack. But I realize now that he really thinks he is helping the Negroes by his actions, and that makes him more dangerous. Those who can find a way to claim that God is on their side have an advantage in any argument. If he truly believes this is a virtuous cause, he'll be more persuasive in his arguments. And when we argue against him, he can make it appear that we are also arguing against God's will. I'm not sure how to counter that."

* * *

Tensions increased even further two days later, when Rina appeared once again to announce visitors. "Massa Eustis be here, Missus Laura, an he be habbin two udder ladies wit he."

"Ladies? Who are they?"

"I don know. He not be sayin. He jis want fuh see you."

Laura went to greet the visitors cheerfully, not anticipating that she would find the ladies already wandering about the parlor, examining the furniture and peering into the cupboards around the fireplace. "Mr. Eustis? What can I do for you? You've missed breakfast, I'm afraid, but I can have Janie put something together if need be."

"Thank you, no, Miss Towne. I'm just delivering these two prospective buyers to you, and then I'll be on my way back. Ladies, I'll be here with the boat to pick you up around three o'clock, when the tide turns." And with that announcement, he scurried off the porch as if he knew that a storm was about to break.

Prospective buyers? What on earth . . .? "Excuse me," she said to the nearer of the two women. "I'm Laura Towne, head of the Negro schools here on St. Helena Island. May I help you?"

"Oh, Miss Towne. The commissioners said we might find you here."

"Might find me here? I live here. And you are . . .?"

"I suppose we are being rather rude. I'm sorry. I'm Mrs. Shaw, and this is my friend, Mrs. Day."

"I see. And you are here because . . .?"

"Because we're going to buy The Oaks, of course."

"You're what? I hardly think so. The Oaks is not for sale."

"Of course it is. The tax commissioners have it listed in the upcoming land sale. Judge Abram Smith showed me the listing himself. We're looking for a place we can turn into a comfortable retreat—somewhere we can go occasionally to get away from the terribly military atmosphere of Fort Welles on Hilton Head Island. Being the wives of army officers is sometimes a real burden, you know. We are constantly surrounded by those hordes of unwashed enlisted men, with their monotonous rows of tents and their dusty streets. And there's absolutely no social life, particularly in the summer."

Laura stood speechless, staring at this clueless woman. "There's been a horrible misunderstanding," she said at last. "Has no one told you about the health dangers here on the island? No white people live here in the summer. There's too much disease."

"That's not what we were told. In fact, Judge Smith said that the woman in charge here—wouldn't that be you?—said there was little or no danger of disease. You won't manage to discourage us with that argument."

"I was just trying to be helpful."

"I doubt it. But whatever your motives, it won't work. We definitely plan to buy this plantation next month. So, if you would be so good as to show us around the house . . ."

"And while we're doing that, you could have your slaves saddle us a couple of horses so we can ride around the property and survey the fields and outbuildings," Mrs. Day added.

"No." Laura had reached her limit of patience. "You may certainly prowl around the house if that's why you are here. The bedrooms are upstairs. You may open the drawers and trunks and snoop in them, too, if you like, but I will not ask my 'slaves' to get you horses. We have no slaves here."

"But surely there are slaves to do the cooking and cleaning, and stable hands and field workers and such? Whatever would we do without any help to manage this huge place?"

"If you remember, Mrs. Day, slavery was abolished as of January 1st. Didn't you attend the celebration? I would have thought you would have enjoyed that . . . social event."

"But I saw all sorts of black faces when we arrived. Aren't they your sl—servants?"

"There are Negro workers here, it is true, but they have legitimate jobs to do, and none of their duties include saddling horses for nosy strangers."

"Well, I've never heard such impertinence!"

"Furthermore, if this plantation goes up for sale, I will bid on it myself and raise any offer you can make, and then I'll give the land to the Negroes who have lived here all their lives."

"Miss Towne, I am fully aware of, and in favor of, emancipation, but I cannot believe you would allow the Negroes to own this house and its lands. Why, they would just ruin it in no time!"

"My, my. What convenient consciences you have when it comes to money matters! I'm through discussing it. Do what you like until Mr. Eustis comes back for you, and be grateful we don't run you off the land and make you swim for it. But I promise you, you will never own this land!"

* * *

One more visitor that week served to remind everyone at The Oaks of the high stakes riding on the land sales. The staff had assembled for dinner on Friday evening. No one had heard from General Saxton, and the longer they waited, the greater was their anxiety. Mr. Hooper had returned from Hilton Head, but he had nothing to report. "I just don't know, Miss Towne. Almost everyone believes that the sales will occur and forthwith solve all the problems of occupation."

"The more fools they," Laura answered. "I find it simply incomprehensible that more people do not recognize the rightness of our position here and the virtues of what we are trying to accomplish."

"The military officers and the whites living in Beaufort do not see what we see every day. They simply hear of an opportunity to purchase land cheaply and . . ."

"Cheaply for them, perhaps, but ridiculously expensive for the poor Negro who simply wants his few acres to support himself and his family."

"Of course you are right, but—"

"Scuse me, missus." Rina stood in the doorway again.

"Rina, please quit eavesdropping on our conversations!" Laura's snappish reaction startled everyone.

"But I aint be droppin eaves, missus. Dat fellow, Ol Harry. You members de one done work fuh Massa Pierce? He be waitin in de kitchen cause he gots a problem an sumbody tole him fuh bring it here."

"Ask him in, Rina," said Mr. Soule. "What's one more problem at this stage?" A few minutes later, Harry shuffled in, hat in hand and looking sheepish. "I sho don want fuh disturb your eatin," he said.

"It's quite all right. Have a seat and tell us what you need."

"No, ma'am. I kin stand. But I tole dat Genral Saxby bout sumptin, an he say fuh ax you."

"General Saxton? What's this about?"

Harry poured out the whole tale of wanting to buy The Inlet on Ladies Island and farm it himself. "It be tree hunnert acres, sho nuf, but I be savin all muh wages an I gots tirty-seben dollar an sixty-tree cent now fuh pay fuh it. But Massa Philbrick, he say I caint buy it cause I be gwine lose all muh money. He say he want fuh buy it heself, an den he be gwine let me work it fuh wages. I don know what fuh do. I tole dat genral an he say fuh ax Miss Towne. So here I be."

For every person sitting at that table, Harry's plight struck a nerve. He was the epitome of the problem of the land sales. They heard the voice of a hard worker with a strong desire to make something of himself. All he wanted was a chance to own his own land. But they also realized that he had no understanding of the economics of land purchasing. They agreed on one point: Mr. Philbrick should not be allowed to destroy Harry's dream.

"Don't trust Mr. Philbrick." Laura spoke for them all. "You must never believe someone who says he'll buy your land in his own name, and then let you use it. That's a slave's bargain. You would be better off with a five-acre farm you could call your own."

"But I gots muh heart set on dat plantation at De Inlet, an I gots lots uh fambly members who be willin fuh hep work it."

"Then I'll offer you another solution." Mr. Hooper walked around the table and offered Harry his hand. "I admire your ambition, and I trust your ability. If the land sales happen, I want you to go to the sale and bid on that plantation until you get it. You put in your money and claim The Inlet in your own name. If you don't have the money to pay the bill, I will lend you the rest of the purchase price, and you can pay me back some day out of your profits."

"Oh, tankee, Massa Hooper. Dat be mos kind uh you. I promises I be gwine pay you back."

Laura blinked furiously, determined not to let anyone see her tears.

32
AN EQUITABLE SOLUTION
February 1863

B y Sunday, Laura's nerves were frazzled. "I swear," she told Ellen, "if General Saxton is not at church, I'm going to go to Hilton Head, track him down, and shake the news out of him. I can't stand this not knowing what is to become of us. And if he hasn't yet done what I asked, I'll do that myself, too."

Ellen grinned. "You would just do that, too, wouldn't you? What a lovely scene you would make. But remember, just a couple of days ago, you were urging me to be patient."

"Yes, but that was you, not me."

"There's a difference?"

"Of course there is. I don't have to pay attention to me." The joking lifted their spirits as the old horse plodded its way toward the Brick Church. Laura caught her breath as their carriage turned into the churchyard and she spotted a familiar white stallion. "He's here," she whispered. "At last we'll know."

"Are you sure you're not just excited to see him?" Ellen teased.

Laura glared at her for a moment before sharing her grin. "You know better than that. But I won't be able to bear it if he doesn't tell me the news this instant." Lifting her skirts indelicately above her ankles, she jumped to the ground and dashed across the grass.

General Saxton watched her approach, making an effort to appear solemn but failing to restrain a chuckle. He grasped her arms to slow her down. "Whoa, there, my dear. I don't want to see you trip and fall on your face before I have a chance to say 'good morning'."

"Is it a good morning, General?"

"It's always a good morning when I get to see my beloved physician."

Laura refused to rise to his bait. "You can be so exasperating. You must know how anxious we all have been about your talk with General Hunter. And we've heard nary a peep from you. Please don't tease any more about it. If he didn't agree to stop the sale, tell me and get it over with."

She looked so wide-eyed with foreboding that Saxton had to force himself not to embrace her. "Of course he accepted your arguments, my dear. And he knew they came from you, by the way. He as much as told me I wasn't clever enough to think of those things without you to coach me along."

Laura missed the slight touch of bitterness in his words. All she heard was the affirmation of her hopes. "So the land sales have been stopped!"

"Temporarily. They will not occur until General Hunter has been assured by Congress that certain plantations will be set aside for two purposes—to meet his military needs and to provide affordable small farms for those former slaves who wish to purchase their land. Judge Smith leaves for Washington on Wednesday to present Hunter's demands."

"And you think Congress will approve?"

"Of course they will. I've helped to draft the petition that will go before the House and the Senate. Hunter used all three of your arguments and added an additional one of his own. Can you believe it? You actually missed a point."

"I'm sorry. What was it?" Laura was beginning to notice the tinge of criticism beneath his words.

"Well, point number four reminds them of the Edisto slaves who were dropped into our lap, and it asks what he is to do the next time a band of refugees from the interior makes its way to our islands seeking the protection of the Union Army. He declared that he must have contingent lands available to him."

"That's a pretty open-ended proposal. Does it mean that Mr. Philbrick's plans will be squelched?"

"You mustn't get your hopes up too far. Hunter's specific requests are for this side of St. Helena. He'll let Philbrick go ahead with his purchases on the far side because he will be a stabilizing influence over there, relieving the Army of any responsibility. But your plantations and your schools should all be protected."

The church bell suddenly stopped its chiming. "We'd best be going in," Laura said. "I have many prayers to send up today. But please come back to The Oaks for dinner after the service. I want to hear every detail."

"I wouldn't miss it."

* * *

If General Saxton was hoping for more time alone with Laura, he was disappointed, for all the Gideonites were eager to hear what had occurred. As soon as they finished eating, they adjourned to the sunny veranda, out of earshot of the servants. "We'll want to be careful about how much we tell the Negroes," Mr. Soule said. "We don't want to get their hopes up and then disappoint them. We'll have to explain carefully how the sales will go, so that they understand that land is not just being given to them."

"I doubt that we'll manage to control the message," Mr. Fairfield said. "They are all such gossips. Nelly, what was the phrase that Rina used? She said she was not 'droppin eaves' when all the time she was listening at the door?"

"Something like that. But they do eavesdrop, of course, when we don't take them into our confidence."

"Let's try to keep this under wraps until we know exactly what Congress decides."

"And I can't tell you that," General Saxton said. "All I can tell you is what General Hunter has proposed. And, mind you, he is trying to appease all sides in this."

"That doesn't make me rest any easier," Mr. Fairfield mumbled.

"I find it reassuring," Laura countered. "We need to present a united front, not one split into warring factions. We've had enough of that sort of thing already."

"Here's the rundown. When the tax commissioners compiled their list of saleable properties, they included all plantations that had not paid their taxes. And that was everybody, with the exception of Mr. Eustis, who is in that strange dual role of Gideonite and Southerner. The new rule will say that a plantation cannot be sold for less than three-quarters of its estimated value. So, for example, the tax records show that The Oaks itself is worth some $5,000, and the lands of the plantation are worth an additional $2,000. A speculator would have to bid at least $5,250 in order to purchase the entire plantation. That's much too much to risk during wartime, when titles to land are so uncertain. So there won't be any bids on the largest plantations, and they will be reserved for the use of the Army and for resettling the Negroes."

"But that doesn't allow the Negroes to buy any land, either. If white land sharks can't afford it, the ex-slaves certainly cannot."

"And what about Mr. Philbrick's consortium?"

"Well, the lands he is proposing to buy are much less valuable at the moment than is a place like The Oaks. Those plantations are, for the most part, small and unimproved. He should be able to claim quite a few, but he'll have to spend most of the consortium's money to do so."

"And the Negroes," Ellen insisted. "What about their ability to buy?"

"Another part of the Hunter proposal asks for a formal declaration of the right of ex-slaves to purchase land they have worked at the rate of $1.00 per acre. It's called preemption. That's enough to provide them with their hoped-for ten acres and a mule."

"When will the sale take place?"

"Right now, Hunter is suggesting February 27th through March 1st. That's a delay of a little more than two weeks, which should give us time to get formal approval from Congress and get the word out, at least to local buyers. Those Northern land sharks everyone has been worried about won't hear about it in time, I'm afraid, which should alleviate some of your other worries."

"Mr. Philbrick won't like it," Mr. Soule said, shaking his head. "He wants the sales done now."

"Whatever happened to that petition of his?" Saxton asked.

"Just as I suspected," Laura said, "those people who have accepted superintendent positions with him signed the petition—Charles Ware, William Gannett, and George Hull among them. But those who work closely with us, particularly Mr. Tomlinson and Mr. Ruggles, refused—quite vehemently, as I understand."

"Well, it matters not now. Nothing will happen until Judge Smith gets back with his report. Right now he's scheduled to return on the 24th."

* * *

Few things happen on schedule, of course, and the land sales were no exception. Judge Smith did return on the 24th, however, bringing word that the sales would go ahead under the conditions General Hunter had outlined. Laura wrote in her diary: "Hurrah! Jubilee! Lands are to be set apart for the people so that they cannot be driven off them."

Another piece of good news came with the appointment of Saxton and Hunter to serve on the tax commission, along with the three original appointees. "We may still be outvoted," Saxton explained to Laura, "but at least we will have a voice in choosing which lands will be marked out for military and educational use."

The arrangements for the sale, however, took longer than expected, and bids were not taken until March 8th. The delay gave a few dissenters time to voice their complaints.

William Gannett disapproved of the set-asides for the former slaves. "I think the government does well enough to offer the Negroes the protection of civil law and education. Beyond those basics, they ought to learn to live with what they have and be satisfied."

Ellen Murray was appalled at his attitude. "Would you not try to repay them somehow for their lost wages—and lost lives—during the last 200 years of bondage?"

"What you are advocating is charity," he answered, "and charity will reduce their independence. Slave owners gave them housing and food and clothing, and those gifts made them totally dependent on their owners. I don't want to see our government making the same mistakes. The Negroes are ambitious, intelligent, and resourceful. We ought to just leave them alone."

Charles Ware fussed against the new plans on other grounds. "Nobody seems to be thinking about the business aspects of all this," he told Mr. Soule.

"You've been listening to Mr. Philbrick for too long."

"At least he thinks like a businessman, not an empty-headed philanthropist. What's going to happen to the live-stock and possessions on land that is sold? What about the buildings, which have a value beyond the land they sit on? I don't see anybody taking those valuations into account. And what about the improvements the government has made to some of these lands? Will their costs be reimbursed? And by whom?"

Nevertheless, when the bidding was completed, most of the residents were satisfied. Among the plantations set aside for military and educational use were The Oaks and Oaklands, where the Hunns had established their sundries store. Near the top of the island, the T.B. Fripp lands and two planta-tions belonging to the McTureous holdings were marked out as guard posts to prevent incursions from the mainland. The four plantations along the road to Land's End and all those along Seaside Road were also reserved for both military and educational use. The common understanding was that they would, at some future date, be offered for sale when their usefulness declined.

Mr. Philbrick fared well, too. For a total expenditure of $7,000, he bought eleven plantations outright and leased two others. His holdings included Fripp Point, Cherry Hill, Mulberry Hill, the John Fripp plantation, and Pine Grove, along with another leased plantation on Ladies Island to be managed by George Hull.

No one was happier than Harry, who was able to purchase his coveted The Inlet with the help of a loan from Mr. Hooper. Laura sometimes remarked that they no longer saw much of Harry, but she and Mr. Hooper both understood that Harry was no longer hanging around because he now had land of his own and had turned into an industrious farmer.

Laura and Ellen still felt a twinge or two over not asking for a chance to purchase Frogmore plantation for themselves. "We could have afforded it," Laura admitted, "but it just wouldn't have felt right to me. I accused Mr. Philbrick of acting in his own self-interest, and then I realized that my desire for Frogmore came from the same impulse. I don't know if I could trust my own decisions if I had to choose between the welfare of my workers and the bottom line of my own balance sheet. And right now, I must put the needs of the people above my own. Perhaps someday . . ."

RINA ON "DESE WHITE FOLK"
February 1863

I sho don unnerstan dese white folk. Oh, I likes some uh dem jis fine. Missus Laura be good an kind to eberbody. When sumbody sick, she kin jis walk inna cabin an de sick person feel bedder. She always hab a cool hand an soft talk, an den she be bringin sumptin outta she black bag dat make de person feel good agin. I admires she mos truly.

An Missus Ellen, she de sweetest ting eber walk dis earth. She be so patience wit we when we be tryin fuh learn fuh read. She never git mad when we be stupid. She jis start ober an splain eberting agin. I aint much good at readin an I caint do dat writin fo ennyting, but she jis tell we fuh keep tryin. I loves de class she be teachin in de afternoon. We kin sit down an work at sumptin dat aint work.

But when dese white folk gits togedduh wit each udder, den dey gits all mad at each udder, an I don like none uh dem. Take what been goin on roun here bout dese lan sales. De folk what live here at De Oaks, dey says dat dey don want dis land sold, cause den dey be havin fuh move away. Dey acts like it be der lan, but it aint. Dey jis be movin in here cause it be empty. Den dey says de black folk need der own lan, but dey not be willin fuh give dem enny.

Den dat Massa Philbrick, he come down here fro Coffin Point, an he say all de lan gwine be sold to he, which make eberbody else

301

mad at he. An General Saxby, he say dat all de lan he gwine go to udder white folk who be comin down fro de nort.

What I wants fuh know, who give enny uh dem de right fuh sell de lan? It neber blong to dem atall. Massa Pope, he done buy dis lan bout ten year fore de Big Shoot an he build dis house special fuh he fambly. When de Big Shoot come, he be takin de fambly up to Aiken where dey be safe fro de big gun, but he aint neber gwine sell dis plantation to nobody. Dat why we all stays here when de fambly leave. We knows dis lan blong to Massa Pope, an we blong to he, too. So how kin dese white folk be gwine sell it? An what gwine become uh we? We sposed fuh be free, but it don sound like it when dey says we kin stay an work fuh de nex white folk what come here.

De wurst part uh all dis be de fightin mongst deyselfs. Dey teach we in chuch dat we gots fuh love we neighbor, but dey don act dat way demselves. Sometime Missus Laura make dat genral so mad he go stompin outta de house an jump on he horse an ride away inna middle uh de conversation. An dey be shoutin at each udder an callin Massa Philbrick sum ugly name.

I ax Missus Laura de udder day bout de lan sale, an she say sumptin dat don make no sense atall. She say, "Don worry, Rina. Nobody gonna buy De Oaks, cause we gwine puts de price up so high dat nobody kin buy it." But ifn dey don wants ennybody fuh buy it, why dey be puttin it up fuh sale?

Like I says, I don unnerstan dese white folk. Some uh dem be good to we, an I likes dem. But sumtime, I wish dey all jist goes way an leaves we alone. Dey be solvin sum uh our trubble, but dey be bringin jis as many new trubble wit dem.

33
VEXATIONS AND DEAD MULES
February 1863

"Laura, what are you doing out here in the middle of the night?" Ellen pulled her shawl more tightly over her shoulders and covered her mouth as she took her first breath in the cold, damp air. "This pernicious fog is going to make you sick."

Laura had been standing at the veranda rail, staring out over the spot where she knew the ocean began, if only she could see it through the fog. Now she turned with a rueful shrug. "I'm sorry I wakened you, Ellen. I couldn't sleep, and I hoped a breath of fresh air might help to settle my thoughts."

"Not this kind of fresh air! I don't usually mind the smell of pluff mud. It can be refreshingly tangy. But tonight it just smells like rotten eggs. Please come back inside. There are still some warm embers in the parlor fire, and we can talk there for a little while. Maybe telling me what's troubling you will help put your mind at rest."

"It's nothing, really." Laura obediently let herself be led back inside, but she was too restless to sit down. "I just happened to hear something Rina said yesterday. She was tidying the bedroom as I passed by, and I heard her mumbling to herself about how she wished we'd all just go away."

"I'm sure she didn't mean that. Rina loves you."

"Oh, she meant it, all right, and she has good reason to want to be rid of us. What good are we doing here? Sometimes I think we're just making everything worse."

"You don't really believe that!"

"Oh, yes, I do. I know that most of us have good intentions, and maybe we've taught a few Negroes to read. But their lives really aren't any better than they were before we came. They still live in those little slave cabins. They're still being asked to do backbreaking work, and we're rewarding them with a few scraps of used clothing not even suitable for this climate. We share our food supplies with them, such as they are, which simply means that we all have a terrible diet."

"We're doing what we can."

"But it's not enough. And sometimes I think we're all headed in the wrong direction. The problems in South Carolina resulted from white ownership of black slaves. How are our white people any better than the ones who came before us?"

"We're different because we care about the Negroes."

"Do we? Does Mr. Philbrick care about the men he's going to put back into the cotton fields to make a profit for himself? Do the soldiers care about them when they drag them off to serve in their army? Do our teachers really care about the children when they fight among themselves over who gets to run the school? Do the evangelicals care about the Baptists when they argue over who gets to take communion? We're making a huge mess. I agree with Rina. I wish the white people would all just go home and leave us alone."

"Laura!" Ellen laughed uncertainly. "You're talking as if you are one of the Negroes. And when you say all the whites should go home, are you including me? I'm one of the white people, you know, as are you."

"I think I feel closer to the Negroes than I do to our own people. Oh, not you, Ellen. You know I'm not talking about you. But sometimes I look at my lily-white skin next to Rina's strong black arms, and I'm ashamed that I'm not dark like she is. Maybe I want to be tan, or light brown, like Lottie."

"We can't change who we are, Laura, but we can change the way we look at one another. Do you remember the other evening when those two colored schoolteachers were here for dinner? When they left, you said you had enjoyed the conversation so much that you forgot to notice that they were black. That's the attitude we all ought to have, and perhaps if we can work here long enough, we'll all forget that there are differences between us."

"And you are a lovely idealist, my dear. But enough for tonight—we're facing another one of those miserable staff meetings over dinner tomorrow. We'll need our rest, as well as a tight rein on our reactions."

* * *

The diners who assembled the next evening were uniformly disgruntled. The previous night's fog had not lifted all day. Everyone who came in looked and felt damp and bedraggled. The chill in the air was one the smoky fireplace could not entirely dispel. And it didn't help when Rina served a tureen full of thin and lukewarm soup. "Can't Janie manage to get the food to the table without it being cold?" Mr. Soule asked.

"Nossir," Rina answered. "I bin out in de cookhouse. Janie be havin trubble keepin de fire burnin in de stove. De wind come down de chimbly an bring de wet long. De logs jis be sputterin. Ifn I was you, I not be spectin a hot dinner tonight."

"I hate this miserable place!" Amanda Ruggles was usually shy and the most soft-spoken of the group, so her outburst startled everyone. "It's cold and wet, and it smells bad. I just want to go home."

Laura and Ellen exchanged a glance. "Every place I've ever lived has had bad weather now and then," Laura said. "It'll be bright and sunny again before you know it."

"It'll still smell bad and be full of bugs and brambles and snakes. I hate it!"

"I'm sure you'll . . ."

"And don't you patronize me, Miss Towne. You're not making my life any better, you realize. You're responsible for my school being such a failure. If I can't have any students, I might as well go home, because I'm not doing any good here."

"I don't know what you mean, Miss Ruggles. What have I done?"

"You've been stealing my children, that's what. They all say they would rather go to Miss Laura's school, and they leave our plantation early in the morning, before I can get out there to corral them. I don't know what you use to lure them away, but I know they'd rather walk all those miles down to the Brick Church than come to my classes."

"I assure you, I haven't . . ."

"Oh, yes, you have. Mrs. Welles says the same thing. We were talking just the other day, and she said she's so tired of fighting you, she just doesn't care anymore. And so am I. You keep all the supplies in your little schoolhouse, and you bribe our children away, just so you can look successful."

"You're making some serious accusations, Miss Ruggles," Mr. Hooper said. "Just what is it you think Miss Towne is doing?"

"Well, for one thing, she holds classes every day because she doesn't do anything but teach, while we other teachers have multiple responsibilities to take care of, and she—"

"That's not true!" Ellen interrupted. "Laura does all the doctoring on the island. She's a lot busier than you are."

"And she teaches them all sorts of fancy stuff, like mathematics, instead of just their ABCs."

"You're absolutely right," General Saxton said. "Holding regular classes, teaching more than just ABCs? No wonder they like her. Sounds like she's doing an excellent job. I'm not so sure about you, Miss Ruggles."

"Come, Eddie. I want to leave. I'm through here." Amanda stood and faced her brother, who was flushed with embarrassment.

"Amanda."

"Don't you give me an argument, too. Take me back to our house. Now!" She stomped out of the room, while Edwin Ruggles raised his hands in a helpless shrug.

"I apologize for her outburst," he said. "She's tired and not feeling well. You will excuse us."

Laura immediately reacted. "Is she not well? Is there anything I can do? Perhaps I should—"

"No, Miss Towne. What ails Amanda cannot be cured by doctoring."

* * *

Laura's brother Will tried to change the subject. "Does anyone have a solution to the problem of slaves who refuse to work?"

"They're not slaves, Will," Laura cautioned.

"Be that as it may, I have a plantation full of black workers who don't work. I've been trying to get them to put a fence around the pasture for months now, and the job still isn't done. They keep telling me they have to get all the rails cut first, but I haven't seen the first pile. And in the meantime, that fool cow keeps wandering off and getting herself lost in the woods. We'll hear her mooing, and somebody has to thrash around through the underbrush and find out where she's got her feet tangled up in the grapevines."

Mr. Fairfield laughed. "I've had the same problem," he said. "There's no explaining the stupidity of a cow. But your slaves may be telling you the truth. Mine were behaving the same way, and I found out that the soldiers were taking their cut wood for their campfires."

"They're not slaves," Laura cautioned again.

"Yes, Miss Schoolmarm." Fairfield wrinkled his lip at her. "You ought to tell them to bring the cut wood into your barn each night instead of leaving it out in the fields, Mr. Towne. Makes it harder for the soldiers to steal."

Mr. Soule stepped into the conversation. "Nor does it help that our workers haven't been paid since October, and some of them not even then. I keep hearing the complaints when I deliver supplies to the plantations under my supervision. We've promised them that they will be paid for their work, but if the government doesn't send the money . . ."

"Yes, yes, Mr. Soule. I'm as aware as you of the problem," General Saxton admitted. "I've sent regular requests to Washington, but there's a war on, and . . ."

"We've noticed the war," Ellen remarked.

"Particularly since that troop of bandits from New York arrived and set up camp down at Land's End. Where did they find those recruits, anyway? They look and act like they just escaped from a jail somewhere," Nelly added.

Saxton grimaced. "You're referring to *Les Enfants Perdus*, of course. They're not called 'The Lost Children' for nothing. They're an independent infantry corps, not assigned to any particular state or army division. They just get moved around from spot to spot whenever someone in the higher echelons decides a heavy hand is needed. They're rough and tough, but they're supposed to be that way. Sorry."

"Perhaps so, General, but their efforts should be directed toward enemy incursions, not innocent civilians," Mr. Eustis said.

"You're having trouble with them at your place, too?"

"Oh, yes. They come creeping through the slave quarters—begging your pardon, Ma'am, but that's what the people call their village."

Laura nodded in resignation at the use of the word slave. "I know, I know."

"Well, anyway, they come around at night and carry off the pigs and the chickens."

"Dey bes not be snatchin muh chikkuns," Rina spoke from the doorway. "I be takin muh broom to um ifn dey duz."

"Rina! You're eavesdropping again," Laura warned her. "Go back to the cookhouse, please."

"You'd better warn her not to go after those soldiers with a broom," Mr. Eustis said. "They've been known to shoot blacks and burn their cabins down if anyone tries to stop them."

"They've been taught to live off the land," Saxton suggested.

"They're not just appropriating foodstuffs and other necessary supplies, General. They're vicious and cruel," Mr. Fairfield said.

"They certainly are. Let me tell you about our most recent incident on Ladies Island," Mr. Eustis said. "Ulysses Jackson has been working for Old Harry, now that he managed to buy up The Inlet. They needed a wagon, and I had an old one I wasn't using. So Ulysses came over to my place with two mules and hitched them up to that wagon to take it home. He didn't get far down the road when some of your 'Lost Children' popped up out of the woods and demanded the wagon, mules and all. When Ulysses refused and flipped the reins to make the mules move on, one of the 'children' pulled out a pistol and shot the mules dead in the road. And they weren't planning to eat them, either. They just laughed and rode away, leaving poor Ulysses standing there, weeping over his dead animals. You've got to do something about them, General."

"Ulysses is probably lucky they didn't shoot him, too. I'll do what I can. Perhaps I can get them transferred to somewhere nearer Charleston—maybe Folly Island or Morris Island. Those areas are pretty well unpopulated. Sounds to me like these men don't need to be anywhere near a civilian settlement. And I apologize for them, for all the good that does."

"There's one more area in which we need some help from the Army, General." This time it was Nelly Winsor who spoke up. "In the last few days, both our school classes and our church services have been disrupted by black soldiers barging in to look for new recruits for Colonel Higginson's black regiment. Not only do they behave rudely, they scare the younger children to death, and they discourage the older boys from coming to class at all, for fear they'll be dragged off and slapped into an army uniform."

"You know we're not taking children."

"Maybe not, but I'm not so sure the young soldiers you send around understand that. They seem to think that putting on a uniform gives them unlimited authority. We've seen them chase a young man clear across a field and then drag him away for resisting their efforts. Some of our people are nearly hysterical over the possibility that they will lose a husband or father or brother to the Army. There must be a better way to gain your recruits."

"We need soldiers badly, I'm sure you realize, but we won't take those who are too young or too old. Nor do we take men whose families really need them. I don't know what else I can do."

"Oh, but if you could just see some of these women, like our Lucy was today, wailing and crying because her Tommy has gone off to Beaufort to enlist. It's really heartbreaking."

"It be foolishness, dat what it be." Everyone turned to the doorway, where Rina was once again poised to jump into the conversation. "De mens makes too much fuss bout listin, an de wimmun cries too much. Dey done forget what life used fuh be, when we'uns be sold up like a chikkun wheneber de massa need sum spendin money. Dat bin de turrible time. Dis be nuttin compare to dat time. I be tired uh listenin to dem silly wimmun."

"Rina! I've told you and told you not to . . ."

"Leave her be, Miss Towne. I think we could all use a bit of Rina's viewpoint. Tell me, Rina. Is your life really better since your owners ran off and we came to take their place?"

"Life not be perfect, nossir, but it be lots bedder wit you white folk den wit de las bunch we hab. When we aint ornry, we be really grateful fuh all you does."

"Thank you, Rina. Now you can go, as Miss Towne instructed." General Saxton stood up from the table and stretched. "As for all of you, I suggest you spend less time griping about existing conditions and concentrate on the good you are doing. Things are going better than you know."

34
SECRETS
February/March 1863

W hen Laura looked back at the month of February, she understood why she had ignored General Saxton's reassurance that "things are going better than you know." The gloomy weather had seemed to affect everyone. Day after day, the fogbanks drifted in over the Atlantic, limiting one's view to an arm's length and drenching every surface with a cold, penetrating dampness that was less than rain but more than mere humidity. On some days, it was hard to tell if dawn had arrived, or if the darkness was really nightfall or just another layer of mist. Monotony can be more emotionally draining than crisis, Laura knew. What she hadn't realized was that in the face of uniform grayness, small changes would take on an exaggerated importance.

The turmoil over land sales was just one example. Anger and fear had spread rapidly, as gossip filled in for lack of knowledge. Then, when General Hunter finally stepped in to alter the rules, euphoria reigned. Mr. Soule, who had struggled with dual loyalties to Mr. Philbrick and to the plantations under his supervision, found new energy once it became apparent that the sales could be completed to everyone's satisfaction. He and Mr. Hooper, who had always believed that

General Hunter would do the right thing, traveled around the island with smiles on their faces. They fairly bubbled with enthusiasm as they reassured the Gideonites that they were not about to be driven out and explained to the more ambitious ex-slaves the possibilities of owning their own land. Others remained skeptical, particularly when rumors of additional postponements circulated.

On a personal level, Laura indulged in some quiet amusement at the expense of Ellen. On Valentine's Day, Reverend Mansfield French and his son William paid a surprise visit to Frogmore, where Laura, Harriet Ware, Ellen, and Lottie had gone to visit Rosie and Will Towne. They had intended only to drop in for dinner, but the settling fog made it impossible for any of them to return home until morning. The impromptu party was jovial, and they sat up late enjoying each other's company before trying to settle into some makeshift sleeping arrangement. All, that is, except for young William French. He was a shy young man in his early twenties. When his preacher father explained that he had decided to drop out of college for a while to see if he could help with the missionary effort, William simply nodded in agreement and studied his shoes. But Laura noticed that he seldom took his eyes off Ellen Murray. When she spoke, he leaned forward with parted lips, as if to capture her every word. And when she tried to draw him into the conversation, he flushed and stammered.

Laura teased Ellen later. "You've made a conquest," she said. "Young Mr. French is obviously smitten with you. Now you'll have to worry about breaking his heart rather than admonishing me about General Saxton."

"Oh, it's not the same thing at all," Ellen protested. "He was simply embarrassed at being in a group of relative strangers. I know I made him blush, but he would have done the same had anyone spoken to him. Saxton, on the other hand, has made it public knowledge that he is head over heels in love with you."

"Aha! There's where you are wrong, my dear."

"No, I'm not. He's made it perfectly obvious that—"

"Wait. I'll tell you a secret if you promise . . ."

"What?" Ellen's face was suddenly somber. "You and he haven't . . ."

"I suspect Saxton's falling in love, but not with me."

"I don't believe it. Who?"

"Tilly."

"No. He wouldn't. Matilda Thompson? She's half his age and doesn't have a brain in her pretty little head."

"That may be the great attraction." Laura laughed. "He was really upset that General Hunter thought I was smarter than he was. I don't blame him for preferring someone who can't argue with him."

"But just last month he was begging you to rescue him from having to spend an afternoon with her. Now he's thinking about spending the rest of his life with her? No!"

"I'm just telling you my own suspicions. I don't know their plans. In fact, I don't even know if they have any plans. As to what would lie behind his decision, I'm only guessing. I hope he's sincere about her, not simply doing it to spite me. But whatever the reason, his attentions have shifted, and so have hers. You don't have to worry about me leaving you for a military man. Although now I have to worry about you being lured away by a handsome young evangelist."

"You're impossible, Laura. But it's nice to see you smiling again."

"Sorry, I know I've been a bit remote lately. Lots of things to worry about, and this infernal fog makes it hard to see beyond the problem to the solution."

"Is there something else going on that I don't know about?"

"I'm a little concerned about Lottie and her attachment to that doctor in the black regiment."

"Dr. Rogers? He has been around here frequently, hasn't he?"

"Yes, he has, and I'm uncomfortable with it. He shows up, and the two of them ride off for the day on some grand adventure, completely ignoring the fact that Lottie has work to do. And they return with silly grins on their faces. The other day, when they came back, they were both draped in clusters of jasmine, as if they had decorated one another."

"I heard her say that they were just old friends from back home."

"Yes, I know. But he's married, Ellen, with a wife and child back home."

"And he's white."

"That sounds as if I'm judging them on their races. What's more important is that he's a white doctor in a black regiment. The black soldiers accept medical treatment from him, but they're not likely to be happy about him courting a black woman."

"Oh dear. Life and love get complicated, don't they?"

"We should know." Laura smiled ruefully. "I also know that when you love someone, you don't hear what others are saying about the two of you. And that doesn't stop me from worrying about Lottie."

* * *

A day or so later, the two women discovered how serious a problem Lottie could be. They were going over plantation accounts when Rina came stomping into the room. "One uh you bedder be gittin down to de cookhouse fore dat new cook kill sumbody."

"Janie? What's she upset about? I thought she was settling in nicely after her move from Edisto Island."

"Well, dat Janie, she hab a knife, an she be wavin it round an pokin it at dat brown gal uh yours."

"At Lottie? Oh, no!"

Laura and Ellen set out at a run. As soon as they reached the slave quarters, they saw the crowd gathered around the cookhouse. "Make way here," Laura ordered, not hesitating to push her way through. "Stop this right now. Go back to your work." Her voice was so authoritative that the crowd melted away, revealing Lottie and Susannah huddling together outside the cookhouse, while Janie stood spraddle-legged in the doorway, moving a large butcher knife in slow circles in their direction.

"Janie! Put the knife down, please." Laura stepped confidently toward the doorway, but the new cook did not waver.

"Tell dat brown gal she gots no bizness in muh kitchen," Janie snarled, punctuating her answer with another poke of the knife.

Laura turned, hoping her authority would carry more weight with the other two combatants. "Lottie, you and Susannah need to return to the house. Now! Susannah, you have work in the bedrooms. Lottie, I'll see you in the parlor in a few minutes. Go!"

This time, when Laura turned back to deal with the cook, Janie lowered her arm and seemed to wilt a bit. "Tankee, ma'am." As she started back into the kitchen, Laura called, "Wait."

"What you want?" Janie was defensive again.

"I'd like to come in and talk, if I may. And I could use a cup of tea, if you happen to have some water heating."

Janie lowered her head in acceptance and Laura made her way into the warm room, only to be shocked at the mess of flour and shattered pottery that greeted her. "What on earth happened here?" she asked.

"Dat brown gal be tryin fuh steal muh food," the cook said, "an dat Zannah, she be helpin cause she hate me fuh takin she job."

"My tea, please, Janie." Laura hoped to settle the cook's anger by putting her back to a simple task. And slowly the story came out.

A few weeks earlier, Lottie had asked Susannah to help her bake some ginger cakes so that she could send a thank you gift to Dr. Rogers. They had come to the cookhouse while Janie was off gathering supplies. They had used up all her molasses and several of her eggs, not to mention the flour. Janie had been angry because she was responsible for the kitchen, and she had told Susannah to stay away. But today the two women had come back, and Lottie had walked straight into the kitchen gathering more ingredients because she and Susannah needed to make two more cakes. The argument had escalated until Lottie told Janie she could have her fired and Janie pulled the knife.

"I'm truly sorry, Janie. This shouldn't have happened, and I'll see to it that you don't have any more problems. But you need to know that we settle our fights with words, not weapons. You must promise me that you'll use that knife only on food that needs to be chopped from now on."

* * *

Dealing with Lottie proved to be more difficult. When Laura confronted her about using household supplies to make a gift for her personal friend, Lottie bristled. "You don't like Dr. Rogers, do you?"

"How I feel about Dr. Rogers has nothing to do with it. I'm sure he's a fine, upstanding gentleman, but . . ."

"He's the finest man I've ever known—so noble, so kind. I am blessed to be able to call him my friend."

"Lottie! That's not my point. What I'm trying to suggest to you is that your behavior toward him is inappropriate. He's a married man. His wife should be the one sending him cakes, if it is cake that he needs."

"But she doesn't. Bell isn't a cook. When I was a patient in his clinic, I used to bake for him, and he was grateful. I'm just doing the same for him here."

"Not any more, you're not. We are often on tight rations here. We can't have you using supplies that may keep us all from going hungry. The Army is feeding Dr. Rogers now. And that will have to do for him."

"What are you going to do about that woman who threatened me with a knife? Have you sent her packing? She was much more in the wrong than I was."

"No, Lottie. I haven't fired her. We struggled for months trying to eat Susannah's cooking. If you had ever experienced that, you'd understand why Janie is so valuable. I've talked to her about the knife, but you'll have to promise to stay away from the cookhouse."

"You're taking her side against mine?"

"I'm trying to keep her from killing you, although I'm tempted to do so myself at the moment. You of all people ought to understand the sense of possession that our Negroes feel about the few things they can call their own. We don't enter their cabins without permission, and we don't take over their jobs or their workspace. It's a sign of respect. You just treated Janie like a slave. That's almost unforgivable."

Lottie burst into tears. "You don't know what it feels like to not belong anywhere. Everybody loves you, and everybody hates me, except for Dr. Rogers. But don't worry, you'll be rid of me soon enough."

"Whatever do you mean?"

"I can't tell you. Not yet. It's a secret between Dr. Rogers and me. You'll know when General Saxton announces it."

Now thoroughly confused, Laura did the only thing she could do under the circumstances. She pulled Lottie to her feet and embraced her. At first Lottie resisted. Then slowly she relaxed as the power of touch worked its magic.

"I'm on your side, Lottie," Laura murmured.

"I'm sorry. I understand what you're trying to tell me, and I appreciate your concern, but it's all so complicated and confusing."

"I think you'd better talk to me."

"I truly love Dr. Rogers, but I don't think it's the kind of love you suspect. A couple of years ago, he saved my life. I owe him everything, and I would do anything for him. Right now he's very homesick, and I'd like to make him happier."

"Maybe he just needs to go home."

"No, he believes in what he is doing, and he'd never turn his back on men who need him. But he's surrounded by strangers, except for me. I can offer him a connection with our lives back home, and he needs that." She paused for a moment and then added, "And so do I."

"Are you still unhappy here?"

"Not unhappy. I find teaching very rewarding. But, yes, I'm lonely. I've never felt quite so isolated. At home I was a part of a large free black community, surrounded by friends both black and white, who cared more about what I did than how I looked. Here I'm some sort of strange half-breed— 'dat brown gal.' The white Gideonites are perfectly polite, but they keep expecting me to be just like them. And the black people cannot understand what I am because I've never shared their experiences in slavery. I don't belong anywhere, except now and then, when I'm with Dr. Rogers. I need him as an anchor in my life."

"But Lottie . . ."

"And I'm not trying to break up his marriage, as you implied. I know Bell, his wife. She's my friend, too, and I would never try to take her place. Dr. Rogers knows that. He even shares her letters with me because he can talk freely to me about her."

"And this secret you mentioned?"

"It's a military secret, not some romantic tryst. You'll have to trust me until the official announcement."

35
THE MORE THINGS CHANGE . . .
March 1863

Contrary to the old saying, March came in like a lamb instead of a lion. Sun, warm temperatures, soft sea breezes, blooming flowers, and rising spirits sent the inhabitants of St. Helena off to church in a thankful mood. Laura, like the others, was at last hopeful that spring would bring welcome relief from the tensions that had settled among them like the fog. Her relief was short-lived.

On Monday afternoon, she was surprised to see General Saxton's carriage pulling into the yard. Why on earth is he back here so soon? she wondered. He was just here for dinner yesterday and didn't mention a repeat visit. First, she realized that there was a woman in the carriage with him. Her heart did a flip-flop. No, he wouldn't bring Tilly here, she thought. Then she recognized the woman and sighed with relief. Mrs. Francis D. Gage represented the Sanitary Commission in Beaufort, and had made a place for herself by helping the Army organize relief efforts in the Sea Islands.

Laura hastily smoothed her hair out of her eyes and went to meet her unexpected guests. "General. Mrs. Gage. How nice to see both of you."

"Sorry to just drop in, my dear, but we're on something of a mission. Is Miss Forten here, by any chance?" It was Mrs. Gage who offered the explanation, while Saxton busied himself with checking the horses' trappings.

"Why, no. She doesn't actually live here, Mrs. Gage. She's finished teaching for the day, so she's probably on her way back to Oaklands. You'll find her either strolling along the road in this fine weather, or perhaps already at Mr. Hunn's store at the Corner. Is there anything I can help you with?"

"No, we have a surprise for her. Her military orders have just come in."

"Orders? Lottie's not in the military." Laura looked toward General Saxton, her eyebrows raised in confusion.

Saxton grinned as he put a warning finger to his lips. "It's still a secret. But I'm sure she'll tell you about it herself. We mustn't spoil the surprise." With that, he snapped the reins and the carriage moved off, leaving Laura standing in dust and befuddlement.

"I hate surprises," she grumbled after the departing carriage, "and I hate secrets."

* * *

Laura's irritation increased a short time later when Mr. Hooper yanked his galloping horse to a stop in front of the veranda and slid out of the saddle, still wearing his captain's uniform from his part-time assignment as General Hunter's attaché. "Mr. Hooper," Laura said. "What on earth is going on? This is a Monday, and we never have visitors on Monday. It's my one day to get some work done. But here you all come—first General Saxton and Mrs. Gage, and now you—all looking like the demons are in hot pursuit. Has something happened in Beaufort?"

"General Saxton was already here? Did he tell you?"

"Tell me what?"

"About the new troop movements?"

"Troop movements? No. He and Mrs. Gage were in high good humor and looking for Miss Forten. I have no idea what it was all about."

"Well, then, it's a good thing I've come."

"Not if you don't tell me what's happening!"

"Sorry. I'm parched from the ride. Can I get something to drink?"

Impatiently she led him into the parlor and sent Rina for refreshments. "Now, start from the beginning."

"General Hunter has just announced that Colonel Higginson's colored regiment, the First South Carolina Volunteers, are setting out for Florida. Most members of their staff have, in fact, already departed. The troops will be boarding ships tomorrow, and Hunter is concerned that if their families realize they are leaving, there will be trouble on shore and more than a few desertions. So he wants all the plantation superintendents to keep their people busy tomorrow and away from Land's End. But it's hush-hush. I don't want to say anything more, in case your maid hears me."

"I doubt that she's back from the cookhouse yet, although you're right about her tendency to eavesdrop. We can move back into the yard if you like, so we can see her approach." Once in the clear, Laura shook her head in confusion. "Why would they be headed for Florida? The Navy has already taken Fernandina, and the last three attempts to occupy Jacksonville have failed miserably."

"The general seems to think that his black troops may be able to do a more persuasive job of it. He's ordered Colonel Montgomery to come up from the south with his Second South Carolina Volunteers, so that the two colored regiments can move in together. And, yes, they'll be headed straight for Jacksonville."

"Well, he's definitely right that our people are going to be upset. We've had a hard enough time convincing the young black men to enlist and reassuring their families that they will not be in any danger. When their wives and mothers find out they're gone, you'll be able to hear the wailing down in Hilton Head."

"I don't doubt it. But there's a good reason behind the move. Admiral DuPont is getting ready to mount a major offensive against the city of Charleston. Hunter hopes the movement of the black troops will be a distraction for any spying rebels, while the fleet gets itself assembled and begins to move up the coast."

"Unlikely. There are too many places where Confederate spies can get a clear view of Port Royal from here, and it's hard to disguise a sailing fleet."

"I didn't come to ask your approval, Miss Towne—only your cooperation."

"Which you'll have, of course. But I'll never understand the military mind. Are you staying for dinner?"

"No, no, I'm headed down toward Land's End to warn the people there." With that, Hooper remounted and rode off, leaving Laura once again in the dust. "You forgot your drink!" she called to his departing figure.

* * *

Although the visitors from the mainland did not show up again at mealtime, several Gideonites did, including Will and Rosie Towne, who had traveled in from Frogmore after they heard the news. "What do you think it all means?" Will asked Mr. Eustis. "You know more about the geography around here than the rest of us do. Will the war be affecting us, do you think?"

"If you mean to ask whether the fighting will come here, no, I don't think so. But will the outcomes affect us? Quite probably. Charleston is such a key location. If our ships can penetrate that harbor and capture the city that started the Rebellion, it could mean an early end to the war. If they try and fail, it could encourage the rebels to put more pressure on the Sea Islands to drive us out."

"And what about our 'friends' in Florida?" Laura asked with a slight eye roll to ward off any direct mention of the black regiment in front of the servers. "How much danger will they face?"

"Probably very little. The troops who gave up their possession of Jacksonville did so more out of boredom than from fear of the opposition. Jacksonville's a nice enough little town, or it used to be, but it has no military importance. Capturing it again will be nothing more than a bully's swagger on the playground. Nobody much will notice—or care."

"I'm relieved to hear that," Rosie said, "because I don't want to seem to be, uh, . . ."

"What?"

"I don't want to look like I'm . . . running away."

"Are you?" Laura looked at her sister in alarm.

"Yes. At least, I'm going away. Oh, Laura, I didn't want to tell you like this, but I need to go home. I've been miserable ever since we arrived. The heat and the damp of this place don't agree with me. I can't shake one cold before I catch another chill. I hate the bugs and the smell of the mud, and . . ." Her lips trembled as she lapsed into silence.

"She's really tried, Laura," Will said.

"I know that. And it's all right, Rosie. Really. I've worried that your constitution was not up to the challenges of our swampy existence. I'll be happy to know you're safe in Philadelphia. Have you thought about when you want to leave?"

"Next week. I've already booked passage on the *Arago* for March 12th."

"Oh. So soon." Laura's voice faltered for a moment before she shook herself back under control. "That's not a problem. We'll just have to get you all packed up in a hurry."

Rosie's announcement somehow put an end to the more serious discussion of the coming military maneuvers, and the visitors left shortly for home. Once they were alone, Ellen reached out to Laura. "Are you very upset, my dear?"

"No, I guess not. I'm not even surprised. The wonder is that Rosie's stay lasted so long. But my world does seem a bit unstable at the moment. I'm not quite sure who's going to pull the rug out from under us next."

* * *

There were more changes to come. Several days later, Charlotte Forten came to The Oaks after school was done for the day. "I need to talk to you and Ellen," she said.

"Are we finally to discover what was behind the secret mission of General Saxton and Mrs. Gage?"

"You knew they came to see me?"

"Yes, of course. They stopped here first looking for you."

"But they didn't tell you . . .?"

"No. And if you don't soon explain, I'll be tempted to throttle you."

"Well!" Lottie took a deep breath, but she could not suppress the smile that lit her face. "I'm leaving here very soon. General Hunter has appointed me to the position of instructor for the troops in his colored regiment. He says that having soldiers who cannot read or write makes double work for their officers, so I am to travel with the regiment and teach the men their ABCs and their numbers."

"But they've already left here."

"Yes, and I'll be joining them in Florida."

"Lottie! You can't be serious! What about your work here? And the dangers of going into a battle zone?"

"What danger? Dr. Rogers says Jacksonville is a whole lot safer—and healthier—than Hilton Head, or Beaufort, for that matter."

"Dr. Rogers! So that's what this is all about."

"It was General Hunter's idea. Dr. Rogers just told him about me when he was asked to do so. And don't look so disapproving. There are two other women who will be going, and we'll be busy all the time with that many students. I think it's a wonderful opportunity, and I don't want you to try to talk me out of going."

"Of course not. It's clear that the decisions are already settled. When do you leave?"

"I'm not sure yet. I'll be going to Beaufort and then to Camp Saxton to meet with Mrs. Dewhurst and Mrs. Hawkes about the arrangements next week. Their husbands are in the regiment—Mrs. Dewhurst is the wife of the adjutant, and Mrs. Hawkes's husband is the assistant surgeon. The men are both in Jacksonville already and making arrangements for our arrivals. And, in the meantime, Mrs. Hunn and I are planning some shopping trips to fill out my wardrobe before I leave. So I'm probably finished teaching at the school. I'm so excited that I'm not sleeping or eating. I can't concentrate on anything else but what lies ahead."

Laura fought to disguise her disapproval, although it showed in the tightness of her facial muscles. "We'll miss you, Lottie, because you're a fine teacher. And I'm sure your talents will be well used in Florida. Let us know if you need anything." It was an obvious dismissal.

36
SOME MARRY, SOME DON'T
March 1863

Since Rosie needed to be in Beaufort by March 11th, and Lottie wanted to visit Camp Saxton, Laura suggested that she, Ellen, and Nelly Winsor spend a last pleasant day with Rosie and Lottie. Mr. Eustis assured them that the captain of the *Arago* would be happy to provide overnight accommodations for the whole party, so that they could all be on hand to wave farewell as Rosie left for home the following morning. They crossed to Port Royal Island via boat and stopped at the headquarters of H.G. Judd, general superintendent for the island, where they lingered over a midday dinner.

"How are things going on St. Helena?" Judd inquired.

"Settling down, now that the land sales are over." Laura shook her head a bit ruefully. "Everyone was pretty much at loggerheads there for a while, but things worked out for the best after all."

"I wish I could say the same for my area," Judd replied. "My people are still having difficulties with marauding soldiers, and I'm being dunned with Army demands for more corn than I can manage to raise. And the threat hangs over my head: Produce the amount of food the Army needs from your fields, or we'll sell the plantations to someone who can better manage them. The tax commissioners just don't understand how difficult our jobs are."

"No, they probably can't begin to understand what's going on out here when they're sitting at their desks in Beaufort, but they've been generally sympathetic to the needs of the former slaves, which I appreciate."

"I wouldn't say that of Brisbane and Wording. When it comes down to it, their primary purpose is to serve the needs of the Treasury Department. Judge Smith, I grant you, is a strong antislavery man, at least when he's sober, but you have to catch him early in the day to get any sense out of him. Problem is, he seldom gets up before a quarter to ten, and he's drinking again by ten."

Most of the ladies simply looked shocked, but Laura laughed. "So I've heard, but at least he's a congenial drunk, not a vicious one. And now we do have Hunter and Saxton meeting with the commissioners and supporting the judge's side. I'm cautiously optimistic that all will work out."

* * *

Mr. Eustis soon arrived with his largest carriage to take the ladies on to Beaufort, where he deposited them near the storefronts on Bay Street near the Arsenal. "Will you ladies be all right for the afternoon?"

"Oh, of course we will. We know everyone in town," Laura reminded him.

"Then I'll pick you up here when the shops close," he promised as he drove off. "Have fun, ladies!"

Lottie was anxious to visit the new sundries store opened by Robert Smalls, and she dragged Nelly with her. Laura and Ellen took Rosie straight to General Saxton's nearby town house, where they hoped to get Rosie's passport stamped and to make sure the rest of her paperwork was intact. Laura didn't really want to talk to the general himself; secretly, she hoped he would already be hard at work out at the camp. But they were not prepared for the sight that greeted them. There, at the curb, was a wagon loaded with pine boughs, jasmine vines, and other flowers. Mr. Hooper was directing traffic as several servants carried the greenery into the house.

"My word! It looks like you folks are getting ready to throw the town's biggest party. What's the occasion?" Laura asked.

"Miss Towne! What are you doing here?" Captain Hooper was suddenly flustered.

But before Laura could answer, James Thompson came bustling around the corner toward them. "Welcome, welcome!" he said. "I'm so glad you could come. This isn't just any party, you know. It's shaping up to be the biggest social event of the season, and the season hasn't even begun yet."

"Excuse me. We seem to have interrupted something. We're not here for a social event. My sister simply needs to get her passport stamped and her paperwork approved so that she can sail back to Philadelphia. If we can just go inside and see the attaché, we'll be moving out of your way."

"Oh, but you'll stay, surely? Tilly will be most disappointed if she hears that you were here but didn't come to her wedding. Excuse me just a moment. Here, you! Those large trees need to be taken over to the church. Just drive the wagon around the corner here and come back along Carteret Street."

"Wedding?" Laura and Ellen looked at one another, communing silently as they were often able to do: Who's she marrying? Isn't it happening awfully fast? Is there any way out of this awkward situation? Whatever shall we do?

Rosie, meanwhile, was looking more and more apprehensive. "Laura, I'm worried about our reservations on the *Arago*. We need to let them know how many we are so that they can reserve staterooms for all of us tonight. Mr. Eustis said I needed to check in with the captain as soon as possible, and he's already taken my luggage to the wharf. Can we take care of my papers before you deal with whatever else is going on here?"

Mr. Hooper, relieved to have something to do, offered his arm to Rosie. "Come, my dear, I'll see to your needs personally."

Laura turned back to Mr. Thompson, hoping that her voice would remain steadier than she felt. "We didn't know that Miss Thompson was getting married," she said. "Who's the lucky groom?" Faintly she noticed that Ellen had laid a reassuring hand on her back, as if to steady her.

"General Saxton, of course. He proposed last week, and Tilly said she saw no reason to delay the wedding. She has always admired the general and did not want their nuptials to interfere with his military responsibilities. They both said they wanted only a quiet ceremony, but I could see the longing in my sister's face. So I'm doing the best I can to make it a festive occasion. A girl only gets married once, and when she's marrying a general she deserves to have all the pomp that can be arranged. The cream of Beaufort society will be here this evening, and now we'll have the most prominent personalities of St. Helena as well."

"Really, Mr. Thompson. I'm sorry, but we can't stay. We have Miss Winsor and Miss Forten with us, and Mr. Eustis will be waiting to drive us all back to the *Arago* for the night."

"That's not a problem. In fact, I saw Mr. Eustis a few minutes ago and invited him as well. He'll join you here. The ceremony is at five o'clock at the Episcopal Church, and then we'll come back here for a light repast. You'll still have time to get to the ship before they pull in the gangplank. See you at the church!"

"But—"

"You might as well quit fighting it, Laura. We've been neatly trapped and will have to make the best of it," Ellen said.

"I'm not upset about it. Just inconvenienced!"

"Of course you're upset. Who wouldn't be? He could have at least been gentlemanly enough to tell you in advance. But be that as it may, we can't avoid attending now. And who knows? We may even get a lovely glass of champagne to warm our drive back to the wharf."

* * *

Later, Laura could remember only small vignettes from the wedding—the overwhelming scent of jasmine, Tilly in her pearl gown and white veil, the surprise appearance of Mrs. Austa French, who sang a long aria in the middle of the ceremony, and most of all, General Saxton's pale and serious face above his fancy dress uniform. The women of St. Helena sat far back in the sanctuary, but even so, Laura was afraid that others would be watching her. She sat ramrod straight, hands folded primly in her lap and feet properly aligned. By the time they boarded the carriage and set out for the shipyard, she was so stiff that she could scarcely lean back on the hard cushion of the bench seat.

Nelly, oblivious to the drama around her, gave a dramatic sigh. "Wasn't that just the most beautiful ceremony you ever witnessed? Oh, I hope my wedding can be half as grand! Were you paying attention to the details, ladies? I'd love to have our church decorated in flowers like that one was. And the refreshment table was ever so elegant. Do you think we can do something like that?"

"Aren't you getting ahead of yourself, Nelly?" Ellen asked. "The last I heard, you weren't even engaged."

"Oh, of course I am. I just haven't told Mr. Fairfield yet. I think we'll marry in May, when the flowers are all at their peaks and the weather is not yet too hot. That will give everyone time to get ready."

"Is there some reason you haven't told Mr. Fairfield?" Laura asked. "Surely he has asked you often enough."

"Oh, we're talking about it, but there are some things he's going to have to concede before I give him a definite answer."

"Such as?"

"Where we're going to live, for one thing. Most of the time now, he bunks with Mr. Eustis, but that little place is certainly not big enough to hold a married couple. He's set on having us take over Frogmore now that you're leaving, Rosie. But there is no way I'd agree to live in that horrible place."

Laura and Rosie reacted at the same moment. "Horrible? How can you say that?"

"Oh, the house isn't all that bad, I suppose, except for that ghastly whipping post in the dining room, but I absolutely refuse to live anywhere where I have to use a haunted road to reach the front door."

"Haunted? For heaven's sakes, Nelly! That's an old slave superstition. You know better."

"I know what I've seen. We took the buggy down that way one night, and I've never been so scared. We were just driving along when up the road came this ball of . . . of . . . I don't know what. It was bright and wavery, like a candle flame, but there was no one there. And when it got to the Hanging Tree, it just floated up into the branches and disappeared. It had to have been a ghost—one of those Graybeards that live in that piece of the woods, I suspect. The place is haunted, all right, and I'm not going there ever again, let alone to live."

"It suited me fine while I was there," Rosie said, "and I never saw anything like what you're describing. In fact, I'm going to miss the peacefulness of looking out across the beach to watch the waves roll in. And the sunrises were glorious beyond description. Oh, maybe I shouldn't be leaving at all!" Rosie's face crumpled as she fought off tears.

"Now see what you've done!" Laura glared at Nelly before she put a comforting arm around her sister's shoulders. "Frogmore will always be there, Rosie, and you'll come back to visit. I promise you that some day I'll buy that land and make it the spot where I can live out my days."

"But I'm going to miss all of you."

"Of course you are, my dear, just as you've been missing Sarah and Lucretia and John Henry back in Philadelphia. Now you'll get to spend some time with them. Think of yourself as having two homes, with the good fortune to be able to travel between them, and with loving family at each one."

Casting about for a way to change the subject, Lottie raised a new question. "Did anybody else wonder where Tilly got that wedding dress?"

"No, why?" Ellen asked.

"Because a dress like that is impossible in Beaufort. Mrs. Hunn and I have been visiting the Negro dressmakers, and not a one of them has anything available beyond serviceable muslin or bombazine. I wanted to have some new dresses made before I leave for Florida, but I've found no one who can help. So how did Tilly lay her hands on pearl-colored silk and a white veil?"

"She probably brought them with her," Laura suggested.

"Oh, surely not, but . . ."

"Why not? The little minx has been shopping for a husband ever since she set foot on our dock. She has just been waiting for some poor fool to step into her clutches. And when she caught one, she wanted to be ready to leap in before he had a chance to get away."

"That's uncharitable, Laura," Ellen cautioned. Then she laughed. "Uncharitable, but probably true."

"It is a very strange match, if you ask me—that old general and that young girl," Lottie said.

"I still think it was a beautiful wedding," said Nelly, not to be put off her favorite topic. "Every woman dreams of the day when she'll be a blushing bride."

"Not every woman," Laura answered. "Personally, I'd rather attend my own funeral."

"Laura! Surely you don't mean that. Everyone needs love."

"And love comes in many different forms. We love our families and friends. We love the children in our classes, the people we take care of, and those who take care of us."

"Of course," Nelly replied, "but I'm not talking about that kind of love."

"Not every woman needs a husband to make her feel complete," Laura said. "Personally, I don't see much need to have a man around at all. Oh, they come in useful when there is heavy lifting to be done, I suppose, but I don't want to share my bed with one just so I don't have to carry the firewood."

In the dark, she felt Ellen's small hand clasp hers with an understanding squeeze.

37
MUSICAL CHAIRS
April 1863

Lottie had moved back to The Oaks, her trunks packed, as she waited for the message that would send her on her way to join the black regiment in Florida. All through the month of March, she had awakened every morning to the expectation that she would be gone by nightfall, only to be disappointed when no word arrived. As tactfully as possible, Laura suggested that she might profitably spend the time in the classroom, but Lottie could not accept the notion that her wait might be a long one.

When the long-awaited letter from Dr. Rogers finally arrived, it brought a huge disappointment. General Hunter had changed his mind about trying to hold the area around Jacksonville and had ordered steamers to pick up all the troops stationed in the area and return them to their former camps. Dr. Rogers tried to explain what had happened: "I suppose this means that we are to protect the Islands while the advance is made on Charleston, if it means anything . . . At the same time I believe the only reason why General Hunter calls us back is because he fears our black troops might be overpowered in the absence of the other regiments . . . At the risk of being reckoned 'suspicious' I must express the conviction that General Hunter has been influenced by pro-slavery counsel. Negroes are now being drafted hereabouts to do garrison duty."

The discontented doctor made several trips to St. Helena in the following days. Each time, he and Lottie borrowed horses or a buggy and went riding out across the island, ostensibly to visit his friends or explore the countryside. Laura pursed her lips but refrained from judgment until Lottie announced that she was going to spend a week or more visiting the camp of the colored regiment.

"I don't think that's a good idea," Laura objected. "With the rumors of an attack on Charleston swirling around, there have been more incursions by rebel spies. You'll be out there fully exposed in that camp."

"And surrounded by a whole regiment of soldiers to protect me. Honestly, Laura, I sometimes think you're just a natural killjoy!"

As if to prove Laura's point, a flurry of action broke out around Edisto Island. Captain J.C. Dutch, whose blockading ship, the *Kingfisher*, patrolled the waters around St. Helena, had word of rebels sneaking onto the outer islands at night to raid abandoned crops. In what Laura termed a bold and enterprising move, Captain Dutch, with a small crew and a dugout, moved onto Bailey's Island and shot the rebel pickets. The crew discovered two Negroes gathering corn and forced them to lead the patrol to their masters' camp. The Union soldiers captured eleven young men, among them the sons of the Seabrook family who had owned most of the plantations on Edisto Island.

Rina and some of her friends had spotted Captain Dutch's ship as he headed down the creek toward Hilton Head with his load of spies. Soon the Negro community had the entire story, and Rina came up to The Oaks with her report. "Dat Capn Dutch, he done ketch a boatful uh sesesh mens. An dey be sum uh de big bugs uh Edisto," she said, with a wide smile that reflected her delight at seeing former owners now suffering.

The incident could not deter Lottie. Escorted by Mr. Pierce, who intended to write an article about Negroes in the Army, she headed for the camp of the First South Carolina Colored Regiment. Laura, trying her best to stay out of other people's lives, made no further comment, although in her diary she recorded her concerns. Shortly after Lottie left, rebels attacked a Union gunboat at the Brick Yard. Several crewmen aboard the *Martha Washington* died, and the ship itself lay disabled in the harbor. "The enemy are threatening the north end of the island, and there is Lottie at the camp. Very unsafe for her, I think," Laura worried in her diary.

* * *

Laura had other matters to disturb her sleep as well. As had happened the previous spring, several Gideonites headed north. Mr. Hooper left because he had contracted a malarial fever and wanted to seek medical attention at home. Mrs. Philbrick decided to take a prolonged leave, pleading an undefined medical condition that required treatment in Boston. Her departure left an important vacancy, for she had been responsible for keeping the household accounts for all the plantations of St. Helena Island. Laura declined to take over but suggested Miss Ware, who proved to be more than willing to have an important role in their organization.

At the next gathering of the staff, Laura invited her to preside at the foot of the table, a position that obviously delighted Miss Ware, who beamed all through dinner.

Laura had hoped that the settlement of the land sales issues would result in more stability. Instead, the Gideonites seemed to be playing musical chairs. First came a visit from Mr. Philbrick and an announcement over dinner that he was giving up the plantation house at Coffin Point.

"I thought you loved that beautiful old house," Laura said.

"Oh, I do, but without Mrs. Philbrick here, I tend to bounce around in all that space. Besides, it doesn't feel so much like home since I've only been allowed to lease it instead of owning it outright."

"I've never understood why the tax commissioners didn't allow that plantation to be sold," Laura said.

"There's a rumor afloat that Mr. Coffin did not abandon the plantation as did the other owners. He may be being held in the Charleston jail on a charge unrelated to the invasion. And if so, he didn't have a clear opportunity to pay his over-due taxes. The commissioners want to clarify the legal ramifications before they confiscate the property."

"If he's been in jail all this time, he's not a particularly desirable property owner."

"Perhaps not, but the commissioners are cautious to a fault. I can do nothing but outwait them, and, in the meantime, I'd rather live elsewhere."

"So where will you go? And who will take over the work at Coffin Point?"

"That's the other thing I wanted to discuss with all of you at The Oaks. You're aware, I know, that Richard Soule is related to my wife. He is coming to work with me on the plantations that my consortium has purchased. He'll be in residence at Coffin Point, keeping an eye on things there as well as overseeing supplies for my other properties. I'll be living on one of the McTureous plantations at least until Mrs. Philbrick returns."

The ladies of The Oaks looked at each other in alarm. As usual, Laura was the spokesperson to express their fears. "Mr. Hooper has already left here. With Mr. Soule leaving as well, who will be overseeing the workmen of our plantation? And who will we have left to defend us?"

"It's my understanding that Reuben Tomlinson will replace Mr. Soule," said Philbrick. "Personally, I don't much care for the man. He's made some very disparaging statements about my 'money-grubbing' tendencies. But you should be content with him, Miss Towne. He comes from a good Philadelphia background, and he is strong in his support of antislavery principles. He's staunchly against the evangelism of some of our more fervent colleagues, and with his solid background in financial matters, he should suit you perfectly."

Laura wasn't sure whether to see that description as favorable or a veiled insult, but she let it pass, preferring to make her own judgments. "There will be just one man assigned here then?"

"No, I'm sure General Saxton plans to assign another. I just don't know who that will be."

Nelly Winsor spoke up. "Mr. Fairfield could come here."

"He has told me that he wants to take over Frogmore," said Philbrick.

"Uh, I'm already running Frogmore," Will Towne pointed out.

"Then you could come here to be with your sister, and Fairfield could take Frogmore."

"Not if he wants me to marry him," Nelly said, bursting into tears and running from the table.

Now Mr. Soule spoke up for the first time. "I hate to be the bearer of more bad news," he said, "but an extra man may not be a problem. I was told in Beaufort today that all of you will soon be asked to move so that the tax commissioners can take over The Oaks."

"Why on earth would they want to do that? Where did this harebrained plan come from?" Laura asked.

Ellen grimaced. "I'm afraid I know the answer to that. It was you, Laura."

"What?"

"Think back," Ellen went on. "We were all at Mr. Judd's for dinner on our way to Beaufort. You and Mr. Judd were discussing the land sales, and you remarked that the tax commissioners couldn't hope to understand how this island worked since they didn't live here. And you know that Mr. Judd is a close friend of Judge Smith. He probably told the judge what you said; the plan could have hatched from that interchange."

"But I never meant that . . . And where would we go if we had to leave here?"

"I believe they plan to send you to Edgar Fripp's plantation."

"Do you mean Seaside? That house is much too small."

"Who told you?"

"Isn't your brother Charles in residence there, Miss Ware?"

"How certain is it?"

346

The questions came too fast to allow rational answers to any of them. It was clear, however, that the suggestion met with unanimous disapproval. Finally, Laura threw up her hands and said, "Enough. We can't allow this to happen. We shall go in a body to General Saxton to protest."

"When do you think we can arrange to see him?"

"Tomorrow. We'll leave first thing in the morning. We can't afford to let this matter wait."

* * *

The group set out in a heavy rainstorm—Ellen Murray, Harriet Ware, Laura, and Will Towne, accompanied by Richard Soule and Frederick Eustis. "How do you know he'll see us?" asked Will.

"Because we're going straight to his house. He can hardly leave us standing there in the pouring rain."

Laura headed straight for the Saxtons' front door, only to be stopped by a uniformed guard who blocked her path. "I'm Miss Laura Towne, here to see General Saxton. Please tell him we are here."

"I have not been told that he is expecting . . ."

"Sergeant! These are friends. Quit harassing them." Tilly stood in the open doorway, looking desperately eager for company. "Come in, do! I'm afraid that the general is not here at the moment, but I expect him at midday, and he would be most upset if he missed you." She bustled about, asking the housemaid to go for towels, demanding more wood to build up the fire in the parlor, and sending word to the kitchen to prepare for guests at dinner. Even when she was flustered, as she was at the moment, Tilly looked gorgeous, while Laura was acutely conscious of how bedraggled they all were from their journey.

As they grew warmer and drier, however, Laura was surprised to realize that she felt quite comfortable with the new Mrs. Saxton, even if that comfort level was tinged with a bit of pity for her obvious loneliness. The assembled group kept up a casual conversation until the sounds of horses in the yard announced the arrival of General Saxton and Mr. Pierce. The two men were surprised to find a house full of unexpected guests, but Tilly's ministrations soon had everyone assembled around a laden dining table.

"Now," General Saxon demanded, "to what do we owe the pleasure of your company?"

"We weren't expecting to stay for dinner," Laura apologized, "but we have a serious crisis on our hands."

"Really? I'm not aware of . . ."

"You aren't? Good. I hoped you weren't involved in this," Laura said.

"Involved in what? What has happened?"

"We have it on good authority that the tax commissioners intend to take The Oaks from us and use it as their own headquarters. We would all be sent to Seaside Plantation, which is certainly not big enough to allow us to maintain our school or manage our surrounding plantations. The house has just two bedrooms and almost no furniture. And what about our slaves . . . uh, our ex-slaves . . . or our animals, or the trees we've planted with our own money, or the crops that are already in the ground?" Laura's words came in a rush.

"My dear lady, please slow down. This is the first I have heard of this plan. Are you sure of your facts?"

"Of course I'm sure!" Laura realized that her voice was getting louder, but she was helpless to control it. "The commissioners told Mr. Soule of their intentions just yesterday, and he came straight to us. You must do something to stop them!"

"Would you care to rephrase that as a respectful request rather than a demand?" The general's voice was suddenly colder.

Mr. Pierce stepped in to avoid a major confrontation. "I hadn't heard of this, either, General, but it doesn't surprise me. The problem with our three tax commissioners has always been that they act first and then consider the consequences, not the other way around. The Gideonites of St. Helena Island have many organizational and manning problems at the moment. They are certainly justified in their fear that such a major disruption might mean the end of their endeavors."

Now properly humbled, Laura tried again. "I apologize for allowing my emotions to overcome my manners, General Saxton. You have always protected our interests, and I assure you that we are grateful. It's just that this is so dangerous a situation that . . ."

"Of course it is, and I shan't allow anyone to run roughshod over your interests. But I do wonder why it has not been handled through proper channels."

"Is there such a thing as a proper channel in the Sea Islands, General? When I first arrived in Beaufort, I asked Mr. Pierce about the system of education the teachers followed. Do you remember what you told me?" she asked, turning to Mr. Pierce.

"I do. It was something on the order of, 'There is no system here. We're all floundering through uncharted territory, just doing what we can.' I'm afraid that's still true."

"Yes. So I'm floundering along with everyone else. I have schools to run, a headquarters to manage with no one in charge, sick and injured patients to treat, new arrivals to assign, food shortages to deal with, the threat of rebel invasions on our homes, heat, bugs, overzealous Army recruiters scaring our Negroes . . ."

"And you think you're responsible for everything." Saxton's words were a statement, not a question.

"It feels that way, yes."

"What were you sent to do here?" the general asked.

"To deliver a shipment of clothing, and then to stay on to use my medical knowledge to help the slaves."

"And to treat your fellow Gideonites if they fell ill?"

"If they were willing to accept my treatment, yes."

"And have you done that?"

"I try to, but I have so many other duties that—"

"And who is it who says you are also responsible for bugs, heat, new arrivals, food shortages, schools, and whatever else you think you have to manage?"

Laura opened her mouth, made a tiny sound, and then shut it again. She had no answer.

"That's my point, my dear. You're trying to run the world without the proper tools or authority to do so."

Will looked fondly at his sister before trying to defuse the argument. "As our older sister always said, Laura, you're arrogant, opinionated, and your feet . . ."

"I know," Laura answered. "Arrogant, opinionated, and my feet are too big. Guilty as charged."

Several people laughed, and the atmosphere lightened.

"I'll make a bargain with you, Miss Towne. If you will get back to doing what you do best—which is offering medical care to your workers and colleagues, including Mrs. Saxton and me—I'll take care of the management of the rest of St. Helena Island."

38
MEDICAL LESSONS
April 1863

It sounded like a reasonable proposal—just go back to doing what she did best, which meant taking care of the sick and injured. Laura started the next week by calling on the superintendents of the St. Helena plantations. She asked about the living conditions of the workers and visited the old slave cabins to locate those who were hiding their ills in silence. What she discovered threw her good intentions into disarray. Sickness and suffering seemed to be everywhere, and all too many of the cases were beyond her limited abilities.

Over at the Capers plantation on Ladies Island, a little girl had fallen into the fireplace while trying to lift a soup pot off the hook. Her ragged dress blazed up around her and caught her oiled hair on fire. Screaming, she had run back into the yard, defying attempts to help her. When Laura entered her mother's cabin the next day, the odor of burnt flesh permeated the room, and beneath it another sweetish odor that warned of worse to come.

"What have you done for her?" Laura asked the mother.

"Don know what fuh do," the mother responded, her eyes brimming with tears. "She be sleepin now, an I don want fuh wake she up."

Laura peered closely at the charred little body and realized that the girl was dead. "How long has she been . . . uh . . . sleeping?" Laura asked, reluctant to break the news.

"Eber since dey bring she in here," the mother said. "I try fuh take she clothe off, but I caint git em loose. You be gwine hep she?"

"I'm afraid there's nothing I can do. Her burns were too serious."

"But you hab all dat larnin. Why you not want fuh make she bedder? Gib she sumptin fuh make she wake up."

"It's too late, Sally Mae. She's not going to wake up. I suspect she was dead when they brought her home."

"No! Don you be sayin dat! Dat be muh onliest lil gal."

"I'm so sorry, Sally Mae," Laura began, but the mother was beyond hearing her. Fumbling in her medicine bag, Laura brought out a small vial of paregoric, which she hoped would calm the mother down and let her rest. But when she tried to administer the dose, the grieving woman struck the vial from her hand.

"Don you be tryin fuh gib Sally Mae nuttin. If you caint take care uh muh chile, you jis gits outta here!" The mother pounded Laura in the chest with her fists and pushed her through the door. Laura stumbled on the threshold and fell backward into the yard.

"Missus Laura? What you be sittin in de dirt fuh? Be you hurt?" The speaker was a grizzled old woman whom Laura recognized from a previous visit to Nelly Winsor's school here on the Capers plantation.

"I'm fine, Beulah. I just tripped as I came out the door. Give me a hand up, will you?"

Laura shook out her skirts and caught her breath for a moment. Then she turned to the old woman. "Do you live here? Do you know Sally Mae?"

"Why you want fuh know?"

"Because Sally Mae needs help. Her little girl just died and she's all alone in there with the body. She needs someone to prepare the child for burial and family to sit with her."

"Sally Mae be jis fine. She don need nobody right now."

"But, surely, she . . ."

"What you know? Dat de trubble wit you white folk. You tinks eberbody gots fuh do tings de way you duz. We hab we own way uh lookin at tings."

"But she seems nearly out of her mind with grief. It's dangerous to leave her alone."

"No, it not. Dat what she need. You jis leaves she be." The old woman started to stomp away and then hesitated before turning back. "Mebbe you really don unnerstan."

"I guess I don't."

"From what I sees uh you white folk, you likes to be lone when you workin. You always be chasin folk outta de room or tellin dem fuh be quiet. But when you faces trubble, you spects eberbody fuh come round an hold you hand. Black folk do tings diffrunt. When we be workin, we be mos always in a bunch uh folk. We works in gangs. We lives in crowded cabins an eats all at de same table. So when we be sad, we wants fuh be alone, cause sad be private."

"I do understand that, but Sally Mae doesn't know that child is dead."

"Course she do. Dat why she shut up inside wit she. She a mam, an she still gots lots fuh teach dat chile. She gwine be sittin dere till she empty she heart uh all dat love. When she finish, den she be comin out, an we takes care uh de buryin. Till den, we leaves she be. She need dis time."

Laura cringed as she recognized the truth of the old woman's description. "I'm sorry. I really hadn't thought of it that way. I'll respect your wishes and be on my way. But if Sally Mae needs me, you be sure to send a message to The Oaks."

"Tankee, ma'am. But dis here trubble aint nuttin you be gwine fix."

* * *

The next day, Mr. Tomlinson approached Laura with another request for medical attention. "There's a woman nameded Sophy out in a camp near Mr. Ruggles's place; she has cut her leg badly. She was chopping grapevine with an axe and missed her swing. Could you go by and see what can be done?"

"Where is this, exactly? I don't remember a camp near there."

"It's actually near the old ruin of the Tabby House. The land is part of The Oaks acreage, but in an area that we have not been cultivating. Old Roger of Edisto came to Mr. Soule just before I took over The Oaks and asked if he and his sixty parents could occupy that land and raise crops there with an eye to buying it at the next land sale."

"Sixty parents?"

"Well, by parents he meant relatives, but you get the idea. They are a hardworking group of men and eager to become independent. Both Mr. Soule and I tried to convince them to leave their families in the village, where they have sturdy housing and government rations, but they were determined to be on their own. Roger insisted that if they were going to succeed they needed to have every member of the family doing their parts. He doesn't want just a farm; he wants a community—a self-sufficient one that handles its own needs. I probably would never have heard of Sophy's accident if her daughter had not happened to meet me on the road to Oaklands."

That afternoon, Laura took the sulky and drove out toward the Ruggles plantation, secretly hoping she would not run into Amanda Ruggles along the way. She probably won't appreciate my interfering with medical problems in her neighborhood any more than she does when I take over one of her students, Laura fussed at herself. But I can hardly allow Sophy to suffer with the kind of leg wound an axe can deliver.

Near the Tabby House, she tied the horse to a tree and set out across the fields. She knew she would find some primitive living quarters, but these little palmetto shanties were much worse than she expected. The concerned daughter, Dorcas, was sitting outside and pointed Laura toward a doorway covered only by a rag that looked suspiciously like a former apron. Laura had to crawl into Sophy's hut on hands and knees because there was not room to stand upright. The suffering woman lay in the middle of the floor, next to a fire that gave off copious quantities of smoke. There was no chimney, so the smoke hung thick in the air, slowly seeping out of the gaps between the palmetto leaves that formed a makeshift roof. The heat was almost unbearable.

Sophy's wounded leg was on the far side from the doorway, so Laura was forced to crawl over the woman to get a good look. Her entire leg was coated with something sticky, and the wound gaped open near her shin. But surprisingly, it did not appear to be inflamed or swollen, and there was no noticeable odor other than a pleasant sweetness.

"What is this?" Laura asked, touching the undamaged portion of her leg. She lifted her hand, and long strands of stickiness followed it.

"Dat be honey," Dorcas answered from the doorway. "Mam tole we fuh find a beehive soon as she gots hurt, an we coats she leg wit it. Dat an de smoke hep keeps de cut fro bleedin an oozin."

"Well, it certainly seems to have worked," Laura said. "How did she know what to do?"

Dorcas shrugged. "I don know. Dat jis what we always does."

"Still, I'd like to stitch up that wound so that it heals better. I think we should move her back to The Oaks so that I can tend to her more easily."

"I don tink Uncle Roger gwine like dat."

Sophy spoke up for the first time. "Ifn I hab fuh go way fro here, I be wantin fuh go back to de village, so's I kin see muh chillun."

"Mr. Fairfield will be the one to make that decision. I'm sure he can persuade Uncle Roger to allow a move, but I'll need to have you close to my care. You can move in with Aunt Phyllis, Sophy. How does that sound?"

"Guess I don gits a choice."

"It'll just be for a little while, I promise."

* * *

Laura's thoughts were jumbled as she drove back to The Oaks. What am I doing? she wondered. Am I any good to these people, or am I just making their lives more confused? I'm trying to treat their physical problems without any understanding of the rest of their challenges. They have a culture of their own and their own way of handling pain and grief. I didn't help Sally Mae or her little girl at all, and I probably made that situation worse. And Sophy's injury is another example. Her family was taking good care of it, even if they weren't doing what I would have done. Now I'm proposing to move Sophy away from the people she loves, just to make my own life easier. I'm not a doctor at all. I'm an interfering old busybody!

She was still stewing that evening at supper. Mr. Tomlinson watched her for a while and then asked, "Have a hard day in the fields, Miss Towne?"

Laura started at the sound of his voice. "I'm sorry. Were you asking me something?"

"You've been a thousand miles away. I was wondering if there are problems I ought to know about."

"Nothing serious. But I've been worried about my interactions with our Negroes. Sometimes I think I'm doing more harm than good."

"For instance?"

"When Sally Mae's child died, I tried to treat her grief, only to have Old Beulah tell me that I didn't understand how their people dealt with sorrow. And of course she was right. I shouldn't have . . ."

"Oh! Beulah!" Nelly interrupted. "I completely forgot. Beulah asked me to tell you that Sally's little girl is going to be buried tomorrow at sunset. She said you could come if you wanted to."

Laura drew a deep breath. "Oh. I've never seen a black funeral. I wonder if I should go."

"It seems to me," Mr. Tomlinson said, "that it would be an insult if you didn't go. But heading out to Ladies Island all alone that late might be dangerous. I'll ride along to make sure you're safe."

"Why don't I go along with you?" Lottie offered. "I've become familiar with several of the people at the Capers place, and I'd like to see how they handle a funeral."

"Thank you, Lottie. I think I should go. I'm coming to realize that I can't treat a person's body if I don't understand that person's feelings. I need to learn how they live . . . and how they die."

"Then I will come with you, too," Ellen added, "and perhaps Miss Winsor should join us as the teacher they know best. We'll stay in the background as much as possible so as not to disturb the ceremonies, whatever they may be. But it will be a good lesson for all of us."

39
A FUNERAL,
A WEDDING, AND A RESCUE
May/June 1863

A s they approached the slave village the next evening, they found a crowd assembling in front of Sally Mae's cabin. Many were people they recognized from other plantations. Some of the men carried blazing pine torches, which cast some faces in shadow and illuminated others. A roughly shaped pine box rested on a brace of sawhorses in the middle of the yard. The silence made the teachers hold their breath, as if any movement might break a mysterious spell.

Out of the crowd stepped an elderly man who spoke a few words in Gullah too thick for the white onlookers to understand. The assembled blacks, however, nodded their heads and then began a kind of chant that grew and expanded as different groups joined in. Laura eventually began to pick up a kind of refrain, but while she still couldn't understand the verses, the grief behind the lament was clear.

Then two men stepped forward, picked up the coffin, and led a procession toward a distant thicket. The people followed slowly, grouped by twos and accompanied by the torchbearers. They kept pace with a complicated but rhythmic clapping until the undergrowth made walking too difficult. Laura and her companions remained at the back of the crowd, so that by the time they reached the worst of the tangled scrub vines, the way had been trampled.

"I thought we'd be going to a graveyard," Nelly whispered. "Why in the world are we headed into this overgrown area?"

"Sh-h-h," Laura cautioned, as the group ahead stopped and surrounded a freshly dug hole.

"But this isn't a cemetery."

"It's a grave, nevertheless."

The bearers lowered their burden into the hole and then tossed the first handfuls of dirt on top of the casket. One by one, the other mourners joined the ritual filling of the grave. Laura finally spotted Sally Mae, looking composed and indistinguishable from the rest of the mourners.

Again, Nelly leaned over and whispered, "Isn't that the child's mother?"

Laura nodded but held a cautionary finger to her lips.

"But she doesn't look any sadder than the rest." This time it was Ellen who frowned and gave Nelly a poke to quiet her.

Once the grave was filled, another ritual began. Now women approached the mound and laid upon it all sorts of objects—a bowl, a broken pitcher, a bottle, a spoon, a makeshift doll, and a variety of shells soon decorated the place of burial.

Again, a song began with a single voice and then became a chant. This time Laura could make out the words:

Like a strong house,
Oonuh keep muh life fuh me.
When oonuh leave fuh de sea,

Take me long
Dat I live foreber wit oonuh.
De water bring we here
De water take we home.

The ritual was finished, and the mourners disappeared into the darkness. As Mr. Tomlinson led the women back toward the road, they puzzled over what they had just witnessed.

"Why at night?"

"Perhaps so that they don't have to miss work," Mr. Tomlinson said.

"You sound like a slave driver."

"And why off in the woods instead of a cemetery?"

"Perhaps because the plantation owners wouldn't let the slaves bury their dead on valuable ground that could be used for agriculture," Tomlinson suggested.

"Why so many conch shells?" Ellen asked.

Lottie knew that answer. "The conch shell is a symbol for water in their folklore," she explained. "And water is very important. Even if their families have been here for generations, they remember that they came to South Carolina from across the sea, and there's an almost inborn desire to return to some ancestral homeland on the other side of the water."

"That certainly is not part of a Christian funeral," Mr. Tomlinson said. "Sounds like they'd rather go somewhere across the water than get to heaven."

"Well, yes, I think that's true," Laura said. "You must remember that we've been teaching them our version of Christianity for only a few months. These rituals have been a part of their lives for as long as they can remember. I think we tend to forget that the Negroes have a culture of their own."

"But we're supposed to be teaching them the right way to do things," Nelly protested. "I found the whole ceremony most disturbing."

"And I, for one, found it very enlightening," Laura said. "Three days ago, I tried to tell Sally Mae how to handle the death of her child. How presumptuous of me—as if black mothers have not been losing their children for centuries! Tonight I saw a mother who had come through the worst of her grief and was handling herself in a sophisticated and intelligent manner. She didn't need me to tell her how to live her life."

"But what if their way of life is wrong?"

"According to whom?"

"Well, obviously, we know more . . ."

"No. Stop right there. We can't begin to know what it is like to be a people who have been enslaved. We can't know what is right for them. We can only help when they ask for help. I've learned this week that I don't know as much about life and its problems as I thought I did. And I've resolved to stop talking so much and start listening more."

* * *

Several nights later, Nelly found Laura standing on the darkening veranda. "May I interrupt your reveries?" she asked.

"Oh, Nelly. Of course. Is anything the matter?"

"No, no. First, I wanted to apologize for sounding intolerant the other night after the funeral. Your observations were quite accurate, and I think you taught us all an important lesson. I only wish I had as much insight into other people's feelings as you seem to have."

"I wish I understood more. I think that struggle is a prime component of our humanity. It's too easy to get wrapped up in our own thoughts and forget that others have different problems."

"Well, I'm certainly guilty of that lately. And I'm afraid I've come to involve you in my personal life."

"I thought you said there was nothing wrong."

"It's not that something's wrong. I need help with something that's right, if that makes any sense."

"Well . . . why don't you just come out with it? How may I help you?"

"I'm getting married, and I don't have a mother."

"I'm not sure I qualify . . ."

Nelly laughed, and her tension seemed to ease. "I just need someone to help me with the arrangements . . . and maybe hold my hand now and then until it's over."

"Hand-holding was a part of my medical training. I can manage that." Laura hesitated, cocking her head to study Nelly's face. "You're sure, then, that this is what you want to do."

"Yes, I think I am."

"You think?"

"It is the right thing to do. I'm almost alone in the world, Laura. You've met my father. You know how elderly and frail he is, and once he's gone there will be no one left to care about me. I need to marry and start a family of my own. I've feared that I would never meet a man I could trust and care about, especially during this war. But Josiah Fairfield is everything

I could want in a husband—hard-working, honest, devout, gentle, . . ."

"Gentle?" Laura could not stop herself from reacting.

"Yes, with me he is. Oh, I know a lot of people don't like him, but that's because he puts on a bit of an act when he's around other men. With me, he is unfailingly kind and comforting. He adores me, Laura, and I know he'll be there whenever I need him."

"You haven't said you love him."

"What's love? I'm not sure I even know what the word means. But I know he's my closest friend. I like him, I trust him, and we work well together. We share the same values, and we want the same things out of life. It will be a good marriage."

"Then I will be happy to do whatever I can to help. May I share the news with Ellen?"

"Of course, and with Lottie, too. I've been thinking I want a simple church service and only a small celebration back here at the house. I want to invite everyone to the ceremony. I've attended so many black weddings that it seems only proper to open my own wedding to our people. But we can't afford a huge reception like the one the Saxtons put on. And if I can't invite everyone, I don't want to pick and choose among my friends."

"But you'll have to have a cake and flowers and a decorated church. Have you thought about a dress?"

"One of the women at Mr. Eustis's place is sewing me a gown of white muslin, and I thought I'd just put some white flowers in my hair."

"Have you chosen a date?"

Nelly giggled. "We couldn't decide, so rather than fuss about it, we sort of drew straws. May 7th is a Thursday, but we thought we could hold the ceremony in the late afternoon when everyone is finished with the day's work."

"Lovely. Leave the rest to us."

* * *

A festive occasion was exactly what everyone needed. Ellen and Lottie took over the decorating chores: polishing the church, arranging bouquets of flowers and hanging baskets around the pulpit, and twining ivy to decorate the pillars. At The Oaks, they cut enough roses to adorn every downstairs room. Laura directed the baking of the bridal cake and contacted the Saxtons to arrange a surprise honeymoon retreat in Beaufort for the newlyweds. On the day of the wedding, Mrs. Phillips, the minister's wife, brought over two iced cakes and baskets of fresh strawberries. Laura arranged all on the dining table, the cakes wreathed by the berries and rose blossoms.

More surprises greeted the guests at the church. One of the army regiments had furnished a band of musicians, who announced the bride's arrival with trumpets and flourishes. Guests poured into the church—among them the bride's pupils, the house staff from The Oaks, and nearly all the Gideonites. The Saxtons attended, along with the Judds, Mr. Hooper, and his guest, Miss Martha Kellogg, a teacher from Hilton Head.

Still, Laura looked about and worried that Nelly would be disappointed at how few adult blacks attended the wedding. "Why didn't they come?" she whispered. "We told every superintendent to invite their people."

"I'm hearing talk that the army recruiters who show up at church services are making the people afraid to come to the church," Lottie offered. "They hold praise meetings at home, instead."

"I hate to say it on a day like this," Ellen said, "but I hear that Sunday school attendance is way down, too, since Mr. Fairfield took over the running of it."

"But the Negroes have always loved Nelly. Surely they would want to see her get married."

"But not to Mr. Fairfield, perhaps."

It was a worrisome suggestion, but Laura pushed it to the back of her mind in order to enjoy the rest of the festivities. After the ceremony, the Judds and Saxtons came back to The Oaks for the cake cutting, but none of the Gideonites, with the exception of Mr. Hooper and Miss Kellogg, were invited. Even Lottie was relegated to helping with the service rather than being treated as a guest. Laura wondered if Mr. Fairfield had something to do with that, too.

I'm being uncharitable, she told herself, and it's not my place to make decisions about who should have been invited. This is Nelly's day, and I shan't spoil it for her.

* * *

A funeral and a wedding had somehow worked together to make spring in the Low Country seem almost like normal life, but the war and its problems were never far from anyone's mind. June opened with another expedition against the Confederates, led this time by the Second South

Carolina Colored Regiment. Colonel James Montgomery commanded only 250 troops, but they were a feisty band, eager to take on their former masters. Accompanying Montgomery was another fiery individual—a tiny former slave, Harriet Tubman, who had come to South Carolina to act as a spy for the Union Army. Together they led their newly recruited black soldiers up the Combahee River and into the interior, where planation owners were still raising rice with slave labor.

Harriet knew exactly where she was going. The groundwork she and her fellow spies had prepared paid off. As their gunboats cruised up the river, slaves began gathering their meager belongings, their children and chickens, and what foodstuffs lay close at hand. They streamed to the riverbanks when the boats blew their whistles, and the troops loaded them aboard before their startled owners could begin to respond. Then, with Montgomery's explicit orders, the soldiers set fire to the crops and plantation buildings. Their clear intent was revenge and destruction.

On the morning of June 3rd, the gunboats pulled into Beaufort harbor and unloaded 727 newly freed slaves—men, women, and children. The Army turned a local church into a temporary shelter, while Montgomery and his recruiters vetted the refugees, inducting into their regiment every able-bodied man. Those not found fit for military service, along with the women and children, then made their way to St. Helena Island, where once more the Gideonites faced the daunting task of clothing, feeding, and housing a band of refugees who had escaped with nothing more than the bits they could carry.

⌒✕⌒

RINA ON "POOR MISSUS LAURA"
June 1863

L an uh mercy! I be worrit bout Missus Laura cause she be so busy wit eberbody's trubbles. Hardly a day go by but she be call somewheres fuh treat sumbody what be sick. Dat Massa Severance call she fuh come see he boy Seymour, but he don listen fuh what she tell he. I hears Missus Laura tell Missus Ellen dat de boy hab consumshun an gwine die, but de fadduh not be wantin he fuh go home.

Den Massa Hooper, he git de swamp feber. One day he be sick fuh die an say he be gwine go home. Den de nex day, he be feelin bedder an he change he plan. Finely, dey git onna boat fuh go to de nort. But by den, dere be mo sick folk eberwhere. Ober at Massa Ruggle place, dere be bad cases uh smallpox, an Missus Laura be worrit bout dem.

Folk goin hungry, too. It be summer an de crops aint reddy yet, so dere aint nuf corn an hay fuh de hosses. Eberbody eatin less cause dere aint no money fuh buy food. De govmint men says dey caint pay what dey owes de workers till de crop come in, but by den we sho gwine be hungry. Genral Saxton be gwine nort fuh talk wit de govmint. An dat Genral Hunter, he be gwine way somewheres fuh good. Now de govmint send sum specters fuh check up on how tings be doin here. Missus Laura done gone to Buford fuh answer dere questions, but she be cot in a turrible storm on de way back an ruint she hat. Dat made she scairt an sad.

She be upset wit Missus Nelly, too. Missus Laura finely gots a box ship fro up nort an in it be a gift for Missus Nelly an Massa Fairfield. Dere be six silber spoon, a ladle, an salt spoon, but Missus Nelly don eben say tankee, an Missus Laura done gots she feelins hurt.

Dat brown gal be causin trubble at de school, too. She be wantin fuh move fuh work wit de color regmint, but dat dere doctor Rogers, he say she caint come cause folks be talkin bout her. Now she be barrassed, I tink, cause she want fuh move outa de Oaks. She be gwine to Seaside, but de Penn School now hab only 2 teacher fuh 160 scholar. Dat make Missus Laura work too much.

An dere be Massa Fairfield. I don unnerstan why Missus Nelly want fuh marry he. He be a nasty man. De udder day, he catch Josie, one uh de stable hand, ridin a hoss he not sposed fuh ride. Josie be usin de hoss fuh race wit de cow. Massa Fairfield an Josie gits intuh a fight, an Massa Fairfield fair choke dat boy fuh dead. Missus Laura hab fuh come out an break up de fight. Now nobody be willin fuh work in de stable, an Missus Laura end up feedin de hosses sheself, which aint right.

Dere be a new lady come here. Dey say she be a famous actress name Margrit Davenport, but we neber hear uh she. Den she marry a genral an be name Missus Lander, but he git heself killt, an now she gots a job runnin de army hospital in Buford. Missus Laura, she aint so sho dey gwine be friend. Missus Lander be English, so she talk funny. She say she be conceited an oberbearin, an she be spectin folk fuh wait on she. She say de army mens at de hospital don like she much an wont let she do she work. Dat make it tuff on Missus Laura, too, cause now de genrals not be lettin enny ladies in de hospital.

Dudder day, Missus Lander come fuh visit. Missus Laura be sittin on de veranda playin wit a lil kitten she hab fuh a pet. An dat Missus Lander done take it home. Missus Laura, she so nice, she say she be gibbin de kitten to Missus Lander. But I knows she miss habbin she own lil cat.

Now she gots more folk what need she fuh doctor dem. We all be glad dose black folk fro de Combahee gots way fro dere massa, but space be gettin cramped roun here. I bin takin in sum uh de black wimmun, so I sees how tire Missus Laura be when she come fuh check on dem.

Dey not be big trubbles, mebbe, but dey all be upsettin Missus Laura, an I don like dat. She seem sad all de time. I be worrit bout she.

40
WAR COMES TO THE ISLANDS
June–July 1863

When Laura looked back on the summer of 1863, what she remembered was fear, pervasive and paralyzing. Disease was everywhere—not just malarial fevers now, but typhoid, smallpox, and yellow fever—with death a common result. The war, which until now had been something happening in the newspapers and on battlefields far away, suddenly became personal and ever present. People she had spent pleasant afternoons with just days before were now casualties of battle. Blood, gaping wounds, and amputations became part of her daily life.

As soon as General Saxton learned that Quincy Gilmore would be replacing David Hunter as commander of the Department of the South, he had assembled the Gideonites to let them know what to expect. "General Hunter has been reluctant to take any offensive action against Charleston since his ignominious defeat at the Battle of Secessionville, which is why you've only seen him running things at Hilton Head. But General Gilmore is of another stripe entirely. He came with the original South Carolina Expeditionary Force and distinguished himself as the general who planned and executed the destruction of Fort Pulaski last April. He's been champing at the bit to strike Charleston ever since. I fully expect to see the attack begin within the month. And it will surely impact all of you."

"Why is that?" Mr. Tomlinson asked. "Charleston is a long way from here."

"No, not as the crow flies. It might take you a couple of days to ride there through all the wilderness and marshland that lie between us, but it's just around the corner if you go by sea. The Navy will begin the bombardment, and you will surely hear every shot. Probably feel them, too."

"Oh dear, that will upset our people who remember the Big Shoot. Some of them still cringe at every loud noise," Laura said.

"They'll have to get used to it. The battle may take several days, and that's just one of the factors that will affect you. A full assault on Charleston will require the participation of almost every regiment stationed here, which will leave the Sea Islands unprotected. If the Confederates suffer losses near or in Charleston, they may retaliate by attacking these islands. You'll need to be prepared for that. There have been serious proposals from Hilton Head about evacuating all these islands for your own safety."

"But we've had those discussions before. We decided last summer that we could not possibly leave here because of our responsibilities toward our Negro population," Laura reminded him.

"This may be different. Snipers threatening individual plantations did not warrant mass panic. But if you find yourselves facing a full regimental attack, you'll have no choice but to run to safety. I'm not saying it will happen, but it's best to be forewarned."

"And scared to death?" Ellen asked.

"No. Just prepared. And, of course, there's another possibility, too. If the battle goes badly for us, there will be inevitable deaths, perhaps even among your people in the colored regiments, and certainly there will be wounded soldiers who will need care. We may have to call upon you and the other ladies, Miss Towne, to help out in the hospitals."

"We'll do what we can, of course."

"Will they really include our Negro regiments in the attack?" Mr. Tomlinson asked.

"Yes, definitely. If I were planning an attack on Charleston, I would want the colored troops to lead the way."

"Why? Are you suggesting that they be sacrificed to protect the white regiments?"

"No, not at all. Southerners have always feared a slave uprising, which is one of the reasons they kept their slaves chained and beaten into submission. An attack led by a regiment of black soldiers would throw them into panic and disarray."

"Are the colored regiments really prepared to lead an attack?"

"Certainly." When several Gideonites looked at him questioningly, Saxton hesitated. "Oh, Higginson's men may not be," he admitted. "The colonel has made sure that his soldiers are well drilled, neat in habits and appearance, obedient, and skillful in what they do, but he is really against violence. He treats his men with respect and is more a father figure for them than a military commander. The general may want to keep them out of harm's way. But we also have Colonel Montgomery's Second South Carolina Volunteers, and that wild bunch is always ready for a fight. Monty has encouraged viciously destructive raids. His tools are terror, hatred for the enemy, strict discipline, and harsh punishment. And then there's the Fifty-fourth Massachusetts. You probably have had little or no contact with them, since they no sooner arrived in June than they were shipped off to join the attack on Darien, Georgia. You'll meet them at the Fourth of July celebration, if not sooner. They're a splendid bunch, recruited by Boston abolitionists from among the most successful free blacks and commanded by officers who are highly educated gentlemen from the upper classes of society. They're a formidable force, and they are ready for serious military action."

* * *

As if the threat of battle had been put on hold, the Fourth of July celebrations were again a success. The teachers had made white rosette badges with a tricolor button for every Penn School scholar. Someone read the Declaration of Independence, several others made short speeches, and the students sang their favorite songs. Then the students and their families had a picnic with bread and molasses water, while the teachers and military staff sat under the oak trees and chatted. At dinner that afternoon at The Oaks were Major Hallowell, second-in-command of the Fifty-fourth Massachusetts, and Major Lincoln Stone, the regimental surgeon, along with Captain Hooper, General Saxton, and Mrs. Lander.

Laura did her best to join in the convivial mood of her guests. She particularly enjoyed talking with Major Stone, who was enthusiastic about everything he had experienced that morning.

"I'm so happy to have seen the people free at last and so well behaved," he said. "Back home, there are still those who don't believe in the Negro's ability to become a full-fledged citizen. If only those doubters could have seen your children this morning! They would have new hope for the future of our great nation, I'm sure."

"Our scholars are charming, I admit," Laura said. "You must see them later this afternoon. They are planning to bring over a load of watermelons for our refreshment, and they'll be performing a little 'shout' on our veranda."

"A shout?"

"It's a unique dance . . . or religious rite . . . or celebration. I can't adequately describe it, but they always want to perform for newcomers to the islands."

"I look forward to it. This whole day has provided a much-needed respite from the preparations for battle."

"About that battle . . . Is it coming soon?"

"All very hush-hush, I'm afraid. But you'll know when it's coming off. One can't easily move four ironclad warships and nearly 1,800 men without someone noticing."

* * *

The major was correct. Within two days the islands were abuzz with rumors of the activity at Hilton Head. Everyone knew when the Fifty-fourth Massachusetts and Montgomery's Second South Carolina troops departed for Folly Island. By Wednesday, July 8th, Higginson and his First South Carolina Colored Regiment marched out toward the railroad bridge over the Edisto River as a diversionary move, and the Gideonites braced themselves for the first sounds of battle.

Instead, a severe line of thunderstorms rolled in during the afternoon, frightening the children—who confused the thunder with cannon shots—and delaying the attack for another day. Laura recorded the first real gunshot on Thursday night at 10 o'clock.

Confusing reports reached St. Helena by July 11th. The first messenger assured everyone that Fort Wagner on Morris Island had been captured, allowing the Union troops to fire directly on Fort Sumter and open the way to Charleston Harbor. The next one brought news of a massive defeat for the Union forces: 49 men killed, another 123 wounded, and 167 missing. The news from the diversionary expedition was no better. The First South Carolina had failed to capture the railroad bridge, and Colonel Higginson had been seriously wounded by a spent shell that grazed his side and caused severe internal injury.

Concern over the casualties gave way the next day to excitement among the freedmen. Higginson's expedition arrived home, bringing with them 500 Negroes they had managed to liberate from the interior. As their small boats had made their way up a narrow branch of the Edisto River, hordes of escaping slaves had descended on them, clamoring to be taken to freedom. By the time Laura reached the Port Royal Ferry, her way was blocked by dozens of impromptu family reunions.

Pompey, Mr. Philbrick's foreman, discovered that his mother-in-law, Charlotte, was among the refugees. Laura found herself pulled into their celebration, much to the surprise of the little black woman, who could not believe that her daughter and grandson were free to talk and laugh with a "buckra lady." Once the initial excitement died down, Laura was able to question Charlotte.

"How did you escape?" she asked.

"We be lone fuh bout a year," Charlotte answered. "De massa an de overseer lef fuh de upcountry. Dey jis says we gots fuh find food somewheres an we gots fuh take care uh weselfs. So we be hidin in de woods an eatin whateber we find growin. We comes out when we see black soljers comin up de riber. Den we runs outta de woods fuh hep."

Laura wasn't sure whether to laugh or cry. Delight that all these people had been rescued competed with the realization that 500 new people to house, clothe, and feed would put a real strain on the Gideonites' limited resources. Some 200 could be housed on one abandoned plantation and put to planting slip potatoes. Many others would reunite with the families from whom they had been separated. The rest would have to spread out across the islands, finding work on individual plantations.

* * *

Worry about the outcome of the Army's foray against Charleston continued. The remaining 1,200 or so Union soldiers had withdrawn to Folly Island until they could be massively reinforced. At Hilton Head, an additional 5,000 troops and eleven ships of the South Atlantic Blockading Squadron prepared to join the battle. Sporadic gunfire shook the ground of the Sea Islands day after day and kept nerves on edge.

Then on Saturday, July 18th, the gunshots rose to a crescendo. From dawn to dusk, they kept up a steady barrage. Those who understood such things explained that the attack had begun. The plan was to shell Fort Wagner into submission before the waiting twelve regiments of foot soldiers rushed the walls. The constant thunder of the naval guns had kept hearts pounding all day, but at dusk, when the guns fell silent, tensions rose even higher—and with good reason.

The word, when it came, was devastating. The Union forces had suffered a great defeat. A total of 1,515 casualties out of 5,000 men told only part of the story. The attack on the fort had been led by the Fifty-fourth Massachusetts. Colonel Robert Shaw, only twenty-five years old, had led the charge on foot. As General Saxton had predicted, the sight of black soldiers had infuriated the Confederates. Shaw and his men reached the top of the parapet, only to be shot at point-blank range. In all, thirty members of the regiment were killed immediately in the battle, and twenty-four soldiers died of their wounds. There were fifteen men taken prisoner, and fifty-two others were never heard from again, their bodies lost in the sea of destruction that overwhelmed the Fifty-fourth Massachusetts. Only 315 members of the regiment made it back to Hilton Head. Nearly every officer had been killed or injured.

* * *

As the wounded poured into the Beaufort hospitals by the hundreds, Laura and the other Gideonites waited to be told what their roles would be. Laura received a message from Mr. Pierce on the 20th, asking her to come to Beaufort to help. Chaos greeted her arrival. Injured men were still being unloaded from the transports. A parade of litters passed her, each bearing a man swathed in dirty, bloodstained bandages. Wagonloads of supplies jostled the soldiers who were on foot.

Almost every vacant house in the city was being used as a hospital ward. The stench of gunpowder seemed to cling to those who had been in the battle, but it was at times overwhelmed by the stomach-turning odors of blood, putrefaction, vomit, and excrement. And then there was the noise. Shouts of instruction mingled with whinnying horses, the clatter of wagon wheels, the screams of the badly wounded, the constant moaning of the unconscious, and scattered cries for help, water, or mother.

Laura made her way to the nearest recognizable hospital, only to be turned away by a young soldier guarding the door. "No visitors!" he shouted at her.

"I'm not visiting. I'm a doctor," Laura said.

"Sure you are, and I'm a camel. Go away!"

Similar treatment greeted her at every doorstep. There didn't seem to be anyone over the age of eighteen in charge. In desperation, she made her way back toward the Saxton house, where she spotted Captain Hooper.

"Miss Towne, what are you doing here?"

"Mr. Pierce sent for my help, but now no one will let me anywhere near the wounded men. Can you vouch for me? Or do you know where they expect me to go?"

"I suspect you're most needed where they've taken some members of the Fifty-fourth—down Bay Street to the Tabby Manse. But I'd better escort you. Come along."

The Tabby Manse, formerly the home of Dr. Thomas Fuller, had been fitted as a hospital by the Roundheads early in 1862, so it was well equipped to receive the most seriously wounded. Captain Hooper's presence eased Laura's way, and she soon found herself in a downstairs ward. If she expected a welcome, however, she was disappointed.

The first soldier to spot her yelled, "Git outta here, Sesesh Lady! We don't need your gloating over our suffering."

Laura was stunned. "I'm not Sesesh. I'm a doctor from Philadelphia, and I'm here to help."

Jeering laughter let her know that no one believed her story. It also alerted an army doctor that something was going on. Laura was relieved to recognize Lottie's friend Dr. Rogers as he pushed his way through the ambulatory patients.

"Miss Towne, what are you doing here?"

"Why does everyone keep asking me that? I'm a doctor, for heaven's sake, and I was sent for. What can I do?"

"Do you have any quinine in that bag of yours?"

"Uh, no, I've never even used quinine. But I have quite a good supply of valerian root powder. That often works as a sedative."

"God help us! Look, Miss Towne. I'm dealing with amputations, sucking chest wounds, and men with their intestines hanging out. We don't have time to deal with your home remedies. If you are determined to help, my recommendation is that you go home. Organize your people to round up their excess food supplies. Watermelons will go a long way to alleviate the thirst of our patients, and fresh vegetables will help, too. And send us some of your superintendents—sturdy men who can do some heavy lifting."

"Watermelons? Is that all I'm good for? Watermelons, indeed! I'm here now, and it's too late to make my way back to St. Helena tonight. Surely there's something more useful I can do."

"I don't know what that might be. Miss Forten and Mrs. Lander might find some nursing duties for you," he said.

"Miss Forten? Lottie? She's already working here?"

"Yes, she came as soon as she heard the battle reports. Mrs. Lander has her mending bullet holes in the men's clothing and helping them write letters home."

"But she's supposed to be teaching at Seaside!"

"I'm just telling you what I know. If you want some advice, though, I'd say let it go."

"Why?"

"Because Miss Forten is struggling to find herself a path between the white side of her heritage and the black side. Until she does that, she isn't going to be much good to you as a teacher. Don't be surprised if she tells you she's headed back to Philadelphia very soon."

"Really? She's that unhappy here?"

"She's that confused about who she is and what her role should be," the doctor said. "Let her go, Miss Towne."

"I understand, but I'd still like to talk to her."

"You'll find both women over at the Smith House on the next corner. At least they'll be able to give you a place to sleep tonight. But then, you might think about going home, too. No one is going to let you provide medical care to men in a military hospital, not even for our black soldiers. Your kind of medicine is useless—worse than useless!"

Laura, who hadn't cried in a long time, felt tears threatening to overflow. Dr. Rogers had just spoken aloud her own suspicion—one that she had been doing her best to ignore. Was her homeopathic training really useless? Was she a fraud? Were her efforts to start a school doomed to failure, too? Should she just give up and go home? Not just to St. Helena, but back to Philadelphia?

41
THE CURSE OF DISEASE
August–September 1863

everal days later, Mr. Pierce confronted Laura at The Oaks. ""What are you doing here on St. Helena?" he demanded. "They need every available doctor in Beaufort. Didn't you receive my message asking you to go there?"

Laura struggled to retain her composure. "I went to Beaufort at your request. I presented myself for duty at every hospital I could find, only to be turned away. Doctor after doctor told me that they needed allopaths, not someone trained in homeopathy. Others said no women were allowed, although clearly some were working as nurses. Even Dr. Rogers told me to go home. He said I could help best by collecting watermelons and delivering them to the hospital kitchens. No one would let me see a patient, although several of our men— none with an ounce of medical experience—were welcomed. So I came back to St. Helena, where at least the Negroes don't question my abilities because I'm a woman."

"Are the Beaufort hospitals objecting to your training or your skirt?" he asked.

"Both, I think. Doctors don't expect women to be educated. And when they learn that I'm a homeopath rather than an allopath, they shy away even further."

"What do those terms mean? Is your training any different from theirs?"

"Yes, actually, it is. Conventional medical training, or allopathy, encourages extreme measures like bloodletting, the use of potent drugs containing mercury and antimony, and amputation to treat the symptoms without getting at the underlying cause of pain or infection. We homeopaths believe in treating the illness, not the symptom, and we encourage the body to heal itself. We use natural remedies, in very diluted amounts, along with paying attention to the patient and trying to relieve as much suffering and stress as we can. And we avoid any treatment that has side effects that may be worse than the disease."

"Like what?"

"Well, quinine, for one. That seems to be the drug of choice these days. When Dr. Rogers learned that I didn't have any quinine in my black bag, he dismissed my alternatives as 'totally useless.' I know that quinine reduces fever and pain, but so do some simple herbal remedies, and they do so without the danger of kidney failure, heart palpitations, and fluid retention."

"Isn't the result the only thing that matters?"

"Oh, Mr. Pierce. You and I are not going to answer that question. What matters is that the doctors in Beaufort don't want my help, and here on St. Helena there are all too many sick people who need me. You know that we have received over 1,200 refugees in the past months, and none of them have had any medical care since the war began. If I could work twenty-four hours a day, I still could not treat them all."

"I suppose that's true, but . . ."

"Then there's the question of who will care for the superintendents and teachers here on the island. Every other doctor is working in the military hospitals, and our own people are going home in droves. Even Lottie Forten just departed on her way back to Philadelphia. Since Mr. Tomlinson is accompanying the wounded who are being sent north and the Fairfields are taking a couple of months furlough, I'm the only doctor our own people have to rely on. I'm afraid we're headed into a period of widespread illness, too. Have you noticed how many people are sick?"

"Well, no, I . . ."

"We may be facing a real epidemic of Low Country fever if this heat does not break soon. Just at Seaside alone, Lizzie Hunn, Mr. Rice's daughter, Mrs. Bryant, and Mr. Walton all have violent and frequent fevers, and I don't have time to sit with them as I would like because of the number of patients I have on the plantations."

"The blacks are sick, too?"

"There's much too much smallpox among them, and even though most of them get only mild cases, it still tends to weaken them. One of my favorite students, Little Marie Mannegault, is very ill. She and all five of her brothers and sisters have just gotten over smallpox and are now suffering from typhoid. Her brother Eneas died today, and I fear Marie will be next. Their mother has no idea how to care for them. She makes them try to get up and walk around to gather their strength, while the poor little things are dying." Laura's eyes brimmed with tears as she remembered the sight of little

Eneas struggling to walk toward her and then collapsing at her feet as he took his final breath.

"You mustn't take these illnesses so to heart," Mr. Pierce said. "You can't hope to save everyone."

"That's easy enough for you to say. You're not responsible for their lives." Laura was crying openly now, her face flushed by embarrassment and emotion. "I'm sorry to let you see the rawness of my emotions, but sometimes I think I cannot go on—not for even one more day."

"Do you really need to take on so many cases?"

"Just who do you think will do it if I don't? A few days ago, I weakened and asked Dr. Wescott to come and see some of the other Gideonites who are ill. All he had to offer were those horrible blue mass pills. Mr. Pearcy asked if they had mercury and calomel in them, and when Dr. Wescott said they did, Mr. Pearcy and Mr. Fordham each refused to take them. Now they are both near death, and I have no time to soothe them or try to ease their passing."

"But surely . . ."

"Would you like to know how I spend my days, Mr. Pierce? I'm up at dawn to visit my patients here, and then I walk to the school, stopping at the plantations along the way. I meet Miss Murray there, and the two of us hold classes for as many as 160 children, because we have no other teachers left. We dismiss school around two o'clock, and I try to get to the other plantations along the road to Land's End. I reach Seaside by five o'clock, so that I can relieve Miss Ruggles, who spends her day there with our patients while Mr. and Mrs. Hunn are running their store. Amanda gives me her report of how all the patients are doing, and I take over the task of examining them, feeding them, and sitting with them until some time after midnight. During those hours, Miss Murray goes back to The Oaks to see our Negro patients and to catch a few hours sleep. In the middle of the night, she drives over and relieves me, so that I can go home and nap until the sun comes up, when the day starts over again."

"Are our people getting better?"

"No, not really. It's the nature of malarial fevers to run in cycles. A patient may feel quite well one day and be prostrate the next. And each cycle tends to be more severe as the patient weakens. I live in cycles, too. I'm weary, anxious, disheartened, and terrified, by turns. There's no end in sight and no solution to our problems. And it does no good for someone like you to keep asking foolish questions, as if all I have to do is come up with the right answer."

"I'm sorry, but . . ."

"Don't you understand? There is no right answer. There's no answer at all!"

* * *

Only to Ellen could Laura admit everything that was troubling her. "I'm going to be eternally grateful to Amanda Ruggles for her help during this fever season, but at the same time, she irritates me every time she opens her mouth. I hate the way she meets me at the door every evening and starts her litany of who is better and who is worse. I find I almost never agree with her diagnosis. I can be sure that if she says Mrs. Bryant is worse, I'll find that lovely lady sitting up in bed making plans to bake cakes or knit stockings. Amanda will tell me that Lizzie is quite well, and I find her only semiconscious. She's so sure of herself, and she's always wrong!"

"We couldn't have managed without her, Laura."

"I know that."

"And she's really trying to be helpful. I think she regrets being so nasty to you about our school."

"Maybe so, but I'm just existing for the day when our patients finally recover and I can send her packing."

"But until then, try to think of more pleasant things. Oh, I know! Come out to the barn and see what I found this morning."

Ellen led Laura to an unused corner of the barn and pointed to a box with high sides.

"Not more kittens!" Laura exclaimed.

"No, not kittens—baby squirrels. I thought you might enjoy them after Mrs. Lander made off with your little cat."

"We don't have time to take care of more animals," Laura said.

"Yes, we do. And we need them as a reminder that life keeps renewing itself. I've named them Bob, Bush, and Bunch. Bush is my favorite because he likes to snuggle. Here, hold him for just a minute so that he gets to know you."

Laura lifted the tiny bit of fur and held it under her chin for a moment. Helpless to stop herself, she smiled, patted the tiny rump, and then planted a kiss on the top of his head. "You're right, as usual. They're quite wonderful. Maybe we can talk Hastings into building them a real cage so that they can see out into the world."

* * *

Laura needed all the cheering up she could find as August gave way to September. Mr. Pearcy died of fever and dysentery on September 2nd, and Mr. Fordham followed him a day later. Within two weeks, two other superintendents died, and when the women at Seaside began to recover, Amanda Ruggles moved back to live with her brother, only to fall ill herself. Miss Rice, now healthy and feeling indebted to Amanda, offered to nurse her. Edwin Ruggles, however, was not happy with that arrangement.

"Miss Towne, you must take on her care. Amanda refuses to have anyone else," he said.

"I can't," she replied. "Almost everyone here at The Oaks is ill. I have my hands full now, and matters will only get worse. Both my brother and Miss Murray are scheduled to take their furloughs this month. The Fairfields are not coming back as expected because he is ill. Miss White needs constant care, as does Mr. Holt. Even Dr. Wakefield is prostrate."

"But Amanda helped you when you needed her."

"I know that, but I can't provide adequate care for everyone . . ." Laura's throat constricted and she fought to swallow. Then the words came out in a rush. "And I can't bear the thought that I might inadvertently be responsible for her worsening condition. Everyone knows that Amanda and I have clashed in the past. People will understand if I don't take her case, but no one will forgive me if I do take it and then something horrible happens. Please don't put me in that position. One of the Army doctors can help her. They may not have seen Low Country fever before, but it is closely related to yellow fever, and they have medicines to treat that."

"She won't have a military doctor. Believe me, I know my sister. If she doesn't have the doctor of her choice, she'll turn her back to anyone else and just lie there until she dies."

He turned and walked out, his slumped shoulders and dragging steps demonstrating his despair.

Ellen rounded on Laura in fury. "You can't do that, Laura! You're a doctor, and Amanda is just a patient who needs you. If you don't go to her now, you'll live to regret it."

"I can't."

"Yes, you can. And you're wrong about people understanding why you won't take her case. If she dies after your refusal, it will be your fault. No one will expect you to work miracles, but you have to try. At least go to see her. I'll come along for moral support, and then we can judge what will be best for her."

* * *

"Thank God you've come." Miss Rice opened the door and pointed to the small room where Amanda Ruggles lay in a narrow bed. Her breathing was shallow, and her chest rattled. Her pale face was blotched with spots of feverish red. Her usually well-groomed hair was lank and tangled with sweat. She showed no signs of realizing that anyone had entered the room. Laura stood silent for a few moments, then pushed her sleeves to her elbows and took charge.

"Someone get me some cool water and a sponge," she said. "Miss Rice, these sheets are already damp, so I'm going to bathe her down right here. See if you can find some clean towels and sheets to remake the bed when I'm finished. Mr. Ruggles, find your cook and ask her to make some tea or broth—whatever she has. And Ellen, I'll need your help to rouse her so that we can roll her over."

"Will she be all right?" Mr. Ruggles asked.

"I can't guarantee that, but we'll make her more comfortable and try to get her to take some liquids. I've brought some medicine that may bring her fever down. And I'll stay with her as long as necessary. That's all I can promise."

Ellen waited until the immediate needs had been dealt with before she touched Laura's arm and whispered, "Thank you."

"You were right, as usual. I need to be here. But you can go home. There's school tomorrow, and you'll have your hands full."

"You can't do this alone, Laura. We'll both stay and spell one another. I've watched you so often that I know what to do. The school will just have to wait."

"I could help with the school," Miss Rice said. "I'm not much good in a sick room. I was afraid to touch Amanda for fear of making her worse. But I can handle a classroom, and I think I can round up some other women to help with the students."

The next three days passed in a blur. Despite Laura's attempts to get Amanda to take some nourishment, she remained in a stupor. Laura and Ellen took turns sitting by her bedside, but her condition worsened.

On Sunday, Harriet Ware stopped by after church to tell everyone that she had arrived home from her visit to the North. "Is there any way I can help?" she asked.

"I wish there were," Laura answered. "I'm terrified of my own lack of knowledge. I've tried everything I can think of, but my remedies are no match for whatever this disease is. I want to send for one of the military doctors, but Mr. Ruggles absolutely refuses to hear of it."

"That's right. I do," Mr. Ruggles said from the doorway. "If I allowed a strange man to examine her, Amanda would be furious with me."

"Well, if you ask me, Amanda will also be furious to find herself dead," Miss Ware said.

Edwin Ruggles jerked backward as if he had been slapped. "She's not going to die," he said, shaking his head. "She can't die."

As if in response, Amanda's breathing became labored. She tossed on the cot so restlessly that Laura feared she would fall off the edge. She moaned and mumbled nonsensical words.

"You can't deny the truth, Edwin." Laura reached out to touch his hand. "She's been unconscious for hours. She's very near death, and there may be no help for her. But if you don't make every effort to save her, you'll feel responsible for the rest of your life." She glanced at Ellen, hearing in her own words the very phrase that had brought her to Amanda's side.

"Then let's send for Dr. Durand. At least she knew . . . knows him. I'll go get him myself."

Dr. Durand arrived with an arsenal of stimulants, but it was already too late. "She's unable to swallow," he said, "and she's fading fast. There's nothing to be done but let nature take its course. I'm sorry, Mr. Ruggles."

Amanda died two days later. Laura, who had not left her bedside in more than thirty-six hours, pulled the sheet over her face and then collapsed on the floor beside the cot. Ellen rushed to her, afraid from Laura's stillness that the two women had died in a single instant. Laura jerked away from Ellen's attempts to lift her up.

"I failed. I shouldn't have tried to interfere. Everyone will think I killed her."

"No, Laura."

"I'm not a doctor. I'm a fraud. They had such faith in me, and I was unable to realize it. How can I go on?"

42
DAYS OF DESPAIR
October 1863

aura and Ellen went home to sleep, but returned early to help prepare for the funeral. Nervous energy carried them through the routines of washing and dressing the body for burial and packing Amanda's things in a trunk. The body lay in a coffin of rough pine draped in black cloth. The room, which had once been used as her schoolroom, was now filled with roses and mourners. The minister spoke briefly of her devotion to the people, and then the ceremony was finished.

Mr. Ruggles approached Laura briefly. "I thank you for what you did for Amanda. I know she had all the help that your skill and affection could give."

"I'm sorry I could not do more," Laura said, close to breaking down from the days of anxiety and lack of sleep. "Will she be buried here?"

"No. This country killed her. I've arranged to take her body home tomorrow. She wouldn't want to spend eternity in a place she hated so much." He turned on his heel and left the room. Laura's face crumpled into tears.

Harriet Ware appeared at her side to hand her a handkerchief and offer a shoulder for comfort. "I want you and Ellen to come back to Coffin Point with us," she said. "You are exhausted beyond endurance. I wish our plantation house had a more suitable name, but we can offer a beautiful setting, a beach to walk on, books to inspire, and music to comfort your souls—provided I can persuade my brother to sing one evening. We'll feed you and provide a quiet setting where you can recover from the strains of these last few days."

Laura was tempted to refuse, but she found she did not have the strength to argue. She allowed Harriet to lead her to the waiting carriage. For the next two days, she and Ellen did what they were told. They found the sea air delicious after the odors of the sickroom. They sat under the trees, picked books at random from the shelves, and rested. Then it was time to go back to work.

As they approached The Oaks, Laura finally allowed herself to laugh. "I have to admit, I've even missed the squirrels. I wonder how they and Rina have gotten along." The cage, however, was not on the veranda where they had left it.

"Rina, where are our new little pets?"

"Dem tings mean! I puts dem down inna barn where dey blongs."

"Did you feed them?"

"Yes'm, jis like you says. But dey keep tryin fuh git outta de cage, an I had fuh lick em back intuh der hole."

"You hit them? Oh, Rina, how could you? They're just babies."

"Dey be de meanest baby I eber see. Dat fuh sho."

Laura and Ellen found the cage just inside the barn door. They both fell to their knees to coo over the tiny creatures, but the squirrels were not interested in visitors. When Laura tried to pick one up, he lashed out at her. "Ow! He bit me!"

"Maybe Rina's right. They do look mean."

"Only because that's what they've been taught, thanks to her lickings."

"Well, for whatever the reason, I don't think they'll ever make good pets. We'll need to release them."

"Are they old enough to be on their own?"

"They'll learn soon enough." Ellen picked up the cage and carried it toward the woods. Under a large oak tree, she eased the door open and watched as the tiny animals scurried to freedom. Bush, Ellen's favorite, went straight for the tree, climbing up the back and then peeking around at them. Bob and Bunch busied themselves with acorns. "I think they're going to be fine."

"Please quit trying to find me a pet. I think I'll just name one of the lizards that climb on the veranda railings."

"You know what we need? A dog!"

Laura shook her head and grinned. "You're incorrigible! I'd love to have a dog, but not while we're living at The Oaks. Maybe someday, when we have our own place . . ." She looked thoughtful as she tried to catch a last glimpse of the squirrels. "I wonder why the Negroes are so cruel to animals. Have you noticed? I'm forever yelling at the men for whipping the horses and pounding on the mules."

"It's not surprising, I think. As slaves, they were beaten their entire lives, and they haven't been able to strike back, except at animals. You've heard the old joke about the boss yelling at his workman—the workman goes home and yells at his wife, who slaps the child, who kicks the dog, who chases the cat, who torments the mouse. It's the same story."

"And so sad! It's another lesson we all need to remember. We teach more through our actions than through our words. Maybe that should be the motto of our school."

"Speaking of school, it's time we start holding regular classes again. Our little scholars aren't going to understand why we keep disappearing on them."

Laura winced at the thought. "You're right, of course, but you're leaving on furlough in just a few days. I'll have to think about how to handle classes while you're gone. I've heard that Lottie Forten has returned to Beaufort, but she hasn't contacted me."

"I've reconsidered my plans to go home," Ellen said. "I was planning to stay only long enough to help my mother and sister get ready to come down here to join us. And that's silly. Mother and Harriet are both grown women. They can handle a trip by themselves. But I'm not so sure you can manage on your own."

"No, Ellen. I won't hear of you changing your plans. You're as tired as I am, and you've not been looking at all well. I want you to go home and take some time to recover your strength."

"I could say the same about you. You should be the one taking leave."

"I'm going home at Christmas, remember? That's why Will is going now. There's no sense in both of us being there at the same time."

"That's another reason I'm changing my plans. I heard you telling Harriet Ware that you are going to be very lonely when both Will and I are gone. I wouldn't enjoy myself knowing that you were miserable here. Now, I don't want to hear any more about it. Besides, it's too late. I already sent Mother a message telling her how to arrange their trip. They are quite possibly already on their way."

Later that night, Laura mulled over their discussion and wrote in her diary: "Ellen says she will not go home this fall. I am afraid it is because just after Miss Ruggles's death I said that, as both she and William were going, I should be quite alone. I should indeed be pretty lonely and, if I were ill, what should I do? The Hunns could not nurse me. Mrs. Fairfield is away; nearly everybody is ill or gone home. Miss Ruggles had to depend almost solely on me, and who could be my nurse if Ellen were to go? I cannot want her to stay for she is not well and needs the change and rest. But I dread her going so much that I cannot urge it."

* * *

For the next couple of weeks, Laura was busy juggling problems—none of them major, but each one a significant distraction. First, there was the question of where Mrs. Murray and her daughter would live once they arrived. Mr. Tomlinson suggested that they take Oaklands, now that the Hunns had settled permanently into Seaside. Ellen quickly vetoed that idea. "It's not healthy," she reminded him. "Everyone who has tried living there has come down with Low Country fever. I'll not have my family put in such danger."

"Frogmore, then," he offered.

"Not unless that horrible whipping post can be removed from the dining room."

"Fine. I don't know why we have let it remain there so long. I'm sure you can get some former slaves to chop it into kindling, if you like."

"But we've just finished moving William out of there and redistributing the furniture," Laura reminded them. "It will take a lot of work to put everything back."

401

"We can do it," Ellen said. "The house needs a good white-washing, anyhow. We can keep the school closed for another couple of weeks and concentrate on getting the house ready for Mother and Harriet. Then, when they get here, we can open the school again and redistribute the students into their classes. If the children are coming back after a long break, they won't mind starting the new session with new teachers."

"Do you think we'll be able to furnish it properly?" Laura asked.

"We'll make it work. We can use some of Will's things that we are storing for him, and I have a lot of lovely furnishings that I have not been able to use at The Oaks. It'll be good for both of us, Laura. We'll have something new and different to think about, along with the excitement of knowing that the family will be here soon to settle into the results of our handiwork. And more than that, I still want us to think about buying Frogmore and living there some day. This will give us a head start on that move."

* * *

The work went more quickly than they had imagined, and within a few days, the house at Frogmore was ready for its occupants. The new problem? No one knew when those new occupants would arrive. The house stood ready—baskets of fresh flowers in the living room, new rugs on the floors, beds made up with clean linens. Tensions mounted as ship after ship arrived from New York without the expected passengers. Flowers wilted. Story after story trickled down from the authorities about missing paperwork or unsigned passes. Ellen tried to remain optimistic, but to Laura's practiced eye, she appeared to be paler and shakier every day. Was she ill or just worried? Laura couldn't be sure, and Ellen refused to discuss her health. Frogmore remained empty.

At The Oaks, they had a much different problem—one of overcrowding. Suddenly, everyone wanted to live there. Mrs. Gage had requested that she be allowed to move her Sanitary Commission office to The Oaks, so as to be situated close to the center of the Negro population while still within reach of the Beaufort hospitals.

"No. Absolutely not," Laura said. "She is violently opposed to homeopathic medicine. I won't be able to handle my patients with that woman looking over my shoulder all the time."

"She certainly is welcome to come here," Mr. Tomlinson corrected her. "We can't afford to antagonize her. At least let's invite her to come and spend a few days before she decides to move here permanently. You have my permission to make her life as miserable as you can, but do it with a welcoming smile on your face so that she doesn't catch on."

Next came Colonel Higginson. He had been released from the military hospital, but his internal injuries from that spent cannon ball had left him with a persistent pain in his side. Not yet ready to return to active duty and let his soldiers see him bent over and wincing, he moved to The Oaks to convalesce. Once ensconced, he settled on the sofa in the parlor and rambled on to anyone who entered the room. He soon figured out that Laura simply ignored his pleasantries. The only way he could get her attention was to say something outrageous. One day, he made constant sarcastic remarks about women doctors. Another time, he criticized General Saxton's military background. Occasionally, he challenged the principles of abolition or the practices of the Unitarian Church.

"If he doesn't get well soon, I'm going to kill him and put both of us out of our misery," Laura said to Ellen one evening. "He's like a mosquito—buzzing around, striking when I least expect it, and constantly annoying."

"Just tell him to be quiet," Ellen suggested.

Laura did just that on a day when the colonel attacked General Saxton again for some minor failing. "Why is it, Colonel Higginson, that antislavery officers never can agree with each other but are always ready to divide themselves and strengthen the hand of the enemy?"

Higginson stared at her for a moment and then grinned broadly. "It's about time you stood up to me," he said. And from then on they were good friends, at least until he went back to his camp. He sent a thank-you note, marred by a request that Laura allow one of his officers, Lieutenant Stone, and his new bride to make their home at The Oaks. Laura and Mrs. Fairfield, who had just returned, put up a united front to reject that idea.

One other problem developed just as Laura dared to relax. It was the last Sunday of the month, and Ellen had gone to church alone. It was Communion Sunday, and Laura was still barred from attending the Baptist ritual. Ellen returned looking worried. "I had a disturbing conversation with Mrs. Phillips, the pastor's wife," she reported. "She asked me when we were going to move our school out of the Brick Church. She said that she and her husband had determined that the church was private property and could not be used as a public school."

"No! They can't do that to us! I'll write a note to General Saxton immediately. He's the only one who has authority over Reverend Phillips."

The very next day, the pastor received a letter from the general, summoning him to Beaufort to defend his interference with the Gideonite project. Instead, Reverend Phillips immediately came to The Oaks, wanting to know why they were complaining of his actions. "I've not interfered with your school in any way," he said.

"Well, Mrs. Phillips suggested to Miss Murray that we might have to move the school, and we need to know if we will be able to continue classes there," Laura answered.

"Mrs. Phillips said that? Pshaw! That's just her talking. She likes to make trouble when she gets bored. I have no intention of disturbing you."

Laura sighed with relief. Now, if only Mrs. Murray would get here, she thought. If only Ellen were not looking so pale and feverish. And if only people would just leave us alone to do the job that needs to be done here! She closed her eyes in a brief moment of prayer and then opened them quickly to be sure she didn't miss the next sign of trouble. It wasn't long in showing up.

43
NIGHTS OF TERROR
November 1863

I t began as a casual comment. Laura and Ellen were headed back to The Oaks from Frogmore after waiting throughout the evening for the promised arrival of Mrs. Murray. They had planned to spend the night at Frogmore, but when once again they were disappointed, they set out for home. "Is this how you felt when my arrival was delayed?" Ellen asked. "The constant raising of my hopes and then dashing them on the rocks has left my nerves frazzled. My hands are shaking for no reason."

As they passed the white bird swamp, Ellen began to shiver. "Is there a lap blanket in the carriage anywhere?" she asked. "I think November is starting off with a real cold snap."

"It's probably the "hants" Hastings is always describing. Or maybe it's this thick mist," Laura replied. "Damp air always feels colder. But you're right. We should have a blanket in the carriage for nights like this."

Ellen complained no further, but when they reached The Oaks, she hurried to bed, burrowing deep under the hand-stitched quilt. "Don't completely bank the fire," she said. "I'm still chilled."

This time, Laura looked at her with concern. "Still cold? Are you feeling ill? Any other symptoms?"

"Just tired. Quit sounding like a doctor."

"It's my job to be a doctor!" But Ellen was already asleep.

She professed to being quite well in the morning, but, as the school day wore on, her energy flagged. Once, when she turned rapidly to answer a student's question, she staggered and had to sit for a few minutes before her head quit spinning. Laura, watching from across the room with her own class, did not miss the signs. She rang a small bell to get the attention of the 150 students in the hall. "We're going to put the books away and close the school until next week," she announced. Ellen did not protest. Thus started a month of escalating danger.

On November 6th, Laura turned to her diary to confess her worst fears: "Last night was one long terror. Ellen was very ill. All day I thought she could not recover. Tonight I hope again." But the next day brought more: "Ellen violently ill all day, nausea, fainting, vomiting blood. She suffers awfully, yet thinks for everybody, telling me what to do if she dies. I am in such a state of alarm and dread that I cannot read my medical books for crying and distress."

The days passed in cycles of hope and fear. Some mornings, Laura awoke to find Ellen alert and bright, only to watch her sink into insensibility as the day wore on. At other times, Ellen was unable to sleep, tossing and moaning throughout the night. Congestion caused her chest to rattle, and the sounds reminded Laura of how Amanda Ruggles had struggled to breathe at the end of her life.

On November 9th, Laura was still awake at midnight, watching to see if the dose of medicine she had just administered would let her patient breathe more easily and help her sleep. A faint knock at the front door announced the long-awaited arrival of Mrs. Murray and her younger daughter. "Where is Ellen?" Mrs. Murray demanded. "The man who drove us here said she was dying." She pushed past Laura, who could only point to the bedroom door. Harriet stood in the hall, weeping openly. Laura led her closer to the fire and held her as she cried out her fears and exhaustion.

"Is my sister really dying?" she asked.

"I don't know," Laura answered. "I'm doing everything I can. Perhaps your presence will strengthen her will to live." But the truth was that Ellen was worse—much worse. Mrs. Murray and Harriet slept on the floor of her room so as not to miss any sound she made. On some days Ellen was quiet, but not because she had found relief. Her stillness came from a congestive chill that was very like death itself.

At other times, Ellen burned with fever. Laura and Harriet took turns pouring cold water over her head to cool her. In the throes of her raging temperature, Ellen became delirious, mumbling certain nonsensical phrases over and over, or lashing out at imaginary visions.

General and Mrs. Saxton came to The Oaks on November 16th to inquire about her health. Laura, released from her sickroom vigil for a few minutes, weakened in the face of their concern. "I can't sleep, day or night, for fear that something will happen," she said. "She has one wretched day after another. When she suffers, I'm sure she is going to die, and each time I believe that she cannot possibly survive another attack. She lies for hours as if dead, insensible to our voices or movements around her. It's been two weeks now, and I am almost crazy with anxiety."

"What can I do, Miss Towne?" General Saxton asked. "Would it be useful to send one of the Army doctors to take a look at her?"

"I don't know. She has always said that she wants no one but me to treat her. I know she would object to having a strange man see her in this condition. But it might be of some comfort to me to know that someone else had taken part of the responsibility for her care. Could you . . . do you think Dr. Rogers would come?"

"Of course he would. He has often spoken of both of you, how kind you have been to him, how welcoming to Miss Forten, how competent you are in treating the Negroes on your plantations. I'll contact him immediately and provide him with a horse. I can have him here by nightfall, if you have room to shelter him overnight."

"Thank you." Laura's eyes brimmed with tears. "I can't tell you how alone I have felt. Ellen decided not to go home for a rest this fall because she didn't want to leave me alone. And now, because of me, she has been taken ill, and I am doubly alone. Funny, the tricks life plays."

"You'll not ever be alone. You're surrounded by more friends than you can imagine. You just need to learn to ask for help. Now go back to sitting with Ellen, and tell her that the doctor is on his way."

True to the general's word, Dr. Rogers arrived before dark. He went straight to Ellen's bedside, checked her temperature, listened to her breathing, and watched her as she slept. Then he motioned to Laura to follow him back to the parlor. "Tell me in as much detail as possible how her disease has progressed."

"I can't tell you exactly when it started. I know she has not been feeling well for some time. I'd think she looked pale or feverish, but then she'd be fine. And we had so many other patients to worry about that I failed to take proper notice of her. But then, two weeks ago, she actually complained of being cold, and almost immediately her symptoms grew worse." Laura went on to outline the progression of the illness up to this day, when her own fears had overwhelmed her.

"Well, she almost certainly has a malarial fever, and, while I respect your homeopathic remedies for mild illnesses, I'm certain that there's only one treatment that has a chance of saving her." He watched Laura's face closely. "I know you don't approve of using quinine, but in this case . . ."

"Go ahead. Do whatever you have to do. Just don't let her die at my hand."

"You mustn't think of it that way. Many doctors approve of your methods. And you've had no part in causing her illness. Your treatments are not responsible for her condition. She just needs more than you are equipped to administer."

"Say what you will, Dr. Rogers, but I can't forgive myself. I am responsible—for bringing her here, as well as for keeping her from going home to rest last month. So if it's quinine she needs, then quinine she shall have. Only . . ."

"Only what?"

"It frightens me because I know how susceptible she is to the effects of medication— to everything, actually. She can't drink—even a sip or two of wine makes her violently ill. And if I give her a dose of homeopathic medication, I have to dilute it even more than usual or she can't tolerate it. Knowing how dangerous quinine can be, even for those with strong constitutions . . ."

"We'll give her just half a dose, then, and I'll leave you with an adequate supply, so that you can judge for yourself whether or not she needs additional doses."

* * *

Laura gave her patient just one grain of quinine and watched as Ellen responded immediately. In her diary, Laura wrote, "It had a strangely powerful effect and acted like a strong opiate. She is so much better that I thought I should go mad or die!" By morning, Ellen had no chills and no periods of insensibility. She was alert and talking normally.

Everyone relaxed. Laura, for the first time in two weeks, had time to consider her own needs. She slept for several hours and took a walk in the woods with Harriet while Mrs. Murray visited with her daughter. Then Mrs. Murray and Harriet were finally ready to go to see their new home at Frogmore. "I do hope they like it," Ellen quipped. "I'm not quite up to the prospect of having to redecorate that house again."

Laura enjoyed the days leading up to Thanksgiving. She was still not willing to leave Ellen for extended periods, but the days passed pleasantly. Ellen was able first to sit up in bed and then to move from her bed to a chair. She bathed while Laura changed the bed, and then she let Laura do her hair, letting it down into her accustomed curls. Laura worried only that she was trying to do too much too soon.

Downstairs, preparations were underway for Thanksgiving dinner. Mrs. Fairfield was baking pies, and Janie was wrestling with the traditional turkey. There would be little company this year, but those who gathered had much to be thankful for. It appeared that the worst ills were behind them. Laura even noted that Ellen was able to eat a little turkey.

That evening, as Laura was helping settle Ellen into bed, Ellen held out her hand and frowned. "What happened to my ring?" she asked.

"Your little cameo? While you were ill, it grew too loose. I put it away in your chest there on top of the dresser. I didn't want it to get lost in the covers."

"Would you get it for me, please? I feel quite lost without it. I've always remembered the day you gave it to me."

Laura handed it to her and busied herself with closing the curtains.

"That's odd!" Ellen said. "This can't be my ring. Why, it won't even fit over my first knuckle."

Laura froze. The words from her medical text rang in her ears: "The danger of quinine is that it can have dire effects on the heart. It weakens the valves, so that the heart cannot push blood to the extremities. The result is fluid retention, evidenced by swelling in the hands and feet. Eventually, fluid accumulation around the heart causes dropsy and certain death."

"Let me see your hands. And your feet," she ordered, pushing the sheet back to examine Ellen by the light of the oil lamp. Shadows cast by the flickering light only exaggerated the puffy folds around her wrists and ankles.

"You do look a little swollen," she said, hoping to disguise the fear that threatened to make her voice shake. "Perhaps you'll have to wait another day or two to wear your ring. You've spent a long time in bed. Your body will have to adjust to being up and about again."

"All right. Put the ring away, then. I guess I can do without it for a few more days."

By the next morning, the swelling was also noticeable in Ellen's face, but she seemed to feel quite well. "I want to try walking around a bit today," she said. Laura helped her move from the fireplace to the window but was careful to steer her away from the room's only mirror. She didn't want her to see how dreadfully different she looked.

Laura was so alarmed by Ellen's appearance that she wrote to Dr. Hering for advice. "Is there anything I can do to reverse the damage the quinine has done?" she asked her former teacher. But she already knew the answer. She also sent word to Colonel Higginson, asking him to allow Dr. Rogers to come back to The Oaks to help with her treatment. Dr. Rogers responded to her note immediately, sending word that he suspected an enlargement of the spleen and telling her not to worry.

But Ellen continued to worsen. The swelling in her arms and legs increased. She began to run a temperature, although not as high as it had been at the height of her illness. When the vomiting began again, Laura summoned Dr. Rogers more vehemently, and this time he came. Using an instrument that looked very much like a trumpet, he listened to Ellen's chest. "She almost certainly has valvular damage to her heart," he said. "I can hear the blood sloshing with every beat. She needs to go home and place herself under the care of a skilled medical doctor."

"But a sea voyage at this time of year . . ."

" . . . could kill her. Yes. That's entirely possible. But allowing her to stay here, with no access to care other than what you can supply at home, is even more dangerous. And if you aren't available . . . Aren't you scheduled to go home soon, Miss Towne?"

"I was, but . . ."

"Then my best medical advice is that you take her north at once. The trip will be hazardous, but she will certainly not recover if she remains here."

RINA ON "IT BE BOUT TIME"
November 1863

I be happy dat Missus Laura finely ax Doctor Rogers fuh come an see Missus Ellen. I unnerstan dat she don trust de soljer doctors. She say dat dey use poison in der medicine an dey do udder tings, like cut off a leg or arm when dey jis needs a good salve an sum stitchin up. Dey sucks blood outta der patient, too, an Missus Laura say dat jis take de life right outta dem. But ennybody what be watchin dis las two week know dat when de soljer doctor gib Missus Ellen he medicine, she perk right up. So dat be a good ting.

But now dat same doctor, he say dat Missus Ellen be gwine die, an dat be a turrible ting. Missus Laura, she run outta de room like a night hag be aftuh she. I neber seed she so upset. She be cryin an gaspin fuh breath. She be white an blotchy roun de eyes. She be stumblin ober tings in she way, like she caint see where she be gwine. I don know what fuh do, but I figgers she don need fuh be alone, so I follows she out to de porch. An I keep watch while she cry sheself silly. Dat be a good ting, I tink. She be holdin it all in fuh too long. She need a good cry.

What Missus Laura gwine do now? I don know, but I hope she strong nuf fuh stand dis. She need fuh take she own advice an take care uh sheself. Fuh de pas two week, she be sittin in dat sickroom all day an night. She don eat nuttin lessin I takes it up dere. She don *sleep lessin she fall sleep in de chair. She don see nobody, don talk to nobody, don let ennybody help she.*

She don do ennyting roun de plantation, neider. She don go fuh see ennybody what be sick in de slave village. She say she only hab one patient an she don want fuh bring enny more sickness intuh dis house. But I tinks dat jis be excuse fuh not leavin Missus Ellen.

Ol Jenny's daughter Elisa, she come ober fro de Capers place fuh see Missus Laura. She be spectin a baby ennytime, an she be feelin sick. Missus Laura take one look at she an send she back cause she gots smallpox. An den Elisa die gibbin birth to dat chile. Dey be gwine bury she here fuh do what she mam say. Dat be Missus Laura fault, I tinks.

She close de school an leave de chillun witout ennyplace fuh go. De poor chillun, dey walk all de way to de chuch an sit onna ground outside waitin fuh de teacher fuh come. An dey don unnerstan why dere not be ennybody dere. I seed sum uh de older chillun tryin fuh teach de little uns dere letters by scratchin in de schoolyard dirt. Dat be sad.

Fuh Missus Laura, de whole world stop when Missus Ellen sick. But de res uh we has fuh keep livin, an dat be hard. It be bout time tings git fixt, one way or tother.

44
REGAINING THEIR BALANCE
December 1863

Rina was not the only one who worried about what was going to happen. Ellen's mother and sister shifted restlessly between their new home at Frogmore and The Oaks, where they could be of some help in relieving Laura's vigil for a while. Mr. Tomlinson had gamely accepted responsibility for the male convalescents whom the Army doctors kept sending to the island to finish their recuperation. He shared his room with them and nursed them without complaint, even while he knew he needed to be out on the plantation. Mrs. Fairfield, who had returned home to find the house full of new guests and the upstairs turned into a hospital ward, chafed at the imposition and demanded to know when everyone was going to be healthy again.

At the request of Dr. Furness, Ellen's former pastor, General Saxton came to persuade Laura to take Ellen north. "He's been talking to your sisters and what they have told him has him very concerned," Saxton said. "He says his wife will be happy to have you both come to stay with them."

"I can't possibly do that, any more than I could take Ellen to my brother's house. Both families have their own people to take care of, and Ellen is my responsibility. Besides, she does not want to be an imposition on anyone."

"Please quit talking about me as if I weren't here in the same room," said Ellen. "I may be ill but I'm not deaf, and I'm capable of making decisions. I don't want to go north, and I won't. My whole family is here on the island, and I'll be fine with my mother and sister while Laura's away."

"And I'm not going anywhere without you. The Towne family gathering will just have to do without me for this year," Laura said, patting her hand.

"Laura! I want you to take your furlough as planned. You need the rest. I won't hear of you staying here on my account."

"It's not your decision. It's mine. Last fall you chose to stay here with me rather than go home to rest. And look what has happened as a result. I will always feel guilty that I am responsible for your illness. I will not leave you now and add responsibility for your death. Doctor Rogers says I should not leave you, and I won't go, no matter what you say."

"Laura, I need you to listen to me," Ellen pleaded. "For most of my adult life, I have longed to die. That's what Christianity really teaches, after all. Life is a vale of tears. Our great reward and joy come only when we can reach heaven. And so I have often hoped for death, prayed for it, even sought it."

Laura was staring at her with horror. "No, Ellen. No, never that."

"But I have always felt that way—until I came here. I saw no purpose to my life. Now, when I have been closest to actual death, I have realized that for the first time I have something to live for." She stopped, trying to take deep breaths and failing to hide how difficult it had become for her to breathe at all.

Laura stood shaking her head, tears streaming down her cheeks. "Ellen, I need you desperately, but I don't want you to feel you must do this for me."

Ellen was shaking her head, still struggling. "It's the children who call me. Theirs is the real need. I must fight to stay longer in life for the sake of our little scholars. And that's how I know I shall be all right. I have found my purpose here. Our school, our children, the training we can offer them—these are vitally important. The whole path of my life has led me here to accomplish miracles, and I will not die until I have achieved that goal. You can leave me without fear."

* * *

But, of course, Laura refused to leave. She wrote to her sisters, describing her disappointment that she would not be spending Christmas with them after all: "Dr. Rogers said he thought she needed the wisest medical aid or there would be no hope for her . . . I told him she had no home in the North and that she was unwilling to thrust herself on my friends. Then he said, 'You must stay with her; she will die if you leave her.' I asked whether he thought it would be long before I could go, and he said hers must be a tedious convalescence—that the responsibility and risk of taking her north made it better for me not to urge her going, but that he must warn me not to go away till she was in a different state from now. So I have made up my mind to it, and I do not dare to think of Xmas at all."

The arguments raged on for several days. Ellen was determined to convince Laura that her health was improving. Every day she made more of an effort to appear well. Once, she even made it downstairs for dinner and appeared to enjoy her meal. Afterward, however, the exertion of trying to return to her room exhausted her, and she had to be helped up the stairs.

"You must stop trying to do so much," Laura scolded. "You only succeed in doing yourself harm. And it won't work, anyway. I have no intention of spending this Christmas in Philadelphia. You might just as well get used to having me here."

Laura's letters, however, told a slightly different story. In a fit of guilt and disappointment, she wrote to her family nearly every day, apologizing for her absence and promising to come as soon as possible. "I shall set out as soon as she is well enough to go to her mother and do without medicine," she assured them—or perhaps herself. Her overall mood was quite clear. She needed "freedom from anxiety." She was "dreadfully worried, beset by care, fear, and self-reproach." She was "grieved and disappointed."

Her excuses grew ever thinner. The weather had turned stormy; even after the storm the sea would be too high. There was going to be a sale of all the furniture at The Oaks, and she needed to be present to claim the items she wanted. Someone might lease the house they lived in while she was away.

Laura dreamed she was trapped in a pit of her own digging, and all she could really feel was a debilitating regret. She sent her family a Christmas greeting: "A happy Christmas to you all, and a bright New Year. You must be merry and make believe I am there." Then she added, "We shall have no Christmas for the school and no school probably. I am so sorry for that."

In her diary she confessed even more. "Life seems very dreary to me, and I am beginning to have a dread of the cares and trials of this place," she wrote on December 18th. And on the 20th, she described Ellen as equally upset: "Ellen for the first time [is] in the deepest despondency. She thinks she will be a burden to others all her life." Deep sadness threatened them both with an end to their hopes and dreams.

* * *

And yet, somehow, Christmas seemed to work its magic. Ellen was well on her way to recovery. Although she occasionally suffered chills, she felt remarkably well most of the time. As for Laura, the end result of her giving up all to care for Ellen was a brief period in which her responsibilities were taken over by others. Mrs. Fairfield was handling the housekeeping, and a new doctor had come to the island to take over most of her patients. While her school classes had been dismissed until the beginning of the new year, the time was being well spent by the local carpenter, Mr. Mockabee, who was building removable bookshelves and desks for use in the church and installing a stove to counteract the unseasonably cold weather they were experiencing.

On Christmas morning, Laura and Ellen had a quiet time in their room. After Rina brought them a pot of coffee, Ellen grinned and announced, "I think it's time for a gift exchange."

"Oh, no. I've had no opportunity to find a gift for you, and I expect none," Laura said.

"This isn't a gaily wrapped package," Ellen assured her. "But I do have a gift—in the form of a solemn promise. I told you that I had discovered that I am in no hurry to die any longer, that I've realized that my purpose in life is to live for the sake of our little scholars. I know you were shocked at the thought that I had longed for death. And I suspect that you were disappointed that I did not say I could live on for you alone. But the important thing is that now I want to live. And I promise you that I will spend the rest of my life right here, making sure that our dream of a full and rich education for our Negro children becomes a reality."

"Then I can offer you no less a confession. If I'm honest with myself, and with you, I must admit that I have never felt that longing for death. Maybe that's because the whole idea of heaven and hell escapes me. My Unitarian background, I suppose. But I have my own bugbear. My whole life has been hindered by fear."

"Fear? You're the bravest woman I've ever known."

"Only on the outside. I've always been afraid that I am not good enough, not wise enough, not strong enough to meet the expectations of others. I've never believed that I was good enough for you, so your statement about the children did not shock me. I blame myself for whatever goes wrong and sabotage my own efforts by second-guessing my decisions. I've always believed that I was responsible for my mother's early death. If I had been a better child, she wouldn't have tried to have another baby, I thought. I've been trying to make amends for it ever since. How's that for a confession?"

"That's why you felt so responsible for Amanda, and why you were so distraught over my illness?"

"Yes, I suppose so. I'm always afraid someone will point accusingly at me and say I should have done more. Then I exhaust myself and try to do too much—none of it extremely well. So my promise to you is that from now on I will do less—that I will work alongside you to make the Penn School a model of Negro education. And I will let someone else worry about the other matters that need to be taken care of. We came here with a specific purpose. Let's dedicate ourselves and our efforts to accomplishing it."

The two women looked at one another with new hope in their eyes. They exchanged a hug and then finished getting ready to go down to dinner. Afterward, Hastings brought the buggy around, and they drove down the street in the slave village. During her convalescence Ellen had been making little woolen sacques for the youngest of the children, and she delighted in being able to pass them out. They finished the afternoon in the parlor, listening to one of their guests, a Mr. Batchellor, play Beethoven's sonatas on their old piano. They took a private tea in their room and retired early, content—at least for the moment—in their new resolutions.

45
EPIDEMICS AND PREEMPTIONS
Late December 1863

Shortly after that idyllic Christmas Day, Nelly Fairfield knocked at Laura's bedroom door. Laura pulled the door open just wide enough to see who was there. She held a cautionary finger to her lips. "I think Ellen has just fallen asleep, and I don't want to waken her. Do you need me for something?"

"I just want to ask a simple question," Nelly said, positioning her foot so that the door could not be closed. "I need to know how soon you and Ellen are planning to leave for the North."

"Leave? Whatever gave you that idea? We're not going anywhere."

"That's not what I heard. I've been told that Dr. Rogers warned you that if Ellen did not return home, she would surely die." Nelly glared at Laura. "And I certainly don't want anyone dying in my house," she added.

Laura's eyebrows arched. "Uh, it's true that Dr. Rogers made that suggestion at one point, but, after due consideration, we decided that such a trip would be much too dangerous. Besides, she's doing so much better now that—"

"Well, if she's doing so well, I see no reason why she can't go to stay with her mother and sister."

"Nelly, what's going on? Are you trying to get rid of us?" Laura ventured a half-smile in the hope that Nelly was joking.

"Miss Towne," Nelly began, "this is my house, and I'm heartily tired of having it turned into a field hospital!"

Laura did not miss the formal use of her name or the lack of friendship that it implied. "Field hospital? It's hardly that," she protested.

"It might as well be. You've got Ellen ensconced up here, with our slaves waiting on her hand and foot. Mr. Tomlinson has his own pet soldiers occupying two other rooms while they recuperate from battle wounds, and there's a steady stream of slaves tromping up here from the slave village to bring you their family members who are poxed and disfigured by whatever is going around. You're vaccinating people on the portico and treating minor wounds in the dining room. It's horrible and discouraging to hear nothing but reports of who is ill and who has just died. I want my house back."

"Your house? That's the third time you've used that phrase. This is not your house. It's the headquarters of the Port Royal Experiment. You only live here on my sufferance. I had arranged to have my brother take over the superintendency of The Oaks, but you were so distraught over Mr. Fairfield's plan to live at Frogmore that I gave up my own preferences to make you happy."

"I lived here before you ever came to St. Helena!"

"Perhaps so, but you weren't in charge of the house. General Saxton appointed me to oversee all our schools on the island from this central location, and he assigned Mr. Tomlinson to live here and oversee the management of all our plantation holdings. It seems to me that you are the extra resident, not we. You're certainly in no position to try to run the rest of us out."

"We'll see about that! Most of your beloved schoolchildren have already fallen victims to the smallpox epidemic. When the plans to redistribute the land become clear, you'll lose this house, and all the other possessions you've laid claim to will be preempted, too. Just you wait!"

Laura watched as Nelly flounced toward the stairs; then she closed the door and threw the latch. When she turned, she discovered that Ellen was awake, her blue eyes round with worry and her forehead creased with puzzlement. "Apparently I've missed a great deal of what's going on around here," she said. "What was that all about?"

"I'm not quite sure."

"Yes, you are. Don't try to shield me from all unpleasantness, Laura. It's too late for that. Obviously, there is smallpox on our plantation, which is bad enough. But what was all that about the land being redistributed? I thought that was settled months ago."

"All right. One thing at a time. Yes, we're in the midst of a smallpox epidemic, not just here but all over the island."

"Didn't you once tell me that Negroes tend to get a milder form of the disease because they've been exposed to it so often?"

"Yes, I did, but the situation seems to have changed. Perhaps it's because they now have more opportunities to travel to new parts of the countryside and come in contact with strangers. Many of our men have joined one of the colored regiments and have been out on maneuvers before coming home to visit their families. Others have mingled with the bands of refugees who have arrived here in the last few months. I can't be sure that they are picking up new strains of the disease, but I do know that dozens of our people have died, and that didn't used to happen. By now I don't think there is a single cabin that does not have at least one patient. I'm vaccinating as fast as I can, but whole families fall sick within hours, and once the little ones have been exposed to the disease it's too late for a vaccine to be effective."

"But you're trying to take care of them? Isn't that dangerous for you?"

"I'm being as careful as I can. I revaccinated myself, and when I go to the cabins, I wear an old plaid dress and a blanket shawl that I remove as soon as I get home. I keep them in the open air on the veranda so that I never bring any contamination indoors with me. And I only see patients if their family members bring them outside, because the cabins are fetid and pitch dark. Try as I may to convince the Negroes that fresh air is beneficial, they insist on boarding up their windows and nailing every opening closed."

"Can you give them anything to help?"

"Not really. There's no cure for smallpox. You just have to outlive it if you can. What worries me most is that many of our people are reacting to the deaths by turning to a witch doctor."

"A witch doctor?"

"Well, they call him a root doctor, but it means the same thing. He's an old man named Lester. He has convinced them to wash the patients with hot pokeroot and salt. Almost everyone who is so treated dies, but they persist in doing it."

"But every part of pokeweed can be a deadly poison!"

"Yes. Lester has already killed two of his own children with it." Laura spoke in a matter-of-fact tone, but her jaw clenched in anger.

"I suppose I know many of those who have died," Ellen said, bracing for more bad news.

"I suppose you do, but I'm not going to give you a list, so don't ask. I've kept all this from you because I didn't want you upset. I still don't. I can promise you three things: I'm doing everything I can to keep as many people alive as possible, the epidemic will run its course and go away when there are no more fresh victims for it to attack, and those who survive will be stronger and as immune as they would have been if I had vaccinated them. This, too, will pass, Ellen."

Ellen nodded and closed her eyes for a few minutes. Then she hoisted herself upright in bed and glared at Laura. "All right. But you still haven't told me about the new land sales problems. Surely that can't be as bad as the smallpox epidemic."

"No, I suppose not. But it's very confusing right now."

"Explain, please."

"Our old friends, Commissioners Brisbane and Wording, have been up to their usual tricks. They've decided that the March sales did not bring in enough revenue, so they are planning to hold another sale of some 16,000 acres of reserved lands. And as you might expect, the Gideonites can't agree on how they think the sales should go, so they are fighting among themselves and trying to influence the tax commissioners to change their plans."

"I'm sure I can guess at the participants."

"And you'd be right. Mr. Philbrick is determined to see the sales go forward as quickly as possible. He wants Northern businessmen to come down here and invest heavily in land. Then, he assumes, they will want to make a profit, so they will hire the Negroes to grow cotton for them, and they'll be willing to pay a high salary to get the best workers. He's willing to see the price of land go sky high."

"But our people can't possibly bid against rich Northern businessmen," Ellen said, "and that makes it impossible for them to own their own land. They'll be hoeing cotton for the rest of their lives. General Saxton must be livid."

"Oh, he is. He's the major force arguing for preemption."

"That's the term I heard Nelly use, and I'm still not sure I know what it means."

"Preemption is similar to the rules for homesteading in the West. It's a legal decision that would allow any Negro who has worked land for six months after the Union Army took over this part of South Carolina to stake out a claim to a twenty-acre or forty-acre farm at a rate of $1.25 per acre. General Saxton is determined that our people have the right to own their own lands, and he's sent Reverend French to Washington to persuade Mr. Lincoln to pass that law."

"Reverend French? Do you think he'll succeed?"

Laura shrugged. "I don't know. He can be persuasive at times, or he can be really annoying. We should know soon."

"But what did Nelly mean about our possessions being preempted?"

"That's one of the really silly parts of the argument. The commissioners tend to agree with a third view. You may remember that back in March, Mr. Gannett was worried about the details of sales that involved not just land, but buildings and chattels—all the animals and equipment and furnishings on the land."

"And he's still riding that hobby horse?" Ellen sighed. "Does nothing ever change around here?"

"Well, people don't. Gannett has managed to convince a couple of the commissioners that before the plantations can be sold, they will have to be restored to their pristine pre-1861 condition. The rumormongers have it that they'll be coming around to take an inventory and undo any changes we've made. It's a good way to attack those who support preemption."

Ellen looked around their bedroom. "We haven't changed anything other than the position of the furniture, have we?"

"No, most of what we are using was here when the Popes inhabited the house. But there are things . . ."

"Like what?"

"Like that marble-topped washstand in the corner. It originated in a Beaufort house. A slave gave it to Miss Susan Walker while she was living in the Hamilton House there. When she came to St. Helena, she brought it along. So technically it should go back, but we have no idea where that slave got it in the first place. Remember the yellow soup tureen that turned up one night at dinner? Hastings brought it up from his cabin. Where did he get it? I don't have any idea. And think about our stable. We have Mr. Pierce's old horse, Charlie, but I don't know Charlie's original owner. The carriage, too, is a mystery. A soldier brought it over from Hilton Head one day. It didn't come with a label."

"So if the tax commissioners insist on complete compliance with an act of preemption, they could effectively nullify the law by forcing us to perform impossible tasks?"

"I told you it was silliness. And you haven't heard the worst. The commissioners are also insisting that the land has to be surveyed and laid out in neat little plots of twenty acres before anyone can stake a preemptive claim. Oh, and they want all the property lines to run at precise right angles, like the grid that was planned for Washington."

"But nothing runs in straight lines on St. Helena!"

"Precisely." Laura smiled and shook her head. "They haven't made much progress, thanks to our pluff mud and marshlands. The plots marked at low tide tend to disappear every afternoon."

Laura turned the kerosene lamp down and began to stir the fire. "It's going to be bitter cold before this night is over," she said. "You need to curl up under those covers and get some sleep. We won't cure any cases of smallpox tonight, and the tax commissioners will have to solve their own differences. For all we know, none of these problems will impact our lives, so let's not lose sleep over phantom threats."

46
MOVING ON
January 1864

On December 31st, 1863, President Lincoln instructed the South Carolina tax commissioners to allow any loyal person who had resided on or cultivated any land owned by the United States since November 1861 to enter a claim for preemption. One or two tracts of twenty acres apiece could be purchased at the rate of $1.25 per acre. A claimant could pay two-fifths of the purchase price at the time of filing, with the balance due upon receipt of the deed. The ruling applied to both black and white, to heads of families or a married woman in the absence of her husband, and to soldiers and sailors who were on active duty in the area or who had been honorably discharged after such duty. These claims were not to come out of the 16,000 acres reserved for charitable purposes. The available land included the active plantations where the former slaves had been working for years. The only exceptions were those lands that had been sold in the sale of March 1863. The decision was not announced until mid-January, but word of the details trickled back to the Low Country almost immediately.

Laura Towne was not one of the first to be informed. She was still trying to gain control of the smallpox epidemic and had resolutely put worries about land sales behind her. In the bitter January cold snap, the disease spread with what she called "fearful rapidity" and "great severity." In her diary, she described making her way down the street, where "at every door and by every hearth sat some bent figure with a blanket over its head, the picture of desolation and pestilence."

Mothers suffering from smallpox gave birth to stillborn infants. Families that would, in different times, have held a wake and a funeral for their departed loved ones now simply carted the body off to be dumped into a hole beyond the reaches of the plantation. Among the men there was hardly a hand to do the necessary work of the place—no one to gather wood for the fires or milk the cows.

Laura was particularly moved by the death of Jenny, that "bright, happy, busy, motherly little body." Jenny was the wife of Dagus, who had always been one of Laura's favorite workers. Jenny and Dagus had six children, and Jenny had ignored her own symptoms to care for her youngest boy, who had smallpox. Now Dagus had contracted the disease, too, and the oldest child, Coffee, sat in a corner, despondent at the realization that he might lose both his parents, as well as his brothers and sisters.

* * *

On January 7th, Nelly Fairfield knocked again at Laura's door in the late afternoon, this time to announce an addition to her family. "I wanted you to know that I have taken two of Jenny's six children, little Brister and Becky, into our house."

"You've done what?" Laura asked. "It's kind of you, but wouldn't it have been better to wait a week or two? They will most certainly have contracted smallpox from their mother and father. If you are not prepared to care for them, it might be kinder to leave them with their own family."

"What difference would that make?" Nelly bristled at any form of criticism. "I want them here. They are the first scholars in my school."

Laura stared at her. What in the world was she talking about? What she had said made no sense to Laura's exhausted mind. "Scholars in your school? What school? I thought you'd given up teaching after you married."

Nelly gave an elaborate sigh and rolled her eyes to the ceiling. "As if you hadn't heard!"

"Heard what?"

Still, Nelly just stared at her with a smug half-smile.

"Mrs. Fairfield. I've been up since four o'clock this morning. I'm worn to a frazzle. If you have something to tell me, please just come out with it. I'm too tired to play guessing games with you."

"So you haven't heard. Mr. Fairfield has leased The Oaks as a school farm, and I expect soon to have every room filled with children."

"What's a school farm? And how is he able to lease The Oaks? I thought it was on that list of land reserved for charitable purposes."

"That's what a school farm is—a charitable organization. We'll be taking in orphaned children and educating them right here where they live. And they will be able to help run the farm by learning to do chores. Now that the decision has been made to allow preemption, this is one of the forms it can take. We've certainly been living and working on the land long enough to qualify. We've made a down payment and will be leasing The Oaks and its chattels until we can pay off the rest."

Many more questions swarmed through Laura's mind, but the only one that she could voice was, "In that case, what is to become of us?" She spoke it half-laughing, unable to believe that she was being expelled from the house she had made available to this woman by denying herself.

Nelly shrugged one shoulder and said, "I don't know."

Laura was slowly waking up to the importance of this discussion. "When you form any plan that will exclude us from this house, I hope you will give us timely notice. It is not easy to provide another home in this department."

"Well, then, I'm telling you now. I have begun by taking these two children, and I intend to fill the house. I will not need your help, and there will be no room for any but the children."

"Very well," Laura said. She watched as Nelly turned and walked away.

* * *

Ellen stood next to the bed, pulled from an afternoon nap by the sounds of the confrontation. "Can they just do that on their own?" she asked. "Can Mr. Fairfield buy this house out from under us?"

"Apparently he can. But permissions don't really matter at this stage. I don't see how we could comfortably share the house after this kind of disagreement. We'll need to be gone as quickly as possible. I probably should take a day to visit our people and tell them we are leaving, but fortunately it won't take us long to pack our things. We should be able to move by the day after tomorrow."

"But where will we go?"

"I was thinking we could go to Frogmore for a while. Will your mother be willing to take in a couple of strays, do you think?"

"Of course she will. It'll be crowded for four, but I'm sure we can make do. You've always wanted to live there. Now's your chance."

"I'm not thinking of anything longer than a temporary stopover. We'll need a place of our own. I don't want to go anywhere where Mr. Fairfield has a chance of lording it over us in any sort of official capacity."

"Where?"

"How about the village—St. Helenaville? There must be empty houses there."

Ellen began to brighten. "The climate is wonderful on that end of the island, and the Edisto settlers have turned the village into a pleasant little town. They have their own church, a grocery store, and a gathering place for the community. It's not too far from our school, either. Thank goodness, Penn School uses the Brick Church, which is out of the jurisdiction of the Gideonites. We'll only have to keep the pastor happy, not the whole cranky cluster of Northern missionaries."

"Are you strong enough to withstand the move?" Laura asked.

"I'm ready whenever you are."

"Well, then, I'll go and talk to Mr. Tomlinson now. I don't know whether he has yet been informed of these new developments, but he needs to be forewarned. I also want him to understand that we are leaving because of the Fairfields, not because of anything he has done. Then I'll send a message to General Saxton, asking if we can have a house in the village. I'm sure he'll agree."

"And I'll send word to Mother telling her to expect us the day after tomorrow."

* * *

It was an awkward time. It was bitterly cold, and Laura felt obligated to visit each of her sick patients to be sure they were warm enough. She spent the morning making tea and gruel and carrying it from cabin to cabin. At every stop, the people clutched her, begging, "Don go, Missus. Don you be leavin we here alone. Who gwine take care uh we?"

Laura did her best to ease their fears and ended up promising to visit often, but, even as she did so, she remained close to tears herself. The slave street at The Oaks had become a second home for her. It was here that she had learned to understand the Gullah language the people spoke. Here she had participated in the shouts and worshipped in the Praise House. Here were her friends and her beloved children. Parting from them was heartbreaking.

Laura intended to postpone a leave-taking with Rina for as long as possible, but Rina was not about to be put off. "Missus Laura! Why aint I free?" The question, shouted from across the slave street, stopped Laura's slow progress down the street and drew an interested audience.

"Rina. Good morning. What makes you think you aren't free?" Laura's heart was beating hard, but she forced herself to remain calm and detached. With so many people watching, she could not afford to let her favoritism for this crotchety old black woman show.

"Dat Massa Fairfiel, he tole me so. He say you leavin an now I blongs to he an he wife. He say ifn I not be willin fuh work, he be kickin me outta muh cabin an sendin me off to sum udder plantation. Do dat soun like free to you?"

"No, it doesn't, and I think Mr. Fairfield told you something that isn't true. Can you trust me for a few minutes more? I need to talk to you, but the slave street is not the place. Would you go back to the house and wait for me in my room? If you happen to see one of the Fairfields, tell them I sent you to find something for me, and then close yourself into my room without talking to them about anything else. Can you do that?"

"Yes'm."

When Laura returned to her room, Rina met her at the door, still poised to defend herself. "What be gwine on?" she demanded.

"Miss Murray and I are moving to a house of our own, leaving Mr. Fairfield in full possession of The Oaks," Laura explained. "As long as you want to stay here in your usual cabin, you will have to work for him, just as he said, but that does not mean you are not free to leave if you wish."

"I kin goes ennywheres? Kin I goes wit you?"

"Would you like that?"

"Yes'm. You be a good person fuh work fuh. I kin do all de tings I bin doin fuh you here, an I kin cook, too. I be likin dat idee." Rina grinned at Laura for a few moments. Then she caught her breath. "But how bout Hastins? We not fambly. We not be marrit nor nuttin, but we's bin livin togedduh fuh long time now. Kin he come long?"

"I don't see why not. We'll need a driver and a handyman and someone to catch croakers for us. Would he agree to that?"

"He be doin what I tells he."

"Well, you two talk it over and decide, but don't tell any one yet. The move won't happen until I find us a house in St. Helenaville and get it ready to be occupied. Until then, do whatever Mr. Fairfield tells you, so he doesn't get suspicious. I don't want him sending you off somewhere."

"Dat what I likes bout you, Missus. You tricky!"

* * *

Moving turned out to be much more complicated than Laura had realized. General Saxton answered her message immediately, telling her that she could claim any unoccupied house in St. Helenaville. He would take care of getting the property deeded to her. He also authorized her to take any and all of the furnishings at The Oaks that she had been accustomed to using. "Make sure you also claim any gifts that have been given to you by grateful patients," he cautioned. "You'll need livestock—particularly your two horses, Charley and Betty, some chickens, if Rina can spare them, and even a cow if you can manage it. The little buggy you've been using is a gift from the Army, and you will be justified in taking a cart, too. It's bad enough that Mr. Fairfield is putting you out of your own home. I won't let him deprive you of your basic creature comforts as well."

Armed with that permission, Laura took her buggy out to St. Helenaville the very next day. She found herself smiling as she noticed how quiet, friendly, and prosperous the little village appeared. This is going to be a pleasant place to live, she reassured herself. The local inhabitants seemed happy to point out unoccupied houses, but once she laid eyes on Aunt Rachel's Place, she knew she had found her new home.

The house was small and single-storied—a basic four-room floor plan with a full front veranda and a southern exposure that offered a view of the river flowing past the front yard. Two small dormers pierced the pitched roof above the veranda. One of them opened to a storage room and the other to a small sleeping area that could be used by a house servant. When Laura walked around to the back of the house, she found an ample yard, housing a cookhouse with a room above for the cook, a lean-to barn, a thriving kitchen garden, fruit trees, and three cabins full of lively black children and their parents, all of whom seemed happy to welcome a new resident.

Accompanied by several of the Negro tenants, she entered the house itself and was momentarily taken aback by how run-down and dirty it was. "Nobody bin livin here since Aunt Rachel move out an go to Hilton Head fuh cook fuh de genral," one of the men explained. "Sand do blow in, but we kin fix dat quick nuf."

Laura was also horrified to discover a sawed-off whipping post with a ring and fastening bit in her new dining room. "That has to go!" she said. "What a revolting idea. It reminds me of the post we had to take out of the dining room at Frogmore."

"I know dat be true. Bot uh dose houses be build by de Fripp brudders, an dey be sum nasty mens. But you don need fuh worrit. We takes care uh it fore you moves in. Dat one chore de menfolk enjoy doin."

"I kin start cleanin de house right way, ifn you wants me fuh work fuh you," a tiny young woman spoke up. "I be Clarissa, an I be de one what clean fuh Aunt Rachel. I kin even sleep in de dormer room in de attic so dere be sumbody livin here permanent-like."

"Thank you, Clarissa. We can sit down and work out your wages after I see how good a job you do. Is that all right?"

"Dat be fine, Missus. I be makin you proud."

Laura was smiling when she returned to Frogmore for the night. "I've found us a little cottage, taken right out of a fairy tale," she told Ellen. "All it needs is a white picket fence. There will be plenty of room for the two of us, and not enough room for anyone to try to share the house or visit for too long—an ideal situation. It comes with a staff, too, and something else you'll really love Besides the three families who are already providing a cleaning crew and raising vegetables that they are willing to share, I've arranged for Rina and Hastings to join us. They will have their own quarters above the cookhouse, since Rina has volunteered to cook."

"Rina? Cook? Does she know how? Have you forgotten about the meals Susannah used to serve?"

"Truthfully, I'm not sure if Rina's ever cooked a meal, but how hard can it be to learn? We can help teach her, if need be. But I'm going to be comforted to have her with us."

"And we'll always have fish to eat with Hastings around. It all sounds wonderful."

"Well, don't pack your bags yet. We're not moving until the house is completely ready and until you are feeling yourself again. But think pleasant thoughts. That will help you get well."

RINA ON "RACHEL'S HOUSE"
January 1864

Missus Laura come to de Oaks dis mornin an tell we dat she be takin Aunt Rachel Place in St. Helenaville. I hab a big ol grin on muh face, cause I knows dat house. De gal she call Aunt Rachel an I grow up togedduh here at de Oaks, least til we start gittin bumps an all dat. I neber be purty cause uh muh twisty ol back, but Rachel—she be a looker. So Massa Pope, he sell she to Massa "Good Billy" Fripp, who be wantin a purty gal fuh teach he four sons how fuh be mens.

Rachel, she hab a hard time fuh while, cause two uh de oldes boys be hateful an mean to she. She hab a couple uh baby, but nobody care who be de fadduh an dey git sold way fro she. Den come Massa Clarence, de son what went way to Columbia fuh learn fuh be a doctor. He be a good man mos times, an when he come home, he buy Rachel fuh he own. De diffrunce be, he love she.

He build heself a lil house on de edge uh St. Helenaville, an when he git it done, he bring Rachel dere an tell she it be she own house. Dey liv dere togedduh in de years fore de war come. Massa Clarence, he tell eberbody dat Rachel be de housekeeper fuh he, but dat not be true. Dey hab two chillun, boy an gal, an Massa Clarence, he proud fuh call dem he own chillun. He not care dat dere skin be brown. He love dem ennyway.

Missus Laura, she be worrit bout de whippin post inna dinin room, but true be tole, it aint neber be used. Massa Clarence, he jis puts it dere so he brudduh don tinks he soft on dat black gal an she chillun.

When de Big Shoot happen, de Fripps all run way, an dey drag Massa Clarence wit dem. But fore he leave, he gib Rachel paper dat say she be free an dat she own de lil house. Den all de Fripps, dey join de army, an Massa Clarence, he tell he brudduh dat he gwine go work in de hospital an he be waitin fuh dem when dey gits demselfs shot. He not be tellin true.

He come back home fuh Rachel. Eber night, he come to she house, an she cook fuh he an clean he clothe. He sleep dere all night, den go out inna maash an hide all de day long. Dat go on til de Edisto folk be movin inna St. Helenaville an it be too danger fuh movin roun de village. Rachel tell he not fuh come dere enny mo.

She start gibbin way all de nice tings to she friends, an den she gib way de table an chair an de bed, too. When de house be empty, she show she free paper to one uh de army mens. He take she to Missus Hayet Tubman, an Missus Tubman take she to Hilton Head. Last I hear, she be cookin fuh some uh de big army mens an gittin paid fuh it. She happy at last.

An I be happy, too. I aint neber goin back to de Oaks, once I gits way fro here. I gwine feel free at Aunt Rachel Place. I tink Missus Laura an Missus Ellen gwine like it dere, too. Dat house be build jis fuh two people fuh share, so nobody gwine bodder dem. An I spects dat de folk what gots Rachel tings gwine take em back when dey find out how nice Missus Laura be.

47
TRANSITIONS
January 1864

For most of January, Laura was too busy to think much about the significance of moving away from the rest of the Gideonites. As she promised, she visited her usual round of plantations, caring for those she thought had a chance of surviving their smallpox. She paused to comfort the bereaved and made sure that the people who had not yet become ill had been vaccinated. No matter what else happened, she reassured everyone who lived in the slave streets that she was not abandoning them.

When smallpox started to spread rapidly among the Gideonites, Laura encouraged them to seek help from the Army doctors. She even refused a request that she move out to Seaside to care for Lottie Forten, who had also contracted the disease. Laura agreed to visit her, but declared her to be not as sick as she had imagined. "You all have access to the government doctors in Beaufort, and General Saxton will see to it that you receive adequate care. But our freedmen have no one but me. I must reach out to those who need me most," she explained.

At least once every day, she traveled out to Aunt Rachel's Place to oversee the work going on there. And every time she went, she added to her mental list of things that needed to be done. Some of the windows would not open, while the door refused to stay shut. Could she find a carpenter to fix them? The floorboards in the parlor had wide cracks between them, and that infernally fine sand seemed to blow straight up and into the house. Could she find a piece of carpet to cover the worst of the gaps? The dining room still sported its whipping post, although she noticed that Rina was right. The post was remarkably smooth, with no marks of a whip and none of the old blood splashes that had stained the Frogmore post. Maybe a carpenter could also saw the post into shelves, she thought. We're certainly going to need somewhere to store our few dishes.

As if she had spoken the wish out loud, a carpenter appeared. A middle-aged black man was waiting for her in the yard the next day. "Be you Missus Towne?" he asked.

"I am. Were you looking for me?"

"Yes'm. I be Edward. When Missus Rachel live here, I makes mos uh she funiture. An when she move out, she give mos uh it back. She say I kin do wit it whateber I wants, but I caint use it. Ifn you needs sumptin, I spects I kin find it fuh you."

"How kind of you! Tell me, do you do repairs as well?"

"If it be sumptin fuh do wit wood, I duz."

Laura could not help but smile. "Can you make my windows open and my door close? I'll pay you well."

"No need fuh dat. I be happy fuh help. It be nice havin sumbody livin here like ole days."

Little Clarissa had already scrubbed the bedroom, Laura noticed, and was now working on a narrow space beyond the bedroom that might provide enough room for a narrow guest cot. Across the hall, a room for provisions appeared to contain some old flour barrels and other supplies. Laura thought about checking the quality of the foodstuffs and then shied away from prying open the barrels. Better let one of the Negro women do that, she decided. I don't know enough about cooking to judge. A narrow passageway separated the rest of the house from the two-story cookhouse that would become Rina's domain. Laura considered urging Clarissa to get the cookhouse ready soon, although she realized that Rina would do all the work over again when she arrived.

In the yard, Laura was delighted to find two pomegranate trees and an apple tree starting to show buds. Greens were flourishing in the large garden plot, and some of the women were already cultivating other sections of the garden in anticipation of more crop planting. Laura made a mental note to be sure the women had an adequate supply of seeds for root vegetables that could be stored for the next winter. There should be enough room out here to feed all of us, black and white, if we plan carefully, she decided.

Laura was not so optimistic about the provisions for the livestock, however. The lean-to barn was situated to block the prevailing winter winds, but it was too small to shelter more than the two horses, Betty and Charley. We won't have to worry about chickens, she realized. They are Rina's specialty, and I'm sure she'll have Hastings constructing pens for them. But what about the cow—if we can find a cow, that is? We're going to need our own milk and butter, because it's too expensive at the store. And, of course, a cow will eventually need both her own shelter and a fenced-in grazing area. We could use a hostler, provided we can find one of those.

Again, when her need was great, an answer appeared. Laura had met Frank on her very first trip to St. Helenaville, but she hadn't bothered to ask about his talents or usual employment because of his advanced age. One day, she drove out to the village with Charley hitched to her buggy. A strange noise startled him, and he reared, threatening to tip the buggy. Laura shouted in alarm, further frightening the already spooked horse. Out of nowhere, Frank appeared to grasp the reins and pull Charley to a halt. He slowly rubbed the horse's nose and whispered in his ear. Laura could see the tension leave the horse's withers as he settled.

"You are a lifesaver," Laura said. "It's Frank, isn't it?"

"Yes'm."

"You're really good with horses. Thank you for stepping in."

"No problem, ma'am. I likes horses, an cows, too. Dey jis simple beasts what needs a slow an gentle hand. I's good at slow dese days."

"Would you be interested in a nice, slow job taking care of our livestock? So far it's just two horses, although I'm hoping to add a mooley cow."

"I kin do dat. I knows where we kin gits you a mooley cow, too. Tankee, ma'am."

* * *

In the evenings, Laura returned to Frogmore, where Ellen was recuperating under the watchful eyes of her mother and sister. "You're starting to look much better," Laura told her. "I was afraid of making this move, but it seems to have agreed with you. Just don't tell anybody else that. I want to make Nelly Fairfield suffer a little more."

"What do you mean? You're a doctor. You're supposed to relieve suffering, not encourage it," Ellen said.

"I'm making an exception in Nelly's case. I stopped at The Oaks today, and Nelly pounced on me, telling me that she didn't mean we had to move out immediately. It seems that when she went to church the day after we left, several people attacked her for turning you out when you were still dangerously ill. Now she's embarrassed and accusing us of turning people against her. I'm sorry, but I'm enjoying watching her squirm."

"Yes, it's a satisfactory result. But what happened to Nelly, Laura? She was a pleasant companion when we were all living there together. I liked her very much. But now she seems like an entirely different person."

"Josiah Fairfield happened to her!"

Ellen shook her head. "I've never understood why she wanted to marry that man."

"I don't know either, but she certainly could have found someone better. For a brief while, I hoped her charm would rub off on him. Instead his nastiness seems to have infected her. A pity!"

"How's he behaving as sole owner of The Oaks?" Ellen asked.

"Abominably! On my way home, I ran into John Driver, his foreman. He asked me if he was obliged by law to plant cotton only for Mr. Fairfield, even though he has bought his own small plot of land. It seems Mr. Fairfield is threatening all his landowning workers that he will throw them out of their cabins if they plant cotton of their own. And he's also telling them that if they do plant their own cotton, they will not be allowed to sell it. I advised John that the law says no such thing and that General Saxton will not let Fairfield throw him off his own land. I also promised him that there would be several people eager to buy his cotton, Mr. Philbrick among them."

"Why does Fairfield want to alienate people?"

"Because he can, I suppose. He enjoys being in power, although that may not last long when he runs out of people to boss around. Our people on the slave street tell me that Mr. Tomlinson is moving out to join Mr. Ruggles on his plantation. And one of the women said, 'Massa Fairfield, he done chased eber bit . . . De house look too lonely, cause no buckra come dere now'."

Laura had one more encounter with Nelly. She had gone to The Oaks to pack up her belongings, and, to avoid an argument, she presented Nelly with the letter from Saxton that authorized her to take her furnishings out of the house.

Nelly, of course, was furious. "Well, you just remember that anything you remove from this house is not really yours. You'll be stealing it from a home for orphans."

"An orphanage? Where are your orphans? Little Brister and Becky are dead from smallpox, I've been told, just as I warned you. And you haven't brought in any other children that I can see. The few items I take from here will be used to allow me to continue working in Penn School, which is already running again and has dozens of students. I find it more important than your pipe dreams."

Laura practiced remarkable restraint as she packed, limiting herself to two place settings of dishes and eating utensils. From the furniture, she chose their bed, a bureau, two chairs,

452

a table, and a sideboard. If we need anything else, I'll ask Edward, she thought.

If Nelly had conducted an inventory, she might have found that almost all the pretty things that now decorated The Oaks had originally come as gifts to Laura from her grateful patients. Laura left them where they were, perhaps because she simply didn't need them. She might have been excused, however, if she thought of this act of apparent generosity as heaping hot coals on the heads of the Fairfields.

* * *

On the last evening before Laura moved to their new home, she and Ellen sat up late talking. Ellen had agreed to stay with her mother for one more week, but she was restless and frustrated by her lack of strength. "I wish I could have provided more help with the move," she said, "but when you tell me about your adventures I can at least imagine it. Do you really think we are going to be happy in St. Helenaville?"

"I'm sure of it. I've learned a great deal by crisscrossing the island every day. I'm convinced there is a magic portal that I pass through between The Oaks and Rachel's Place. I can be angry and insulted one minute, and the next I find myself relaxed, humming a silly tune and grinning. I can't wait for you to discover how different the village really is."

"But what makes it so? Is it just the absence of the Fairfields, or the presence of our new neighbors, or something else that happens at that magical portal?"

"I can't put a name to it, but it's a real enough difference. One of the things I've come to realize is that there has been an air of contention at The Oaks ever since I arrived. On my very first day in South Carolina, I asked a question about the program the Gideonites were following, and I was told there was no plan. Everyone was just bumbling along without any clear purpose. When I arrived at The Oaks, I found a hot-bed of disagreement. Two of the ladies were already packing to go home, and, mind you, they had only been there for three weeks. Miss Susan Walker was a dominating force in the house, but it was Nelly who was actually doing the work while Miss Walker complained about how much she had to do. She had established her own rules, which demanded that the other women take turns doing the more disagreeable tasks rather than the jobs to which someone else had assigned them. She put me to work as housekeeper, although I had been sent to oversee clothing distribution, for example. She second-guessed every decision Mr. Pierce made, including his decision to go home himself. And when she couldn't convince him to stay, she practically raced him to the wharf to catch the next ship going north."

"But that could just have been because the venture was still so new. By the time I arrived, everyone seemed friendly enough," Ellen said.

"Only on the surface, my dear. Do you remember your first service at the Brick Church? I tried to tell you then that there were religious squabbles going on that threatened the Port Royal Experiment. You didn't see them until the great Closed Communion flap made them obvious. There were—and still are—evangelical missionaries who believe that Unitarians are devils incarnate. Others feel the same way about Baptists—especially black Baptists."

"Those are the pious souls who want the Negroes to stay put in their own churches and not darken the doors of the pure white congregations. I have seen that and deplored it. But it's not the whole story."

"No, I suppose not. We have a common goal to educate the freed slaves and their children. Or do we? How many arguments have you heard about what we should be teaching? Remember Amanda Ruggles accusing me of stealing her children by trying to teach them some mathematics? Or the black man who protested in Sunday school that we were telling Bible stories instead of teaching them their ABCs?"

"Neither of us have mentioned the arguments over land sales and preemptions, either. I see what you mean. We Gideonites have been so busy fighting each other that we haven't accomplished much." Ellen's face mirrored her disillusionment.

"I'm afraid that we've only managed to teach the former slaves that freedom means permission to disagree. We've provided terrible examples of Christian behavior. Unfortunately, anger only begets more anger, so that by now the very atmosphere of The Oaks seems poisonous to me."

"I can't deny that."

"In contrast, St. Helenaville grew up as a summer resort. No one was trying to teach anybody anything. Nobody wanted to be the boss or take control or make money. A summer home was just a place to relax and enjoy a beautiful day. That attitude still prevails, thank goodness, and it's what makes the village so charming. The slaves of St. Helenaville were completely free long before Lincoln proclaimed emancipation, and because no one has been ordering them around, they are more willing to work—if that makes sense."

"Does that prove that Mr. Philbrick's theory is correct—that the Negro will work if you pay him enough?"

"Not necessarily. I think it's more important that they take pride in their work. They are willing to share their labor if others recognize their efforts. That's why Clarissa is scrubbing her knuckles raw to clean our little house; why Edward is bustling around with a handful of nails and his trusty hammer as soon as the sun comes up; why Frank has been out checking every family—black and white—to find a spare cow. It's even why Rina and Hastings are willing to leave the only home they've ever known and come with us to St. Helenaville. Praise and gratitude make an enormous difference in how a person feels about himself. And when he feels good about himself, he treats others well."

"That's where the Gideonites got it wrong, isn't it? They came to criticize and change the way the slaves had been living. And that made the slaves feel bad about themselves."

"That's at least part of the problem. We have much to learn from the Negroes of St. Helenaville—those the Gideonites have not managed to harm."

48
AN INDEPENDENT HOUSEHOLD
February–March 1864

llen joined Laura in their new home a week later. It had been a busy week, and Laura had much to report. They moved to the veranda after a pickup supper to watch night fall on the river. "This may be the most peaceful spot on the island," Laura said. "I sit out here almost every night, drinking in the stillness and beauty."

"Somehow it feels safe, too," Ellen said. "Instead of an encroaching swamp, we have neighbors with lights in their windows and a church with a steeple to point our way."

"I agree. I like that feeling of being part of a community. We're private here, but within shouting distance of others if we need help. And help would come, too. I can guarantee it. Everyone has been welcoming and generous. The white curtains in our parlor are just one example. Clarissa turned up with them one morning, saying nothing except that 'sumbody send em'."

"What's that?" Ellen asked, pointing to a shadow that had appeared in a corner of the porch.

"Oh, that's Puss. No, don't make a face at me! I know I promised you that we could have a dog some day, but one of the women from the cabins brought Puss up to the house, and I couldn't refuse to accept her without being rude. She's just a barn cat who hangs around looking for mice, which is a useful occupation, you must admit."

"What does Rina think? Isn't Puss interested in her chickens?"

"Not so far. And if I have to choose between Puss and Rina's hens, we'll be eating lots of fried chicken. The women planted one whole area of the garden with early spring onions, lettuces, and peas, and those chickens picked the lock on their coop and dug up every seed in the garden. They're getting so fat, we may even have to roast them instead of frying them."

"Well, I can certainly see that you're not at all fond of that cat." Ellen was now laughing harder as the little cat wound her way around Laura's ankles, rubbed her furry cheek on Laura's shoe, and then leaped to her lap, settling in with a deep, throaty purr.

"All right. We'll try to find a dog for you, too. All you'll have to do is go out into the yard and mention that you'd like to have one around for protection. You'll be tripping over puppies before you can get back to the house."

"Did you try that method for getting a cow? That's what we'll really need."

"Don't talk to me about cows right now," Laura said. "I did suggest it to our new hostler, and by the next day he reported that Mr. John Alden—one of our superintendents out here—had an extra one that he would send over. In just a couple of hours, here came Mr. Alden leading a skinny old cow and her calf. We put them in the stable out back with Charley, but the first time I went to feed them, that cow lowered her head, shuffled her feet back and forth a bit, and then charged right at me. I ducked to one side, but she still head-butted me and sat me right down in the dirt."

"No! What I would have given to see that, provided you weren't really hurt, that is."

"Just embarrassed. But it didn't make me very fond of her. And then the next day, Bossy proved to be a jumper— sailed right over the fence, leaving her little calf behind and sashaying down the road with a purpose. We haven't seen her since, so, instead of having a supply of free milk, we now have to buy extra milk to feed the calf she abandoned."

"This new house is beginning to sound like a zoo," Ellen giggled.

"It is that, and getting worse all the time," Laura replied. "Bossy's disappearance reminded me of last spring, when Betty wandered off. We put her out to pasture one morning while she was in heat, and she disappeared. I wasn't too worried because she was so little that I didn't think any of the soldiers would want to steal her. Sure enough, she came back in a day or so, no longer in heat and looking very self-satisfied. She had found herself a beau down the road. I suspect we'll have a colt before spring is over this year. Maybe that's what Bossy is up to, as well."

"That would be fun, but in the meantime, no milk and butter for us?"

"None except what Mr. Thorpe lets us buy from his supply. Mr. Alden promised to bring another cow, but I haven't accepted his offer. If Bossy comes home with another calf on the way, I don't think we could afford to feed them all."

Once again, Laura's words proved to be prophetic. A few days later, Bossy the cow meandered down the road. She was home—worn, dirty, weary, and milkless. "What good are you?" Laura demanded. "Just another hungry mouth to feed."

Laura was justifiably irritated, for fodder was in short supply. It had turned cold again in March, and the animals were suffering. Laura had twenty-five bushels of corn to use as feed, but she rationed it carefully, hoping to make it last until the next harvest. On the bitterest day of the cold snap, however, she set Rina to grinding some of the corn and mixing it with hot water and molasses to feed the livestock. When Laura appeared in the stable with this hot mash, Frank the hostler leered at her. "You aint gwine gib dat good stuff to dese anmals, is you? I kin tinks of a bedder place fuh put it."

"Oh, Frank, you wouldn't eat this. It's horse food."

"I aint gwine eat it. I gwine put it in muh still an make likker outta it. Dat gwine warm we fuh a good long time. Den when I's finished wit it, you kin still gib de cooked corn to de anmals. Dat way, eberbody happy, eben de horse an de cow."

Laura could not help but smile. "No, thank you, Frank. Charley is quite frisky enough without you turning him into a drunk."

"Me neider, I spose."

"You suppose correctly. Now help me portion this out to the horses and cows."

"Waste uh good corn, you ax me," he mumbled as he did what he had been told.

Laura enjoyed describing the incident to Ellen. "It's another example of how different things are here. Our Negroes may work for us, but you don't see any of the fore-lock-tugging, shoe-shuffling deference we used to get from the former slaves at The Oaks. These people look us in the eye and dare to challenge us, even though they respect us."

* * *

Laura and Ellen had returned to teaching their classes in mid-February, but as often as possible they avoided discussing the affairs of the island. On the other side of St. Helena, however, arguments continued to rage.

Mr. Brisbane, the tax commissioner, had listened to General Saxton announce Lincoln's decision on preemption without argument, but he had secretly sent his own agents to Washington to plead his case with Congress. On February 9th, he had announced that the land sales would go on as scheduled, and he warned that preempted claims might not stand. Two days later, he made good on the threat, canceling all the preemptions. The Negro claimants were still reeling from that shock when, a week later, the land sales were stopped again.

Reverend French appeared at the Brick Church on February 21st to preach a sermon directed at the black parishioners. "This land is yours," he told them. "You have earned it with your hard labor, and you have paid for it with your blood and sweat, as well as with your money. Take the land you need. Plant your own crops, not somebody else's, and defend your rights with your hoes, if need be."

A visiting pastor, Mr. Barrows, had been dropped into this confusing controversy without much preparation. After the service, Laura stayed to talk with him for a long time. She filled him in on the history of the land disputes with Philbrick, whose actions Reverend French had denounced in his sermon, and on the current mood of the people, who had paid their filing fees in good faith and now stood to lose their investments. "I fear that the advice Reverend French gave may do great harm to our people and to this island," she said. "It is not my fight. I have nothing to lose one way or the other. But I do care about fairness and doing what's right. I hope you will be careful in what you say, lest you fan these sparks into flames."

* * *

The once shabby little house was looking better, but it still needed a lot of work. Laura paid a visit to the smallpox hospital and bought a chaise longue that they were not using.

"Aren't you afraid of getting poxed?" a hospital attendant asked.

"No. It's been aired out thoroughly, and everyone in my house has a fresh vaccination. Besides, I'm a doctor, and I've been treating smallpox patients all winter. If I didn't catch the disease from my patients, I'm surely not going to catch it from a chair."

She put it on her cart and wheeled it home, where she retrieved from one of her boxes a length of scarlet upholstery material. Then she called upon Ed the carpenter. "Do you think we can cover this chaise with the new material?" she asked.

"No problem, Missus. I gots lots uh dose polstry tacks. I jis pull de ol ones out, use ol material as pattern fuh cut new covers, an tack it back on. I be glad fuh de work."

"I insist on paying you."

"No, Missus. Dis not take no work tall. Ifn you wants fuh spend you money, I still gots dat furniture dat Rachel gib we. I be willin fuh sell you dat."

"All right. Let me see what you have." At the end of their bargaining, Laura found that she had purchased a sideboard for the dining room, one with drawers and shelves beneath to store all her packets of medicine. She also bought two small pine tables and a green sofa for the parlor.

The additions nearly filled the small house. Rina was so excited by the new furniture that she began pulling out her own treasures to finish the decorating. She added paintings and wall hangings, vases and figurines, curtains, doilies, and small throw rugs—what she called her "purty tings."

"Where did all these things come from?" Laura asked. "What do I owe you for them?"

"I don member where dey comes fro," Rina said. "Some uh dem be in muh fambly fuh a long time, an I aint sellin you nuttin. Dis be muh own home now, an I neber spect fuh hab anudder one. So we's all gwine joy dem togedduh."

"Together." Laura repeated the word to Ellen, almost tasting it. "What a wonderful concept. And what a delightful family we have formed here out of mutual trust and respect. Why can't the rest of the world learn how to live this way?"

49

A SCHOOL OF OUR OWN

Spring 1864

The biggest threat to the existence of the Penn School had always been their free use of the Baptist Church's building. Whenever controversies arose among the various denominations over such things as communion, the arguments tended to spread to educational issues. The evangelicals among the Gideonites had always considered their mission to be the spreading of Christianity, and their own brand of it at that, while the Unitarians were teachers who cared foremost about education. Such disputes had frequently threatened to close the doors to Laura's school. With the help of General Saxton, she had managed to avoid direct confrontation only because the general intimidated Mr. Phillips.

Then, on February 12th, Pastor Phillips died of smallpox. Laura's medical advice had not been consulted, which did not surprise her, given their ongoing conflicts. She also knew his death did not mean that the threat to the school had passed. Mrs. Phillips, the pastor's wife, had made it clear that the school issue was far from settled. Laura watched with alarm to see who would take Phillips's place.

Immediately after the funeral, Laura and Ellen reopened the school, knowing that it would be harder for a new man to evict them if their school was up and running. Both women were delighted to be back in the classroom. Penn School had been closed for three and a half months—first because of Ellen's illness, and then due to the smallpox epidemic. Empty chairs were sad reminders of the children who had died, but those who had survived were bursting with new energy. Laura had to banish only a few ruffians to sit in the churchyard until they could behave. The rest had had enough of idleness and were eager to learn.

All across the island, leasing deals had given rise to the availability of school farms. New teachers were arriving, which led to staffing changes and some confusion as to who would attend each school. Penn School picked up those whose needs could not be met on their own plantation and soon had a full complement of scholars again. Laura, Ellen, and Ellen's sister Harriet each had a class of some fifty children.

At the beginning of March, two boys arrived at the door of the Brick Church to ask if they could attend school there. They introduced themselves as William Gregory and Henry Mack from Mr. Ruggles's plantation.

"Aren't you supposed to be attending class at The Oaks?" Laura asked. "I thought all Mr. Ruggles's children were going there."

"We be wantin fuh come here, cause we aint larnin nuttin at de Oaks," Henry explained.

"Obviously not." Laura winced at their heavy Gullah tongues. "I'm sorry. We can't take you here unless you bring a letter from Mrs. Fairfield. She will have to put your names on it, tell us how long you have been in her school, and give you permission to come here instead of there. Can you take care of that?"

"Yes'm. We kin do dat."

The next day, they came back with a scribbled note from Nelly Fairfield:

"William and Henry are supposed to attend my school, but I have no class for children their age. In fact, I have given up teaching altogether. You can have every one of my students, for all I care."

Laura and Ellen exchanged looks that spoke of both self-satisfaction and exasperation. While they were too kind to laugh at this new development, neither was surprised that Nelly's grandiose plans had failed. "What will that mean for Mr. Fairfield's lease?" Ellen asked when she and Laura were alone. "If you hold a lease for a school farm, aren't you required to fulfill the school part?"

"Well, for that matter, I'm hearing that he's not doing so well with the farm part, either," Laura said. "After Reverend French's tirade at church, only a few of the Negroes are willing to work for him. But that's just gossip, and unbecoming of me. By now, I really don't care what problem the Fairfields have, so long as it doesn't affect people I'm fond of."

* * *

The new Baptist pastor, Mr. Parker, arrived in mid-March. He was an elderly man, pulled away from a looming retirement in his small Connecticut town to serve this unknown parish. Laura met him for the first time when he appeared at the school.

"I understand from Mrs. Phillips that there have been hard feelings between your staff and the church," he said. "I thought I'd drop by and reassure you that I have no intention of disrupting your arrangements here. I believe strongly in education. May I visit your classroom? I'm interested in what you are accomplishing."

He watched for a bit, and then asked if he could question the children. Laura agreed. He picked a child at random and asked, "What do you have in your head?"

"Sense," the child answered.

"No, that's wrong. You have brains in your head."

The frightened child rolled her eyes at Missus Laura to see if she had made a terrible mistake.

"And how do you get knowledge into your brain?" Parker asked.

"God put him dere," another child volunteered.

"No," Mr. Parker said. He launched into a complicated explanation of how the five senses all provided sources of knowledge. As he spoke, he waved his hands about, pointing to mouths, eyes, ears, noses, and fingers. His voice, unfortunately, was so low-pitched that the class could not hear him. All they could see were those waving hands, and they soon were giggling and pointing to each other. It was sheer disaster.

Laura eased him out of the room as kindly as she could. "I apologize," she said. "One of the problems we have is overcrowding that makes it hard for teachers and students alike to hear what's going on. I'm sure the children were trying to please you."

"If they were, they would be the first ones since I arrived here," he said. "I only want to be useful. I came here expecting peace and sincere religious zeal. I thought I was joining a band of people who lived in harmony and who worked with combined effort. Instead, I find nothing but friction—friction in every quarter: religious, military, and philanthropic. I don't know what is expected of me or who to believe."

"You'll have to judge that for yourself, I'm afraid. I can tell you that every person I know holds sincere beliefs, but we are all quite different. I, for example, am a Unitarian, which makes me a suspicious person to all the Methodists and other evangelicals among us."

"A Unitarian? Really? I don't think I've ever met one of those."

"We aren't dangerous," she said with a smile.

"But, oh, my dear, I'll be forced to convert you."

"You're welcome to try, so long as you don't also kick my school out of your church. It's the only place on the island that can hold all of us."

"I promise I have no intention of doing so," he said. "And I didn't mean to complain. I'm just a little homesick for my quiet old parsonage, I suppose, where at least I could get something to eat."

"What?" Laura was confused at the sudden change of subject. "Are you hungry?"

"I'm always hungry here. I can't eat pork and beans. They give me gas. I had never even seen an oyster, that slimy thing that shows up at every meal, and sweet potatoes give me dyspepsia. You people don't seem to eat anything else."

"I'm afraid that's about all we have, at least until the summer crops start coming in. I can get you some eggs, though. And there will be fresh fruit soon. Do you think you could survive on watermelon?"

"Looks like I may have to."

The two parted as friends, although Laura doubted the old gentleman's ability to defend her interests against entrenched opponents who did not approve of her school.

* * *

One promise of relief arrived in a letter from General Saxton. "I've had an inquiry from the Philadelphia Commission asking if there is any need of schoolhouses in the department. I'm hoping you and Mr. Tomlinson will each write to them, giving them your opinion."

Laura's memory of Pastor Parker's visit was still sharp as she wrote her answer. She couldn't speak for the school farms, because she had no real experience with them, and she squelched her first reaction, which was to call them "sheer folly." Instead, she concentrated on the needs of Penn School.

"We are in great need of a dedicated schoolhouse for several reasons. We are using the local church on sufferance from the pastor, whoever he happens to be, and that means we are in constant danger of expulsion. We cannot have desks or blackboards because the church must also be used for religious services. And we have the noise of three large schools in one room—three teachers and as many as two hundred scholars, all speaking loudly to be heard. The overcrowding strains our voices; I have frequently developed laryngitis. Our students do not get our full attention, and the situation is fatal to keeping good order in the classroom. We feel like orphans, searching for a home of our own."

As she wrote, she was reminded of the usual chaos at the Brick Church school, which had been partially responsible for driving Miss Forten away. *I wonder how she's doing?* Laura thought, and, almost as if in response, Lottie arrived one morning at the beginning of April for an impromptu visit.

"I've been wanting to see both of you," Lottie said, greeting Laura and Ellen with generous hugs. "Now that I'm feeling so well again, I wanted to tell you personally that I will be returning to teach at Seaside. I miss my little scholars more than I could have ever imagined."

"I completely understand," Laura replied. "While everyone was so ill, we closed our school, and it felt as if there were a huge hole in our lives. Children can be annoying little imps, but they do have a way of burrowing their way into our hearts. I'm delighted to hear that you are feeling quite well again, with no ill effects except for . . ." Laura stopped herself in horror as Lottie raised her hand to her cheek.

"You can feel free to mention my pockmarks," she said. "I know I'm badly scarred, but it's only skin, not my soul." As Laura stammered to make amends, Lottie patted her hand. "I've learned a lot these past few months. One of the lessons I now hope to pass along concerns the nature of skin itself. Just as smallpox scars do not change who I am, so the color of my skin does not make me different from you or from our children. It's just wrapping, and, like a birthday present, if you want to enjoy the real gift, you have to get past the wrapper."

"Oh, my dear, I'm so glad you're back!" More hugs and more than a few tears marked the successful reunion.

The response to Laura's letter came quickly. The Philadelphia Commission would be shipping a partially pre-constructed three-room schoolhouse for the use of Penn School. She was delighted. Then came a follow-up letter from Mr. McKim, bemoaning the size of the building and predicting that it would be much too small to be of any use. Gloom jousted with anticipation.

Laura had planned to go home for the summer, because she had so neglected her family the previous winter. They feared for Laura's health and stamina, and their letters had started to sound more than a little aggrieved that she constantly chose the needs of her South Carolina people over those of her own family. Now Laura hesitated again. "It would probably be better to stay on St. Helena until the schoolhouse arrives and we can get it all put together. If I go home, I'll just be sitting there worrying about how big it is and how to get it ready for use."

Ellen, who often acted as Laura's voice of reason when situations threatened to overwhelm, advised her not to wait. "You've been in South Carolina long enough to know how things get done here. You've been told the building is coming; you have not been told when it will arrive. If it comes while you are gone, which is highly unlikely, the engineers can put it together. It may be larger than Mr. McKim expects. If so, we'll find more students to fill it and enjoy having elbow room at last. If it's too small, we'll round up our own carpenters and build additions. Until we see it, we cannot judge. And nothing that is going to happen will require your presence or your worry. Go home, Laura."

Laura agreed at last, for she well remembered how homesick she had been over Christmas, but she also had a list of responsibilities that needed to be taken care of first. She had been waiting for almost a year to see the results of Betty's escape from her pasture. Like a doting grandmother, she wanted to be present for the birth of the colt. The classes at Penn School needed to be reorganized to balance them more evenly. New teachers were waiting for assignments to school farms. And, most important, the site of the new schoolhouse had to be established.

Betty was the most cooperative. On May 10th, she produced a perfect little chestnut colt. Laura named him Saxby. "I didn't say Saxton," she pleaded as Ellen made fun of her for naming the tiny animal after the general, but they both knew that the blacks often substituted the name Saxby for Saxton. Was Laura making a connection between Betty running off to find her own stallion and the general's sudden proposal to Tilly? Laura would never admit it. The colt, however, was a delight. He skipped around playfully and chose Ellen as his special person. Whenever she quit playing with him, he would leap at her and nip at her dress or fingers until she gave him her full attention again. On the last day of school, the two women took Betty and her colt to school with them, where the children had a fine time learning about baby horses. Then they led the horses down the road to the pasture at Mr. Ruggles's plantation, where they were to spend the summer.

Laura did her best to prepare for the next school year, promoting her own students to Harriet Murray's class, letting Ellen take over Harriet's old students, and arranging for Ellen's youngest sister, Fanny, to join them in the fall. Since General Saxton also expected her to oversee the other school farms, she tried to make the rounds. But she didn't bother going to The Oaks. Rumor had it that the Fairfields were packing up to go home. She did, however, take time to talk to one of the new black teachers about trying to do too much. She warned Mr. Lynch that he was risking his spirituality by trying to be both the preacher for the black church in St.

Helenaville and the only teacher at his own school farm in the village.

"It's not that you are not doing a good job," she explained, "but I know from my own experience that when I tried to be both doctor and teacher, I did not enjoy either occupation. I've now decided that my greatest love is teaching, and I've been more than willing to turn over most of my patients to the new homeopathic physician on Ladies Island. You may need to make the same sort of compromise."

Finally, she turned to the most important decision of all, the location of the new Penn School building. When preemption had seemed a certainty back in February, she had staked out a claim at a spot on Coffin Point Road, east of the Baptist Church. It lay on Mr. Pope's property near the signal station. Then the multiple reversals of that ruling had wiped out her claim. With Mr. Tomlinson and Mr. Ruggles, her greatest supporters, she toured the island.

Mr. Philbrick stepped forward to offer his own land. He would, he promised, lease the land at a minimal rate, so that they would have more money to spend on finishing and furnishing the new building itself.

"No," Laura said. "I have always advised our Negroes to buy their own land rather than relying on the promises of another landowner. I can do no less when I'm dealing with my own needs."

"Are you afraid that I'll take the building away from you?" Mr. Philbrick asked. "I could almost be insulted by your lack of trust."

"I don't think you would take it away," she answered, "but it would still be your land, and I would expect you to want to retain some control over it. We've already had that kind of relationship with the Brick Church, and I won't do it again. I appreciate your offer. I believe you make it in good faith. I will welcome students from your plantations. But the land we choose must belong to the school."

In the end, they chose a plot in a field directly across the road from the Brick Church. "Are you sure you don't want to move the school to a place closer to your home—somewhere that would shorten your travel?" Mr. Tomlinson asked.

"In St. Helenaville? No. I don't know whether we'll stay there, or move to Frogmore or to another of the plantations. That will depend on which old owners come home to reclaim their land after the war. But in any event, the children who must walk to school are more important than my own convenience. This is the central location and the place they are used to. We'll stay here. All that really matters is that we have a school of our own."

50
THE WAR WINDS DOWN
Winter 1864–Spring 1865

Laura spent a relaxing summer in Philadelphia. She enjoyed reading newspapers again and catching up with political news and the latest reports on the progress of the war effort. She did not enjoy the heat and grime of the city, the constant noise, and the overcrowded streets. By September she was itching to return to her lovely St. Helena, where there were giant trees instead of tall buildings and the air smelled of nothing stronger than pluff mud.

Ellen was standing on the Beaufort dock to meet her when she disembarked from the *Flora*. Across the river, Hastings waited with the buggy to drive them home. "We have to take one small detour," Ellen explained. "We've scheduled the opening of school for October 19th, and I want to make sure Mr. Parker is aware that we need access to the church a couple of weeks earlier than that."

Exhausted from her voyage, during which she had been seasick the entire time, Laura leaned back, closed her eyes, and breathed deeply of the soft, warm air. Within minutes, she dozed and did not awaken until Ellen tugged at her hand and said, "You might want to open your eyes, Laura."

She yawned, shook her head, and mumbled, "Sorry." Then she sat straight up, gasping at the sight before her. "It's here? It's really here!"

The new schoolhouse stood in the middle of the field she had chosen, shaded by spreading live oak trees with their waving Spanish moss. The porch at the front door faced the church across the road. On either side of the porch a long classroom wing stretched out, giving promise of generous space within. The boards had been freshly whitewashed, and they sparkled in the sun.

"Dreams do come true," Ellen whispered.

"They do indeed. It's beautiful, and larger than I expected. Can I see the inside?"

"You can, if you insist, but you might be disappointed. The building is completely framed, but the inside remains unfinished. The shipment included only a few desks, we haven't decided where to mount the blackboards, and the outbuildings await a construction crew. It's here, but not yet ready for occupancy."

"I don't see anyone working."

"No. Welcome back to the South, Laura, where everything gets done tomorrow."

"But school starts in two weeks and . . ."

"And we'll be back in the Brick Church, at least for a while. Mr. Wilson, the government contractor who has been assigned to us, says that he and his men have not been paid for the past six months, and he cannot keep them working any longer."

"Does General Saxton know?"

"I'm hoping that your persuasive voice will help push him to demand action. We need you here, Laura."

* * *

478

Despite that initial disappointment, Laura was happy to be home. Aunt Rachel's Place had gained a new name—Teachers House—and was now fully furnished. Ellen had even managed to find a small stove for the dining room that allowed them to enjoy their meals in comfort, even during the fall's coldest and stormiest days. The parlor provided a cozy haven just big enough for the two women, and the central wall's fireplace provided heat for both parlor and bedroom.

School, too, was going well. They opened with one hundred and ninety-four scholars and four teachers, one in each corner of the church. The children were eager to get back to their studies. Laura awoke every morning in good health and vigor. She found that she still loved teaching. Her greatest pleasures came from those moments when the face of a puzzled child suddenly lit up with understanding. If a student smiled, so did his teacher.

The fall was always a time of plenty. Eggs and vegetables were in good supply. The earlier berries were gone, of course, but watermelons still waited in the fields, and the fruit trees were weighted down with a heavy crop. Whatever will we do with this many pomegranates? Laura wondered, but she soon found that the children were eager to pry open the hard-skinned fruit; they considered the seeds a special treat.

Laura wrote home to reassure her family that all was well. "I am getting my South Carolina health back—eat like a horse, sleep like a top, do any amount of work, and read nothing; that last is too bad and greatly to my regret. We have begun reading in the carriage on our way to school. The weather is exquisite, the school flourishing, household matters comfortable, living good, and all things smooth at present." She spoke only of her own affairs, and her optimism did not extend beyond the borders of St. Helenaville.

As usual, the island itself buzzed with rumors. The ever-present tax commissioners were talking of re-leasing the school farms, so as to put them into the hands of government-supplied new teachers rather than the old volunteers. They had access to a whole new crop of teachers, now that the war was winding down. Most of the new volunteers, of course, were actually looking to get their hands on land before the former owners could reclaim their property, but the commissioners saw only people who were willing to work at low governmental salaries. What would happen to volunteers like the Murrays? No one seemed to have considered that.

In previous years, Laura would have been raging with indignation at the shortsightedness of the Beaufort bureaucracy. Now, however, in her newly found serenity, she was a voice of reason. "All is as uncertain as ever, but I do not trouble myself," she wrote to her sisters. "The uncertainties down here all smooth themselves into very good order in time, and so I do not fear any serious vexations in the new school arrangements on the school farms."

As December arrived, Laura had even more cause for optimism. The carpenter was back at work in the schoolhouse, taking measurements for new seats. He promised that all would be ready soon, perhaps allowing them to start school by the new year.

The teachers did not wear themselves out with Christmas decorations this year; they were too busy packing things up in the church and planning the move across the road that was scheduled for the week between Christmas and New Year's Day. They did, of course, hold a party for the children on the day after Christmas, during which they distributed some 250 small gifts that they had prepared for the students. At home they baked ginger cakes for all the children in their own yard, and distributed gifts to their workers. At dinner they entertained two newly arrived Negro teachers who were awaiting assignments to their new schools. It was a quiet but enjoyable holiday.

* * *

Another restful period had prepared Laura and Ellen for the excitement of the new schoolhouse, but they had not anticipated all that would be involved in the move. Already, on January 8th, 1865, Laura wrote home with a major request—they needed a school bell. Mr. Tomlinson was expecting to be reassigned, and he had suggested that he could get a belfry put up before he left if there was a chance of a bell arriving soon. Laura's letter to her brother revealed a touch of rivalry between schoolmarms. Laura's longtime friend, Harriet Ware, had just purchased a bell for her own school at Coffin Point. It weighed twenty-five pounds and had been delivered on one of Mr. Philbrick's schooners. It was already ringing across the Coffin Point plantation, calling students from a mile and a half away.

Laura wanted one twice that size, since she estimated that her students came from five or six miles away. She was unwilling to ask Mr. Philbrick for help in delivering it, so she suggested that her brother appeal to some of the other cotton merchants who intended to purchase the current crop, or to the Philadelphia and New York commissioners. Surely, she thought, one of them would be willing to bear the cost of transportation, so long as she paid for the bell itself. Then she needed a wheel and a rope, she added. By March, Laura's inquiries were more pointed. The government workers were shingling the roof. If the bell did not arrive before they finished she would have to pay for shingling the belfry roof herself.

In the end it took almost five months, but the bell did arrive, a handsome copper specimen that could be heard over much of the island. Laura also paid for the belfry and the hanging, rather than ask further help from the government. By then, she was hoping for a fence around the playground.

In the same letter as the request for fencing, Laura included a description of her new school's accomplishments: "The children have read through a history of the United States and an easy physiology, and they know all the parts of speech, and can make sentences, being told to use a predicate, verb, and adverb, for instance. Ellen's class is writing compositions. We are going to have a grand school exhibit before we close, with dialogues, exercises in mathematics, in grammar, geography, spelling, reading, etc." It was a fine demonstration of how far the Port Royal's educational experiment had come in less than three years, and Laura was justifiably proud.

* * *

Elsewhere across the island that spring there was excitement of a different sort, for it was obvious that the war was coming to an end. Sherman had completed his march to the sea, reaching Savannah on December 22nd, 1864. Refugees from all over Georgia followed his army and now poured into the Sea Islands, seeking the basics of shelter, clothing, and food. Laura petitioned her old sponsors in the Commissions for help, which this time was slower in coming. General Saxton announced his intention to reopen Edisto Island and send the new refugees there. The announcement appealed to many of the residents of St. Helenaville; quite a few of them had come from Edisto two years ago and now saw a chance to go home.

Such a move caused a tremendous upheaval among the white officials as well. General Saxton was appointed a major general and given complete control over all the freedmen's activities in the Department of the South. Saxton, in turn, appointed Mr. Tomlinson his second in command, to be stationed in Beaufort. Mr. Williams took over St. Helena Island, and John Alden went to Edisto. More locally, Mr. Hunn and his family went to establish a store on Edisto, and the tax commissioners replaced Miss Hunn's school farm with government teachers at Seaside. The Fairfields had left The Oaks, so Mr. Ruggles leased that house and offered to share it with the Murrays. Laura was appointed superintendent of all the schools run by the Philadelphia Association and agent for the Pennsylvania Freedmen's Relief Association in South Carolina. For the most part, the decisions were wise. Competent people now held the most important positions in the department, but it would take them a while to get used to their new responsibilities.

April 14th, 1865, was a grand day of celebration for several of the Gideonites who traveled to Charleston to witness the handover of Fort Sumter to the Union. For these people, who had been involved in the hardships of war since 1862, it was a sign of their long-awaited triumph, and they gloated a bit as they witnessed firsthand the devastation that had wrecked this once beautiful city. A few days later, they were despondent to learn that on the very day of their celebration, Abraham Lincoln had been shot. Still, everyone knew that the war was effectively over.

Many of the old plantation owners were already drifting back under the assumption that they would be able to reclaim their lands, and, in truth, there was a possibility of it. Lands that had been confiscated for unpaid taxes might well be reclaimed, provided they had not been legally sold. So, for example, young Gabriel Capers came back to his Ladies Island plantation, which the government was still reserving for purchase by the Negroes. Gabriel warned his former slaves that he would eventually get it back and that he would be more favorably disposed to those who cared for him by providing a place to stay until then. Rina allowed him to move into her old cabin at The Oaks, simply because she felt sorry for him.

Others reacted with similar sympathy. In St. Helenaville, Dr. Clarence Fripp came back, hoping to find his little love nest awaiting him. When he learned that Rachel had sold it to Laura, he claimed the house next door, which had also originally belonged to the Fripp family. Laura's brother Will was already renting that house, and he was forced to stand by as Dr. Clarence moved into the other half. They made strange housemates and neighbors.

For most of the Gideonites, the end of the war signaled that it was time to go home. But for Laura Towne and Ellen Murray, the end of the war meant that the Port Royal Experiment was about to face its greatest challenge. It had been relatively easy to help the former slaves learn about the meaning of freedom when Northerners were the only teachers around. But what would happen when those teachers went home and South Carolina was reclaimed by its former white masters?

"Our Penn School is more important than ever now," Laura commented one evening. "It's vital that black children receive the same comprehensive education as white children, so that they can meet one another on equal terms."

"You don't have to convince me, my dear," Ellen said. "I would be disappointed in you if you suggested we give up now. But how can we manage to do any more than we're now doing?"

"Well, there's an advantage to my title as superintendent of schools run by the Philadelphia Association. I can recommend to them that the only way they can protect the investment they've made over the past years is to make sure that our schools continue to run."

"We really have only one school—our own," Ellen reminded her.

"I've been thinking about making that two schools. I've already written to Mr. McKim, asking that the Commission finance the purchase of Frogmore plantation. It can't be reclaimed by Thomas Coffin because it was never confiscated by the government; rather, it was legally sold several times for taxes."

"So it will be sold to Philadelphians this time around?"

"Not exactly. The house and surrounding two acres will be sold to me. Then I will turn the deed over to a board of trustees, of which I will be one, for the purpose of establishing Frogmore School. General Giles from Hilton Head will bring his team of Army engineers at once to construct a substantial building, similar to Penn School but much larger. As soon as the building is completed, we will hire good Northern teachers to open the school for elementary students. Then we can turn Penn School into the high school for the island."

"You really have it all planned out! But where will the money come from to keep both schools running?"

"The land. The Philadelphia Association will be purchasing the whole thousand acres of Frogmore plantation. That land, minus the two acres holding the house and school, will grow ever more valuable and can be sold as needed to support our efforts."

"So we will be moving to Frogmore!"

"Some day, I hope. Right now, I don't think it's possible. Frogmore is in much better shape now than it was when I first came here, and I loved the little house then. But to make it our permanent home, it will need a lot of work, including a rebuilt second story. It needs a new well, and it could use some sheltering trees and some fruit trees, too. We can't afford all of that right now."

"We can afford neither the money nor the time, I agree. But some day . . ."

"Yes, some day. The road to Frogmore may not be haunted, as I've been trying to tell our people for years, but it's a lot longer than we realized. It will be a journey of years, but with a noble purpose at its end."

RINA ON "SWEET CHARIOT"
Summer 1865

D at Missus Laura. She jis be a miracle, sho nuf. When she fust come intuh muh life, I likes she well nuf, but now I loves she. She done change muh whole life an de people in muh life. I don know where I be ifn it not be fuh she. We be fambly, cause we takes care uh each udder.

I be gittin ol. I hab bad pain in muh stummik. Sumtimes I caint eben stan up. I caint walk cross de floor witout stoppin fuh breathe. Missus Laura, she pertend not fuh notice, but I knows she see muh trubble. She neber say nuttin, but she be hirin new gals fuh do muh work fuh me. I preciates dat.

She be takin care uh muh fambly, too. She gib Hastins one job ater anudder, so he gots plenty uh wages. She take care uh muh lil gal Lizabet, too. Lizabet be de onliest chile I eber hab, but she not be right in de haid. Sumtimes she git confuse, an den she act wild an git in trubble. An she husban, Jack Brown, he be sick fuh so long. Missus Laura visit he in hospital an set up he soljer wages so Lizabet hab sum money.

I be hearin dat ol sweet chariot comin fuh me mos enny day now, but dat all right. I knows Missus Laura be safe. She be habbin Missus Ellen wit she, an now she be ownin Frogmore, too. I neber unnerstan why she be likin dat place so much. I still tinks it be full uh hants, but she say no. So she gots two places fuh live—Frogmore *an Rachel Place. She gots she own school, an eber chile on de island fuh love. She gwine be all right, eben when I not here no more fuh take care uh she. An bout Missus Ellen, she eben got her a dog now.*

When I looks back on muh life, I sees dat I be purty silly sumtimes. De Big Shoot come, an I be scairt cause I tought we all gwine die. Den Missus Laura come, an by an by all de tings I fears gots bedder. It like we larnt fuh sing dat ol spirichal:

"Jehoviah, Hallelujah, de Lord will perwide,
De foxes dey hab holes in de groun',
An de birds hab nests in de air,
An' ev'ry thing has a hidin' place,
But us po' sinners ain't got nowhere . . . ."

Dat remin me dat I gots me a home wit Missus Laura, an I knows de Lord gwine perwide.

A NOTE ABOUT THE AUTHOR

Carolyn P. Schriber is a Professor Emerita in the History Department at Rhodes College in Memphis, TN. Since retiring she has written several other books on the Civil War in South Carolina: *A Scratch with the Rebels* (paperback or Kindle edition), the award-winning novel, *Beyond All Price* (paperback or Kindle edition), and a collection of short pieces, *Left by the Side of the Road: Characters without a Novel* (Kindle edition). She has also written a handbook on publishing called *The Second Mouse Gets the Cheese: How to Avoid the Traps of*

Self-Publishing (paperback or Kindle edition). Read more about her work on her publishing company website. She now lives near Memphis with her husband and five lovable but opinionated cats. When she is not engaged in her duties as president of Mid-South Lions Sight and Hearing Service, a non-profit charity connected with Lions Clubs International, she writes and enjoys traveling to do more research in the Low Country between Charleston and Savannah.

A SHORT BIBLIOGRAPHY

Primary Sources:

Allen, William Francis, Charles Pickard Ware, and Lucy
 McKim Garrison. *Slave Songs of the United States*.
 New York, 1867; reprint, University of North Carolina
 at Chapel Hill, 2000.

Forten, Charlotte. *Journals*. Edited by Brenda Stevenson.
 New York, 1988.

Forten, Charlotte. "Life on the Sea Islands." *Atlantic*, May
 and June 1864.

French, A[usta] M. *Slavery in South Carolina and the Ex-
 Slaves; or The Port Royal Mission.* New York, 1862.

Higginson, Thomas Wentworth. *Army Life in a Black
 Regiment*. New York, 1869; reprint 1984.

Letters from Port Royal: Written at the Time of the Civil War.
 Edited by Elizabeth Ware Pearson. New York, 1906;
 reprint 2010.

The Penn School Papers. University of North Carolina at
 Chapel Hill. Library. Southern Historical Collection.

Rogers, Seth. "Letters of Dr. Seth Rogers, 1862-1863."
 Massachusetts Historical Society Proceedings, Vol. 42
 (Boston, 1910).

Towne, Laura Matilda. *Letters and Diary of Laura M. Towne:
 Written from the Sea Islands of South Carolina, 1862-1884.*
 Edited by Rupert Sargent Holland. Cambridge, 1912.

Towne, Laura M. *Diary*. Xerox of handwritten copy (Penn School Papers, # 3615). University of South Carolina, Carolingiana Library, Columbia SC. 1963.

Walker, Susan. *Journal, March 3d to June 6th, 1862*. Edited by Henry Noble Sherwood. Cincinnati, 1912.

Secondary Literature:

Butchart, Ronald E. "Laura Towne and Ellen Murray: Northern Expatriots and the Foundations of Black Education in South Carolina, 1862-1908." In *South Carolina Women: Their Lives and Times*. Edited by Marjorie Julian Spruill, Valinda W. Littlefield, and Joan Marie Johnson. Athens, GA, 2010. 2:12-30.

Cooley, Rossa Belle. *School Acres: An Adventure in Rural Education*. New Haven, CT, 1930.

Crum, Mason. *Gullah; Negro Life in the Carolina Sea Islands*. New York, 1940.

Dabbs, Edith M. *Sea Island Diary: A History of St. Helena Island*. Spartanburg, S.C, 1983.

Davidson, Chalmers G. *The Last Foray, the South Carolina Planters of 1860: A Sociological Study*. Columbia, SC, 1971.

Harris, Yvonne Bailey. *The History of the Penn School under Its Founders at St. Helena Island, Frogmore, South Carolina, 1862-1908*. Michigan: University Microfilms International, 1998.

Jacoway, Elizabeth. *Yankee Missionaries in the South: the Penn School Experiment*. Baton Rouge, 1980.

Johnson, Guion Griffis. *A Social History of the Sea Islands with Special Reference to St. Helena Island, South Carolina*. Durham, NC, 1930.

*Northern Money, Southern Land: The Low Country Plantation
    Sketches of Chlotilde R. Martin.* Edited by Robert B.
    Cuthbert and Stephen G. Hoffius. Columbia, SC, 2009.

Porcher, Richard Dwight and Sara Flick. *The Story of Sea
    Island Cotton.* Charleston, SC, 2005.

Rose, Willie Lee. *Rehearsal for Reconstruction: The Port Royal
    Experiment.* Oxford, 1964.

Trinkley, Michael. *Of Freedom unto All: An Archaeological
    Examination of the Port Royal Experiment.* Columbia, SC,
    1987.

*War of the Rebellion: Official Records of the Union and
    Confederate Armies*, Series I, Vol 14. National Historical
    Society. Harrisburg, PA, 1971.

Wright, Roberta Hughes. *A Tribute to Charlotte Forten.*
    Michigan, 1993.

Journal Articles:

Billington, Ray Allen. "A Social Experiment: The Port
    Royal Journal of Charlotte L. Forten, 1862-1863."
    The Journal of Negro History 35 (Jul., 1950):233-264.

Curry, Richard O. "The Abolitionists and Reconstruction:
    A Critical Appraisal." *The Journal of Southern History* 34
    (Nov., 1968):527-545.

"The Freedmen at Port Royal." *The North American Review*
    101 (Jul., 1865):1-28.

Matthews, Donald G. "The Abolitionists on Slavery: The
    Critique Behind the Social Movement." *The Journal of
    Southern History* 33 (May, 1967):163-182.

Ochiai, Akiko. "The Port Royal Experiment Revisited:
    Northern Visions of Reconstruction and the Land

Question." *The New England Quarterly* 74 (Mar., 2001):94-117.

Pease, William H. "Three Years among the Freedmen: William C. Gannett and the Port Royal Experiment" *The Journal of Negro History* 42 (Apr., 1957): 98-117.

Rachal, John R. "Gideonites and Freedmen: Adult Literacy Education at Port Royal, 1862-1865." *The Journal of Negro Education* 55 (Autumn, 1986): 453-469.

Roper, Laura Wood. "Frederick Law Olmsted and the Port Royal Experiment." *The Journal of Southern History* 31 (Aug., 1965):272-284.

Taylor, Kay Ann. "Mary S. Peake and Charlotte L. Forten: Black Teachers During the Civil War and Reconstruction." *The Journal of Negro Education* 4 (2005):20.

Westwood, Howard C. "Generals David Hunter and Rufus Saxton and Black Soldiers." *The South Carolina Historical Magazine* 86 (Jul., 1985):165-181.

Wolf, Kurt J. "Laura M. Towne and the Freed People of South Carolina, 1862-1901." *The South Carolina Historical Magazine* 98 (Oct., 1997):375-405.

15687254R00269

Made in the USA
Charleston, SC
15 November 2012